Also by Harold Burton Meyers:

Geronimo's Ponies

Reservations

The Death at Awahi

A HERO OF BRAG

A Novel

Harold Burton Meyers

A Hero of Brag

© Copyright 2021 by Harold Burton Meyers

ISBN 978-1-7368333-4-6

Published by Steven Key Meyers/The Smash-and-Grab Press

The characters appearing in this book are fictitious, and any similarity to real persons, living or dead, is coincidental.
 Cover: East View Cemetery, Vernon, Texas

SMASH
& GRAB press

to Jeannie

A Hero of Brag

I. The Tunnel

1.

"BOY, WHO THE HELL you think you are?"

"Pa, I don't know."

Pa lifted the jug, tipped it. The walnut in his neck popped up, popped down. He wiped his lips with the back of his hand.

"You ain't worth the rope to hang you, you know that?"

"I know that, Pa."

"You killed your ma, boy."

"I didn't mean to, Pa. I was just getting borned. I didn't know no better."

"What business you had, getting borned?"

"I don't know, Pa."

"Here's something to know. Come daylight, I don't want you around no more. You got that, boy?"

"Yes, Pa."

"And don't you go pestering your brothers'n sisters, neither. They don't want you around no more'n me."

Pa slapped him across the face and booted him past the falling-down tobacco barn into the road. His brothers and sisters had places of their own nearby, but Pa was right. They wouldn't want him around, never had.

He stayed the night in the woods with ghosts. Next day he went down the road to Cannady's store.

A man in uniform called him over to a table by the pickle barrel.

"Hey, you boy, how old you?"

"Seventeen."

"Sure it ain't 15, maybe 14?"

"I'm sure."

"You want to be a soldier?"

"I reckon."

"Why?"

"I don't like them Yankees stealing our slaves."

"You own any slaves, boy?"

"Sure do. Lots."

"You give your slaves shoes?"

"Damn right."

"How come you ain't got shoes?"

"Well—"

"Never you mind, son. General Lee won't. Sign here."

The boy made his mark.

SPLIT-RAIL FENCES SNAKED over low hills and chalky outcroppings on either side of the lane, enclosing fields overgrown with weeds and bushes. Spotting a rail that looked loose, the boy broke ranks and worked it free. He'd be able to get a fire going when they stopped to make palatable the boiled mule meat issued as marching rations. Some of the fellows who'd been in the war since the beginning told how people back then thrust food on them as they marched—apples, bread, fried chicken, thick slices of ham or bacon, even pies and puddings. But those days were long gone, if they had ever existed. The boy had never been offered so much as a rotted spud. He hoisted the rail onto his shoulder alongside his musket.

An officer rode past.

"Sergeant McCandless!" the officer shouted. "What's that man doing with that rail?"

Sergeant McCandless came at the boy red-faced.

"You, there, what's your name?"

"Amos Gower, Sergeant."

"What company?"

"Yours, Sergeant."

The sergeant stared at him with a look that Amos had seen on his face before, a melding of sneer and snarl.

"Of course you'd be mine. You're just the kind of stupid butternut who's always in my company. Drop that rail."

"But—"

"I said drop that rail, Amos Gower. And you're on sentry tonight, all night."

Amos dropped the rail. Hoots rose all around as he scurried to catch up. Everyone was glad of this break in the monotony of marching—especially glad, he felt, because it was he who had been targeted. He looked back and saw Jess Fellows returning to the line carrying the rail that he had been forced to give up. Jess was another of the young'uns like Amos, given cast-offs as uniform and an old smooth-bore musket instead of a rifled gun. But nobody stopped Jess from stealing the rail. The officer had ridden on. Sergeant McCandless still had his eye on Amos.

Amos shuffled on, breathing dust, his canteen dry, with no prospect of heating his boiled mule meat to make it go down easier. With every step he got dustier, thirstier, hungrier, and angrier. He was, he told himself, mad as a wet hen. First time he was in a battle, he'd just happen to be pointing his musket at Sergeant McCandless when he fired. He'd clip off the officer next, if by unlikely chance that personage should happen to be in the vicinity when bullets began to fly.

He put the canteen to his lips, hoping for a miracle, but got only a drop, not enough to clear his throat of the dust raised by the column shuffling along the country lane ahead of him. The sun burned down. Under his bare feet the ground felt too hot for the time of year, hot enough to fry eggs. His thirst sharpened at every step. He lifted the canteen again. It was as dry as his mouth. He hoped the column would soon ford a creek, so he could dip his canteen into cool water as he crossed. He wanted the stream to be shallow, though. He hated walking through water up to his chest, holding his musket and powder box over his head, while his haversack and blanket roll threatened to float away.

He had grown since he joined up and was taller than any man around him, but scrawnier. His scraps of uniform if ever new had been so long before they came to him.

The drooping brim of his slouch hat had pulled away from the crown in several places. It might have fallen to his nose had his ears not blocked its descent. His pants, blue when taken off a Yankee corpse by a Confederate forager, had faded to near gray by the time they came to him. Held up by frayed rope suspenders, the pants fell short of his shins but were so big in the waist that they could have held another Johnny Reb his size. Holes in the knees and seat exposed patches of unwashed skin. His butternut shirt was out at the elbows and nearly buttonless. It had gone unwashed for so long and bore so many stains of sweat and of soot from long-extinguished campfires that it was nearer black than the yellowish-brown color a walnut-hull dye had once given it. Intended like his pants for someone short and heavy, the shirt drooped tent-like off his shoulders, except where his rucksack's straps clutched folds of excess cloth to him. The shirttails barely reached his waist. The sleeves stopped short of his wrist bones.

He was barefoot by preference. Square-toed brogans dangled from his neck on frazzled leather laces, but they had been shaped to another man's foot before they came to him and were not shoes to be worn with comfort. In months of marching here, there, and someplace else, but not yet into battle, he had slogged through mud and water so often that the leather had stiffened and cracked. He couldn't walk a mile in them without rubbing blisters on his feet. He had no socks to ease the rubbing—had never had money to buy any or anyone to knit him a pair.

A rumor had spread through the ranks a day or two earlier that General Lee had issued an order exempting shoeless men from going into battle. Amos had aimed to shed his brogans at the first chance of doing so without being seen. Before he could do it, however, the same rumor reached Sergeant McCandless. Another order came down, delivered forcefully and in person by the company commander: Any man caught shoeless would be shot as a deserter, battle or no battle. No one had to wear his shoes all the time—merely had to keep them by him, ready to be put on when the order came to do so. And there the shoes were, rapping his chest at every step.

Around a bend and over a rise, the column came to cultivated fields around a burned-out house with columns. Only the columns and one end of the house still stood. Its front wall was missing, exposing empty rooms with floors sagging into blackened ruins below. The roof had mostly caved in. Around the ruins of the house, a couple of barns or stables survived, as did a row of small outbuildings that might once have been slave cabins. Beyond the cabins, a neat white fence surrounded a small burying ground with granite gravestones. A spring flowed from the base of a steep chalk cliff that was overgrown with brush and vines and wild azaleas in bloom. The water looked clearer and wetter than any Amos had ever seen. He licked his cracked lips.

The officer who set Sergeant McCandless on Amos had stopped to talk with a one-armed man leaning on a gate in the split-rail fence. Behind the one-armed man a tree-lined lane led toward the burned-out house. The man wore overalls and a cavalry officer's broad-brimmed hat. He held a short-barreled saddle rifle in his one hand. Beside him stood the tallest black man Amos had ever seen. He was dressed like his master, except for the hat. A holstered pistol dangled from his belt, its barrel seemingly as long as that of his master's rifle. Amos was shocked. Arming a slave! He had never heard of such a thing.

Ranged along the gate beside the two men and hanging on it were a dozen children, black and white. One girl looked near to Amos's age. Their eyes met. Amos thought he saw her smile. He couldn't tell if his raggedy state brought the smile or if she was just being friendly. She had blue eyes and brown hair that glinted red in the sun. She wasn't pretty in his eyes—she was too freckled, too skinny, too bony. But he liked the way she looked at him.

"You there, soldier," the one-armed farmer yelled, gesturing at Jess with his rifle, "where'd you get that rail?"

Jess hollered back, "Brung it from Georgia, I did. I growed up with this here rail."

Everyone laughed and hooted, all but Amos. He shuffled along thinking, Ain't that just like Jess Fellows? He done just what I done, but he can laugh it off, get away with it. Ever we stop, Jess is going to get right down to breaking up that rail and getting his mule meat hotted up and decent to eat. I'll be lucky to get the smell off it.

The one-armed farmer was not laughing nor was the officer. "Sergeant, bring that man over here."

Sergeant McCandless stopped the column and marched Jess Fellows over to the officer. Jess still had the rail on his shoulder.

"Sergeant, get this man's name," the officer said.

"That there's Jess Fellows, sir."

"Well, tell Jess Fellows to hand over that rail." The officer spoke loudly, meaning to be heard. "I will not stand for theft by any soldier under my command, especially not of a rail from a fence belonging to an officer who has fought bravely in our noble cause, a hero who will soon rejoin us despite grievous wounds." Speaking directly to Jess Fellows for the first time, the officer added. "I'll deal with you later, soldier, after we're long past this gentleman's property. In case you don't know, you can be shot for stealing that rail."

The column moved on, no one laughing. Amos looked back as he went, back at the skinny girl hanging on the gate beside the one-armed farmer in the cavalryman's hat. She was staring at him. He was sure of it.

When the company fell out by a stream that had been dammed to form a small pond, Amos forced his way to the forefront. The water was already roiled and muddy but he filled his canteen anyway. The mud would settle out. Sergeant McCandless assigned two men as guards to march Jess Fellows off to see the officer. Jess swaggered away with a grin on his face. He still swaggered when the guards brought him back, but the grin was gone. He was red-eyed and pale. The guards said the officer had mouthed Jess hard. They said Jess broke down and cried, begging for mercy. In the end the officer decided to let him go with a warning instead of having him shot as an example, but he told Sergeant McCandless to keep Jess on extra duty for a month. The guards said Jess fell to his knees and tried to kiss the officer's boots in gratitude.

Jess told a different story. He said he'd looked that damn officer in the damn eye and told him he didn't have no damn right to do a damn thing to him just because he'd picked up a damn fence rail that was lying loose on the damn ground, just asking to be picked up. Wasn't a damn thing the officer could do, Jess said, but let him go. Nobody believed his version of what had occurred, and Jess conceded that the officer had said some hard things.

"Sticks and stones," Jess said, "sticks and stones."

Sergeant McCandless put Jess on lookout with Amos.

THE CORPORAL LED Amos and Jess Fellows along a creek bed with bushy banks till they came to a road where two trails from the north converged into one westward-tending dirt road.

"Federals is coming at us whatever way you look, or so I hear," the corporal said, "foot and horse both, spoiling for a fight. Watch both trails and the west road, too. Don't take nothing for granted. These boys is tricky. Can't tell where they'll spring up next."

The corporal settled them in a thicket on a brush-covered hillside. "Keep out of sight. You're here to see them and not them to see you. They come along, one of you slip away and scoot back to camp. The other one wait to see how many more is coming along. Stay awake. And quiet. Them folks ain't bringing nothing you want."

Jess asked, "Where we at, you reckon?"

"Mississippi, by now, I should think, Tishomingo County maybe. Or maybe somewheres around God don't know where, the way we been skipping back and forth, trying to keep away from them Yanks till we get there, wherever there is."

Jess had another question. "What we going to do when we get to this place that you and God don't know the where of?"

"Fight, boy, fight. There ain't much to count on in this man's army but you can count on that in the end. We'll fight there if we can make it there, or here, or someplace else if we can't. And about time, I say. We been dodging around too long."

"Bring 'em on," Jess said. "We'll give 'em hell."

"You boys keep your eyes open."

Amos and Jess Fellows made themselves comfortable, more or less. Sergeant McCandless had given them a big hunk of bread, not more than two or three days old. He gave them each an onion, too, along with what might once have been an apple but was now so shriveled and rotted that Amos wasn't sure if he meant it as a gift or an insult.

Amos thought they might risk a little fire around on the other side of the hill away from the road to warm what little was left of their boiled mule. Jess said no. If the smoke didn't attract a Yankee scouting party, which they sure as hell didn't want, it would be bound to call the corporal down on them — Sergeant McCandless too, perhaps. They didn't want that either. Hidden in the bushes on the hillside, they swatted flies and skeeters as they ate their cold meat, bread, and onions. Both took a bite of apple and spat it out.

Jess said, "Wisht I had me a woman."

"Me too."

"You ever had you a woman?"

"Sure. Lots of times." Amos never had, but that was not something a man could admit. "How about you?"

"Lots."

Amos didn't believe him but Jess went on, talking about things he had done to women or they to him. Amos didn't believe much of that, either. But one of these days, he told himself, one of these days. He called to mind the girl on the gate.

Darkness came down on them. One minute Amos could see a good long way and the next minute he couldn't pick out his hand in front of his face. An owl hooted off in the woods and in the distance dogs bayed.

"I don't see no reason we both of us got to be awake at the same time," Jess said. "I'll stretch out here a while, then you poke me up and I'll watch." He spread out his canvas ground cover. Soon he snored, flat on his back, mouth open.

When Amos came awake he was stretched out full length on the bare ground, with his slouch hat rolled up as a pillow. The moon was full and well up. He sat up, yawning, and put on his hat. He saw a troop of Union cavalry coming down the nearest branch of the trail, almost up to them, coming slow with a jingle of bridles. Grabbing his gun and haversack he crashed through the brush to a cave-like thicket at the top of the hill. The noise he made woke Jess and caught the ear of the Yanks.

A Union officer spurred up the hill.

"What's this?" Jess said, looking up at the officer. "What's this?"

"What this is, is this," the officer said.

Leaning from the saddle he drove his saber into Jess's neck and drew it across his throat, one ear to the other. Blood spurted over Jess's face, making him look like he had pulled a red mask over his head. His eyes rolled back until only the whites showed. Waving arms, kicking legs, he flopped over the ground like a headless chicken. The officer's horse danced backward at the smell of Jess's blood. The officer kept his seat, watching Jess, sword ready for another thrust.

Amos remembered the brim of a hat etched in sharp outline against the sky. A shadowed face with a moonlit beardless chin. Blue shoulders, similarly moonlit. A glint of steel. A strangled scream. A flood of blood. Jess's eyes and teeth gleaming white in a moonlit red mask. Nothing more.

The Union soldiers rode on. Amos crept out of his thicket and down the hill to see what Jess had in his rucksack and pockets. No use letting someone else get it.

2.

AMOS HEARD THE GIRL calling, *"Chickee, chickee."* He lay on the dirt floor of the tumble-down shed and peered out a foot-high hole at the base of a rotted-off board.

"Psst," he said. *"Psst."*

He had been in the shed two nights. At dawn of the morning after he watched Jess Fellows die he had heard distant gunfire. As he listened he dreamed of the heroic things he would have done had he been there. Then the guns stopped. However the fight had come out, his company would be gone somewhere else, he didn't know where — Sergeant McCandless, the officer, and all the rest. Jess Fellows, too.

He had seen the girl at a distance but this was the first time she had come close to the shed. She held her apron out in front of her, making a basket of it, and scattered cracked corn.

"Here, *chickee. Chickee, chickee.* Here, *chickee."*

"Psst." He stuck his hand out the hole. *"Psst."*

Now she heard. She looked around, just long enough to see his hand. She backed toward him, bent over like she was looking for eggs in the weeds that grew along the side of the shed, chickens fussing after her. As she bent her skirt lifted. He saw the back of her leg almost to the knee. She wasn't more than a foot away. He could have reached out and grabbed her ankle. She backed past the rotted board and looked in at him.

"So it's you. I saw you the other day, marching along the road."

"I'm hungry."

"Come on out. I'll take you down and Mother'll feed you and Father will help you get back to your company. He's going back to the war soon himself."

"I can't do that."

"Why not?"

"I just can't."

She was bent over, peering at him through the hole. Her expression changed. It reminded him of Sergeant McCandless. She stood up.

"Don't let Father see you. He won't stand stragglers on the place."

"I ain't a straggler."

"Don't talk so loud. Father's milking in the stable. He'll hear. I'll be back later."

"I ain't ate in two days."

"Shush now. I'll be back."

He lay dozing on the hard-packed dirt floor of the shed, thinking about his stomach. The last thing he'd put in it was the final bit of rank mule meat and half an onion he'd found in Jess's rucksack when he searched it after the Federals rode on.

She was back. Through the opening in the rotted board, he saw the gray skirt that hid her legs to the tops of her shoes. She dropped a chunk of bread, a fried chicken leg, and a raw carrot on the ground within his reach. She didn't stop or say anything. The next day, the girl brought him more food — pickled pigs' feet and fried mush wrapped in cornhusks, along with an apple and two thick cookies, chewy ones. Amos couldn't remember when he had eaten so well.

This time the girl paused in front of the opening. "You've got to leave. Father's going to rebuild this shed, turn it into a storehouse. He says it'll give the Yankees something to steal so they won't go looking for the rest of our stores, should any more come by after he goes back to the Army."

"I got no place to go."

She backed up against the shed, like she was resting and dropped ribs, two biscuits, and an apple. He could see a bit of leg above the shoe and below the skirt. He reached through the hole in the shed and stroked her leg. She jerked away.

"You've got to get out of this shed or you'll be sent back to the Army. Tonight you slip out and go up on the hill, this side of the stream. There are three trees there. You go behind the tree on the right—you know your left from your right?"

"I know."

"You go behind the tree and there's a shallow cave. From the outside it doesn't look like it goes anywhere. But you go in and look to the right and you'll see a tunnel. You crawl through that tunnel—it turns a lot—to a big cave and wait for me. I go there every afternoon. It's my special place. You can't stay, though. You've got to go."

That night he found the three trees and the shallow cave in the steep hillside behind the trees. He didn't see the tunnel at the back of the cave until he was right on it. The opening was small, under a ledge. He crawled blindly in on his belly and inched forward, head first, bit by bit, fearing to trust the girl but having to. A little way in, the tunnel turned once and then again, the second time sharply. It was black as a boot, but after a third turn he found himself in a dimly lighted cavern. Looking up he could see moonlight filtering through crevices far overhead. He could hear nothing but the muffled sound of water running.

He lay down and tried to sleep, but every time he dropped

off he saw the Union officer slip his sword into Jess Fellows' throat. When he shut out that image, another showed up that he liked no better — of a one-armed man, the girl's father, wearing a cavalry officer's hat and carrying a short-barreled rifle. He stood at a gate with an armed slave, a giant, beside him, guarding a little farm that was all that remained of what before the war must have been a great plantation. Once asleep, he dreamed about the smooth skin of the girl's leg.

The next morning he awoke in a limestone cave with curving walls and a vaulted ceiling. From its roof dripped what Amos thought looked like icicles, which reflected streaks of sunlight angling in from overhead. At the back of the cave he saw the dark mouths of three small tunnels. Several books lay on a table at one side of the cave. Beside the table were a chair and a doll's bed with a doll in it, covered by a blanket except for its head. Against another wall he saw trunks and wooden boxes, many of them padlocked, a stack of blankets, and piles of turnips, carrots, sweet potatoes, and cabbages.

It was afternoon when the girl came. She brought him a ham shank, two roasted potatoes, and a jar of milk, along with half a loaf of fresh-baked bread. She put the food on the table and sat in the chair, cradling the doll in her arms. Sunbeams fell on the table.

All else was shadowed, making it seem that the light created a separate room for the girl. He sat cross-legged on the sandy floor ripping strips of ham off the shank with his teeth.

"Make it last. I nearly got caught."

"What is this here place?"

"This cave? It's where we're supposed to hide if Federal troops come again. They burned or stole most everything — my piano, my pretty clothes, everything except some cows and chickens — mules, too — that were in the woods. But they didn't find this cave. Father stored these boxes up here for safekeeping before he left for the Army, along with things he wouldn't need, like his ordinary clothes. So they didn't get any of that, either. The Federal officer asked the slaves where the silver and such was. Father had left Scoot in charge of the place—you saw him when your company went by the other day. Scoot spoke up, pretending not to talk good, 'Ya'all done got it a'ready, suh.' So they went away. Most of the field hands followed along, thinking the Yankees had come to free them and provide for them. Scoot stayed and so did some others."

"That big slave—Scoot, you said—he had him a gun. Was it real?"

"Of course it's real—it's a Remington—but Scoot's not a slave. Used to be, but not anymore. After Father lost his arm and came home to get well, he said, 'All that time in the hospital, I decided the preachers are right. No man's got the right to keep another man his slave. It's immoral and against God's will.' So Father freed the ones who stayed and pays them wages."

"He freed slaves? He's a traitor! Somebody hear talk like that, they'll hang him."

"He is not a traitor! He's a cavalryman, a major, wounded in battle. General Lee himself went to the hospital and gave him a medal. Father's a hero. Anyway, Father says the war shouldn't be about slavery but states' rights."

Chewing noisily, he gnawed the shank in his right hand and stuffed bread in his mouth with his left until his cheeks puffed out.

"Don't choke it down like that. Nobody's rushing you."

"What's your name?" he asked, his mouth full.

"Minnie," she said. "Minnie Wilkes. What's yours?"

"Amos Gower. I'm seventeen."

"I'm fourteen, almost fifteen. Were you in the battle?"

"You bet."

"We could hear the guns all the way here. Your company came by again early today. The officer said your company was attacked from behind in the night by Federal cavalry they didn't even know were around. He said one sentry who might have warned them was killed and there was no sign of the other. They think he deserted."

"That ain't true, Me and Jess Fellows, we was on lookout. We was the first that seen the Federal cavalry come along and we held them off best we could, picked them off one by one as they come over the hill, But then Jess got hit and I kept on till I didn't have no more powder. I couldn't make it back to my company through the Federals and come here."

She listened big-eyed—believing every word, he was sure. He believed it, too, in a way.

Amos choked down the last of the ham and sat back, rubbing his belly.

"That was right good," he said. "I never ate better ham."

She stared at the back of his hand. "What's that on your hand?"

"A louse." He picked it off, crushed it with his thumbnail against his middle finger. He flicked it toward her.

She scrambled away. Again she looked at him as Sergeant McCandless had.

"Everybody's got them. Can't get rid of them. We call 'em our Yankee visitors."

"Father says it's just a matter of keeping clean."

She went to a box along the wall and pulled out a brick of brownish soap. She picked up a blanket too.

"You go back in that middle tunnel. It goes along a way and turns down. You'll come out at a little pool. It's not deep and it's cold but you get in there and scrub top to bottom. Scrub your clothes and blanket, too. And then wrap up in this blanket till your clothes dry."

She was bossy but he thought that was a good thing. When she was bossing him she didn't talk about him leaving. He took the soap and blanket and crawled in blackness along a twisting tunnel. After a couple of sharp turns the sound of running water grew stronger. He came out into another cavern, smaller than the other but like it, with light from crevices overhead. The stream had cut a narrow channel in the stone floor and gouged a saucer-like depression in the middle.

Amos stripped off his clothes and scrubbed them with the brick of soap in icy water elbow deep. The soap stung like fire where he had scratched bites on his arms. Black flecks floated up and slowly drifted away with the current. When he finished rinsing clothes he wrung them out and laid them to dry on the rocky shelf beside the stream.

The water was so cold he considered not washing himself. But Minnie wouldn't like that. Using his hands as a dipper he poured water over his legs and rubbed vigorously. When that began to feel bearable he put first one foot and then the other in the water. He soaped his hair and body from the top down and eased into the pool all the way. It was just deep enough to cover him. The cold took his breath away, but it felt good, too. He couldn't remember the last time he'd been clean and free of lice.

He wrapped himself in the blanket and crawled back through the tunnel to the outer cavern, thinking of Minnie, ready for her. He wished her hair was golden, not ordinary reddish-brown, and given a choice he'd want her to have a soft pretty face, not brown and freckled. He wanted a girl with meat on her bones, a girl he could dig his fingers into, bounce on, like Jess Fellows had talked about doing.

Minnie was all bone, skinny as a rail. But she was who was there. He'd have to take what he could get. Now, he thought, I'll do it now, she like it or not. It's time I had me a woman. She ain't all that pretty and not much to her, but she'll have to do until I find me one I like better.

She wasn't there. He crawled out to the end of the tunnel, blinking against the bright light. He opened his blanket and let the sun warm his bare body. He looked down the hillside, where wild flowers bloomed everywhere in the underbrush. He thought about Minnie, imagining her with flesh on her bones, somebody to rest against, bounce on.

The next day when she crawled into the tunnel he was waiting for her after the second turn, in the darkest part. He pressed against the side of the tunnel, not breathing, and let her crawl up to him on her hands and knees. He came up over her from the side, knocking her flat.

She shrieked and rolled over on her back, scratching and kicking, pounding on his chest. She kept slipping out from under him, but there was no room for her to get away. He pulled her skirt up, not sure what he would find under it. And then it was easy. It was like he knew just what to do. She shrieked as he plunged into her but he held her hands over her head and put the weight of his body down on her and let her buck and twist and holler all she wanted. He was in her good and solid, all the way in, and nothing she could do. It was just like Jess said it was.

He rolled off, pleased with himself. Nothing wrong with me, by God. I'm man enough for any woman.

As soon as he was off her she was gone, gasping and sobbing, scooting backward through the tunnel, dragging the clothes he'd torn off her. By the time he got turned around and went after her, she was far down the hillside scrambling through the azaleas, straightening her clothes.

3.

AMOS FEARED THAT Minnie's one-armed father might come after him with his short rifle, but he didn't know where he could go if he left the cave. He spent days creeping through the dark tunnels that honeycombed the cliff, looking for places to hide and ways to get away if need be. He found caves of all sizes. Many contained stores stashed away by Minnie's father—everything from cabbages and carrots to smoked hams, plenty to last through a winter. He also found more openings to the outside, some of them mere cracks that only someone as skinny as he would be able to squeeze through. He could not easily be cornered inside the cliff.

When no one came looking for him he decided that Minnie had kept secret what he had done. The more he thought on it the more likely it seemed that he was safe. She'd be ashamed of what she had let him do, he reasoned, and wouldn't want anybody to find out about it. She'd know that nobody would believe she hadn't asked for it some way or other. And as he thought about it he realized there was an added reason why she couldn't afford to mention what he had done. No man worth having would marry her if she let it be known that she wasn't a virgin. He felt proud of himself. He'd got himself a cherry.

Not even Jess Fellows had claimed that.

As a farm-reared boy he was handy with snares and traps, and he was able to catch rabbits and squirrels in the thickets outside the caves. He roasted them over small fires he got going with flint and steel in a cavern far back in the network of tunnels. He didn't think there was much chance of anyone seeing smoke rising from the hillside at night but just in case he snuffed out his fires as quickly as he could. He missed the chicken wings and bread that Minnie had brought him. But he was eating better than he had on the march—or at home, for that matter.

He munched raw turnips, carrots, onions, potatoes, cabbages, and apples from the stores in the hillside. He was careful not to take too much from any one pile and stayed away from the hams and slabs of bacon, sensing that Minnie's father knew the exact number he had hidden and would be quick on the trail of a thief should so much as one disappeared. In what he thought of as his home cave he hefted the padlocked boxes stacked along one wall. Several felt heavy enough to contain the silver the Union officer had inquired about. Restrained by fear of Major Wilkes, Amos resisted the temptation to break into them.

What he missed most was Minnie. He wanted her under him again. His hand wasn't enough to please him anymore, now that he knew what it was like to have a woman, even a skinny little thing like Minnie. He could still feel her sharp hipbones poking as she struggled to keep him out of her. He had supposed that after she got over the first shock of it she'd start feeling the way he did, that she would want more of what he could do for her, like Jess had said women did. But she did not come back.

He grew comfortable but not content in his caves and tunnels. He knew no more about what was going on than he had in the Army — if anything, knew less. In the Army there had always been *somebody* around who claimed to know something, which was comforting even if he didn't believe a word the *somebody* said. Hungry for information, he spent hours every day outside the cave looking down on comings and goings and other doings at the farm below. He saw Minnie feeding chickens, saw her father with his forehead pressed against a cow's flank, milking one-handed. He watched black men, slaves no longer, working in the fields, and Minnie's mother working right alongside former slave women churning butter or scrubbing clothes. For all his watching he couldn't tell much of what was going on. People would come and go and he had no way to find out where they came from or went, and why.

On a sunny morning after days of rain, Minnie's father came out of a cabin dressed in his uniform, braid on his shoulders and sleeves, one sleeve folded back over the stump of his arm. The brass handle guard on his curved saber shone like gold. He stepped on a mounting block and swung himself one-handedly onto a black mare that skittered about before allowing him to guide her back into place. He leaned down from the saddle and kissed his wife and Minnie as they stood on the mounting block. The smaller children were held up to him and he bent to touch his lips to their foreheads. He shook hands with Scoot, the big black man who had carried a long-barreled pistol the day Jess Fellows had been made to give up his fence rail.

When Major Wilkes rode out of the yard on the high-stepping mare, an ex-slave Amos had seen working around the place followed, mounted on one mule and leading another. The second mule was loaded with leather-covered boxes and camp equipment. Far down the muddy lane the major and his servant, no longer slave, paused to wave before riding on. All this went on and Amos, cast away on the hillside, knew only what he could see. He hungered to know more.

Minnie came up the hillside. The azaleas had quit blooming. He considered slipping back into the tunnel to catch her again by surprise as she crawled in. Jess was right. She was coming back for more. But she had made him wait too long. He would punish her, pretend not to want her, make her beg for it. She climbed slowly with her head down, but even if she had looked up she would not have seen him.

She lifted her head. He was shocked. If she had been thin before, she was now a skeleton. She looked like an old woman, with dark circles under her eyes, which were red and puffy from crying. The tip of her nose was also red and looked even redder because the rest of her face was so pale under the freckles. He hadn't thought her pretty before. Now he thought she was downright ugly.

When her eyes fell on him, her expression again reminded him of the scornful way Sergeant McCandless had looked at him the day he tried to steal her father's fence rail—an unanswerable look combining disdain with distaste and hatred.

"You got to marry me," she said.

He stared at her. He had not spoken to anyone in weeks and he croaked, "What?"

"I got your baby in me." She sounded country, not city like she usually did.

"I never. Why you talking that way? I don't like it."

Sergeant McCandless snapped onto her face. "You got to marry me, hear?"

"I can't marry you."

"Why not?"

"I'm married a-ready."

The sergeant knew better.

"I shouldn't never have trusted you," she said. "I seen you marching by with all them others and you looked like you was playing soldier. And when you come back like you done I felt sorry for you even if you were a deserter. That was dumb of me."

"I weren't no deserter—I told you what me and Jess done."

She shook her head. "And the first chance you got, you done that to me. And now you got to marry me."

"I ain't going to marry you."

"Yes, you are. If you don't, soon as I tell Mother, Scoot'll take you back to the Army and you'll be shot. If you try to get away Scoot will track you down and shoot you himself. Father says he's the best shot he ever seen, in or out of the army."

He believed her.

"All right. But if I'm going to marry you, you got to do what I tell you, starting right now."

Sergeant McCandless!

"Come on," she said. She crawled through the tunnel into the cave that had once been hers and was now his. She lay down on his blanket.

"Take off your clothes."

She stood up and stripped, not looking at him. She stretched out on the blanket again and folded her arms over her face. She opened her legs and he lay down on her. She was stiff as a ramrod, every muscle rigid. But he was, too, and he didn't mind. He didn't mean to marry her, though. He could feel her bones sticking into him. He wanted a woman with meat on her bones.

Every afternoon she came to him, bringing a chicken leg or pork chop and stale bread, sometimes milk and, when he demanded it, an occasional piece of pie or cake.

He accused her of feeding him table scraps. She looked at him, *Sergeant McCandless* on her face, saying nothing. He ate and then she stripped and folded her arms over her face while he got on her. He told her to take her arms down. She refused. When he exposed her face by force, he was surprised at the strength it took to move those pipe stem arms. She kept her eyes closed even then. If she did look at him, he knew it would be with her *Sergeant McCandless* look, but he needed to know for sure. It seemed like something was missing if she wouldn't look at him when he was inside her.

"Open your eyes," he said.

She clamped her teeth. She wouldn't open her eyes, any more than she would willingly take her arms down. It wasn't until he was done that she looked at him, a quick, contemptuous glance. *Sergeant McCandless!*

She picked up her clothes, silently dressed, and silently left, leaving him with the uneasy feeling that it was he who had been bested. Her silence bothered him as much as her *Sergeant McCandless* look or her talking country. He wanted her to tell him things, what was going on at the bottom of the hill, what she felt and thought. If she spoke at all, it was in monosyllables, communicating little, volunteering nothing, and most of the time not even answering questions. Her not speaking made him feel he was not connected with her, even when he was.

He did not understand what had gone wrong. Why wasn't she as soft-seeming and friendly as she'd been? Why did she look at him as she might at a cow pie in her path, something to be stepped over and otherwise ignored? She had asked for it, hadn't she?

He began to suspect there were things Jess Fellows had not told him about women, things that she could tell him, if only she would. But she wouldn't say a thing, or at least nothing that mattered. She had the answers, he was positive, and could have told him, but she would not. Now and then he grew angry and drew back his hand to hit her. That made her look him square in the face, but *Sergeant McCandless* made him bring his hand down. He did not dare do otherwise.

The only thing she would talk freely about was marriage.

"When?"

"Not yet. And next time, bring me some pickled pigs' feet."

Instead of pigs' feet, she brought her mother.

Amos lay on his belly and peered through the weeds as they climbed the hill to the tunnel. Her mother was no taller than Minnie, but broader and heavier—a sturdy figure, wearing a white bonnet that kept him from seeing her face, a high-necked gray dress that reached to her shoe tops, and a starched white apron. She came up the steep hillside easily, without hesitation or pausing for breath. There was something imperious in her bearing. Here she was, a woman and not a large one at that, striding through the underbrush like a colonel. He scuttled through the tunnel back to his cave and then into other tunnels, hiding. When he came out Minnie and her mother were gone.

The next morning when he rolled out of his blanket the black giant called Scoot was squatting by Minnie's table. He was too big for her chair. The long-barreled Remington rested on his knees.

"Who you?" Amos asked, though he knew.

"Scoot. I'm Scoot, and I'm taking you to see Miz Wilkes."

Amos decided to pretend not to be scared, though he was. The man with the gun had been a slave—in Amos's eyes was still a slave—and therefore would be accustomed to obeying orders.

"Get outa here. I ain't going to have no slaves in here."

Scoot threw back his head and laughed, a deep laugh resonating far down in his chest. He stood up and gestured with the pistol.

"Up, boy." His voice was as deep as his laugh. "Miz Nellie, she wants to see you and I'm taking you to her."

It wasn't right, a slave ordering a white man around, but Amos couldn't think what to do about it.

"Move them feet, boy."

Scoot crawled through the tunnel after him. Once outside Amos had a moment or two in which he might have run away. But he remembered Minnie's saying that Scoot was the best shot her father had ever known. He slouched down the hillside ahead of Scoot, trying to look nonchalant. Children peeked around doorways. Some of the children were black and some white, the white ones being Minnie's little brothers and sisters.

Amos felt shamed by having a slave, even a freed slave, herd him along like a criminal, and nothing he could do without getting shot.

Scoot rapped on the door of the last cabin.

"Come in," a woman called.

Scoot threw open the door and pushed Amos inside with his gun. "Take off your hat, boy."

Amos snatched off the remnants of his floppy-brimmed slouch hat. The only light came from the open door and small windows high on either side of a fireplace. Minnie's mother sat, rocking and knitting. Scoot prodded Amos to stand where the light from the doorway fell on his face. He could not see Minnie's mother very well at first, but when his eyes adjusted to the dimness he saw where Minnie got her *Sergeant McCandless* look.

But she was polite.

"I am Nellie Wilkes, Minnie's mother."

"Yes'm."

He darted his eyes around the cabin, not wanting to look at her. The cabin was much like the one Amos had grown up in, but this one was whitewashed and clean. There were pictures on the wall and rugs on the floor, which was of hewn boards and not of packed dirt like the one at home. The bed was made and the table was neatly set.

"What is your name, young man?"

"Amos, ma'am. Amos Gower."

He didn't mean to call her ma'am, but she drew it from him like a claw hammer draws a nail.

"How old are you, Amos?"

"Eighteen, ma'am."

"Minnie said 17, but I don't believe that, either. How old are you, Amos?"

"Sixteen, ma'am?"

Sergeant McCandless.

"Close on, ma'am." Every time he opened his month, a *ma'am* he didn't know he had in him leapt out.

Knitting needles clicked.

"Who are your people?"

My people, ma'am?"

"Your parents. Who is your father?"

"Pa's a farmer, ma'am, but he's got him a bad back."

"What is wrong with his back?"

"It hurts, ma'am."

"So he doesn't do much?"

"No, ma'am. Not much. His back hurts right smart."

"He sits around and drinks?"

How did she know that? He wiped his palms with the hat he clutched. His throat was dry as a dusty road. He said nothing.

"Where is this farm? Where do you come from?"

"Georgia, ma'am."

"Where in Georgia?"

He stared at her. She repeated her question.

"I don't know, ma'am."

"You don't know?"

"No'm. Nobody never told me. There weren't no place to give a name to, ma'am, just old man Cannady's store down the road a piece."

"How much schooling have you had, Amos?"

"I went to school, ma'am. I can write my name, ma'am."

"Can you read?"

"Yes, ma'am!"

She picked up a Bible from the table beside her and opened it, taking a moment to find the passage she wanted. She handed it to Scoot, who tucked his pistol under one arm and held the Bible open in front of Amos.

"Read the Sermon on the Mount," she said. "Matthew, Chapter 5."

"I don't know no Matthew."

She laughed. So did Scoot.

He stood silent, hating her, hating them both.

"Read him a bit of it, Scoot. Perhaps that'll help him get started."

Scoot turned the Bible around and read, booming out the words like a preacher. "And seeing the multitudes, he went up into a mountain: and when he was set, his disciples came unto him: and he opened his mouth, and taught them, saying, Blessed are the poor in spirit: for theirs is the kingdom of heaven."

Again Scoot held the Bible in front of Amos.

"I can't make it out, ma'am. It's too dark in here."

"The truth is, you can't read. Isn't that so?"

"I can write my name, ma'am."

"An educated man," Mrs. Wilkes said. She laughed, Scoot too. Amos shuffled his feet and turned his cap in his hands.

"Tell me more about your family. Tell me about your mother."

Her commanding manner would have kept him in the room even if Scoot hadn't been standing there, six-shooter in hand.

"My ma's dead, ma'am. Pa, he said get out."

"Brothers and sisters?"

"Yes'm."

"Older or younger?"

"I'm the baby, ma'am. Ma, she died a-borning me."

"Your father sent you away. Didn't your brothers and sisters take you in?"

"No, ma'am. Pa said he didn't want me pestering my brothers and sisters. He said they got troubles enough without me, ma'am."

"And now you've got my poor little Minnie with child, sweet, dreamy Minnie."

"I never, ma'am. No, I never."

Sergeant McCandless. Scoot lifted his pistol. Lifted it slowly, as though he were about to aim it.

"Young man, were my husband here, he would horsewhip you and send you back to the company you so shamefully deserted during battle. You would almost surely be shot or hanged at once as a coward and deserter, as well as a rapist. But he is gone and I don't know when or if he will return. So I must handle this."

He swallowed hard at every word. *Horsewhip. Coward. Deserter. Shot. Hanged.*

His Adam's apple jumped like his pa swallowing rotgut.

"Yes, ma'am," he said, though she had said nothing to say yes to.

"Minnie has persuaded herself that there is nothing for her to do but marry you, and she insists on doing it. She is a stubborn child despite her dreaminess — the most strong-willed little person I have ever known.

"She will not change her mind. She does not love you, you must understand, but Minnie has always been a romantic. She has supposed all her life that someday a prince would come to her. She would marry her prince and live happily ever after. You have destroyed that dream, childish and foolish though it was, and she cannot believe that any man worth his salt will ever look at her again without scorn. Thanks to you, she feels dirtied. Perhaps she is."

Amos wanted to protest but did not know what to say. He turned his hat in his hands, shuffled his feet, and stayed quiet.

"I have told her she does not have to marry you or anyone else. Gossiping tongues cannot hurt her for the simple reason that we will pay no attention to them. I have told her I would prefer she did not marry you, because a brutal, ignorant boy can only grow into a brutal, ignorant man who will do nothing but make her unhappy. The only difference between what you are today and what you will be in three or four years and all your life is in height and weight and strength."

Again Amos felt the need to protest her description of him, but he couldn't manage more than a strangling sound in his throat.

"I have warned her that by marrying you she will only suffer and that her child would be better off with no father than with such a father as you. But Minnie feels that she was at fault for putting herself in a position that allowed you to do what you did. She also feels that if you were to be shot she would be responsible for your death. She cannot bear the thought. She is a soft-hearted child—always has been. She once stepped on a frog and held a funeral for it. She buried it next to her grandmother and put a little white cross on the grave. Rather than see you killed, as you deserve, she is determined to sacrifice herself for the mistake she made when she took in a deserter about whom she knew nothing and of whom she should have expected nothing but what happened.

"She learned too late that when you touch dirt you come away dirty."

Amos did not feel he should have to bear insults like that. This rich lady with *Sergeant McCandless* on her face and highfalutin' language in her mouth had no right to call him dirt, no right that he knew of. But he did not have the words to say what he had in mind to say. And Scoot was there with his pistol. There was no way for him to grab her and slap her the way he felt he should.

She stared at him — would have stared him in the eye if he'd let her — and said all those ugly things calmly, without raising her voice. She might have been discussing a pig wallowing in the mud, or a slave. That was it, he decided. She was talking to him like he was a slave, a nothing. When she paused, waiting for him to speak, it took time for him to find his voice.

"I ain't going to marry her. I don't have to and ain't nobody going to make me — ma'am."

"I see there is one thing we agree on. You understand as well as I that it would be better for both you and Minnie if you didn't marry.

"But the rest of it we may think differently about. You can marry Minnie or you can go with Scoot to the nearest Confederate regiment to be turned in as a deserter and a rapist. You would be dead within a day. That would please me. I would not be pleased to have you marry my daughter."

"I ain't going to do neither one," he said. He turned toward the door.

Before he had gone a step he was on the floor with Scoot's foot on his chest, holding him down.

"Put him in the root cellar, please, Scoot. We'll keep him there until he decides what he wants to do."

Scoot lifted three boards on the floor and rolled Amos into a dark hole.

He fell on a mound of what he took to be sweet potatoes. He fell hard, the breath knocked out of him. Scoot threw his hat in after him and put the boards in place. Amos heard a scraping noise and a thump overhead as Scoot moved a box or chest over the boards. Cracks between the boards admitted strips of light except where Scoot's feet and the box blocked it. Amos could see nothing. He could hear voices, however.

"Not a prepossessing young man, do you think, Scoot?"

"No ma'am, he's not a boy I'd want my girl to wed."

"Nor do I, but she's in a family way and he's the father, for better or worse, and Minnie insists on it."

Amos heard feet moving overhead, heard the voices, but could not tell what was being said. He knew only that as usual somebody was deciding his fate and he had nothing to say about it.

4.

AMOS DID NOT actually see the mouse — it was too dark in the root cellar for that — but tiny feet scampered over his cheeks and around his mouth and nostrils. What could it be if not a mouse?

Somewhere he had heard of an animal that could draw your breath away and kill you. He couldn't recall what animal it was, but a mouse seemed probable. He did not want to take any chances. He tried to brush it away, whatever it was. Nothing but the scampering was there. It was not a mouse trying to draw his life away but what was worse, the ghost of a mouse.

Day and night he sat on the potatoes with his back against the root-cellar wall, his mouth pressed against a knee, and a hand cupped over his nose. Beset in the dark hole by fear of breath-stealing mice or their ghosts, it came to him that the world was in a bad way when a colored man and a woman could hold a white man prisoner in a root cellar, making him sleep on potatoes hard as rocks. He brooded about that and the choices Mrs. Wilkes had given him. Not marrying Minnie meant going back to the army and certain death. Marrying Minnie would mean facing Major Wilkes when that officer returned from the war — and then certain death.

To Amos any officer was a mysterious being to be feared

and kept away from. A corporal was as highly ranked an embodiment of authority as Amos had been able to face without anxiety. Officers strode around—or more often, rode—sowing difficulties in the path of lesser beings like Amos. Officers were invariably imperious, self-satisfied, and knew what was going on and why. They were ever willing to discommode as many men as were under their command by ordering them to do difficult, unpleasant, and even dangerous things at inconvenient times, without apology or remorse or telling them why it was necessary that they should do whatever it was they were told to do.

The thought of facing an officer who was also Minnie's father made Amos feel as though he'd just gulped down a big hunk of spoiled mule meat that would not lie easy on his stomach. He did not expect the major to be any more pleased than Mrs. Wilkes at the prospect of a common soldier as a son-in-law, in particular a soldier who before the marriage hád arranged for the Wilkeses to become grandparents. The major would most likely kill or maim him in righteous wrath, son-in-law or not, but if for any reason he didn't kill him outright it would only be so he could send Amos back to the army to be shot or hung. Mrs. Wilkes had offered him nothing but a choice of sure deaths.

He had to escape. He would stay alert and wait for a chance to kill Scoot. It would not be easy. Scoot was not only big. He had the intimidating bearing that Amos associated with officers and Minnie's mother. Attacking Scoot head-on had no more appeal than going back to the army or marrying Minnie. He was not afraid of Scoot, of course. A white man scared of a nigra? Amos had never heard of such a thing. It was good sense, not fear, that made him wait for a chance to get rid of Scoot that did not risk damage to himself. Or so he told himself.

His thoughts drifted to Minnie. He missed her—not so much

missed her as missed having her under him to plunge into. As he thought about her, he considered with pride the baby she said he had given her. He regarded it as proof of his manhood. He was as good a man as any, capable not only of bending a woman to his will, but also of leaving his mark upon her, she want it or not.

If only Minnie had a little meat on her bones. If only she would take her arms down from her face and look at him as he lay on her. If only she did not have a Confederate major of cavalry, described as a hero, for a father, who was bound to want him dead. If only she did not have a mother who looked at him as she did, despising him with all the force of Sergeant McCandless.

Except for all those ifs, being married to Minnie might be all right, at least until he could figure a way to get away safely. Thinking about Minnie under him, he stretched out on the sweet potatoes, took one hand down from his face, risking the mice, and put it inside his pants.

Scoot lifted the boards over the root cellar. He laughed and flashed white teeth when he saw what Amos was doing.

"You want me to come back later, boy?"

Amos rolled over on his side to hide himself from the big man's view while he got his pants tied together again. He had long since lost all buttons. I'll do it, by God. I'll kill him. Laughing at a white man! That nigra don't have no call to laugh at me, 'gardless.

There was no one around as Scoot took him to the privy. There never was. It was as though everyone had been warned to hide when Amos came out of his hole. Amos saw a pickax leaning against a shed that served as a stable now that the barns were burned. He veered over toward it, as though avoiding something he saw in the trail. He glanced over his shoulder. Scoot was there behind him, not even carrying his long-barreled pistol, not paying attention.

Why not? All he had to do was get close to that pickax, make one sudden leap, grab it and swing the ax, driving the point home in the big man's back. Scoot wouldn't have a prayer.

Amos made the leap and got his hand on the pickax handle. Before he could lift it he was on his back in the weeds, having smashed his head against the side of the shed on his way down. Scoot pressed the pickax against Amos's Adam's apple and smiled down at him, a smile that Amos took no comfort in.

"You got a touch more spirit than I reckoned, boy."

He pressed on the pickax. Gagging, unable to breathe, Amos pulled at the pickax with both hands but couldn't move it. Pinned to the ground, Amos thrashed like Jess Fellows in his death throes.

"Short on good sense, though," Scoot eased the pressure of the pickax enough for Amos to catch his breath. "What little Minnie wants with the likes of you, I wouldn't know."

He nudged Amos with his foot.

"Up, boy, and no more nonsense."

Amos got up and staggered to the privy, clutching his throat and choking with rage and frustration. That black man had laughed at him, Amos Gower, a Confederate soldier. No, he thought, letting his rage turn to the fantasy he had first sketched for Minnie in the cave. A hero. That's what he was. Not just any hero but a Confederate cavalryman hero. Scoot seemed far away and unimportant as he daydreamed of himself ahorse, fighting battles and performing deeds that caused men to cheer in admiration.

Amos and Scoot were on the way back from the privy, with everyone out of the way as usual, when Major David McGehee Wilkes came home. The black servant who had followed Minnie's father out the gate now led him back, a canvas-wrapped burden on the back of the skittish mare. His saber, its scabbard missing, gleamed under the ropes that bound his shroud. Other belongings followed on the mule that had carried them away. Whatever had happened to the major, the horse and servant had been spared, mules too.

"Ho, Henry," Scoot called. "You hang back there whilst I tell Miz Wilkes."

Before he could go to her, Minnie's mother came out of a cabin next to the one she lived in and where Amos was kept penned under the floor. Amos had wondered where she spent her time while Scoot got him out of the hole, because she was never around then. She was pale and biting her lip, but made no sound. She ran to the mule and laid her head against the canvas bag. After a moment she stepped back, keeping one hand on the bag.

Amos thought she should be crying but she wasn't.

"Are you all right, Henry?" she asked.

"Yes'm, right fine."

"Put the boy away, Scoot, and then bring the major."

"Move along, boy," Scoot said, gesturing at Amos with the pickax.

All around were loud screams and lamentations as women and children poured out to surround the black mare. Minnie was among them, looking scrawny as ever, a bulge at the waist the only showing of the baby she claimed to have in her belly. It was the first time Amos had seen her since he was put in the hole. Her face was screwed up, crying. If she saw him, she gave no sign.

Back in his hole, Amos heard the feet overhead, the coming and going of wailing women, the quiet voice of Minnie's mother soothing them. Late in the day he heard Scoot report that he and Henry had finished digging the grave. Then he heard their footsteps as they bore the major across the floor and out the door. The next time Scoot took him to the privy Amos saw a new wooden cross and fresh mounded earth in the burying ground at the base of the hill. Scoot did not speak to him and no one else was around. The quiet seemed eerie. There was no crying, not a sound, coming from the cabins where everyone retreated when he came out of the hole. He hungered for news. What had happened? What would happen next?

He was put back in the hole and in the night he heard the quiet moaning of Minnie's mother overhead in the cabin, where the smell of death in a hot climate lingered.

In what seemed like minutes after he fell asleep, Amos woke up with the mouse—he was sure it was a mouse this time—sitting on his face, drawing away his breath. He screamed and kept screaming. The ghost of Minnie's father had taken the form of a mouse and was there in the hole with him, determined to suck his life's breath away as punishment for what he had done to Minnie.

In his terror Amos stood up and pushed with his back against the boards that kept him prisoner. Suddenly the box or chest holding the boards down slid aside. He was able to stand up, waist deep in the hole.

Mrs. Wilkes stood before him in her nightgown, holding a candle. Her hair was tangled, her face pale.

"Get out," she said. "It's up to me now. I won't have you on the place. If you're still around in the morning I'll send you back to the Army."

Amos went out the door in a rush. Only after it closed behind him and he found himself outside in the dark did he recollect that ghosts could go anywhere. He pounded on the door, yelling to be let in. Scoot was there in a minute. He threw Amos down and for the second time that day planted a foot on his chest.

"Who're you? Who're you?"

He ground his foot into Amos's chest.

Mrs. Wilkes opened the door.

"It's the boy, Scoot. I want him gone."

"He's gone," Scoot said. He took Amos by the seat of his trousers and the collar of his shirt. He hustled him to the gate where Amos had first seen Minnie, lifted him over the gate, and dropped him in the road.

"Git, boy," Scoot said. "I see you around again, you're dead."

Amos clung to the gate.

"I'll marry her," he screamed. "I'll marry her."

Scoot left without a word.

Amos huddled against the gate all night, fighting ghosts, not falling asleep until the sun came up. Well into the morning, Minnie came out and opened the gate, waking him.

"Come on," she said, in a mix of city and country, "I done made Mother change her mind about sending you back to the Army. She says I'd do better to have the baby and no man than to have you around the rest of my life. She's right but I said, 'Mother, it isn't right, a baby without a name.' She said, 'You'll never be happy with a lout like him.' I said, 'Mother, I know that.' So Scoot's done gone for the preacher."

It was bright day now.

"I ain't going to marry you. I don't have to and I ain't going to."

Sergeant McCandless.

"Come on. Mother said clean you up and give you one of Father's suits to wear."

He stood a moment, not following her, thinking. He began to see an advantage to marrying Minnie, scrawny though she was. With the major dead, he would not have to face an irate officer whose child had been misused. And one day Minnie would be rich, and her riches would be his. If he didn't like being married to her, he could be on his way any time he chose, with money in his pocket.

She said over her shoulder, sounding more like him than herself, "You come on, hear? Scoot, he ain't a-going to stand for no nonsense."

He obeyed, but said, "You hadn't oughta talk like that, not if I'm going to marry you."

"Ain't it the truth? I hadn't oughta."

It was the first suit of clothes, matching pants and tail coat, that Amos had ever put on. It didn't fit, of course, because tall as Amos was for his age, he wasn't yet as tall or as broad as the major had been. Amos had to fold back the sleeves of the coat and turn up the legs of the trousers, while cinching the pants in folds around his waist with a piece of rope—the major's belts were much too big. But the material was fine. Amos felt well dressed for the first time in his life. He also tried on a pair of the major's shoes. They were expensive ones made before the war of soft leather. Amos had already got his growth in his feet and hands. The fit was perfect. For the first time in his life, he had socks to put on.

The ceremony was held outdoors in front of a burnt-out church. The preacher, a fat man with rosy cheeks and a drooling lower lip, wore overalls under vestments that were spotted with cinder burns. When the time came Amos said, "I do," almost cheerfully.

The preacher shook Amos's hand. "Now kiss the bride."

Amos turned toward Minnie. She was wearing a long white dress and a little cap with a veil. She did not lift the veil or offer her lips when he tried to kiss her. He wound up pressing his mouth against stiffly starched lace. She lifted the veil only when her mother came to her.

Her mother was crying. Minnie cried, too.

As Minnie and her mother clung together, Amos stood by, feeling confused. Mrs. Wilkes had not cried on learning of her husband's death, but now sobbed bitterly at her daughter's wedding. Something was out of kilter.

His confusion only deepened as her brothers and sisters, all younger than she, and a variety of relatives and friends came up to weep with Mrs. Wilkes and Minnie. Not one spoke to him or even looked at him.

At last her mother turned to him and shook his hand. She did not offer to kiss him.

"Try to be a good man."

"Yes ma'am," he said.

5.

IN THE YEARS THAT followed Scoot worked him hard and Amos grew muscular as well as tall, his body finally catching up with his hands and feet. He was not lazy or dumb when it came to farming, and he enjoyed the work.

Scoot taught him more than he had learned in all his life before. He learned what crops to plant when, and much more. How to plow a straight furrow, help a cow give birth, treat a collar sore on a mule, shoe a horse, build a silo, repair a fence, butcher a steer, tan a hide. He learned to spread mutton tallow on the stinging cracks that cold weather and damp put in his knuckles, to look for the telltale bent blade of grass or the thorn-caught hair or thread that said a deer or man had gone this way and not that. How to estimate the seed needed to plant a field and the number of bricks to fire for a chimney high enough to draw well.

By the time Amos passed the six-foot mark, Scoot had taught him everything Amos felt he needed to know to work the land, harvest and preserve the crops, care for his animals, and house his family—everything, that is, except why Scoot, the patient teacher, refused to call him anything but *boy*. You, *boy*. Now, *boy*. Ho, *boy*. Over here, *boy*. Why Minnie's mother still looked at him with her *Sergeant McCandless* look and never spoke to him except with a scarcely veiled scorn that kept him aware how little she liked him. Why Minnie would not take her arms off her face and look at him when he mounted her. Why she would laugh and play and cuddle with his children and smile at anyone else in the world, even a black child she didn't know, but offered him only her *Sergeant McCandless* look. Why to anyone but him she talked like her highfalutin' mother, while when she spoke to him she sounded just as country as he.

He knew she was mocking him, but he dared not ask why; he feared she would tell him. In the night after Amos rolled off her, she pulled down her nightgown and turned her back on him, dropping off without a word. He lay beside her in the bed hungering for something more, not sure what it was he lacked or why it was denied him.

He soon had three sons, but not an Amos among them. She made a point of giving each child two names, at least one of them Biblical. Duncan Ezra ("Dunc") was the eldest, followed by Benjamin James ("Ben") and William Nathan ("Nate").

Amos reminded her that his name was Biblical—she had told him so. Wasn't it time she used it? Minnie refused to explain why she wouldn't use his name, except to say, "I ain't going to call one David, neither." Amos couldn't understand that. She had loved her father and she loved her children. Why wouldn't she name one of them David? Or at least Wilkes?

Whatever her reason, Amos knew beyond a certainty that Sergeant McCandless was mixed up in it and it was aimed at him, not the children.

Once they left babyhood, his boys became an amazement to him. Until then he paid them no mind. They were broad-shouldered little fellows with enormous hands and feet. Every one of them, Amos was proud to note, looked like him, with broad faces, big ears, black hair growing low on protruding foreheads, recessive chins, deep-set eyes of so dark a blue that they appeared black, and large fleshy noses—arched but doughy. Even Amos could tell at a glance that no one but he could have fathered them. All were healthy and strong as horses, except for Dunc having weak eyes that kept him from seeing much farther than a hoe's length in front of him.

As he grew sure of his competence in the art and science of farming, he felt it was time to assert his rights. By then, thanks to Minnie's insistent tutoring, he had learned to read and write a little, though laboriously.

By then also he, Scoot, and Henry, the former slave who brought the major home, had built four smaller houses where the big house once stood. Two of the houses were larger than the other two and formed a rectangle around a shared court. Mrs. Wilkes lived with Minnie's younger brothers and sisters in one of the large houses on the long sides of the rectangle. Scoot occupied the other. Amos and Henry occupied the smaller houses with their families. Amos resented the inequity.

Minnie did not.

"I ain't aware we need more room," she said.

One evening Amos happened by as Minnie's mother sat rocking on her front porch, knitting baby garments.

"Evening, ma'am."

She nodded.

"I been doing me some thinking, ma'am."

"Have you, now?" She did not bother to conceal her wonder at such an assertion coming from the likes of him, even if he was her own son-in-law, a six-foot-four man with a thick black beard and a wrangle of sons pushing out the walls of his house. Dunc, Ben, and Nate had just been joined by twins, Donald Noah and Robert Joseph.

"I been thinking, ma'am, I'm 22 now—"

"Or perhaps you mean, 'Close on, ma'am'?"

He remembered their first meeting. "Yes'm, close on, ma'am. But it's time I took over this here farm and run it, place of Scoot."

She rocked along, looking out toward the distant river, knitting, saying nothing. "We ain't working but a smidgen of land, ma'am. But if we gotten us a few more hands—lots of folks is begging to work for next to nothing but keep, or maybe shares—just a few more hands and we could get ever last bit of our land planted again."

The rocking chair stopped. She stared at him over stilled knitting needles.

Sergeant McCandless!

"*Our* land?"

"Your land, ma'am. I misspoke myself."

"So you did."

"I reckon it's time, me being your son-in-law and all—"

"I had nothing to do with that."

"It's time I run the place, ma'am. Ain't right, a nigra telling a white man what to do, and him your son-in-law."

"Negro, if you please. Scoot is a very capable manager, the very best I know. I am extremely pleased with his work and do not plan to replace him now or in the future."

"Well, now, ma'am," he said, "I don't reckon to work for him no longer, him a Negro or not. What I got to tell you is, if'n I ain't going to run the place, me and Minnie is going to Texas."

"What a good idea, though I'd rather you left Minnie and the children here. When can you start?"

BEFORE AMOS WAS on his way to scout out the lay of the land in Texas, planning to send for Minnie and the children later, there was time to get in another crop and for Minnie to become pregnant with still another child, who would be born in his father's absence and be named Jefferson Peter.

He went off well-dressed in clothes of Major Wilkes that now had to be let out instead of taken in to make them fit. He was mounted on a black mare, daughter to the horse that had carried Major Wilkes to war and brought him home twice, once less an arm and once as a canvas-wrapped corpse. The saddle he used was Major Wilkes's and he kept the major's rifle ready to hand in a saddle scabbard. The major's sword was tucked in a bedroll. No one knew that it was not some thieving passer-by who had stolen it.

There were other things he was taking with him that no one knew about, including a thin-bladed knife concealed in his boot, Scoot's long-barreled pistol, and two jugs of corn whiskey produced in a still hidden in the woods without Mrs. Wilkes's permission or Scoot's knowledge.

When Amos had his truck loaded on a mule, he looked around for someone to say goodbye to. Scoot and Henry were building a shed to shelter a new-fangled hay rake Mrs. Wilkes had agreed to buy on Scoot's recommendation. The twins were in their cribs.

Dunc, Ben, and Nate were underfoot but too young to be interested in anything but themselves. In the common courtyard edged by the houses, Minnie bent over a tub set on a low bench, scrubbing boys' pants on a washboard, sleeves shoved up past her elbows, hair falling around her face, cheeks bright with exertion, perspiration beaded on her forehead.

As Amos came up, she tossed a pair to Mrs. Wilkes for rinsing in tubs of hot water. Picking up a long pole with a hook on the end, she snagged another pair of pants out of a big iron pot in a pit of hot coals.

"Well, I reckon to be off."

"You still here? I thought you'd be halfway to Texas by now." Minnie held up the pants and studied a stain. "Where do you suppose that boy got into axle grease?"

"No telling," Mrs. Wilkes said. "He's just like his father, poor child."

Amos remembered the day Major Wilkes had gone off to war. Everyone had said good-by to him, taking turns standing on the mounting block.

"Well," he said.

He felt the heat from the fire pit on his face. He lifted his cavalryman's hat, which had once belonged to Major Wilkes, and wiped sweat off his forehead with his shirt sleeve. Amos had taken the hat from a trunk over Mrs. Wilkes's protest after he learned that she proposed giving him only $500 in gold to start up in Texas. That was a large sum for the times but not near what he had hoped for. Minnie had said it was plenty as far as she was concerned and she would not ask for more. He knew it was no good him pressing Mrs. Wilkes for more, so he took Major Wilkes's hat instead.

He combed his beard with his fingers. "Well, I reckon to be off."

"I swear," Minnie said, "here's more grease. Those boys!"

Amos mounted his horse and left with no further notice from anyone. He had to open and close the gate for himself. As he rode he puzzled over the difference between his going and Major Wilkes's. He concluded that the difference was accounted for by the fact that the war was four years over. He felt aggrieved that his wife and his mother-in-law had forgotten in such a short time what respect was due an officer, a cavalryman, and a hero of the Confederacy.

IN VICKSBURG AMOS found his way to the Planters and Merchants Reorganized Bank. He handed the letters Mrs. Wilkes had given him through the teller's grill. He then leaned against a marble wall and admired the polished paneling and brass of the grandest room he had ever been in. The place was crowded, but in a few minutes a little man in tail coat, starched shirt, and black tie, bustled out and pumped Amos's hand as though he was drawing water.

The little man identified himself as John Comfort, president of the bank. Talking the while, Mr. Comfort guided Amos past important-looking gentlemen waiting in the outer room and through swinging gates to a paneled inner sanctum, which turned out to be the president's office and nearly as grand as the main banking room.

Seated with a cigar in hand and lighted, Amos learned that Mr. Comfort had looked after the Wilkes family's business affairs since before the war. By dint of hard work, reputation, and certain friendships, Mr. Comfort had managed to recreate his bank since the surrender. He mentioned his joy at being able at any time to be of service to the Wilkes family. He inquired in turn about the health of Mrs. Wilkes and each of her children by name, including Minnie, without pausing for an answer.

"And Mrs. Wilkes tells me you and little Minnie are going off to Texas with your fine young family," Mr. Comfort said.

"If'n the sun comes up and the river don't rise," Amos said, pouring country into his speech beyond even his natural bent. "We sholy 'preciate Miz Wilkes's hep to get us theah."

Mr. Comfort sighed and rang for his clerk. The rest of the business was conducted rapidly, with a minimum of ceremony. Amos knew that he had fallen in Mr. Comfort's estimation from the status of a once-rich but still prosperous lady's well-dressed son-in-law to that of poor-white adventurer preying on that same lady's daughter. When it came time to sign a receipt for the gold Mr. Comfort handed over, Amos drew an X rather than sign his name, which he could have done, though it might have taken time.

From the bank Amos found his way to a riverfront hotel that Mr. Comfort assured him was cheap but clean and respectable—cheap being all Amos had asked for, clean and respectable thrown in by Mr. Comfort.

The hotel had survived Federal shelling during the war, but not without damage that had been only crudely repaired. The building was small, with a butcher shop sharing the first level with the hotel's public rooms. Creaky stairs rose on the outside of the building to the second floor, where Amos was able by paying extra to get a bed to himself in a room with two beds. No one was around, but the landlord said his was the last unspoken-for bed available in the establishment that evening and congratulated him on his good fortune in securing it.

Amos's horse and mule went into a stable across the alley behind the hotel.

Countryman that he was, he worried about the safety of his belongings in the big city. He gave a one-eyed stable boy a dime and a mean look to watch over his packs. To indicate what might happen if a pack were disturbed, he pointed the rifle at the youngster and pretended to pull the trigger.

"I'll keep my eye on it," the boy promised.

The room came with meals. After a supper of pigs' feet, sauerkraut, and cornpone, Amos wandered the streets for a time. He was awed by the scurrying people and vehicles. He wondered where all those people were coming from and where they were going so urgently. As usual he felt that everyone but he knew something he had missed. He decided he didn't care for city life—especially the crowds who seemed to know better than he where to go, what to do, how to do it.

He went back to the stable and dug a jug of corn whiskey out of a pack. He lit a candle and sat on the edge of his bed. The cornhusk mattress rustled every time he lifted the jug to take a swig. He thought about finding a brothel, but he was no fool even in his cups. If a woman had come to him, a well-upholstered woman with pads of flesh over the sharp bones and angles that Minnie presented uncushioned, he would have been glad to use her. But he was not willing to risk even a sliver of his $500 in gold in the saloons and whorehouses of Vicksburg.

The second bed in the room was still unoccupied when Amos put down his jug, blew out his candle, and stretched out fully dressed, not even pulling off his boots. He dropped quickly into stupefied sleep.

Sometime later he awoke with a start. Moonlight filtered in through the window overlooking the alley. He heard a scratching at the door. Heart pounding, thinking his gold was threatened, he slipped his hand into a boot and pulled out the knife he carried there.

By the time the door opened wide enough for a dark figure to creep into the room Amos was standing beside the door.

The man who tip-toed in held what looked to Amos like some kind of revolver. Amos seized the man's wrist and twisted it. He heard the bone crack. The revolver-like object went flying. He aimed a kick at a face bending toward him in agonized surprise. By the time the intruder made his first small sound, no more than a low moan, he was flat on his back in a corner of the room with Amos's knee on his back and Amos's knife deep between his ribs.

When Amos rose, the man was dead. In the moonlight Amos saw that he was a young man, a small man. With his head thrown back and blood trickling from his open mouth, he looked in the moonlight like Jess Fellows. The pistol turned out to be a candleholder with an oddly shaped handle full of curlicues. The candle had gone out or perhaps had been blown out by the young man to avoid disturbing anyone as he entered the room to stretch out on the other bed.

Amos wasted no time. He picked up the body and shoved it through the window. On Vicksburg's waterfront, he reasoned, one more dead man in an alley was not likely to cause a stir. He listened for steps in the hall. Hearing none, he seized his belongings and crept down the outside stairs. No one was in the alley. He took the body by the heels to drag it to a new location behind another building.

Catching a glimpse of the river between two sheds, he decided to dump it over the cliff. First he emptied the dead man's pockets, netting several coins, a thin wallet, a palm-sized derringer, a pair of dice, and a pack of cards. He heard the splash as the body hit the water.

Just at dawn a river man ferried Amos, his horse, and his mule out of Vicksburg and across the Mississippi. Standing at the front of the raft, Amos scanned the murky surface of the river for the body. He saw no body, but the dead face of the young man who looked like Jess Fellows seemed to float on the muddy waves wherever his eye fell.

Turning away from the sight, he opened the wallet, finding little in it worth keeping except a few bills, a letter, and a photograph of a round-faced young woman. He dropped the wallet into the river, along with the dice and cards. After a moment's hesitation he threw the derringer in, too.

In the dim light of a not yet risen sun, he studied the letter, hoping to learn something about the man he had killed, hoping at least for a name, but he could not make sense of what he tried to read. It would require more time than he had just then to dig out words he could take hold of and shape into meaning.

He turned to the photograph, which told him almost more than the words but still not enough. The young woman stared out at him with an expression that seemed bold and yet vulnerable, simultaneously inviting and rejecting his scrutiny. Her lips were pressed together, straight full lips that seemed to shelter a smile. Heavy eyebrows shadowed her eyes, drawing attention from the eyes themselves, which nonetheless seemed to be looking directly into his. She had a strong chin and full cheeks and her dark hair framed her face in a soft cloud. Looking at her made Amos think of bedding her, as though by killing the young man in Vicksburg he had somehow gained the right to use the young man's woman as he wished.

She looked like she might be a big woman with meat on her bones, which interested Amos. He wished the photographer had shown more than just her face and a hint of shoulders. He felt certain, with no evidence but the photograph itself to go on, that the woman was the young man's wife. While the young man was surely a gambler, judging by the cards and dice and little pocket gun, the woman looked respectable, solid. And yet, there was that ambiguity in her face and smile. It suggested to him that she would not be one to cover her face when her husband mounted her.

Amos did not blame himself for having killed a man—he had done what seemed at the time to be what he had to do—but he wondered how the young woman would fare now that her man was gone. He knew it was a foolish thing to do, perhaps a dangerous thing, but he slipped the photograph and letter into his rucksack. The dead man's face faded from the waves.

By the time the sun was overhead, Amos was in Louisiana and riding hard for Texas.

6.

THE TRAIL WAS WELL-MARKED and heavily traveled. Amos could have hooked up with any number of Texas-bound folks, some on horseback, some walking, others trudging alongside wagons or oxcarts bearing families and household goods. But he saw greed and treachery in every face and kept to himself, avoiding the crude inns and taverns along the way to camp in the woods. As he rode he pulled out the photograph and letter, which had been refolded so many times before he got it that the creases were worn.

The photograph told him little more than he had gleaned when he first scanned it.

But the letter began to make sense as he studied it. It was a long letter, written on both sides of lined paper in the sort of cursive script that had flowed so readily from Minnie's hand when she tried to teach him to write. Amos found it hard to decipher, though block printing would not have helped him.

The letter was to a man named *F* from a woman named Mary Pollard, who lived in Amesville, a settlement on the trail he was following to Texas. Amos felt sure that *F* was the young man who was now dead and Mary Pollard was the woman in the photograph. He decided *F* had been Mary Pollard's sweetheart, not husband, and she was likely a schoolteacher — she mentioned holding class, used a lot of big words, and wrote a long letter.

He puzzled out the words letter by letter, but they did not always come together well enough to make sense. It was as though a dark veil stood between him and the letter. The exact meaning of the words kept slipping beyond his grasp just as he thought he'd caught it. Best as Amos could make out, Mary Pollard was urging *F* to give up cards and drinking and get religion. Otherwise she would marry someone else and not send *F* any more money.

> Dear F, Well I am fine and holding class like always. Things has slowed down in Amesville because of the railroad not coming throu afterall but plenty of pupils. Sue the new girl from Kansas City who helped out while I and you was together is gone on to Santonio but lerned me things before she left you wont find in your schoolbook. The boys cant get enough & twice as rambunktous as ever. Its quick easy & I charge extra so the money rolls in twice as fast in half the time and trouble.
>
> You said maybe we can pare up again after the comotion over what you done to the blacksmith dies down. Well F maybe we can if that should be what you want. But first you got to get religion and lern your busness like Im lerning mine. I dont want my hard erned money going to the Devil with somebody who dont even know how to deal off cards without somebody tumbling to it and grabbing your hand & the pot like that blacksmith done. What it is with you F is drink. You got to do the same as me & keep in mind your working when everybody else is playing & you got to make them think your playing too. This is not like being in church as you wouldnt know & its not somthing your doing with a bunch of old friends. You got to keep in mind it's a job just like teaching or selling mens shoes &

you do it for money & its them has got the money. It dont help to swear at the cards. If you dont get the cards you want its because you dont deal them proper. Or think of it like school & your the teacher like I do. You got to give the boys what they come for to get what you want. Do what I do & work on doing it better so they keep coming back. What youve got to cure yourself of F is funning around when your working. You know I never take a drink except with you & maybe another special frend.

Im sending the money you asked for but F there aint any more where this come from. Im saving up from now on & when a good man comes along willing to forgive & forget Im going to buy me a farm & settle down & raise a family. I wish you could be the good man but that dont seem likely the way you wont stick to busness. You can come back here any time you want though. The folks who fussed with you about what you done to the blacksmith with that little gun has mostly gone on to Texas now and them thats still here dont care so come on home and let me show you what Sue showed me. I won't charge you. With you its all on the house F even the extras. Your right at the head of the class with me like always. As ever your frend.

Mary Pollard

Amos decided to look up Mary Pollard once he got to Amesville, if he did. What the purpose of looking her up might be he couldn't say. He didn't plan to make himself known to her, but he felt he owed it to himself to see what kind of woman the young man he had killed, this *F*, had been able to attract.

He studied the direct-looking eyes and the lips that now seemed to be smiling and now were not.

He imagined Minnie as well-fleshed as he took Mary Pollard to be, imagined her looking up into his face with eyes open and maybe a smile. Amos had listened to a lot of rough-talking men besides Jess Fellows, and the wisdom he had gleaned was that there were women other than whores who did eagerly all the things a man dreamed of. Mary looked like she might be such a one. Or perhaps not, her being a schoolteacher and from the looks of her letter as quick with words as Minnie, which Amos had long since concluded was a drawback that could make a woman too full of herself to submit sweetly to her wifely duties.

Amos puzzled along, wondering again why Minnie wouldn't show him her face when she lay under him. Had Mary Pollard shown her face to *F*, assuming that she had allowed him on her before marriage?

He dozed off in the saddle, dreaming first that it was Minnie and then Mary Pollard who bumped, bumped, bumped against him.

BY THE TIME he reached Amesville Amos traveled an almost deserted trail. It was raining and cold. Rain was common in that part of the country at that time of year. Cold was not.

He had two pair of pants and three shirts with him and put them all on. To fend off rain he wore Major Wilkes's cavalryman's hat and draped a canvas over his shoulders. It reached on either side past his stirrups.

Amesville was in piney woods at a river crossing. It was a settlement of scattered cabins built of logs that no one had troubled to strip of bark. One cabin had "MARSHEL" carved over the door. Beside it was a smaller cabin about the size of a three-hole privy. It had a barred window and "JAIL" over its door. A couple of the bars had been wrenched apart. An enterprising man put in jail could be free in the time it took him to get from the door to the window.

Next to the jail Amos saw a cluster of structures lacking signs: a stable, a corral, an open-faced shed of peeled pine poles, and a lean-to hut, also of peeled pine, with a door, but no window. The door was ajar. Neither corral nor stable held a horse or other animal. In the open-faced shed Amos could inventory at a glance all the tools and equipment a blacksmith might need for a going business, including anvil, forge, bellows, hammers, and tongs. Around the shop and hut stood wagons needing wheels or axles, rusted plows with broken points, rakes, logging chains, and a pile of hinges. No one had replaced the blacksmith Mary Pollard's *F* had put out of business with his little gun, and his services were missed.

Amos decided on the spot to look into pausing in Amesville to add to his stake, using the skills Scoot had taught him. Without dismounting he rode across the muddy road to a largish building of unpeeled logs. It had a covered porch and a three-word sign over the entrance: "STORE, SALUN, HOTEL." One of the white columns flanking unpainted double doors bore the remnants of a cardboard sign that had once read "GIRLS." Someone had crossed out the *S*.

In a smoky lobby lit by two high-hanging coal-oil lanterns, three men wearing broad-brimmed hats sat on a bench by a potbellied stove, whittling on small chunks of wood. All three suspended their knives in mid-air as they looked Amos over. Behind a pine-board bar running the length of the room, a man in a green eyeshade and bulky sweater looked up from an account book.

"Come in, friend," he said. "You might's well join the wake."

He paused, his pen poised in the air, studying his account book. Amos said nothing. He leaned his rifle against a wall and stood near the stove, hands spread to catch the warmth.

"Now that you didn't ask," one of the whittlers said, "the wake's for a newly deceased town. First we lose us our card dealer—"

A second whittler broke in, "Oh, Frank'll be back. He was just skeered of what the blacksmith was going to do to him after he shot him in the foot with that little gun of his."

"Maybe Frank'll be back but the blacksmith won't," the first whittler said. He also paused for a question but went on when Amos stood silent, rubbing his hands together over the hot stove. "Died, the blacksmith did. Took a pus in that foot. Old Doc, he sawed it right off, of course, but he was gone in a week, the blacksmith was, smelling like he'd died in the war. Looked at the right way, I suppose, we was probably fortunate to keep him in town at all, dead or not. Preacher that said the good word over him, he left not two days after, along with the sawbones that taken off that foot. The schoolteacher and marshal too. Even the bartender is up and gone."

Amos finally bit. "Where'd all them folks go?"

"Downstream or on west," the third whittler said. "Amesville has done had its day of glory. Time was, less'n three months ago, we had the best river crossing you could find in a hundred miles and seemed like nothing could stop us. This here was the hell-raisingest town 'twixt Kansas City and Houston. People poured through here like shit through a sick mule. Why, we had a town council made up of us three, and every comfort of a metropolis, including a professional gambler, a right handy blacksmith, two whores, one of 'em from Kansas City, and a doctor who didn't know nothing about pills but could saw like a logger.

"Then some feller finds what he says is a better crossing downstream a ways and that's where the new railroad is going to go. Now we've got us a missing card shark, a dead blacksmith, and only one whore, not the one from Kansas City. No doctor. No preacher neither, but that don't signify."

"You most likely will be near the last of the folks who'll be coming this way, as word gets around," the first whittler said. "Ain't nothing going on in these parts no more but a bunch of loggers chopping trees to float down river and nesters trying to put in cotton on land the loggers clear."

Amos was curious as to why the three whittlers stayed when everyone else left.

Amesville's hold on the property-owning storekeeper seemed clear, but he didn't understand what the others were doing there. It came out at last, without the rudeness of questioning, that the first whittler was the undertaker who had buried the blacksmith. The second was the town banker, whose office was under his hat, and the third was the postmaster for a post office that was authorized but not yet built. They were farseeing men, buying up the property of departed settlers for next to nothing, in the belief that big as the country was, it wasn't big enough to absorb all the folks heading west. One day, they expected, the backwash would start and more nesters would come back to Amesville to stay, having exhausted their hopes of striking it rich out among the Indians of Texas.

Amesville's growth would no longer be rapid, but no telling, said the undertaker, how valuable the land would be in time, assuming all those land-hungry settlers could stay fed and out of the hands of doctors long enough to buy it.

Amos asked about the blacksmith's shop. "I'll sell it to you," the storekeeper said.

"You own it?"

"No, sir, but I'll sell it to you."

"If'n it's all the same to you, I'll pay for it with scrip just as good as your title."

"Sold," the storekeeper said. "You know how to shoe a mule? If so, you've got a living just from loggers."

He went out into the rain and rode back across the muddy road. He put his horse and mule in the stable, which was well stocked with hay. He also found a stack of burlap sacks and wiped down his animals. When he took his belongings into the lean-to he disturbed a woodchuck and several families of rats and mice. A fire laid in an iron cook stove awaited his match, and dry wood was stacked against the wall. Several battered pots and a frying pan hung on the wall behind the stove. The place was furnished with a table that had three sound legs and one that was broken but still serviceable, two stools, and a plank bed. A jumble of bedding, stinking of long-spilled blood and pus, was piled on the planks.

Amos surmised that somebody had been laying a fire for the wounded smith when the man expired, making it unnecessary to light the fire.

After throwing out the bedding, disturbing another rat or two, Amos tossed his bedroll on the planks. He lit the fire and got the place so warm that he stripped off his extra pants and shirts before he investigated the smithy. He found a supply of coke and quickly got a fire going in the forge. The bellows seemed sound enough. Its action was a trifle stiff but it made the coals glow. He was in business, fully equipped so far as he could tell, and not a dollar invested.

He plodded back across the road through the mud. In the store a young woman had joined the three men around the stove. She wore a flowered wrapper and had dark hair pulled away from her face and falling down her back.

Amos recognized her at once as *F*'s letter-writing friend Mary Pollard, though the photograph had not done justice to her youth, the fresh color in her cheeks, and the alertness of her eyes. She sat in a rocking chair, leaning toward the stove. The wrapper fell away to reveal her breasts, either of which represented more flesh than both of Minnie's, even with milk.

"We done scared up a new pupil for you, Molly," the undertaker said, still whittling. "This here's Mr.—Mr.—well, I ain't sure—Mr. Who?"

"Wilkes," Amos said, for reasons he couldn't have to put tongue to. "Amos Wilkes."

She eyed Amos up and down. A smile played about her lips.

"There looks to be enough of him, but that don't always mean a lot. You'd be surprised at how little some big men is in places that count."

She looked at the banker.

"Or maybe you wouldn't be surprised."

The other two whittlers hooted, the storekeeper joining in. The banker laughed, too, but weakly.

Amos lifted his hat to the woman. "How do, ma'am."

"Well, he knows his manners anyway. An officer and a gentleman, like my pa, according to the hat and manners. Was you in the war, Mr. Wilkes?"

"Yes'm, cavalry," he said.

"Pretty good at riding, I reckon?"

"Yes'm."

The other men laughed, slapping their knees. Amos didn't know what they were laughing about, but after a moment a laugh rumbled up from deep within his chest and boomed forth as though he knew exactly what the joke was and relished it.

She stood up, big boned, nearly as tall as he. Sturdy thighs, solid enough to hold up a bank, thrust against the wrapper.

"Well, come along then," she said. "First time's on the house. Sample of the merchandise, so to speak."

"Man needs a drink first, Molly," the undertaker said, as Amos stood silent, turning his hat in his hands.

She went behind the bar and poured whiskey from a stone jug into a mug. "The drink's not free. That ain't my department."

"That's all right," Amos said. "I'll pay."

He slapped a coin on the counter. She poured him a second drink.

"Let's go. Free don't last long around here."

Amos followed her through a curtained door at the back of

the store and along a dark hall.

"Leave your boots out here. I don't want mud in my room. Coat and hat too."

The room was small and warm, centered around a big bed with tumbled covers. A tub of water steamed on a range in the corner and a flowered pitcher and basin stood on a washstand beside the stove. One wall was covered with women's dresses and other clothing hanging from pegs. There were more ladies' shoes and boots lined up on the floor under the dresses than Amos had ever seen before, even in a store.

"Get your pants off. Shirt, too, you want." She went to the stove and ladled hot water into the basin.

Amos did as ordered, breathing hard. She came to him and shocked him by grabbing him and pulling him toward the washstand. He went suddenly weak in the knees.

"Damn, you're fast," she said. She pumped a little to help him finish. "Most folks wait till they're in."

She washed him as he diminished. Amos found the attention pleasant.

"You want to try again?" she asked. "You've had your free shot, by rights, but it don't seem like it ought to count, being caught in mid-air so to speak. I'll make the next one half-price and throw in something extry for nothing."

Amos nodded, ashamed at having fouled her hand. He was startled when she bent over him. Jess Fellows had talked about this, but he'd thought Jess was just talking, like he did so much.

After a moment, she drew away. "Reckon you're ready to go."

She fell on the bed with her wrapper open and clamped powerful legs around him. It was like being pulled into a tub of butter. He couldn't feel a single bone. But she didn't look at him. She turned her face and stared at the wall. He tried to bring her face around. She knocked his hand away and closed her eyes. She was as much a mystery as Minnie.

It was over quickly. He decided that even with the extry she'd thrown in there hadn't been a whole lot more to it than if she'd been Minnie, except for no bones sticking him.

"Well, come again any time," she said. "I'm here day and night."

Amos crossed the street to the smithy and dug out Mary's letter to *F*. He unfolded it but did not look at the words before dropping it on banked coals in the stove. Its edges browned and crisped, curling toward him.

Words seem to rise from the darkening paper, seeking escape, until it burst into flames. He touched the black remnant with a poker and watched it fall apart, a thousand bits of nothingness.

He didn't need her letter anymore.

7.

THE BLACKSMITH BUSINESS slowed once Amos worked his way through the backlog he found on his arrival in Amesville.

He soon left in a wagon a young nester had been unable to reclaim. It was pulled by a young team purchased from another luckless settler. Trailing along behind, tied side by side to the tailgate and blinkered to overcome their animosity, were the black mare and the mule that he had brought from Mississippi. With him he also took the smithy equipment, a deal more cash than he'd had when he arrived, and Mary Pollard.

She was tired of a place where free spending travelers no longer turned up and her customers were mostly regulars. It was like being married to a dozen different men, she complained. She always knew what to expect with every one of them, right down to the time and services required and the conversation before and after. There was no real interest in it.

Before leaving Amesville Amos wrote to Minnie for the first time. It took him several hours spread over two days. Pleased with the ink-smeared product, he showed Mary the letter.

> Dere wive
> Im inn Amsvil gon to Texass. saved 25 doler Cash

Mony. bisnis Slow movin to beter plase.

Yr husbin Amos

"I reckon that done it," he said.

"I just reckon it did," Mary said.

It did not occur to him that the glint in her eye might be amusement or that the note, spelling aside, would bring more puzzlement than enlightenment to Minnie. Where was Amsvil? Why had he stopped there for so long without writing? Why had he addressed the envelope to "Misus M. Wilkes"? And what business had added $25 to his capital but was now slow? (The actual sum was closer to $50, but Amos saw no need for precision.)

Mary Pollard was pregnant—by Amos, she said, though he hadn't been in Amesville long enough to be responsible for the size of her belly. But he said nothing. He regarded it as a convenience to have Mary around, especially now that she was not charging him even for extras. She was an amiable companion, uncomplaining, compliant, and a good listener.

At night as they lay in the back of the wagon between the anvil and the bellows, Amos sat up now and again to lick a jug. As the rotgut took hold he talked like he was thinking aloud. Nigh on to everything he'd thought or done in his whole life— and a deal more that he hadn't—poured off his tongue.

He told her about battles he had been in and what General Lee said when the greatest military leader the world had ever known pinned a medal on him for his exploits at Vicksburg. The deaths of Jess Fellows and Mary's gambler friend *F* did not figure in his musings, nor did he think it needful to mention that his name was not Wilkes, he had been a deserter and not a major in the cavalry, and he had never been decorated by Lee or anyone else for leading a cavalry charge against Grant at Vicksburg or for any other reason.

Otherwise Amos told her most everything, even about Minnie and the tunnel and *Sergeant McCandless* on her face. When he started talking about Minnie and puzzling over the sources of her scorn for him, he couldn't shut up.

Mary surprised him by being shocked at his Minnie stories and his willingness to tell them. She was indignant at his failure to understand the wrong he had done to a dreamy little girl and her tender nature. He had treated that child like she was a grown woman and a practiced whore, Mary said—and even a whore, she added, didn't care for surprises like he'd given Minnie in the tunnel.

Amos listened but didn't agree. What Mary had to say didn't jibe with what Jess Fellows and other men of experience had said on the subject of women. Amos was inclined to believe they knew better than Mary what they were talking about, being men and hence stronger-minded than any woman. It didn't seem fair that Mary tried to put the blame on him for what happened in the tunnel. He'd only done what Minnie wanted and what any man would've done, or tried to do. She must have liked it or why did she make him marry her when he didn't want to? It was only a way of coming back for more, like Jess Fellows said women did. He blamed something unnatural in Minnie for the way she'd turned angry with him and stayed angry.

Mary brushed his reasoning aside. She pointed out that, by his own telling, jumping on the girl in that dark tunnel had been his idea, not Minnie's. He had knocked all her girlish dreams of romance out of her head when he seized her and thrust himself on her. What he had left her, other than the baby in her belly, was a dreary certainty that no decent man—or woman—would look at her with anything but scorn once she bore a fatherless child.

Maybe her mother was right in saying that the girl didn't

have to marry but little Minnie wouldn't have felt that, Mary argued. She would think of all the pointing fingers and clacking tongues. Gentle dreamer that she was, she would have shrunk from the notoriety she faced. She would have feared, Mary said, that she could not survive the gossip that would spring up around her as her expanding belly made her plight public.

Even marrying Amos would have seemed better than that to a frightened little girl—an assertion that Amos found belittling.

"Now, here," Amos said. "Now, here. You don't know Minnie. She ain't skeered of nothing and nobody. Never has been."

Mary ignored him. She had a theory of her own and lectured him with no more regard for his feelings than Minnie or Mrs. Wilkes. In that day and age, Mary told him, life without some sort of man, however worthless, was pitiful hard for a woman, a fact which Minnie would have known in her bones. There were few ways for a woman to make a living that did not have to do with a man. She could be his wife or his whore.

There were not many other choices, and Mary did not see a lot of difference between the two states in most cases, but a woman had to be powerful strong to stand up for herself without a man, especially when she was pregnant. Minnie might have managed it, because her mother stood by her, but the child had not yet known her own strength. She had probably felt dirtied and blamed herself for her plight. Marrying someone like Amos must have seemed a just punishment on her for having gone into that tunnel in the first place.

"Now here," Amos protested again. "Now here."

Mary ignored him and told her own story.

She said she had come from folks who had been rich before the war. They had lost much of their money but not their pride or position. As she told it, she had been a giddy girl, a reluctant student and a reckless social butterfly with a liking for worthless young men. She was caught in bed with the Episcopal bishop's married son, a family friend. Mary had thought to brazen it out, she said, but her own mother called her a whore and turned her out of the house. And here she was — whore, but her own woman.

The difference between her and Minnie, she said, lay not only in the reaction of their mothers — though that had been crucial for her — but in the fact that she'd had a choice in bringing on her downfall, and Minnie had not. She knew just how Minnie must have felt about what Amos had done to her — how, for that matter, she probably still felt.

As for herself, she said, she was content with her lot, at least for the time being. It was better to be her own woman, even if it meant living as a whore, than to be dependent on a single weak, foolish, and treacherous man.

Amos did not take comfort in any of this and began to regret that he had told Mary so much. It also troubled him that he couldn't seem to get away from Minnie. Even when Mary clamped him to her with powerful thighs he puzzled over Minnie, remembering the sharp little bones pressed against him, the arm over her face, the flatness and bitterness and anger of her. Mary said he had sentenced himself to Minnie in that tunnel. In that, at least, Amos thought she might be right.

AMOS SET UP his blacksmith shop in a little town in East Texas cotton country. He was soon prospering again. Mary passed herself off as Mrs. Wilkes and joined the Women's Missionary Circle at the Methodist church, which she attended every Sunday and occasionally forced Amos to attend as well.

One Sunday she recognized a former customer in a pew several rows ahead of her. She didn't think he saw her but she told Amos she wanted to move on, just in case. Amos thought

Texas must be populated by men who had been with her in Amesville on their way west, but he also was ready to move on. He wrote to Minnie, again under Mary's amused eye, to tell her where he had been but not where he was going—not to keep her in the dark, necessarily, but because he didn't yet have a more specific destination than somewhere further west in Texas.

One night on the trail, with little advance notice, Mary gave birth to a son. It was not an easy birth, but Mary directed Amos every step of the way. He had never been in the room or even nearby when his own sons were born. But under Scoot's direction he had assisted many a cow to bring forth its calf and many a mare its foal. Nothing about the birth of a child seemed particularly strange or frightening or even wonderful—not the blood, the gradual widening of the cavernous opening, or the sudden appearance of the child's head. The baby was a boy—a big one.

When Mary declared that the child looked just like him, he accepted the assertion without protest, though both knew that it could not have been his by several months. He had never paid close attention to babies and this baby looked to him like any other, including his and Minnie's. Amos suggested that Mary name the child for him, but she settled on Eph Wilkes, explaining to Amos how Eph was spelled. Amos could see no difference between *F* and *Eph* except on paper, but he did not bring that up. He pretended it did not matter to him what name Mary gave the child.

Mary started a garden in every town they stopped in, but she often spotted a former customer before the first onion could be pulled. Amos did not mind moving on. Each move carried him closer to West Texas, where grasslands were being opened for settlement through the removal or decimation of Indians. He was in no hurry, however—he wasn't eager to head into Indian territory before he was sure the hostiles were cleaned out for good. He kept tabs on what was going on out there by chatting with eastbound travelers who brought him a horse to shoe or a wagon axle to repair.

Time slipped past. His informants reported that the Indian threat was about over. Amos began preparing for the last lap of his journey. He did not mention his intentions to Mary, even when he was drunk and got talkative in bed, nor did he pass along the reports he got about what was happening in West Texas. When it was time to go he meant to go alone, without Mary and little Eph. He had put by a goodly sum. The size of the ranch he expected to be able to establish had expanded with his savings. He hoped to expand it still more by taking with him the money Mary had saved from her working days. So far as he knew she had not spent a dime of it since she joined him.

He decided he had been paying for her services after all, having laid out a tidy sum for her bed and board and Eph's. It seemed only fair that she cough up her share of their expenses, willingly or not. As the time neared for his departure, Amos searched Mary's belongings when she wasn't around, looking for what he now regarded as his money. Finding nothing, he concluded that she had disregarded his warnings about banks and put her savings in one, beyond his reach.

He felt cheated.

AS AMOS OPENED the gate, he found Mary and Minnie on the front porch, rocking like sisters or best friends. Minnie cuddled Mary's little Eph on her lap. The laughter died. The two women — one knife-thin, the other overflowing her chair — stared at Amos as they might at a stranger they felt no desire to see. Amos stood at the bottom of the steps as if barbed wire kept him from joining them on the porch.

"Isn't he a sight?" Mary said.

"Isn't he though?"

The two women started laughing again. Amos couldn't recall ever seeing Minnie laugh. He'd heard her, but it was always with her mother or children, never with him.

Now she laughed so hard that her freckled cheeks grew rosy and her blue eyes sparkled with tears. For the first time he realized that she was a beautiful woman. And she was laughing at him.

"Now, here," he said. "Now, here."

"You just be quiet. Ain't nothing you say going to matter, not from now on."

"I'm glad he's yours and not mine," Mary said. "Fastest man in Texas. Couldn't please a nanny goat."

"Never could," Minnie said.

"Now, here! That ain't no way for ladies to talk."

The two women were off again, laughing so hard they had to pull out handkerchiefs and wipe their eyes.

"Cavalryman!" Mary said.

"Major Amos Wilkes!" Minnie said.

"Hero!" they said in unison. "General Lee!"

"I ain't going to stand for this."

"Yes, you are, Amos Gower."

"How'd you — ?"

"Mary writ me. She said you was fixing to skip out."

"I never. No, I never."

He saw *Sergeant McCandless* on two faces.

"Ain't right, the both of you sitting there like that."

"If you know so much what's right, what about the tunnel?"

He had no answer and doubted he ever would.

"FLAT AS A SKILLET, dry as a broom, and windy as all get out," an east-bound traveler told Amos, speaking of West Texas. Amos didn't mind flat or windy and didn't hear dry.

What he saw in his mind was a sea of green grass rippling in the breeze and tickling the bellies of grazing cattle as far as the eye could see, all his.

Once in Owchicta County, however, he quickly added brown grass and blowing sand to flat, dry, and windy in the litany. But there was land for Amos to seize and seize it he did. His $500 in gold and the even greater sum he made in smithing went far on the empty frontier. He built his herd quickly—and his family, too. Micajah Moses joined Dunc, Ben, Nate, Noah, Bobby Joe, and Jeff ten months after Minnie turned up.

At first they lived like nesters in sod burrows sunk in the prairie. But after two successful years in a row Amos was able to borrow enough money from Mr. Hines at the new Owchicta County Cattlemen's Bank to build a two-story house for Minnie on a knoll that was not very high but higher than any other within a day's ride. When Amos came riding home from a trip to town he could see Minnie's house thrusting out of the prairie miles ahead, a monument to his success and prosperity.

As he liked to point out, the house was larger and grander than anything in the entire town of Owchicta, except the new Methodist church, with its towering steeple, the new courthouse with its white columns, and the new Cattlemen's Bank, which not only had white columns in front but also a cupola with a clock.

Amos didn't see much use for a cupola if you weren't going to put a clock on it. Columns were a different matter. They sent a message of power and importance that no one could miss. He vowed that one of these days, by God, he'd give Minnie columns to go with her house.

"This ain't Mount Vernon," she said, "and I ain't Martha Washington."

Even without columns her house was impressive for its time and place. On Sunday afternoons Owchicta families drove out from town in buggies and wagons to stare from the road, sometimes stopping in if the ladies of the family were Methodist, the church Minnie went to when she had the chance. Minnie's sitting room was not crowded, though it held two sofas, six stuffed chairs, and a loveseat, plus a grand piano with more carvings on its legs than the one burned by Yankee guerrillas back in Mississippi.

The house boasted a curving staircase with banisters the children slid down if Minnie wasn't around. The dining room table accommodated enough chairs—all matching—to seat the family and plenty of guests at one sitting, except that there were never guests to entertain and the family always ate in the kitchen, at a similarly large table. Four bedrooms took up the upstairs, with room left over for a central play area and an office that Amos never entered and only Minnie used.

Minnie had her own outhouse near the kitchen with a graveled path to keep her feet dry in the worst of weather. Amos and the boys shared a three-holer out by the bunkhouse. Their old sod houses provided spacious root cellars and doubled as cyclone shelters. Minnie also had a deep well and windmill that delivered plenty of alkaline but acceptable water and a henhouse snug enough and big enough to outshine half the residences bragged about by the Methodist ladies of Owchicta.

"That tells you something about them snootballs," Amos always added when he bragged on Minnie's new house, but he never said what the something might be.

Dunc, Ben, and Nate moved to the bunkhouse as they grew older, and Minnie claimed a bedroom for herself, assigning Amos another. This did not keep Amos out of her bed, but as she told him, at least she didn't have to put up with him one minute longer than it took him to do his business, which fortunately was always over so quick that if she didn't look sharp she'd miss it.

"Now, here. You hadn't oughta talk like that," he protested. *Sergeant McCandless.*

Minnie had no female companionship on the ranch, except that of the ignorant young daughters of nester families, who helped around the house and with the children.

So far as Amos could tell, she did not seem to expect or want companionship. She did not complain, which was all that Amos had to go on. Every time he went into town, however, she had letters for him to take to the post office. The letters went chiefly to her mother and to Mary, who at first had kept the name Wilkes for herself and little Eph but was now Mrs. Valentine, respectably married to a railroad man in East Texas. Eph was also a Valentine now, which Amos resented — what was wrong with Wilkes? Each time Amos returned from Owchicta, he brought letters from Minnie's mother and Mary Valentine.

He never knew what either of them had to say, any more than he knew what Minnie was writing to them. Amos did not think a decent woman like Minnie should correspond with a former whore. When he presented Minnie with this notion she said, "Ain't it the truth?" and kept on writing to Mary.

Each spring Minnie took those of her brood who weren't old enough to be useful on the ranch to Mississippi on the train. Going and returning, she stopped off to visit Mary and her railroader. Mr. Valentine, Minnie told Amos, was all that a husband should be — quiet, sober, a great reader, and altogether unlike Amos in every respect.

"Every?"

"So Mary tells me."

Amos was sorry he asked.

As for Mary's son Eph — she and Mr. Valentine had a near-annual dividend of other sons, with an occasional daughter — he was a paragon, to hear Minnie tell it. Eph Valentine was unfailingly polite and thoughtful, brilliant in his studies, as morally upright a child as any Methodist mother like Mary Valentine could dream of. He was always tall for his age, good-looking, and sweet-tempered. He was kind to his inferiors and had no superiors. He was destined for success every step of the way. Year after year Amos yearned for news of clay feet, which never arrived.

MINNIE TOOK TO barring her bedroom door. But every so often, after an evening of sitting with a jug and a coal-oil lamp at the kitchen table, brooding over her refusal to soften toward him, Amos crashed through the door and found his way to her bed. His bulk filled the room, and the intensity of his striving, brief though it was, made the house shake, to the boisterous delight of the boys old enough to understand what was going on.

One winter night Amos heard Noah shout toward the bunkhouse, "Hey, Dunc, Pa's in the saddle again."

He heard little Micajah ask, "What's Pa doing to Ma?"

Dunc, his voice recently changed, answered raucously. Amos heard, but missed the words.

"Can I do it too?" Micajah asked.

With a violent shudder, Amos rested on Minnie. Her eyes covered with her arm as always, bones poking, she said, "Fast? I swear! Mary said you was the fastest man she ever knowed, not a bit like Mr. Valentine."

Amos leaped up, pulled down his nightshirt, and rushed down the hall. He hauled Noah out to the barn, picking up Dunc at the bunkhouse on the way.

"What you young bucks thinking of? You hadn't oughta talk about being in the saddle, not where your ma can hear."

"What about Micajah?" Dunc said, sniffling.

"It was you and Noah started all that yelling."

"Pa, I can't help it if some damn fool's gonna yell at me when he hadn't oughta."

"I'll learn you to help it."

Dunc went first, being the older. Amos bent him face down over the workbench. He had nailed a short length of rope to the wall at either end of the bench. Amos looped the ropes around Dunc's wrists and drew the loops tight until the boy's arms were stretched out as far as they would go. Amos pulled Dunc's nightshirt up to his shoulders. Getting the range, he flicked a time or two with the old rein that he used for a strap. Then he let fly as hard as he could until Dunc's bare bottom turned redder than a West Texas sunset in a dust storm. The boy held out until the red was turning purple before he started sobbing and carrying on so much that he couldn't get his breath. After Amos untied the ropes and pulled Dunc's nightshirt down, the boy stood blubbering against the workshop wall until Amos, breathing hard, was done with Noah.

"By God," Amos said, "you boys ain't going to forget this trip to the workshop, not for a good long while. You ain't going to be sitting much neither, not if you can help it. The idea! Talking like that where your ma can hear! Right in front of Micajah, too. You got no business putting ideas like that in the boy's head."

Out of that encounter, Minnie produced another child, another boy, delivered by a midwife Amos fetched from town a week or so before Minnie expected to need her. The two women had a grand time visiting and laughing and singing hymns in the sitting room while Minnie played her piano. Once again Amos hoped that this time Minnie would name the child for him.

"I got eight sons, with this here one," he said, "and not one named for me. It ain't right, me being the father and all. This one, by God, is going to be Amos."

Minnie named the child Ephraim Ezekiel and decreed that he should be called Eph.

"There's already an Eph," he said.

"So there is, Mary's boy."

"What's wrong with Amos?"

"There's already an Amos."

8.

ALL THE OLDER BOYS but Dunc, who despite weak eyes had become Owchicta's town marshal, continued to work on the ranch after they grew up and married early, usually at the end of a shotgun. Their wives were town girls—flibbertigibbets, in Minnie's eyes.

Their houses were untidy, their cookery inedible, their children unmanageable, and their conversation—interspersed with giggles—intolerable. Minnie was glad that none was willing to live at the ranch, though it meant that the boys had to take turns visiting their families in town.

In 1888 Dunc finally married a sharp-tongued schoolteacher named Lorena. At last Minnie had a daughter-in-law she could abide. Unlike the flibbertigibbets, Lorena kept a neat house, cooked tasty meals, and was welcome at the ranch. She and Minnie played duets on the piano and discussed books, the evils of drink, and the pressing need for women to get the vote.

Dunc and Lorena's first and only child arrived ten months after their marriage.

Dunc wanted to name the boy after Amos. Lorena would not stand for it. Minnie backed her up and suggested "Major Wilkes," for her father, the child's grandfather. Knowing it to be an honor, Lorena seized on the name.

"That boy oughta be Amos. That's what Dunc wants," Amos complained.

"Maybe so, but Lorena and me decided there ain't no need for it."

Little Major Wilkes had eight uncles at birth and three years later gained an aunt. Minnie named her daughter Mary Nell—a pretty name, Amos thought, though its parts came from an ex-whore and a dreaded mother-in-law. The baby who bore it was his instant angel. For the first time there was an infant in the house that he enjoyed holding and rocking.

"Ain't she the sweetest little thing you ever seen?" he said, bending over her crib. The brown juice from a wad of tobacco stuffed in his cheek dribbled out a corner of his mouth and ran down his beard. He wiped it away with a finger.

Mary Nell grabbed the finger.

"Damned if she ain't just the prettiest damn little thing I ever seen," he said.

She pulled his finger into her mouth.

"Strong, too. Just look at that!"

Mary Nell pushed his finger away. She began to cry.

"Aw, now, what you crying about, little sweetheart?"

"She don't like dirty things," Minnie said.

Amos lifted her out of her crib. "Come to Papa, darling."

Mary Nell screamed and held out her arms to Minnie.

MINNIE DECIDED a ranch ten miles from town was no place to bring up a girl. Using money provided by her mother, Minnie bought a five-acre plot near Dunc and Lorena's cottage at the northern edge of Owchicta. Her land had the remains of a burned-out house on it, along with a henhouse and a barn, both untouched by fire. The barn provided a tack room, a hayloft, two stalls for cows, and two for horses. The henhouse was cleaned up, painted, and restocked with laying hens and a haughty red rooster.

Minnie built a sprawling one-story brick bungalow with running water, wide porches, and a bathroom complete with porcelain tub and toilet, a first for Owchicta. A windmill lifted the water from a deep well to a wooden water tank towering on steel legs. It was a large house, but except for the running water not nearly as grand as the one at the ranch. Still, it had several bedrooms and a sitting room roomy enough for the grand piano, a sofa, the loveseat, and several overstuffed chairs.

As at the ranch, the kitchen was the biggest room in the house. It had a boardinghouse-sized coal range, plenty of cupboards and countertop work space, a table with benches seating 16, and a sewing nook with several rocking chairs. A storeroom off the kitchen served as a pantry, with shelves of Minnie's home canned string beans, peaches, and apple butter on every wall. The pantry also held a bed and chiffonier for Amos when he found it necessary to stay overnight. He never saw Minnie's bedroom, which she equipped with a double-barred, two-inch oaken door.

Thanks to her mother's lawyers, the title to the property was fixed in Minnie's name. Amos could have no claim on it, which he resented. He had always understood that God and Texas law decreed that whatever a wife brought to a marriage or came to her after the wedding belonged not just to her but to the husband as well.

The lawyers he consulted assured him, however, that Minnie's mother's big-city shysters had wormed their way past the Lord and Texas law by way of trusts and other nefarious devices, and there was nothing Amos could do about it. The house was irretrievably Minnie's and beyond his reach, as were certain funds held for her in trust by the Vicksburg bank once presided over by Mr. Comfort and now headed by his brother.

From the time Minnie moved into town, she took part — or meddled in — in church, civic, and cultural affairs. Lorena had done the same after she quit teaching to marry; the county did not employ women who had husbands to support them.

The two made a formidable team. They started small — a book club here, a Bible study group or musical circle there — and built a network of active women who would spot problems and do something about them. Over the years Owchicta's voteless women forced the males who ran the town and the county to establish a city park, a library, and a county school system that eventually included a four-year high school.

Each winter Minnie moved the younger boys into town with her for schooling.

Eph was the only one who took to books willingly, but they all had an instinctive understanding of arithmetic, especially if it involved numbers with dollar signs attached. It was, Minnie said, the one civilized talent that Amos had given them. But he believed that his sons' facility with figures came from her side of the family, which was so sharp and greedy it could keep a respectable married man from claiming property that in the eyes of the Lord and the laws of Texas was rightly his.

FOR YEARS AMOS campaigned to have a memorial honoring Confederate heroes placed in the Owchicta town square. At last the city and county jointly authorized the project.

As the ranking Confederate officer in Owchicta County, Amos was made chairman of a committee to select an affordable monument from a St. Louis drummer's catalog and see to its unveiling with suitable ceremony on Remembrance Day, 1895. At the committee's first meeting, the mayor of Owchicta, a member of the body, pointed out that the county was filling up with northern newcomers. Maybe it would be better to consider something more neutral than a Confederate memorial? Perhaps a bronze plaque displayed in the monument salesman's catalog? It showed two clasped hands beneath a United States flag and the emblazoned words, "Together for a Glorious Future."

Amos called that a mealy-mouthed misrepresentation of history that only a no-good Yankee traitor would favor. He insisted that nothing would do but another item in the catalog, the statue of a Confederate cavalryman seated on a rearing horse and waving a sword. The mayor saved his skin from flaying only by denying that he had meant what he said; it was only a joke and nothing less than a Confederate cavalryman seated on a rearing horse could express the reverence he felt for the brave heroes who had died on the right side of history. But it turned out that a single bronze horse, without saddle or rider and with its four hooves planted on the ground like a plow horse, would cost more than a good-sized herd of real horses, times being what they were. The only statue in the drummer's catalog within the committee's budget was a Zouave rifleman.

Amos said he wouldn't stand for it.

"It was us cavalry could've won the War," he said. The capital *W* was right there in his voice. "The damn infantry lost it."

The St. Louis drummer urged him to take another look at the Zouave—an actual photograph, the salesman said, and identical to the one that would be cast in purest bronze for Owchicta's town square. Finger-combing his beard, Amos saw that the Zouave was no more an infantryman than he himself had been. He was a dismounted cavalryman, not a foot soldier—"look at them boots." Amos said he recollected seeing a troop of Louisiana cavalry decked out like that with those very boots in one of the battles he was in—Shiloh, maybe. Or was it Vicksburg? He couldn't say offhand which battle it was, but he remembered the boots, baggy pants, and funny hats them *A*-rab

Johnny Rebs wore as they dug in their spurs and charged a line of Federals, a-whooping and a-hollering.

The St. Joe drummer studied his catalog.

"I do believe you are right, suh. That there's no infantryman. I'll speak to our catalog folks."

The Remembrance Committee agreed that an affordable cavalryman like the Zouave, though dismounted, would be a suitable symbol of devotion to their noble—if for the moment lost—cause. The drummer began filling out the order form.

Amos voiced another reservation. It seemed to him, he said, that it was hard to tell at a glance that the catalog Zouave was a Confederate and not a Yankee. The St. Joe salesman told him not to worry. Their Zouave would be Southern as cornpone. He'd order their statue cast with a "CSA" on the fez so large that nobody with eyes in his head and the ability to read plain English could possibly mistake the Zouave for a New Yorker.

To cinch the deal, the salesman threw in a polished granite base with a standard message engraved on it. Any deviation in or addition to the inscription would naturally be extra, which seemed fair to all concerned. The message was suitable for North or South, though the salesman did not point that out.

SACRED

to the MEMORY

of

OUR GALLANT BOYS 18 6 1-65

ON REMEMBRANCE DAY, Amos left the ranch at daybreak and rode into Owchicta to unveil the Confederate statue in the town square. The day was warm, the wind still, though it would pick up later in the morning. Sweet peas bloomed along the white picket fence of Minnie's place. Swinging off his black

85

mare, joints aching from the ride, he heard Eph boom out in the deep, speechifying voice he had recently cultivated, "Pa's here!"

Eph was 15 and about to complete the eighth grade—the first of Minnie's sons to stay in school so long. For weeks he had been polishing the valedictory address he was to deliver at graduation. Amos had heard him orate several times, proving what Amos had long alleged—Eph could talk himself out of a tunnel with a train coming on. He rolled out his sentences like he was chewing sugar cane, with the conviction of a carnival barker and all the style imaginable, sounding not a bit country.

The speech, entitled, "Owchicta and the Good Ship *Enterprise*," was about salesmanship, progress, and the bright commercial prospects of Owchicta. Amos was awed by the learning Eph displayed. He predicted a great future for the boy as a politician, or maybe a drummer. Eph could sell a hairbrush to a bald man.

Eph was not only educated and a good talker. He was also a young man who knew how to dress. Except on occasions such as today's dedication of a memorial to the Confederate cause, his brothers and Amos mostly wore bib overalls and denim shirts, with clodhoppers on their feet, farmer straw hats on their heads, and red or blue kerchiefs tied around their necks to pull up over their faces when the cattle or the wind kicked up dust too thick to breathe. Their hair rarely knew a comb except perhaps on Sunday. Eph carried a comb in his pocket and slicked his hair down with a middle part, whatever the occasion or day of the week. He sported peg-leg pants, checked ones sometimes, and starched white or purple shirts, along with high white collars, and black string ties, even at the ranch.

Eph was purely a sight for sore eyes, as Amos often said, especially if the eyes happened to be in a female head. In recent months Amos had bought out two nesters, who claimed that Eph had put the watermelons under their young daughters' aprons. Eph denied it in both cases, of course, but the evidence against him was overwhelming.

"Don't come crying to me," Amos said to the nesters. "It's up to you to watch your girls just like it's up to me to watch mine."

He went to Mr. Hines down at the Owchicta County Cattlemen's Bank and borrowed to the limit to buy the families' holdings so they could go packing westward with their shame. Amos was well pleased. Though times had turned tough in the cattle business, he was still expanding and glad to have the nesters' land. A man could never have too much land.

Besides he was tickled at the idea of Eph, young as he was, scattering his seed the way he was doing. Wasn't a girl in the county safe from Eph—or a woman, for that matter. It was not thought to be for tea and cookies with Mrs. Rinehart that Eph stopped by the Western Union telegrapher's house most every afternoon on his way home from school, while Mr. Rinehart wore a green eyeshade and tapped out other people's messages at the telegraph office downtown.

RIGHT AFTER EPH shouted that Pa had arrived, Amos heard Minnie's mother reply, "Well I guess it can't be helped."

He had forgotten that Mrs. Wilkes was scheduled to visit. Scoot had died and she had moved to Vicksburg to be near her city-dwelling sons and daughters, leaving management of the plantation in the hands of Scoot's oldest son. Now she visited Minnie every spring and Minnie went to Mississippi, stopping off to visit Mary Valentine, only in the fall. But some things never changed. Mr. Valentine remained a paragon and Eph Valentine the best this and top that of the universe, most recently as a graduate of the University of Mississippi law school.

Amos heard Mary Nell complaining in the house and

Minnie scolding. "Now, girl, you stop that whining. He's your Pa and you're obliged to kiss him, even if his beard is sticky."

Amos spat his chaw on the ground and scrubbed his beard clean as he could with his bandanna.

"Young lady, quit squalling and give him his kiss. He's your Pa and it's too late to do anything about it."

Mary Nell appeared on the porch, wiping her eyes with her fists—the prettiest little girl ever seen on God's good earth. Big hazel eyes, yellow-flecked and near green at times—"cat's eyes," Amos teased—rosy cheeks, a dainty nose like Minnie's, dark hair glinting red in the sun. Her white dress flared around her, spotless. She might have stepped straight from heaven.

Amos couldn't help himself. He grabbed her, hugged her, tossed her skyward, rubbed her face with his. Mary Nell screamed. He couldn't stand to see her cry. He held her tight, trying to comfort her. She cried harder than ever, kicking and elbowing in her struggle to get away.

"Let me go! Let me go."

Mrs. Wilkes came out on the porch and took her from him.

"Well, I see you never learn." *Sergeant McCandless.*

Amos went into the house to relieve himself, which gave him greater pleasure than usual because he could do it on a flush toilet. He was prouder of the inside plumbing in Minnie's house than of almost anything else in the world but little Mary Nell and the way his Eph was turning out.

Flushing the toilet, he filled the tub with hot water from a faucet—no hauling of buckets from the kitchen in Minnie's household—and lay in soapy water with his beard floating and one leg draped over the side of the tub, which barely contained his bulk.

His contentment was such that he stayed in the tub until the water was cold.

His sense of well-being grew as he dressed in a new black

suit, stiff-collared white shirt, and calf-high black boots with two-inch heels. He wrapped a gold sash around his waist and across his chest and stuck Major Wilkes's sword in it. Pinning a couple of medals to his lapel by their faded ribbons — he had found them in a Fort Worth pawnshop — he clamped his cavalry-officer hat on his head. The hat was stained and battered, but it was the only part of his father-in-law's uniform that still fit him. Amos thought that with the medals and sword, the hat was ample evidence of the service he had rendered to the Confederate cause. He had long since forgotten that the hat and medals had not always been his.

After he was dressed Amos went downtown. During the night the statue had been set on a polished granite pedestal in the middle of the town square facing the courthouse. A tent-like canvas tarp, held in place by pegs driven into the ground at each corner, would conceal the Zouave from all eyes until the courthouse clock struck 12:00 o'clock. At that signal Amos, as the ranking Confederate officer in Owchicta County, would spur the black mare and yank the shroud away to give the county's citizens their first sight of the monument that the Remembrance Committee had selected from the catalog of the St. Louis drummer.

When Amos arrived at the square, only the "1861-65" on the granite base showed beneath the shroud. To prevent unauthorized peeking, Marshal Dunc Gower had guarded the statue all night. He didn't recognize his father at first.

"Now, y'all just stay back. Ain't nobody going to get him a look-see afore Pa says it's time."

"It's me, Dunc, your pa."

"I was afeared it was them dratted boys again. They been buzzing around here like flies on a cow pie ever since sun-up, trying to get them a peek."

"Which boys is that, Dunc?"

"I dunno. Couldn't get close enough for a good look. Ever time I chased one boy, a half-dozen run around behind, yanking at the cover. I been around and around this here statue till my legs is about give out. Only thing done any good was them boys got tired, too."

The ceremony started at 11:00 o'clock, with the sun high and hot. The square was jammed with wagons, buggies, and more people than Amos or anyone else had ever seen in Owchicta at one time. They had come from all over, many on a three-car special excursion train from Wichita Falls to the flag-stop ten miles east of town. The livery stable made a fortune running farm wagons as buses.

Four grizzled Confederate veterans dressed in whatever scraps of uniforms they could fit into stood at attention at the corners of the statue. Each held one of the ropes anchoring the Zouave's shroud against the wind. Now and again a gust ballooned the canvas, and the veterans had to use both hands to keep it from sailing away.

As the ceremony got underway, the wind turned out to be a peace-keeper. It whipped away and made harmless the words of the dunking-Baptist minister, who had won the drawing to decide which of Owchicta's ministers would give the invocation. After asking God to bless the town, the statue, and such of his listeners as came regularly to the proper church and were up to date with their pledges, he declared that it was the Lord's duty to open the misguided eyes of sprinkler Baptists as well as Methodists to the error of their ways and bring them into the total-immersion fold before it was too late. He did not mention Presbyterians or Episcopalians, who were too few to bother with, and uppity besides.

Had his words carried far beyond his lips, certain offended members of his audience might have heated the tar and stripped feathers off a flock of setting hens to have at him right there, never you mind its being Remembrance Day, Decoration Day, Memorial Day, or whatever Day you'd care to call it. The wind made certain that only God heard the preacher's exhortation, and only He could be offended by it.

The mayor gave the principal address. In it he chose to revisit the proposition that it was time for North and South to draw together as one nation. Again the wind blew so hard that his ranting didn't reach even the ears of Amos and other dignitaries seated behind him on the platform. Had he been able to hear the message, Amos might have hotted up another tar bucket.

Following the mayor's address, the wind died down. The crowd had no difficulty hearing the new Owchicta Grade School Marching Band blast out *Oh, Our Blessed, Blessed Southland,* a hymn-like number composed for the occasion by the bandleader. All six instruments—three trumpets, two trombones, and a bass drum—got started and finished within a breath of the same time. Mr. Hines, president of the Owchicta County Cattlemen's Bank and treasurer of the Remembrance Committee, as well as commander of the newly formed Owchicta chapter of the Sons of the Confederacy, rose to introduce Amos.

The wind was quiet and Mr. Hines was loud as he pictured noble warriors with unflinching spears and golden eagles with shining talons fastened in evil foes. It turned out that he was describing the exploits of Major Amos Gower in defending the South during the War of Northern Aggression. When the time came, he declared, as between General Robert E. Lee and Major Gower, who had been decorated by Lee himself, he would choose the major to lead the risen-again South to victory. He did not mention that General Lee was no longer in the running, having already gone to his reward.

On hearing Mr. Hines link his name with that of Lee, Amos

stood at attention and saluted with his sword in the direction of Minnie and Mrs. Wilkes, who were sitting in Minnie's new buggy at the side of the square. The crowd cheered. Mr. Hines paused to catch his breath. The cheering stopped. In the sudden stillness Mrs. Wilkes shouted into Minnie's ear. Her words could be heard all over the square. "Who in the world is that man talking about?"

Minnie put her hand to her face and rocked back and forth. Amos knew that she was laughing, but he hoped everyone would suppose that Mrs. Wilkes was merely deaf and confused and that Minnie was embarrassed by her mother's remark. He put her out of mind. He wasn't going to let Mrs. Wilkes spoil the happiest moment of his life.

The ceremony moved along with military precision. As Mr. Hines neared the end of his encomium, Amos mounted the black mare, who as always skittered a bit. The Confederate veterans who held the front ropes of the shroud handed them to Amos, who tied them to his saddle horn. The veterans holding the rear ropes stood at attention, prepared to let go when Amos spurred the mare to pull the canvas off the statue. Mr. Hines concluded: "Three cheers for a noble cause and Major Amos Gower, the Confederate hero of Owchicta!"

The crowd responded with Rebel yells. The courthouse clock began striking 12:00. At the third note the wind gusted. The statue's shroud flew up several inches to reveal the Zouave's boots and a bit of trouser-leg. Ear-piercing whistles punctuated the Rebel yells. At the seventh strike of the clock the mare jerked her head, fighting the bit.

Enthusiasts in the crowd fired their pistols. *Dixie* exploded from three trumpets, two trombones, and a bass drum. On the clock's twelfth stroke, Amos spurred the mare. She reared, bucked, and bolted, taking Amos and the shroud with her. Ropes whipped around Amos's throat. Sitting on six inches of air between returns to the saddle, he clung to the horn with one hand, waved his sword with the other and—choking—sailed out of the square under full canvas, aboard a black mare plunging like a schooner in heavy seas.

II. The Hex

9.

ON A WARM SPRING DAY in 1898, four strangers rode into Owchicta out of a dust storm. Bandannas covered their faces from sand-rimmed eyes down. At the granite base of the Confederate statue, Dunc Gower fanned himself with his sweat-stained Stetson as he chatted with the old fellows who sipped corn whiskey and whittled at the Zouave's feet. What with the dust in the air and hat-brim shadows on their faces, the strangers' bandannas did not seem out of place, or maybe Dunc didn't notice them.

"Where you boys from?" he inquired. His marshal's star glittered on his chest.

"Not here," one of the strangers answered, without pulling his bandanna down.

"Not Here? I never been there."

"Over past Far Away," the stranger said. "Gotta run to the bank. How about you hold our horses?"

"Glad to."

"Won't be long."

The boys from Not Here over near Far Away hobbled across the square to Mr. Hines's Owchicta County Cattlemen's Bank in high-heeled boots made for riding, not walking.

As they entered, one of them announced their presence with a shot at the bank's tin ceiling. The horses Dunc was minding spooked and tried to jerk the reins out of his hands. Not knowing who fired the shot or what at, he and the whittlers hunkered down behind the Zouave. Inside the bank Mr. Hines and his tellers grabbed rifles and started shooting. Without touching another trigger, the would-be bank robbers stumbled back to the Zouave, zigging and zagging among the bullets like newly hatched chicks fleeing the rooster. They snatched the reins from Dunc just as one bullet in a volley fired by the bankers glanced off the Zouave's bronze boot and took off the top of Dunc's head.

THE UNDERTAKER BROUGHT Dunc home and stretched him out in the front parlor on a sheet-covered platform placed over two sawhorses. When the pocket doors slid open, Dunc lay on his back in his best black suit with his hands clasped on his chest, new cream-colored Stetson on his head, and his marshal's star propped between two fingers. He was too long for the platform and overhung it at both ends. The soles of the fancy boots Lorena and Major Wilkes had given him on his last birthday were still shiny.

Major Wilkes nudged his mother. "I never seen Pa lay down with his hat on.

Boots, neither."

"He never did." Lorena didn't correct his grammar.

"Lucky thing Dunc was good and tall so he hangs off my platform," the undertaker said, "Otherwise I woulda had to cut off the back of the brim to make him lay natural-like with his hat on. Woulda looked funny, and it seemed a shame to mess up that brand new Stetson. As it is, your boy'll have a nice-as-new hat when he's big enough to wear it. And don't ol' Dunc look like he's just fixing to jump up after a little nap with the top of his head still in one piece, 'stead of being blown to Kingdom Come like it is?"

"You sure done it, Mr. Ross," Amos said. He combed his fingers through his beard. "I swear he's ready to sit up and start cussing out them murdering bank robbers any minute now. Same ol' Dunc!"

Minnie grabbed Lorena's arm before she could spit out what she had on her tongue.

"Very nice, I'm sure, Mr. Ross," Minnie said. "Now please leave. And Amos, don't you say another word."

Amos took Major Wilkes to the town square to look at the nicks left on the Confederate monument by the bankers' bullets.

"That's where it landed, boy." Amos pointed at a dent in the Zouave's bronze boot. "Right there. The bullet bounced off that there foot and right into his head. Kilt him dead."

Major Wilkes touched the dent Amos pointed out. The tip of his finger just fit the depression, which looked to the boy more like a graze than a dent. The bronze felt cool, though the sun was on it.

"Right there," Amos said. He took his flask out of a hip pocket and saluted the monument with it. "Your pa was a hero, Major Wilkes."

"My pa's dead."

"Course he's dead. That's what makes him a hero. Kilt in the line of duty, trying to stop them bank robbers. Doing his duty as town marshal, like any Gower would."

"Ma says he wasn't no hero. She says he was a near-sighted damn fool too dumb to stay down when bullets was flying. She says that when those men rode up and asked him to watch their horses while they went to the bank, he said he'd be glad to. Never noticed that the man didn't pull his bandanna down before he started talking."

"Your ma said that?"

"Yessir."

Amos took a swig from his flask and then one more.

"Major Wilkes Gower, you tell that woman—"

He stopped, not finishing his thought. Major Wilkes was a direct little fellow, not scared of man, beast, or even his mother, who was famed for being able to skin a man with her tongue at 40 paces. Young as she was, Lorena was almost as adept a man-skinner as Amos's own Minnie, whom he rated a 50-footer if ever there was one. He knew that if he kept going Major Wilkes would almost certainly tell Lorena what he said, which was the same as telling Minnie. He wasn't sure he felt up to facing the wrath of the boy's ma as well as his grandma.

One or the other, perhaps. But both at the same time?

"You tell your ma your grandpa says it maybe takes a hero to know one."

"Ma says you ain't no hero either and not even a cavalryman. She says you was in the infantry in the War and nothing but a private and a deserter to boot. That's what Grandma says, too. Grandma says you just tell big-mouth stories about doing things you never done. It was Grandma's daddy who I'm named for was the cavalryman, the officer, and the hero."

It was too much, the boy bringing up his name like that. Amos grumbled off, taking out his flask as he went.

Major Wilkes leaned against the statue's base, tapping his front teeth with a finger. It was something he did when he was thinking hard, just as his grandfather combed his beard with his fingers before making a pronouncement.

He touched the dent in the Zouave's boot again. It still felt cool.

"I be damned," he said.

The boy walked home slowly, still tapping his teeth. He

went around to the privy in back before going into the house, where his mother was sitting by his father's side. It looked like she was holding his hand, but he couldn't be sure. As he got closer and stood opposite her, he saw that he was right. Her hand rested on Dunc's. The marshal's star was now in its proper place on the lapel of his coat.

"I'm going to be a marshal like Pa or maybe a deputy when I grow up."

She smiled but her eyes were red.

"That's all right, Major Wilkes. Just remember to keep your head down when somebody's shooting at you."

"I told Grandpa what you said about him not being a hero and all."

"And what did he say?"

"Not much. He started to, but didn't."

"I shouldn't have said it, not to you, but I was mad about your father getting himself killed and looking like a fool. Never been to Not Here! Watching their horses!"

"He couldn't help it. He couldn't see."

"That's the point. A marshal so blind he couldn't tell the difference between an ordinary bandanna and a robber's mask should at least have had the sense to wear spectacles. But not your father. Didn't look manly, he said. So now here he is, stretched out on a board, wearing his boots and a half-brimmed hat. A Gower to the end!" She waved a hand at Dunc's corpse. "I hate him for it, but I loved him, too."

"You want to take it back, what you said?"

"Not for a minute."

The boy reached out and touched his father's face with the tip of the finger that had filled the dent in the Zouave's boot. Dunc's cheek felt colder than the statue's bronze. It felt like he had been packed in ice. Major Wilkes was nine years old and the man of the house now. He went out to the stable and climbed to the hayloft to cry where no one could see or hear him.

ONLY ONE BANK ROBBER was captured—a baby-faced young fellow, not yet bearded, whose head was topped by curls. No one knew his name, and he refused to give it.

Prosecutors identified him as "Curly Head." From the moment Curly was caught it was clear that he would wind up with a rope around his neck. But he was so grievously wounded by bankers' bullets that it took months for him to recover enough to make it worthwhile hanging him.

Not that he had pulled the trigger or anything like that. Neither he nor any of his fellow bandits had fired another shot after putting a hole in the bank's ceiling, which now drew sight-seers from as far as Waco. The young man would be hanged because it was clear to all right-thinking Owchictans, including the twelve who served on his jury, that if Curly and his companions had not attempted to rob the Cattlemen's Bank, Mr. Hines and his tellers would have had no cause to open fire at the robbers as they ran for the horses whose reins Dunc held, and Dunc would not have died.

It was Owchicta's first execution, and Sheriff Barnes wanted to do it up right. But the sheriff had never seen a hanging that involved anything more than throwing a rope over a tree limb, setting the condemned man on a horse's bare back, and smacking the horse's flank. Such informality did not seem appropriate for an up-and-coming West Texas county seat (pop. 1,532) that had a courthouse with a Confederate statue in front, a state-certified judge, a full-time sheriff, seven deputies, and two lawyers. Sheriff Barnes formed a Hanging Committee of outstanding citizens, Amos among them.

On the day the Hanging Committee met, Amos came in from the ranch and Minnie fed him breakfast before she left for a WCTU meeting with Lorena. Since Dunc's death Amos had felt responsible for keeping the boy, now ruled by women, on a manly track. Do him good to be in on plans for hanging his daddy's killer, Amos thought—toughen him up. With no one at home to tell him not to, Amos went over to Lorena's to pick up Major Wilkes on his way to the committee meeting.

Sheriff Barnes asked if anyone knew the proper way to hang a duly convicted criminal. Amos spoke up. "I recollect two hangings during the War—no, three it were. Couple of deserters and a Yankee spy. I was in charge for the spy."

"Was them hangings done regular, gallows and all?"

"We done everything regular in the War. General Lee wouldn't do it no other way."

Sheriff Barnes commissioned Amos to build a proper gallows at the foot of the courthouse steps, facing the Zouave. From there the robber would be able to see both sites of his double crime—bank robbery and murder. The sheriff made only one demand.

"Make it so everybody can see," he said. "We'll put the children right up front. Nothing like a hanging to show youngsters like your grandson here—what's your name, boy? Major Wilkes?—that they're on the road to hellfire and damnation like this here bank robber when they go to cussing, tipping over privies, and smoking behind the barn, that sort of thing,"

"That's right," Amos said. "And the next time them robbers want to rob a bank, they won't try it here. They'll by God know Owchicta ain't a town to fool with."

Amos had never seen a gallows or a hanging. But he had learned a lot about building under Scoot's tutelage. He constructed the legs, frame, and crossbeam with railroad ties, cast iron straps, and 10-inch bolts. Flooring the platform with two-by-twelve boards, he put a trapdoor in the middle and, as ordered, left the platform open on all sides to provide good views from every angle. He made the stairway so it could be moved away from the platform and let everyone watch Curly Head after he dropped.

Amos's biggest problem was how to keep the trapdoor from dumping the prisoner as soon as he stepped on it, before it was time to spill him. He tried and discarded a number of ideas, but finally worked out a simple but acceptable solution: He drilled two holes in the trapdoor, one on either side, and threaded a second stout rope—the first being the hanging rope—from the crossbeam down through one hole and back up through the other to the crossbeam, thus forming a U-shaped sling for the trapdoor to rest on, like a swing.

As Amos explained it to the sheriff, Curly Head would stand between the ropes holding the trapdoor up and directly under the hangman's rope. The sheriff would put the dangling noose around Curly's neck. At a nod from the sheriff, someone would cut the trapdoor rope with one quick swipe of a sword. The trapdoor would fall. The murderer would dance on air where everyone could see him.

"He won't be able to dance. We'll tie his legs together," the sheriff said.

"That don't signify. He'll bounce around one-legged," Amos said. "And I want to be the one to cut that there rope. Dunc was my son. Seems to me I got the right."

"If you want to do it, sure," the sheriff said.

"It'll be an honor."

AMOS AND MAJOR WILKES sat on the porch of Lorena's house in the afternoon sun, letting their Sunday dinner settle.

"I got me an idea," Amos said. Looking over his shoulder to make sure neither Minnie nor Lorena was there, he took a swig from his flask.

"What idea is that, Grandpa?"

"I'll put you up on that there platform with me. Crowd'll go wild when they see Dunc's son hand the sword to Dunc's daddy to cut the rope to send Dunc's killer to his maker. Really spice things up."

"I don't think I want to, Grandpa."

"Nonsense, boy. You'll have every lady in the square crying her eyes out."

"Ma won't let me, Grandma neither."

Amos took out his flask again. "Don't worry about them. We'll go in right now and tell 'em what we're going to do, and that'll be that."

He clamped his fingers over Major Wilkes's head like a cap and guided him into the kitchen, where Lorena and Minnie were cleaning up, one washing and the other drying. Standing just inside the door, gripping Major Wilkes's skull, Amos combed his beard with the fingers of his free hand.

"Me and Major Wilkes has decided that he's going to hand me my sword to cut the rope when we hang that murdering bank robber."

Minnie was drying a platter. She looked at him with more than just *Sergeant McCandless* on her face. It was as though she was looking at a scorpion in the potato bin.

"I've waited all these years for that man to show a single lick of sense, and I'm still waiting," she said, talking city. Amos might have been a mile away instead of right there in the kitchen with her.

"They say patience is a remedy for every sorrow," Lorena said, scrubbing a pan.

"Whoever said that never met Amos Gower. Patience won't touch him. The man's a fool, and there's an end to it."

"Now here—"

"I said, there's an end to it."

Back on the porch Amos sat rocking beside Major Wilkes, sucking on his flask, saying nothing. He dozed off. Suddenly his head popped up. He wiped his mouth with the back of his hand.

"*Sergeant McCandless!*" he said.

"Sergeant McCanass, Grandpa?"

"That look. All over her face. All these years." He unscrewed the cap of the flask and took a nip. He dozed off and snored, just once. His head popped up again.

"Never said a decent word to me, the sergeant didn't, not the whole time. Looked at me like I just shat my pants."

He tipped the flask to his lips. It was empty. He let it fall into his lap. His head drooped.

"Weren't you an officer and gentleman in the war, Grandpa?" Major Wilkes said. "That's what you always say, even if Grandma don't."

"What you talking about, boy?"

"What you said just now about some sergeant—McCanass, it sounded like."

"You hearing things, boy. I ain't never said a word about Sergeant McCandless and ain't going to, not to my dying day."

TO MAKE IT CONVENIENT for everyone who wanted to watch the desperado swing, the judge set the hanging for a Saturday. The event drew the biggest crowd in Owchicta's history—displacing the unveiling of the Zouave Confederate monument as No. 1.

People came from as far away as Dallas to watch, many by an excursion train and the livery stable's farm-wagon buses. It was a sunny day with an autumn feel—a good day to hang a man, everyone agreed, though a pity he'd gone wrong so early in life. Picnicking families spread blankets under the courthouse trees. Lemonade stands staffed by ladies from various churches did a brisk business. Barkers hawked souvenirs, including hangmen's knots tacked to boards bearing the legend, *"Curly Head Bandit Hanging Owchicta Sept 10 1898."*

Territorial disputes broke out here and there, but the mood was festive, and the arguments were settled short of fisticuffs except at the Zouave and its base, where out-of-county boys competed to find places. Though it was not a school day, the town and county school officials viewed the hanging as an opportunity for both educational and moral instruction. They decreed that any Wilbarger County pupil not present would be expelled for a year. Special deputies sworn in for the day roamed the square, nervously patting the pistols drooping from their waists. They were primed to repel a rumored rescue of the condemned youth by his gang of desperadoes.

The Owchicta Grade School Marching Band, augmented by a tuba, played *Oh, Awful Wages of Sin Paid Today*, a dirge composed for the occasion by the bandleader. Behind the band the county's school children marched class by class to their favored position directly in front of the gallows on which the young robber and presumed murderer would pay for his sins. Minnie and Lorena publicly opposed forcing children to watch the hanging, but in the end they sent Mary Nell and Major Wilkes to school as ordered, rather than have them lose a year's education.

Amos arranged for Mary Nell, as Dunc's sister, to occupy a place of honor in the front rank of first graders, giving her an unobstructed view. He made a similar arrangement in the fourth grade for Major Wilkes, who declined it. Amos had not insisted. Major Wilkes had skipped a grade and was younger than his classmates but so much taller that no one standing in front of him would be in his way. Eph, almost 20 now and selling insurance, stationed himself by a leg of the gallows, hoping to get a close-up look at the dying man.

Sheriff Barnes ambled down the courthouse steps with Amos beside him and the prisoner hopping along just behind, shackled hand and foot. The county commissioners had presented the sheriff with a braid-laden uniform, but he said hanging was just part of a lawman's job, nothing special, and insisted on wearing his work-a-day clothes—denim pants held up by red suspenders, laced-up riding boots, a collarless white shirt, and an unbuttoned blue vest with his lawman's star pinned on it. Amos was dressed in black, from new Stetson to shiny new boots. He carried his father-in-law's sword upright in his right hand. The prisoner wore bib overalls and no shirt.

Two senior deputies steadied the prisoner by his elbows as he struggled down the steps to the square and across to the gallows, where they lifted him step-by-step up the stair to the platform. His curly hair was soaked with sweat and clung to his skull, as though he'd just taken off his hat after working in the hot sun. His face looked whitewashed.

In deference to their congregations' outrage over Dunc's death, the pastors of Owchicta's established churches had all declined the $10 fee for comforting the murderer in his final moments. An itinerant evangelist leaned over the curly-headed bandit's shoulder, open Bible in hand, and appeared to nibble at his ear. Four deputies brought up the rear with cocked rifles, ready to foil those rumored rescuers. When the prisoner was safely on the platform, other deputies removed the stair.

Held in place by the rope sling that Amos would slash at the appropriate moment, the trapdoor sagged when the doomed man hopped on it with the aid of two deputies.

His weight made the trapdoor's front edge fall two inches or more below the gallows' floor. To keep the prisoner from pitching forward, the deputies had to hold him upright while the sheriff pulled the noose down and drew the knot tight under his left ear. The sheriff and deputies stepped aside. The crowd fell silent. Amos stood at attention, sword in hand.

The evangelist prayed long and loudly. Only those who stuffed fingers in their ears could fail to hear. As he painted a vivid picture of the hellish flames into which the sinner would soon fall, delicate ladies in the crowd reached for smelling salts and hardened drinkers for their flasks. Children sobbed and screamed.

When the prayer ended, the stench of sulfur and burning flesh seemed to pollute the air.

Amos held the sword high. The Owchicta Grade School Marching Band blew a fanfare, or something like it. Amos dipped the sword toward Mary Nell and Major Wilkes, as though saying, "This one's for you." The shiny blade caught the sun as he lifted it to slash the rope supporting the trapdoor. A reflected beam from the sword flitted over the upturned faces of the crowd.

Amos slammed the sword against the taut rope. The blade bounced back like a scared hen hitting a chicken-wire fence or a bullet grazing a bronze Zouave's foot. Again and again Amos slashed at the rope, without parting a fiber.

Amid catcalls and shouts ("Take your time, old man, he ain't in no hurry"), Amos used the sword like a saw. One small strand snapped. Men in the crowd howled, slapped knees, and poked elbows into their neighbors' sides. His head cocked to the side by the hangman's knot under his ear, the prisoner splattered Amos's new boots with his last meal — sunny-side up eggs, country bacon, pork chops, biscuits, and grits with red-eye gravy. There might have been apple pie, too, had he not lost his appetite before he got to it.

Mary Nell shrieked, "Let go of me!" Everyone in the silent square heard her.

Amos saw her shake off a teacher's restraining hand and rush blindly through the crowd, away from the gallows.

"Mary Nell, come back, you'll miss the hanging!" Amos yelled. "Eph! Go get her, Eph. Bring her back."

Eph plowed through the ranks of children and rushed back to his post by the gallows leg with Mary Nell under his arm. She battered him with fists and feet, screaming.

Red-faced and sweating, Amos gave up on the sword. He drove its point into the platform floor and left it. He took out his pocketknife and tested the blade's edge with his thumb.

The crowd laughed. Someone yelled, "If that don't work, just choke the sonabitch." Someone started chanting, "Choke him, choke him," and the crowd took it up.

The boy standing next to Major Wilkes said, "Ain't that your grandpa up there?" Major Wilkes struggled for an answer, but found none.

The knife was sharp, but the rope was thick.

As Amos sawed strands parted slowly. The trapdoor sagged more and more. The prisoner's shackled feet skidded into sight below the gallows' floor, gradually followed by knees, hips, rope-bound throat, and at last the tortured face fighting for breath, tongue protruding. The crowd's clamor stilled. Mary Nell struggled in Eph's arms. Her screams were the only sound.

Amos leaned over the open trap to watch Dunc's killer dance on air with no place to put a foot. He could see only sweat-drenched curls, but he could hear the young man choking, fighting for breath.

"Grab his goddamned legs, Eph! Give him a good yank!"

"Can't, Pa. I got me a hellcat here."

"Break his neck, Eph! Yank him!"

"Mary's kicking me in the balls, Pa. Takes both hands to hold her."

"I said break his goddammed neck, Eph. Now do it!"

Strangling at the end of the rope, the dying man spoke. His words rang through the square, each word distinct, but in a language never before heard in Owchicta. *"Crwrgh! Eeghwr. Hrckk. Hrckk. Crwrgh!"*

Mary Nell lay limp in Eph's arms.

Eph told Amos later, "Feller's tongue comes in and out of his mouth like a big chunk of raw meat, all bloody, pushing out them words like corks out of a bottle. Could of been the Devil hisself talking. *'Crwrgh! Eeghwr. Hrckk. Hrckk. Crwrgh!'* Too bad Mary Nell fainted. She missed the best part."

"Her own fault," Amos said. "I done all I could for her."

AT THE OWCHICTA Methodist Church on Sunday the pastor, who had watched the hanging but had no role in it, opened his sermon with a window-rattling shout. *"Crwrgh! Eeghwr. Hrckk. Hrckk. Crwrgh!"* He then built his homily around the notion that the dying man was speaking in tongues, repenting and cleansing his soul of sin at the moment of death. He urged his flock to do the same, but in advance of the event.

Major Wilkes told Amos what the preacher said.

"He got it wrong," Amos said. "He weren't speaking in tongues. It was Polish, most likely, maybe Gypsy. That young feller done put a hex on me. I feel it in my bones."

10.

WHEN AMOS LOST the ranch he didn't think it was sufficient to blame the weather, though the elements had been against him for a long time, no question about that. Nor could he lay it solely to Mr. Hines at the Owchicta County Cattlemen's Bank, who called in his paper at just the wrong moment. So many things went wrong all at once, so fast that only one thing could fully explain the disaster—the pox that Dunc's murderer put on him. *Crwrgh! Eeghwr. Hrckk. Hrckk. Crwrgh!*

Amos threw whatever he could beg, borrow, or steal into the effort to save his land. He didn't touch the house in town only because he could find no way to undo the work of Minnie's mother's slick Vicksburg lawyers. The property and everything connected with it remained fixed in Minnie's hands. No matter how he pleaded, cajoled, threatened, and ordered, she wouldn't give up any of it to help him out, not even her smart new buggy or the handsome grey that pulled it around town.

Nor would she dip into the nest egg held for her at the Vicksburg bank, which hatched enough income each year for her to live comfortably without help from Amos. But her fortune was as inaccessible to him as her bedroom or her house. In any case, house and nest egg combined could not have stopped the avalanche of demands on him. Once started it took no time at all to reach catastrophe.

First came powerful winds, blowing harder and steadier than ever before. They sucked all moisture from the ground and filled the air with dust, which formed crusts around the eyes and nostrils and mouths of cattle and men alike, giving them hideous masks of dried mud. Dust mounded against the ranch house outside and on the window sills inside. One notable storm, perhaps even a cyclone, was the worst Amos had ever seen. The wind was so violent that it sent everyone in Owchicta County into root cellars for safety and drove a straw through a calf's throat, killing it.

Or did the drought come first? Amos could not make up his mind. It was a dry country by nature, of course, but always before there was enough moisture to hold down the soil and bring grass in the spring. No more. Amos had to buy hay at higher and higher prices to feed his steers and dig extra wells to water them. Windmills whirred, but the wells went dry and the cattle troughs filled with sand and tumbleweed skeletons. His lines of credit dried up, too. He couldn't borrow to deepen wells or pay for the feed.

Herds that didn't starve to death died of thirst. The few steers that survived were so scrawny and weak it wasn't worth driving them to the new auction house at the railroad flag stop east of Owchicta.

Amos fell behind on the loans that had enabled him to buy land from nesters, including those whose daughters Eph had impregnated. Mr. Hines, the banker who had nominated Amos to lead the risen-again South in a new fling at glory, would not extend the loans even when Amos brought up General Lee — would have liked to, he said, but could not because of a financial panic gripping the country.

Mr. Hines had no doubts about who had brought Amos to

his knees. It was not him, nor was it his bank, Mr. Hines said. It was Wall Street shenanigans by Eastern money men—the likes of Morgan, Gould, Harriman, and Rockefeller. Rothschild, too, of course.

Representatives of a rich Englishman—a duke or maybe an earl, it was believed in Owchicta—sent land-buying agents through the county, driving buggies equipped, or so it was said, with greenback-packed chests. Forced to sell, Amos tried to hold out for gold or at least silver, but in the end took the paper. He had the stacks of bills in his hands only long enough to pass them to Mr. Hines, who said that when discounted for currency's loss of value against gold since he'd lent the money, the greenbacks offered by Amos, all he had, were not sufficient to pay off his debt. It was news to Amos that the lien he signed said anything about discounts.

Minnie looked at the contract. "That's what it says, all right. Pity you didn't let me read it before you signed."

Amos took the contract to a lawyer, who said Minnie was right. There it was in print—not big print, it was true, but size didn't count when it came to a legal document.

Amos lost even his blacksmith tools to Mr. Hines. About all he was able to take with him when he moved to the storeroom off the kitchen of Minnie's house in town were the clothes on his back, the ancient buckboard wagon with twelve-inch sideboards he had picked up before he left Amesville with Mary Pollard, his old black mare, and the workbench on which he had once tanned the backsides of misbehaving sons. Just for old times' sake he also took along the bit of rein he had used as a strap.

The best job he could get was as night jailer at the courthouse. He emptied chamber pots when he came on duty at eight o'clock every evening and again just before he left at eight in the morning.

The rest of the time he sat at a desk with a big key hanging on the wall behind him, which he took down to open the bullpen door when a deputy brought in a drunk. Some nights he was the only person at the jail. Nipping at bottles of confiscated rotgut as he guarded empty cells, he dozed in a chair tipped back against the wall, hat sloped over his eyes and boot heels cocked on a desk or hooked on the rungs of his chair.

On such nights he brooded over the puzzles in his life — why he had jumped up instead of staying put in the brush beside Jess Fellows. Why Minnie still held a grudge about what happened in the tunnel. Why that young card shark *F* had chosen to slip into his Vicksburg hotel room carrying a candleholder shaped like a revolver. Why strangers had the power to rip his land and cattle from him without his having any say in the matter.

However Amos sorted through the rubble of his life, he could not understand why he should be at the beck and call of others as though he had been in the army all these years with Sergeant McCandless ordering him around. It wasn't right, he felt — a man his age having to sit up all night trying to stay awake when he should be home sleeping like everybody else, honored and quiet in his own bed. And there was not a thing he could do about it.

He found nothing to blame himself for. He could not fault himself even on the bank loans. It had made sense to buy all that land from nesters with unwed pregnant daughters. He not only rescued Eph from the clutches of immoral young women who willingly opened their bodies to men not their husbands, he also gained good grazing land on which to expand.

As for unknowingly signing a lien with a discounting provision tucked away in the fine print — well, what was a man to do? Allowing Minnie to read the contract for him would have been tantamount to asking a woman, with all a woman's weak-mindedness in matters of business, for permission to do what he had already decided to do. What kind of man could put up with that?

All his pondering led him back to that hex—that *"Crwrgh! Eeghwr. Hrckk. Hrckk. Crwrgh!"* No doubt about it. The curly headed young man choking to death at the end of a rope had let it out of the bag. Amos had been living under a hex his whole life. Hadn't his mother died a-borning him?

AFTER THE HANGING Mary Nell hid whenever Amos tried to get close to her. He rushed through the house in the belief she was playing hide and seek.

"Who's got my Mary Nell?" He looked under rugs and on top of doors.

"Leave her alone, Amos," Minnie said.

"We're just playing."

"Mary Nell's not playing. She isn't a baby anymore. She's six years old and doesn't want anything to do with you, as anybody but you would know. So leave her alone."

Minnie fed him his meals on time and washed his clothes, but she was mostly silent as a doorknob when he was around. With the ranch gone her old feistiness toward him was replaced by indifference. Most the time she didn't bother to talk country when she dressed him down, though her tongue lost none of its sharpness. *Sergeant McCandless* didn't turn up on her face nearly as often as he once had, but Amos sensed that it was only because, having been reduced to emptying slop jars at the county jail, he didn't amount to enough in her eyes for her to bother scorning him. She had declared victory over him without even consulting him. He almost missed the sergeant.

After a night of nipping at jugs confiscated from drunks in the bullpen, he staggered home, determined to have it out with Minnie.

"Drunk again, I see," she said as he stumbled up the back steps and opened the kitchen door. *Sergeant McCandless* may not have been on her face, but Amos sensed his presence. "Why don't you just stay down there at the jail and sleep it off with the rest of the boozers?"

What could a tired man say to that after a long night on the job? Putting his eggs-over-easy on top of his grits and drenching them with black-strap syrup, Amos postponed the showdown with Minnie and Sergeant McCandless to another day.

AMOS WORRIED THAT Lorena and Minnie might sissify Major Wilkes and spent as much time with the boy as he could. They worried that Amos would be a bad influence on him, but were reassured when Major Wilkes continued to get good grades in school and did his chores at home without much complaint. He milked the cow, chopped the wood, fed the chickens, and groomed the horses—his pony and Dunc's black mare. She was yet another distant descendant of the one that had carried a Confederate hero to war and brought him back a corpse wrapped in canvas. The boy didn't enjoy shoveling manure or spading the garden, but did both cheerfully enough when asked.

Most of all, his mother and grandmother were reassured by the fact that when he was caught doing something he wasn't supposed to—tipping privies at Halloween, throwing spitballs at his friends during school, or taking the Lord's name in vain—he never tried to lie out of it.

"Yes'm. I done it."

"Did it, please, Major Wilkes."

"Yes'm. Did it. I won't do it again, Ma."

And he would smile, melting whatever wrath might linger in Lenora's heart. That smile! It could douse anger like water on an ember. It was truly the smile of an angel, Lorena and Minnie agreed, taking no note of the possibility that the angel knew it and used it to his advantage.

Nor did they notice, though he did, that his repeated pledge not to do it again was ambiguous. It could be construed to apply to the grammar of his admission rather than to the particular deed he was admitting to. Was he promising to give it up, whatever "it" might be, or was he merely promising not to say "done" in place of "did"? The boy favored the latter interpretation, but he never tried it out on his mother and grandmother.

WHENEVER MAJOR WILKES had a question, Amos had an answer.

"Grandpa, why does the sun always come up in the east?"

"Why—" Amos combed his beard with his fingers— "because the sun's like a railroad train on a one-way track circling around us."

"Miss Coggins says the sun don't go around the earth, the earth goes around the sun." Miss Coggins was his teacher.

"Major Wilkes, that old maid don't know no more about the sun than she knows about men. You go out in the prairie sometime, not a house or a fence anywhere in sight, and you watch the sun come up. It's clear as the nose on your face. The sun's coming up, the earth ain't going down—any fool can see it. You tell her that, boy. Tell her your Grandpa said so."

"Yes, sir."

He didn't tell Miss Coggins or anybody else, though he was mostly open about what he saw, did, and heard with Amos. He spoke freely—or, at least, with the appearance of freedom—of their excursions, except when he was told, "Now, boy, don't say nothing about this, hear?"

Whether from forgetfulness or from recklessness after too

many nips at his flask, Amos sometimes failed to repeat the caution. So on many unlikely topics Major Wilkes felt free to chatter away at home.

"Ma, what's a whore?"

"Major Wilkes! Where did you hear that word?"

"Oh, with Grandpa, down in the square."

"I might have known."

"They were talking about whorehouses they'd been to and arguing about which ones were best. Most everyone said either New Orleans or Kansas City. Grandpa claimed San Francisco was the best, but he said there's one up at Mingus in Indian Territory that's almost as good."

"Your grandpa's never been near San Francisco."

"I know that, but he's been to Mingus. It's just that I couldn't figure out what they were talking about."

"Just as well."

"All I got was that it's where whores live. But they never said what a whore is."

"Ah!"

"So I wondered. What is a whore?"

"Well. Let me see. A whore, I guess, Major Wilkes, is—well, is a bad woman."

"Why's she bad, Ma? What'd she do?"

"Things nice women don't do."

He mulled it over. She waited for the next question.

"Oh," he said.

Lorena told Minnie about this conversation. Minnie discussed whores and whorehouses with Amos.

"I never," he said. "No, I never."

IT WAS SUMMER, 1900. School was out. Major Wilkes sat on the steps of Minnie's porch, elbows on his knees, whittling nothing in particular. Fresh from his mid-day breakfast, Amos sat in the swing with his boot heels resting on the railing.

"You been to the carnival, boy?" Amos asked. He spat over the railing.

"Grandma don't like you spitting tobacco juice on her plants, Grandpa," Major Wilkes said.

"Don't you worry about your grandma, boy. You leave her to me. I asked you, you been to the carnival?"

"No, sir. There's one here now, though."

"I know there's one here now. That's why I asked you. You ain't been to it?"

"No, sir. I ain't never seen a carnival." Major Wilkes was not always careful with his grammar when he was with Amos. "Ma says I ain't old enough. That's what Grandma says, too."

"How old are you, boy?"

"Eleven, Grandpa."

"Plenty old. Them women!" Amos spat over the railing again. "Where they gone to?"

"Book club."

"Be a while yet, you think?"

"Good while."

"Let's go to that there carnival, boy."

Bright pennants and flags, U.S., Texas, and Confederate, waved over a dusty field just outside of town. Faded letters on stained canvas strips stretched between the flagpoles proclaimed, *"Happy Harry O'Harrigan's Circus of Wholesome Entertainment for All the Family."* Two rides, a carousel and a barrel roll, stood ready, and off at the edge of the field were sundry travel wagons.

Scattered around a big tent were three smaller tents and an elongated wagon with five axles, which bore a narrow red house-like structure without windows. A varicolored but faded sign identified it as *"The Hall of Mirrors."* Posters outside one of the small tents pictured *"The World's Strongest Giant,"* bare-chested and dressed in tights, lifting what appeared to be the world's smallest elephant. On another tent a poster invited *"Gentlemen of Refinement"* to view dances by Little Egypt, pictured as a lithe young beauty half-clad in numerous sheer veils. A line at the bottom added, *"Private performances by appointment only."*

A barker in checked pants, top hat, and a dusty tailcoat invited Amos and Major Wilkes into the big tent to watch what he described as "a grand parade and the most daring show this side of San Francisco." They took seats in front of a small ring. A dozen or so men, who might otherwise have been whittling around the Zouave's base, sat with them on bleachers that wobbled whenever anyone shifted a leg or eased a buttock.

A juggling clown led the grand parade. Behind him another clown, wearing green coveralls with red polka dots, puffed out his cheeks to trumpet an ear-splitting march that sounded something like *Dixie*.

The clowns were followed by the bare-chested giant, who looked smaller than Amos to Major Wilkes, and two hefty but scantily clad women with sashes draped across their bosoms. The sashes identified one as Miss Justice and the other as Miss Liberty. Miss Justice carried scales and wore a blindfold over one eye. Miss Liberty held a flickering torch aloft. In their wake, a man with a black eye-patch and dressed as a pirate waved a scimitar, as did several others wearing baggy pants like the Zouaves. ("A-rab pirates," Amos whispered, nudging Major Wilkes).

The barker brought up the rear. He carried a whip and pulled a small cage bearing a sign on the side: "Danger! Beware the Dwarf Javanese Tiger!" In the cage slept an animal that Major Wilkes identified as a puma.

Miss Justice and Miss Liberty dropped out of the parade to pose on platforms of baled hay. The trumpeter sounded *Charge!*

Two trapezes, each bearing a large woman in a gauzy gown, dropped from the top of the tent. Swinging back and forth, the women pumped now and again to keep up speed, displaying more female flesh than Major Wilkes had hitherto encountered. The spectators, all except Major Wilkes, cheered and whistled, none louder than Amos, as Miss Justice, Miss Liberty and the two trapeze artists bowed, waved, and mouthed kisses. The barker delivered a spiel touting the ferocity of the Javanese tiger and then poked the animal with his whip. It lifted its head and snarled before dropping off again. Miss Justice and Miss Liberty each recited a series of poems with many winks and gestures which seemed to delight the men but which seemed pointless to Major Wilkes, except for certain words that he knew well but was forbidden to use.

After the show Amos bought Major Wilkes a sticky candy cane from an Arab vendor.

"How you like your carnival, boy?"

"It's all right."

"All right! Why, boy, you won't see a better one this side of Kansas City."

"I don't think Ma and Grandma would like it."

"They don't need to know everything. Don't tell 'em."

Amos gave Major Wilkes two dimes to ride the carousel and the barrel roll.

"You go have you a good time while I take me a gander at Miss Egypt."

Major Wilkes handed his dime to the strongest giant in the world and mounted a wooden pinto with a painted mane. He scrunched up in the saddle to get his feet off the floor and into the stirrups. He was the only rider.

"You hold on to that there pole, hear? The pony goes up and down on it. Folks get throwed off, they don't hang on."

"What makes the horse go up and down?"

"Me, I reckon."

Bending from the waist, the world's strongest man thrust his head and shoulders through a horse collar attached by ropes to a horizontal pipe that stuck out from the carousel. He seized the pipe with both hands and plodded forward, pushing against the collar to pull the carousel around and around. The pony rose and fell on its pole. The only sounds were the giant's heavy breathing and a clanking noise. Major Wilkes thought it was almost as exciting as sitting on his mother's front porch.

Major Wilkes tried the barrel-roll ride next. Like the carousel, it was jerry-built. A wooden barrel, five feet or so in diameter, was mounted horizontally on a framework of pipes. One end of the barrel was solid, with an array of gears and a crank. The other end was open except for one upright board, which supported one end of a shiny steel pipe running the length of the barrel in front of a shelf-like bench.

The world's strongest man, still puffing from his exertions at the carousel, took Major Wilkes's dime.

"You ever rode a barrel roll before, young fella?"

"No, sir."

"You sit on the bench, grab the handrail in front of you with both hands and hang on for dear life. Get too much for you, pound your feet and yell. I'll stop the roll if I hear you."

"What makes it go?"

"Same as before. Me."

He showed Major Wilkes the gears and turned the barrel over with the crank. He let Major Wilkes try it.

"Don't seem hard."

"Ain't, until three or maybe four folks loads into it all at once. Then you'll grunt."

"What happens when I go over the top?"

"Just when you think you're going to spill like a marble in a jar, I crank you 'round the other way."

Major Wilkes climbed up a couple of steps and crawled inside the barrel. It smelled musty, like wet hay. Resting his back against the curved wall, he seized the handrail and was surprised at how cold the steel pipe felt. It reminded him of his father's cheek.

"You ready in there?"

"Yes, sir."

The barrel creaked. Major Wilkes rolled slowly upward. Just as he felt that he was about to slide off the seat and be left hanging on the handrail, the barrel reversed and swept him down and then up the other side, losing speed as it rose. Back and forth he rocked, clinging to the pipe as instructed. His stomach rolled with the barrel. By the time the barrel stopped he was as sweaty as the world's strongest giant.

"Want another ride?"

"I don't have any more money."

"That's all right. I'll give you a free ride."

"I reckon no, thank you."

Major Wilkes waited outside Little Egypt's tent until Amos came out, buttoning his shirt. Major Wilkes got a glimpse of Miss Justice behind him. She looked nothing like Little Egypt on the poster.

Amos took him next to *"The Hall of Mirrors"* in the red house on wheels. Signs above the entrance at one end promised *"101 Laughs for All the Family"* and an opportunity to *"See Yourself as You Truly Are."*

Miss Liberty took their money wordlessly and gestured them up the steps. Inside coal oil lamps and candles overhead cast eerie shadows in a blue-curtained maze.

As the door closed behind them and his eyes adjusted to the dim light, Amos got his first laugh. One mirror showed him tall and thin, while in a second mirror he was short and fat with cheeks like cantaloupes and, when he turned just so, buttocks like pillows.

"Look at me, boy, look at me. You ever see anything so funny?"

Major Wilkes laughed, at his own image as well as Amos's, but without smiling.

The sign outside had promised that he would see himself as he truly was, and he was seriously interested. Amos rushed on ahead, unable to restrain his eagerness to see what the next set of mirrors would make of him. Major Wilkes lingered before each mirror, tapping his front teeth with a thumbnail, pondering each image and ignoring Amos's booming laughter at each turn of the curtained corridor and his cry, "Hurry up, boy. You ain't never seen the like."

Major Wilkes hadn't known there could be so many ways to view himself. If he was seeing his real self in each mirror, which if any was the true Major Wilkes? Was it possible that each image was true and he was really all these grotesqueries? He heard the outer door at the far end open and close. He was alone as he came to the last set of mirrors and saw himself disassembled, fragmented, refracted, and reflected as discrete bits and pieces—a brow atop an ear, an eye looking out a mouth. He was sunlit glass shards of many glittering shapes and colors falling in a void, forming images iridescently, randomly, each image disturbingly familiar. He was looking at himself shattered in a kaleidoscope. He rushed out and hurled himself at Amos.

"I want to go home, Grandpa," he said.

11.

AMOS INSTRUCTED Major Wilkes in what he regarded as the practicalities of Texas manhood. How to break a wild horse to saddle. How to rope and brand a maverick calf, whether heifer or bull, without being accused of stealing it, even if you were. How to turn a young bull into a steer with surgical precision. How to best the other fellow in a horse trade, a goal that required perfecting the art of crafty lying—a subversive art for which Major Wilkes displayed the innate talent of any child living in an adult world. His favorite subject in Amos's curriculum was how to hit a target while firing a pistol from the back of a running horse.

Far out on the open plain, where there was only a prairie dog to see or hear, Amos threw a green glass jar into the air as Major Wilkes raced by on his cow pony, reins in one hand and a Colt in the other.

He fired one shot. The jar blossomed in a sky rocket of green shards glistening in the sunlight.

Amos let out a whoop. "First shot! I never seen the like."

Major Wilkes turned the pony and trotted back.

"Boy, I'd like to see you do that again, but I only brung that one target."

"We can use prickly-pear ears, Grandpa. That's how I learned."

"You done this before?"

"Lots of times, Grandpa."

"Your ma know?

"No, sir."

Major Wilkes dismounted and tore a pad off a cactus. He handed it to Amos. "Watch them needles, Grandpa."

Amos threw the cactus ear into the air. Major Wilkes hit once, missed once, hit two in a row. The pad fell apart. Amos tore off another cactus pad.

"Now, boy, let's see you do it t'other handed."

He hit the target only once in six left-handed tries.

"Don't you worry, boy," Amos said. "A little practice and we'll get that left hand up to snuff. I never seen nobody could match you, boy. Them big hands on you, they're gun-slinger hands, ever I seen any. If times wasn't so goddamned tamed down, I could make you into Billy the Kid."

In the stable behind his house Major Wilkes wiped down his pony and his father's black mare, which Amos had ridden to give her some exercise. Amos sat on a bale of hay, chewing on the stub of a dead cigar. He combed his fingers through his beard, thinking hard.

"Your pony ain't a bit gun shy, is he?"

"No, sir."

"And you rode him for the boys' calf-roping contest you won last year?"

"Yes, sir."

"So you could handle him if'n you was shooting with both hands?

"You bet."

Amos jumped up and paced back and forth, sucking his cigar, spitting tobacco juice. "Everybody'll think I'm funnin' when I enter you in the contest."

"What contest's that, Grandpa?"

"The county fair contest."

"You mean running and jumping?"

"Nope, not this year."

"Calf roping? Bronc busting?"

"Gun slinging from the saddle. I thought first to make it bareback, but wouldn't no one want to enter. Folks ain't hard-assed enough no more for bareback. Don't say nothing about it, though, not even to your ma, and I'll wait to enter you till the last minute, so her and your grandma won't know what's going on. I'll make me a bundle, if'n you shoot like you done today."

"I never heard of a contest like that at the county fair, Grandpa."

"Ain't nobody else either. Come to me in a flash, just like that." He snapped his fingers. "It'll be fast-draw, rapid-fire, two-handed. One rider at a time, twelve shots at twelve cactus ears, riding flat out against the clock."

"Wouldn't tin cans or bottles be better, Grandpa?"

"Loose cans and bottles is hard to find. Prickly pears is all over the place. You got to think of these things, boy."

Major Wilkes pointed out another problem. "All that shooting from the back of a horse. Somebody'll get killed, Grandpa."

"We'll do it east of the fairgrounds and shoot out over the prairie. Ain't nobody to get in the way out there."

"But you'd have to have twelve people out there tossing cactus ears in the middle of running horses and all that shooting. Who's going to want to do that? And anyway it wouldn't be fair. No two tosses would be the same."

Amos scratched his beard again, thinking. "We won't toss 'em. We'll nail them cactus ears on sticks in the ground. Replace 'em as needed."

"I'm really good at targets that ain't moving."

The next day Major Wilkes proved his boast. He was better with his right hand than with his left, but his two-handed score was so good that Amos called off practice sessions. That left hand still needed work, but he saw no need to waste ammunition.

The county fair committee bought the gun-slinger idea right off, after Amos explained that it had been a favorite event for cavalrymen in the War. He'd seen it many a time. Even won it now and again.

"You going to enter?" the chairman asked.

"Nope, wouldn't be fair."

"But you'll run it for us, fix up the track and the targets, all that?"

"Glad to," Amos said.

On the county fair committee's behalf, Amos hired a man with a mule team to drag railroad ties through the sagebrush to clear a straight track, a quarter-mile long and away from the fairgrounds. The committee agreed to supply a tent, and Amos arranged for tellers from the Owchicta County Cattlemen's Bank to collect $5 from each entrant to make up the purse, winner take all. The committee also paid for posters advertising the event without revealing who was behind it. The posters were illustrated with a drawing of a bow-legged gunman wearing chaps. His pistols spewed smoke and flames, framing the message:

FIRST ANNUAL OWCHICTA GUN-SLINGER CONTEST!
SHOOT FROM THE SADDLE!
TWO GUNS, 12 SHOTS!
RACE THE CLOCK!
ALL RIDERS WELCOME!
WHO'S FASTEST? HIM OR YOU?
FIND OUT AT THE COUNTY FAIR!!!!

On the fair's opening day, speeches, and kids' events—sack races and the like—filled the morning. Lunch followed, with food available at booths manned by ladies from church auxiliaries. Each booth offered a specialty. Fair goers could buy fried chicken from dunking Baptists, barbeque from sprinkling Baptists, and slices of angel food cake or cherry pie from Methodists, with all proceeds going to worthy Christian causes.

Minnie and Lorena had charge of the Methodist cake and pie booth. Nearby the newly-founded Moose Lodge set up a tent for gentlemen only and—or so the church ladies whispered—lured prospective members with alcoholic beverages.

Amos's Gun-Slinger Contest was the first event of the afternoon, ahead of calf roping, bulldogging, and bronc riding. The deadline for entering was 12:00 o'clock, a half-hour ahead of the starting time. Ready money was short in Owchicta County, but syndicates formed. By ten minutes before 12:00, seven riders had found backers and put up the $5 entry fee at the Gun-Slinger tent, where a sign said, "OPEN TO ALL RIDERS."

"We got a good field here," Amos said.

Five minutes before the deadline he brought Major Wilkes to the tent through a crowd of onlookers.

Laughing, he said, "My boy says, what the hell, he'll give it a try."

The bank tellers laughed, too. But they wouldn't take his money.

Major Wilkes pointed at the sign on the front of the table. "It says right there, sir, OPEN TO ALL RIDERS. I'm a rider, and I got my $5 right here."

"The young'un's right," a bystander shouted, amid backslapping and laughter. "Let'im enter."

Others took up the cry. The fair committee conferred and ordered the tellers to accept Major Wilkes's entry.

"Seems a shame, taking the young fella's money," the head teller said, but he put Major Wilkes on the entry list as No. 8.

"He's a good shot. Good rider, too," Amos said. "I'm betting on him. Anyone want to make a little side bet, step right up. You bet a dime. My boy lose, I give you your dime back and pay you another. He win, I get your dime and you pay me five more like it."

The fair committee told the tellers to record and hold the sidebets. The first man to lay down his dime shouted, "Hey, boys, Old Man Gower's giving away money."

Amos had scraped together $24. Bettors rushed to get their share of a sure thing, wagering from ten cents to as much as a dollar each against the boy. They were still jostling one another to keep places in line when Amos ran out of cash to cover them. The tellers refused to accept his IOU's and betting ceased.

Word of Amos's largess and Major Wilkes's participation spread quickly, but did not reach Lorena and Minnie at the Methodist pie and cake booth until well after they heard gunfire. By the time they pushed through the crowd at the Gun-Slinger track, two riders had been disqualified for drunkenness after too many trips to the Moose Lodge tent and four others had already made their run. Two of the four had missed every cactus pad, one had hit two, and the fourth had scored with four of his twelve shots and was already being hailed as the champion. The seventh rider was at the starting line. Major Wilkes was in the saddle with "No. 8" pinned on the back of his shirt. All Lorena and Minnie could do was watch.

No. 7 held a cocked gun in each hand. His reins lay loose on the horse's neck. The horse was jittery, tossing its head. The starter fired into the air. The horse reared. No. 7 slid backward out of the saddle. As he hit the ground his fingers tightened on both triggers. No one got hit, but the twin blast sent the horse speeding riderless across the prairie, stirrups flapping. No. 7 was disqualified for careless handling of a loaded firearm and lack of a mount.

Amos led Major Wilkes's pony to the starting line.

"Go do it, boy. Bang, bang, bang!"

"Yes, sir," Major Wilkes said.

The starter holstered his gun and sent the boy's pony off with just a slap on the flank instead of a shot. Major Wilkes spurred down the track as though in pursuit of a calf with a lasso whirling overhead. It was an old game for both rider and pony. His right hand Colt scored five shots, the left two, for a total of seven out of twelve.

"Got more work to do on that there left hand," Amos said.

There were complaints, of course. Amos had devised the contest, set the rules, and secretly trained Major Wilkes, while few of the other entrants had heard of such an event before they signed up for it at the fair, or so they said, and had been given no chance to practice. But the fair committee ruled that the competition had been properly conducted—there had been posters all over town, after all—and no restrictions had been put on age. It didn't matter that Major Wilkes was only eleven. He was Gun Slinger Champion of Owchicta County, fair and square.

Amos collected the purse as well as the side bets. The committee took a cut of the side bets for expenses, which Amos had not expected and did not think was fair, but he still came out with the purse and more than $100 in bets—more money than he'd seen at one time since he lost the ranch. When Minnie and Lorena scolded him for exploiting a little boy, he gave Major Wilkes a dollar of the purse.

Minnie wouldn't stand for it.

"Amos, you hand all that purse money, every penny, over to

Lorena for Major Wilkes this minute. He's the one who won it."

Amos protested, but not too much for fear Minnie would make him give up his side winnings as well. Lorena allowed Major Wilkes to keep the dollar Amos gave him. She put the rest into the savings account she maintained for the boy at the Cattlemen's Bank.

Looking ahead to the next year's county fair, Amos planned a more challenging event. He began training Major Wilkes to guide his pony through a prairie-dog town at top speed while firing at the little nuisances. The first time Major Wilkes scored two kills out of twelve shots, none with his left hand. The next time it was four with the right, two with the left.

But when the time came to plan the next year's events, the county fair committee refused to sanction Amos's *"Champion Prairie Dog Killer"* gun-slinging contest. The committee feared that more participants than prairie dogs would get hurt, what with the danger of horses stepping in holes and spilling their riders. Besides, prairie dogs came out of their holes in random and unpredictable ways. No one could be sure where the riders would be firing, endangering spectators. The committee's adverse decision cost Amos a fortune, the way Major Wilkes's left hand was shaping up.

BOYS LIKE MAJOR WILKES—who had to be dragged from a book to the supper table, who picked out tunes on Minnie's piano, and who sang in the church choir—were liable to hear the dread cry, "Sissy!"

But Major Wilkes was spared that humiliation. He was not only big for his age, he was a good fighter, even though he eschewed the eye-gouging, knee-in-the-groin tactics Amos tried to drill into him. Besides, he was a good-natured boy who did not tease or bully and got along well with his peers. His manners were good, too. Lorena and Minnie had seen to that.

He could be relied upon to say "please" and "thank you" without giving it a thought and to stand up when a lady entered the room. He could eat soup without slurping and a sunny-side-up egg without dripping yolk down his front.

By the time Major Wilkes was 13 years old, he was man-sized and growing fast. After school and during holidays he worked for farmers and small ranchers around Owchicta. Before long he was an experienced field hand, skilled and strong enough to plow unbroken sod, stretch a fence, cut and rake hay without supervision, and handle just about any other farm or ranch chore that came along. He could ride, rope, and bulldog as well as cowhands who'd been at it for forty years. He branded as though he'd been born with a hot iron in his hand and was slick as a surgeon at turning bull calves into steers.

When haying or roundup time came, he could pick and choose whom he'd work for.

Major Wilkes emerged from high school in 1905 at 16, a highly educated man by Owchicta standards. Amos refused to attend the graduation exercises.

"Ain't no point to all that high-school folderol," he said. "Eight grades is more than enough. I never went to school a day in my life and see where I got."

AMOS HEARD THAT Old Man Vanderwagen, the biggest ranch owner in Owchicta County other than the rich Englishman who bought Amos's spread, needed wranglers for a cattle drive to Ringle in Indian Territory, where a new auction house was said to be drawing buyers from as far away as Chicago. Without consulting Lorena or Minnie, Amos approached Vanderwagen about taking on Major Wilkes.

"Sixteen, you say? Well, I don't know," Vanderwagen said. He was a short fellow with bowed legs, a Bible-thumper with no liking for Amos. "He ever work a trail drive?"

"No, but he's a fast learner and big for his age. Ain't nobody better with horses and cattle—worked for lots of folks around here. You ask them."

"He a drinker?"

"Never touched a drop."

Vanderwagen said the best he could do was half wages, but if Major Wilkes did a man's work he'd get a man's pay. Lorena had reservations about allowing her boy to join a cattle drive, but Amos argued that it was time the boy saw a bit of the larger world.

Major Wilkes had never been out of Owchicta County. Lorena consulted with Minnie. In the end they agreed to let him go. What settled the matter for them was not Amos's rationale for the trip, but what Major Wilkes said about it: "I want to go, Ma." It helped that Vanderwagen was known as a straitlaced old fellow. He wouldn't lead the boy into trouble.

Before Major Wilkes left, Amos slipped him two dollars with a wink and a jab in the ribs.

"Now, after the drive and you get paid off," Amos said, "the boys'll go out and have themselves a time. It's the custom. There ain't nothing in Ringle but alkali water and cattle pens, so they ride up to Mingus. You just go along. And if you meet somebody called Tessie, you give her my best, hear?"

Major Wilkes proved his worth and got his man's pay, like the other trail hands. Only three steers out of hundreds died on the drive—one of exhaustion or maybe old age and two in the treacherous Red River crossing. With the herd sold, Vanderwagen left off Bible-thumping to lead the whooping, hollering group from Ringle to Miss Emma's Home Away from Home for Respectable Ladies and Gentlemen in Mingus, the county seat, for an evening's celebration.

Vanderwagen shushed them before they reached the town.

"Lots of good church people here," he explained. "Don't

want to get 'em stirred up before we've had our fun."

Miss Emma's boarding house stood alone in the middle of a small forest of cottonwood trees just past Jolly Roger Road, the last platted street in Mingus. It could be reached (or escaped from, in case of need) by any of several trails that wandered to it from different directions. It was a big house with many barred and heavily draped windows and numerous doors, only one of which could be opened from the outside, and that only after a knock had called someone to unlock it from the inside. Wide porches and balconies adorned with filigreed iron embellishments surrounded the house. Towers and a widow's walk topped it. No light showed as Vanderwagen and his crew tied up their horses at hitching posts tucked among the cottonwoods.

"Now, men," Vanderwagen said, "behave like God-fearing gentlemen. Miss Emma don't stand for rough stuff."

MAJOR WILKES STOOD gripping the brim of his hat, rolling it up.

"Sixteen, your friends said?" The woman was young but large, wearing a red dressing gown of some sheer material.

"Yes'm," Major Wilkes said. He looked over the top of her head at the walls, which were red and covered with pictures in gilt frames. All the pictures were of women wearing even less than the woman standing in front of him.

"First time, your friends said."

"Yes'm." Major Wilkes averted his gaze from the pictures and looked around for his friends. They had all vanished.

"You're a big'un for 16."

"Yes'm."

"Not many fellas I have to look up to."

"No'm."

"Let's go up. I'll show you the ropes, then it's up to you."

"Yes'm."

She turned and went up the stairs ahead of him. The steps were covered with the thickest carpet Major Wilkes had ever seen. Like the walls and her gown it was red. Her haunches reminded him of a mule's behind. One of the trail hands had described the pleasure of following a willing woman up stairs. "I like to reach out and pat her ass," he had said.

Major Wilkes thought about doing it but decided not to. The woman said over her shoulder, "Fellas said your name is Gower?"

"Yes'm."

"I got a friend Amos. Amos Gower. You know Amos?"

"Yes'm, he's my grandpa."

"Well, he's a good'un, Amos is. Decorated by General Lee in the war. Don't see him much anymore, but his son Eph is one of my regulars. Reckon you know Eph?"

"Yes'm, he's my uncle."

Major Wilkes was shocked, not about Amos, whom he thought capable of anything. But *Eph?* He was married to Muffie Wadkins, who had dropped out of school for him. Why would *Eph* come to a place like this?

"He's dealing in oil leases hereabouts, Eph is, and always comes by when he's in town, sometimes all night. He's going to be a rich man, one of these days, Eph is, you just wait and see. Famous, too. Thinking of running for state representative up to Wichita Falls, so I hear. You say 'hi' to Eph for me, next time you see him. Your grandpa, too. Tell 'em Tessie says 'hi.' They'll know who you mean."

"Yes'm," he said, though he wouldn't know what to say to Eph, much less Amos.

"Well, here we are." The woman was puffing. The stairs were steep. "Now you take off your pants and boots. Shirt, too, if you want, or just unbutton it. I don't care for buttons digging into me."

"Yes'm."

The room was small with red walls, a wide bed with a red cover and a mirror in the ceiling overhead and a nightjar under it. The walls seemed to be thin. He could hear grunts and heavy breathing in nearby rooms.

The woman spread out a towel on the bed and lay down, opening her gown. "All right, sonny, let's get going."

"Yes'm."

Later, as he pulled on his boots, he said, "I'd appreciate, ma'am, if you didn't mention me to Eph or my grandpa."

"You can count on me, sir. Come see me any time."

When he got home he told his mother and grandmother all about his trip, except his visit to Miss Emma's. Listening to him, Lorena and Minnie congratulated themselves for letting him go. He seemed so much more grown up for having seen something of the world—less tentative, somehow. Even his voice seemed deeper, more like the man he wasn't quite, or so they believed.

He gave Amos back his two dollars. Amos asked if he'd seen Tessie.

"Who?"

12.

INSTEAD OF SLEEPING after a night of guarding drunks and nipping at confiscated liquor, Amos — bone tired, hardly able to keep his eyes open — waited at the courthouse to testify as a prosecution witness in a theft case.

He had reported seeing a prisoner rifle another prisoner's pocket while they were in his custody. But the defense lawyer said in his opening statement that both prisoners would testify that they had seen Amos pocket the missing money while booking them for public drunkenness and fighting. Legal wrangling and the testimony of the officer who arrested both the victim and the perpetrator of the alleged robbery took up most of the morning. Waiting outside the courtroom to be called, Amos kept himself going with the aid of a flask he had filled before going off duty. He didn't testify until mid-afternoon.

It took only a few questions for the prosecutor to get Amos's story. In the middle of the night, he testified, he had happened to look into the bull pen and had seen the accused robber get off the cot where was sleeping off his drunk and creep over to the victim's cot.

[From the transcript:]

> Q. And what did he do when he reached Mr. Lewis's cot, Mr. Gower?
> A. He taken that there wallet and got him some money out of the wallet.
> Q. And you saw him pocket that money and throw the wallet into a corner of the cell?
> A. Yes, sir, I did.

Right from the start the defense attorney came at him like Sergeant McCandless making him return a fence rail to a one-armed Confederate officer, who turned out to be Minnie's father.

> Q. Mr. Gower, were you asleep or awake when you saw the defendant steal that money about two-thirty in the morning?
> A. I were awake, like I said. I wouldn't seen nothing without my eyes was open, now would I?
> Q. Perhaps not. Now while your eyes were open, Gower, did you ever see three $1 bills and two four-bit coins in John Lewis's wallet?
> A. No, sir. I never did, so help me God. But I seen the defendant take that money out of that there wallet.
> Q. Is it your duty as night jailor to remove and log in all valuables from the person of your prisoners before you place them in the bull pen or a cell?
> A. Yes, sir.
> Q. Did you do that with Mr. Lewis?
> A. No. sir.
> Q. And why didn't you?
> A. He had horse shit—
> Judge Pearson: Watch your language, please, Mr. Gower.
> A. Horse manure, he had horse manure all over him from rolling around in the corral, fighting.

Q. And you didn't want to get all dirty?
A. I sure didn't.
[Laughter]
Q. Was Mr. Lewis all dirty the next morning when he reported the theft?
A. I don't know. I were home sleeping by then.
Q. Were you inebriated when you went home, Mr. Gower?
A. No, sir! I don't never drink on duty. Not never. Everybody knows that.
[Laughter]
Q. You're sure you'd remember if you had taken that wallet out of his pocket before locking him up?
A. Course I'd remember.
Q. And you're quite sober now, are you, Mr. Gower?
A. Damn right. You want to smell my breath?
Q. I think not, thank you.
[Laughter]
Q. Mr. Gower, did you or did you not take that wallet off John Lewis when you booked him and did you or did you not take three dollar bills and two fifty-cent pieces out of it and throw the wallet into the corner of the bullpen, where it was found the next morning by the day jailor?
A. You come outside and ask me that.
Judge Pearson: The witness will answer the question.
A. Course I didn't.

Amos left the stand red-faced and sweating, thirsty, too. He leaned against the Zouave's base in the square, nipping at his pocket flask. He had been confident that the jury wouldn't take the word of a prisoner over that of a sworn officer of the law, but now he wasn't at all sure what the verdict would be. He hadn't had any luck since that murderer spinning at the end of a rope put the hex on him. *"Crwrgh!"* the murderer had cried. *"Eeghwr. Hrckk. Hrckk. Crwrgh!"* If that wasn't a curse, Amos didn't know what it could be. The way he had been humiliated that morning proved it again.

The prisoner who had been on trial emerged from the courthouse with his family. They laughed and shouted and threw hats in the air. Amos saw that it wasn't enough that he'd lost his land and had to stay awake all night emptying chamber pots for criminals while other men slept. Now even justice had turned its back on him. That hex had done it again. The man he had accused of theft had gone free and he himself stood all but accused. He took out his flask and finished it off in one long gulp.

Across the square Mary Nell and a crowd of youngsters carrying book bags came from the soda fountain in the drugstore next door to the bank. There were six or seven in the group, mostly girls but with a couple of boys in their midst.

One of the boys coming out of the drugstore made a deep bow to Mary Nell. The other students gave way, clearing space. She curtsied and hid her face behind an out-spread hand. The boy dropped to one knee and opened his arms wide. Mary Nell threw herself at him, knocking him over. Both of them went rolling over the boardwalk locked in each other's arms. Mary Nell's legs flashed out of her petticoats. The other students laughed and applauded.

Amos was there before Mary Nell got her skirts pulled down. She was laughing. Her eyes sparkled and her cheeks were flushed. He grabbed her arms and pulled her from the clutches of the boy on the sidewalk.

"Slut!"

Mary Nell jerked away.

"Pa, it's only out of the play."

Mary Nell was not only president of the freshman class. She had also been chosen for the part of heroine in a play being put on by the high school's newly formed Thespian Society.

"You get yourself on home, young lady. I ain't going to stand for this."

The boy whose arms she'd jumped into struggled to his feet. "Mr. Gower, we're only rehearsing."

Amos hit him on the nose, saw him fall. Blood flowed over the fallen face. He looked like Jess Fellows after the glint of a sword in moonlight. Grabbing Mary Nell's arm Amos dragged her toward home. At the gate she twisted away and darted down the road. He chased her, caught her.

"You old drunk," she screamed, kicking at him.

"Don't you speak to your pa that way." He aimed a slap at her bottom.

"Drunk, drunk, drunk."

She swung her book bag, catching him between the legs, knocking the wind out of him with the pain of it. She was on the steps going into the house when he caught her again.

Minnie came flying out. He pushed Minnie away, almost knocking her over, and tucked Mary Nell under his arm. Carrying that little girl to the tack room in the stable was like hauling a sack of wildcats, all sharp nails and teeth. She bit his arm and raked her fingers through his beard from cheek to chin, scratching his face as well as pulling whiskers. He dropped her on the dirt floor in front of the old workbench he had moved in from the ranch and barred the tack room door.

Minnie pounded on the door. "Amos Gower, don't you touch that girl."

He spread-eagled Mary Nell face down, pressing himself against her to hold her, and grabbed the ropes hanging on the wall at either end of the bench, just as they had at the ranch long ago, when he whaled the daylights out of Dunc and the other boys. He looped the ropes over her wrists and drew them taut. The old piece of rein still hung at the side of the bench, though Amos hadn't had cause to give anyone a licking since the last of the boys left home. He had never before even thought of taking the strap to Mary Nell.

"Pa, don't. Please don't, Pa."

She turned her head to look at him over her shoulder. He saw the tears in her eyes, heard the agony in her voice. It pleased him that she knew what was in store and feared it.

Minnie banged on the door, a steady beat, screaming.

He spared Mary Nell the indignity of having him lift her skirts. He slashed at her with the strap through the cloth. She stopped crying at the first stroke. She had her head turned to one side, flat on the bench. Her lower teeth clamped her upper lip. Her eyes were closed. Not a muscle moved. No matter how hard he whipped her he could not make her cry or change expression. She held out longer than any of the boys ever had. It was like she was dead or was being miraculously protected from the force of his blows.

His arm tired. He stopped.

"I hate you, Pa," she whispered. *"Drunk, drunk, drunk."*

He saw he would have to treat her as he had the boys, pit the strap against bare flesh. No more cushioning fabric to ease the pain of the whip. He yanked up her dress and petticoat and pulled down her bloomers. He was shocked. The dress had not protected her at all. Her little rump was crisscrossed with bloody welts. Ugly black blotches were forming along the edges of the welts. He'd never seen worse, not on any of the boys.

He reached out and touched her, gently, sadly. She screamed and jerked away.

"Don't, Pa. Please don't."

He gaped at her, taking a long time to understand what it was she was thinking he might do. She found some slack in the rope. She twisted first one hand free and then the other. She had the bar off and the door open and was weeping in Minnie's arms before Amos had recovered from the shock of realizing what a mistaken view of him Mary Nell had.

From then on Mary Nell would not stay in a room if Amos

was there and never looked at him or spoke to him as she left. He told himself that she would get over her mad. He was sure she would realize after a while that she had deserved the whipping. But she didn't. In long nights at the jail, Amos puzzled over her obstinacy. It wasn't so much that she would not speak to him or look at him. It was that *Sergeant McCandless* was back in residence, not only on Minnie's face but also on Mary Nell's. No matter what Amos said to either of them, the sergeant leaped into the room, snarling.

Around dawn at the jail, his flask near empty, the hours still ahead before his night's work was done seemed to stretch longer than had all the hours of the night behind him.

In that dreary interval he pondered a dark question that lurked in his mind. There in the stable he had taken down her bloomers and seen what the strap had done. His heart breaking with pity, he had put out his hand to stroke away the hurt. And she had pulled away, screaming, terrified by what she thought he meant to do. The question he pondered in bleak hours before dawn was: How had the sweetest, purest little girl in all the world learned about the thing she feared he was going to do?

The question tormented him.

After he got home he stayed at the kitchen table after eating the grits and eggs and bacon that Minnie had put before him when he got home from the jail. He slipped some corn whiskey into his coffee cup when she wasn't looking, one last drink before going to bed. Mary Nell came through the kitchen, book bag over her shoulder, and went out without a word. She slammed the door as she left.

"That little old girl, she ain't right, somehow," he said.

Minnie was filling a basin with water to do up his dishes.

He struggled for words.

"She thought I were going to— to—"

He couldn't get it out. The shock of it was still on him.

"She thought—"

"So did I," Minnie said.

"But how'd a little old girl like that, no bigger'n my thumb, how come she'd know about something like that?"

Minnie swished her hands through the dishwater, working up suds with the bar of brown soap.

"What'd make her think—"

"Amos, you're a fool. Always were."

He went to bed with further dark questions for company. What had he been about when he reached out to stroke her bruised flesh? Had she in her innocence divined in the instant of his touch a terrible truth he could not even now bring himself to face? Had she sensed that lust would follow the blinding surge of pity he felt when he saw the livid streaks his strap had left? Harshly as he had beat her, lightly as he touched her, had she recognized that what she had to fear from him was something worse than the whip? How could she have known?

For Amos, all the questions came down to one last question, the darkest of all.

What might he have done had she not freed herself and got away? He feared the answer and dared not seek it.

Amos Gower felt a stranger to himself.

13.

NOT LONG AFTER Major Wilkes visited Miss Emma's Home Away from Home, Owchicta County Sheriff Barnes hired him as errand boy and spittoon cleaner at the jail, a position that ranked only below Amos's.

Within months the boy was doing all that and most of the things a deputy might do as well. He settled fence and water disputes between nesters and ranchers, broke up family fights at isolated homesteads and talked the embattled participants back to good sense. He served summonses, calmed drunks, and tracked the occasional rustler. He made arrests and guarded defendants at criminal trials. He took over the sheriff's office chores, straightening out files and bringing records up to date with an efficiency that drew praise even from the clerk of the County Court, who for years had deplored the sloppiness of the sheriff's procedures.

Sheriff Barnes gave Major Wilkes a star to wear, but never got around to raising his pay or promoting him to deputy. Major Wilkes pushed him on it, but for two years the sheriff said, "Be patient, son. You're mighty young. We don't want to rush things." Away from the office he boasted so publicly about his young jewel of a non-deputy and his willingness to work for next to nothing that Sheriff James of Hardcastle County in the brand-new state of Oklahoma heard about him. He wrote Major Wilkes, inviting him to come see him in Mingus.

THE DEPUTY on duty said, "You got here fast."

"That's right," Major Wilkes said. "I did."

The deputy went over to a door on the sunlit side of the half-basement sheriff's office.

Major Wilkes heard him say, "Fella's here you told us about."

"Send him in."

Sheriff James pushed back from his desk but didn't get up. He was a big man gone to fat, with white hair and a belly that overhung his belt buckle like a 50-pound sack of rice. Sunlight streamed through barred windows behind him, making it hard for Major Wilkes to see much more than a dark silhouette. The windows looked to have been unwashed longer than the courthouse had been standing. Leaning back in his chair, the sheriff lifted a boot toward the top of his desk. He couldn't make it with that leg and tried the other. No luck. He sighed, settled back in his chair, and lifted his left leg over his right knee with both hands.

Once settled, he questioned Major Wilkes closely, revealing by his questions that he already knew a great deal about him. Fifteen minutes into the conversation he picked a lawman's star off his desk and waved it before Major Wilkes, who sat on the edge of his chair in front of the desk, rolling the brim of his Stetson. The star reflected a sunbeam onto the wall above the sheriff's head, where it danced like a halo.

"This here star's yours if you want it. Eighteen's young to be a deputy, but I reckon you're bigger than anybody who's likely to debate the point with you."

Sheriff James said that if Major Wilkes accepted the star he would spend six months or so in Mingus, on trial but at full pay, learning the ropes and getting acquainted with folks.

Then he would go down to Ringle in the southwestern part of the county and run his own show in a township covering nearly a third of the county, though a sparsely populated third. It stretched from near Mingus to the cane breaks and quicksand of the channel-shifting Red River, at that point the border with Texas.

Away from the river, the sheriff said, Major Wilkes's territory was chiefly open but rugged range, dry as a cowhand on his way to town on a Saturday night with money in his pocket and a thirst that would take a quart of corn whisky to quench. A few long-established big ranchers had run their cattle on the open range, with or without permits or deeds, since the rough-and-tumble Texas days, and they wanted to keep it that way. The sheriff warned Major Wilkes that he would spend much of his time dealing with clashes between those ranchers and latecoming nesters who fenced off their homesteads with barbed wire.

Constant quarrels over property and grazing rights were, in fact, the reason why he needed a deputy at Ringle.

"Sounds fine," Major Wilkes said.

As Sheriff James pinned the star on him, he said "Major Wilkes" was too much of a mouthful for day-to-day use. "Confusing, too. Major ain't a name. It's a title, less'n you explain it. We'll call you Wilkes Gower, Will for short."

"I reckon I can answer to that," Major Wilkes said. But he continued to think of himself as Major Wilkes.

WHEN MAJOR WILKES got back to Owchicta, Lorena invited Minnie and Amos to Sunday dinner to celebrate. She invited Mary Nell, too, but the girl refused to be in the same room as her father. Major Wilkes was decked out for the occasion almost up to Eph in sartorial splendor—black suit, celluloid-collared white shirt, black string tie, and shiny boots. He had recently managed to grow a neatly trimmed mustache, which drooped around his mouth and looked, his friends said, like a croquet wicket—croquet being the newest fad from back East to strike the fancy of Owchicta's younger set. Major Wilkes had not yet told Amos about the new job, so there was no mention of it until the two were alone on the front porch.

"When I was up in Mingus the other day, Grandpa, Sheriff James offered me a deputy's job, full pay."

"You ain't going to take it, though?"

"Thinking about it."

Amos shook his head. To him Oklahoma remained a lawless wilderness and Mingus a raw little town with nothing but Miss Emma's establishment worth noticing. Besides—though he said nothing of it—with Minnie and Lorena always nipping at him, his sons grown and wrapped up in their own family affairs, and Mary Nell refusing even to look at him, Amos felt like an old buffalo bull driven out of his herd. Major Wilkes was the only one who treated him like he was important. He didn't want the boy to leave him.

"Major Wilkes, there ain't nothing up there and ain't going to be. Hardcastle used to be part of Texas, you know, just like Owchicta, but it was so worthless we let 'em stuff it into Indian Territory a few years back. Nobody much up there but outlaws and renegade Indians. If one don't shoot you, the other'll scalp you."

"It's growing, Grandpa. Nice solid people. Oklahoma's going to be a state in a few months."

"Yeah, growing. So's Texas growing, and we been a state and growing since before the War. Whyn't you stay where you belong? You might could be deputy one of these days, and people know you here. Hell, you could be sheriff after a while, elected on your own."

With Lorena and Minnie still cleaning up the kitchen, Amos felt safe in pulling out his flask. He offered it first to Major Wilkes, who declined.

"Like you say," Major Wilkes said, "I could probably get to be a deputy here in Owchicta one of these days.

"But Grandpa, I've been picking along for two years, getting flunky wages for a deputy's work. Sheriff Barnes keeps saying, 'Wait till you're older and settled down. Don't rush things.' Now Sheriff James wants me as a real deputy, with a place to live and full pay. And he wants me now. Nothing said about being older."

Amos found it a hard argument to answer. It was true that only his age was holding Major Wilkes back.

"Well, I reckon you're going to do it. But I wish you wouldn't."

They sat in silence.

"Your ma know what you got in mind?"

"So does Grandma. They both think it's a good idea. I'm leaving in the morning."

"Well, then. Reckon it ain't no good me saying nothing."

"That's right. I'm sorry, Grandpa."

Amos didn't care how sorry the boy was. He felt betrayed.

AFTER TWELVE HOURS of sitting with his feet cocked up on his desk while he tried to keep his eyes open, Amos headed home. He had finished his own flask early and then pretty well killed a confiscated jug of white lightning. In front of the courthouse he saw Sheriff Barnes out front, arms akimbo and his hat pushed back, hobnobbing with early arrivals. Amos didn't feel up to a hobnob. He ducked his head and scurried by while the sheriff's back was turned.

In the square a soldier sat cross-legged on the Zouave's

pedestal with his hat beside him, the sun on his face, and a book in his hand. A ready-made cigarette drooped from his lip, unlit. As Amos passed, the soldier looked up from his book.

"You got a light, Pop?"

He was little more than a boy, a tall but scrawny buck private in a uniform too big for him and a haircut so close at the sides that his scalp showed. His freckled face had yet to feel a razor's stroke, and his hands and feet were outsized for the thin wrists and shanks that connected them to the rest of him.

Amos saw that someday the young man would be just as broad-shouldered and big-bellied as he himself had become with the years. The fair hair would darken and finally turn gray and thin. The boyish face would disappear beneath a carpet of beard. But that was all future. Right now the soldier was just a skinny youngster feeling his oats, aware of his coming power but not yet able to assert it.

To Amos, reading seemed a strange thing for a soldier to do—indeed, a queer thing for any man to do in Owchicta. Besides, real men rolled their own cigarettes. He walked up to the soldier, crowding him on the pedestal.

"What did you say, young fella?"

"I said, you got a light, Pop? That means, I wonder if you got a match, Pop."

"That ain't no way to speak to an officer," Amos said, loud as he could.

"I don't see any officer. I was speaking to you, Pop."

"When you speak to me, Yankee, say *Sir*," Amos's voice carried throughout the square. On the courthouse steps someone laughed.

A throbbing in Amos's temples reminded him of footsteps overhead in a Mississippi root cellar and of Minnie banging on the workshop door. He knotted his fist in the soldier's shirt. The uniform that had been too big grew tight over the young man's chest and shoulders as Amos twisted it.

"Now, here, Pop, you've got no call—"

Amos yanked him off the pedestal. "*Sir*. Say *Sir*."

Sheriff Barnes yelled from the steps, "What's going on down there?"

Someone yelled back, "Old Man Gower's got hisself a load on and is fixing to kill hisself a soldier."

Still clutched in Amos's grip, the soldier twisted around to put his book face down on the pedestal, careful not to lose his place. Amos shook him a little. The soldier took the unlit ready-made off his lip and placed it on the book. He looked Amos in the eye and kneed him hard. Amos went to his knees, grabbing himself. The soldier chopped him on both sides of his neck with open hands. Amos couldn't breathe. He felt like he had a noose around his neck and a coyote gnawing at his privates. Bent over, almost to the ground, he rocked back and forth and groped at his tortured groin, gasping for air.

The soldier kneed him again, this time under the chin. Amos straightened up and fell backwards, and lay stretched out full-length on the ground with the soldier standing over him.

Amos heard the sheriff say, "Looks to me like that there soldier is fixing to kill hisself Old Man Gower."

Everyone laughed. Sheriff Barnes came down the steps and helped Amos to his feet.

"Come on, Amos. Get yourself on home and sober up. Can't have my night man sleeping off a drunk in the public square."

The soldier was standing, ready to start in again. Amos staggered away. He was going to throw up and didn't want to do it in front of everybody. With jaws clamped together to hold back the vomit that was already filling his mouth, he headed blindly out of the square.

How word of his wrangle with the young solider traveled so fast, Amos couldn't understand. By the time he dragged in the kitchen door with his manhood aching from the soldier's knee, Minnie knew every detail. She sent him back outside to clean his boots.

There was vomit on his pants, too. He took them off and dropped them on the porch for Minnie to wash. He went into the house in his droopy-seat long johns. Mary Nell was in the kitchen. Now he faced a pair of Sergeant McCandlesses, one young, one old. He hoped Mary Nell would leave as usual. He didn't want her to see him in his present state. But she stayed.

"Your pa was fighting with a book-reading soldier," Minnie said.

"That must be Jimmy Weston. Lucy Hines's cousin brought a bunch of friends down from Fort Sill for a few days. Jimmy's read more books than any boy I've ever known."

"Well, he's a fighter, that young man. He got your pa down in no time and sent him home whipped."

"He never," Amos said.

Minnie slammed his plate of eggs, pork chops, and grits in front of him as though he was late to the table and not there yet. The sight of food, sunny-side-up eggs, cooked just the way he ordinarily liked them, made his stomach roll over. But he poured blackstrap molasses over the grits and pricked the eggs with his fork.

Mary Nell said, "Ma, I don't want to go to school, not today, not after this. I don't want to face people."

"You go. Just pretend you don't know the old fool."

"But I do know him."

"Then let people know that you know just as well as they do that your pa's a drunk and a fool and it doesn't have a thing to do with you because you aren't either of those things. That's what I've been doing all these years."

Amos closed his ears and choked down his food as fast as he could, wanting nothing in this world but his bed and solitude.

Before he fell asleep he grieved over Mary Nell. She had turned into a grudge-holder, just like her mother. He couldn't see why. It was one of the multitude of things Amos could not sort out. It was as mysterious to him as the loss of the ranch had been or why Minnie had always kept her arm over her face.

When he finally fell asleep he dreamed of Jess Fellows lying in moonlight with his throat slit by the Union officer's sword, his face a bloody mask and his teeth glittering. In the dream Jess sat up as Amos was going through his pockets.

"What you doing, Amos? That there's my watch you got."

"You're dead, Jess. You can't sit up like that."

"Well, I done it," Jess said. He got to his feet. His head, held on by nothing but a stretch of skin, tipped back. His neck gushed blood. He kicked Amos between the legs.

Amos woke up screaming, but no one came to him. He lay on his cot with his groin aching. He didn't know if the pain was from Jess's kick in the dream or the Yankee soldier's in the square.

After a while he went back to sleep. He had the same dream again.

He sat up in bed so wide awake that he got dressed and went down to the Moose Lodge, where he and other old-timers tilted chairs against the wall, swapped war stories, and spat tobacco juice at the closest spittoon.

No one mentioned Amos's brush with the young soldier. They'd all had their bouts with the bottle and were willing to let bygones be bygones. The town's younger citizens might think of Amos as a no-count has-been. The Odd Fellows had memories that went back before yesterday and treated him with the respect due Major Amos Gower, a cavalryman in the Army of the Confederate States of America, an officer and gentleman, and a hero with medals pinned on him by General Lee to prove his heroism.

Minnie couldn't take that away from him, however hard she tried. Nobody paid attention to a woman who scorned her husband.

14.

ON MAJOR WILKES'S first day on the job, Sheriff James called all his deputies in from their districts to meet the new man. The meeting had just started when gunshots sent them scrambling out the door into the square. A hatless old man aimed a Colt at a marble statue of Justice standing in front of the courthouse. Blindfolded, both breasts demurely draped, Justice held a pair of scales aloft in one hand, a downward pointing sword in the other. The gunman steadied his gun on his forearm and fired, shattering the tip of Justice's sword. He gave a rebel yell, followed by an Indian war whoop. Holding the gun behind his head, barrel up like a feather, he stomped around Justice, whooping and firing into the air.

"Old Man Fincus," Sheriff James said. "On the warpath again. He ain't got this drunk for a long while. Stay back."

The wind ruffled Fincus's wisp of hair. His clothes wrapped around him in folds.

Major Wilkes saw that he had once been a much larger man. He thought of Amos.

Sheriff James called, "Put it away, you fool. You'll kill somebody."

Fincus stopped prancing and took aim at the phalanx of

lawmen. They rushed up the broad wooden steps to the building's porch to shelter behind the courthouse columns, two to a column except for the sheriff. He was too wide to share. While their backs were turned, Fincus reloaded.

"Hate to do it, but looks like we'll have to shoot the poor old cuss," Sheriff James said from behind his column. "Too bad. He used to be a real somebody. Come up here from Owchicta County maybe 25 years ago while we was still part of Texas and done real good. But he lost his ranch a few years back. Never got over it. Lives at the county poorhouse now."

From the next column over, Major Wilkes said, "Let me try to talk him into handing over his gun."

"He'll shoot you before he'll do that, Will."

"I don't think so. Pure chance if he can even hit the courthouse, let alone me."

"Hate to risk it."

"I know a lot of old fellows like him, my grandpa for one."

"Well, reckon, if you want to. But keep your gun ready and use it if you have to."

"I won't need a gun."

Major Wilkes unbuckled his gun belt and handed it to the deputy sharing his column. He stepped into the open, hands up.

"Mr. Fincus!"

The old man spun around and fired two shots. One produced a burst of dust in what might have been the courthouse lawn, had any seed been scattered there that year. The second shot sent splinters flying from the lowest courthouse step.

Major Wilkes clasped his hands behind his head, elbows spread like batwings or enormous ears.

"I surrender, Mr. Fincus. Wouldn't want to fool with you."

"Better not. You fool with me, I'll punctuate your gizzard."

Major Wilkes eased down the steps. "That's what folks tell me, Mr. Fincus, sir. They say you're the best damn shot in Hardcastle County, or so I understand. But I'd like to talk to you."

"What about?"

"I think maybe you know my grandpa."

"What's his name?"

"Amos Gower. Lives down at Owchicta."

"Sure, I know him. Big man. Tall. Shoulders wide as a mule's ass. Had a good-sized spread."

"That's right. Lost it, though. Bank foreclosed. Grandpa took it real hard."

"Them goddam bankers! They done it to me, too."

"That's what I heard, Mr. Fincus. I'd like you to tell me about it."

Major Wilkes was in front of the old man, only a couple of steps away.

"All right, but stay back. No tricks."

"No tricks, Mr. Fincus, I promise. My grandpa's pretty down in the mouth these days. If I knew your story, I could tell it to him. It'll maybe make him feel better knowing he ain't the only one the bankers robbed. He always had a lot of respect for you. Speaks well of you to this day."

Waving his arms, Fincus poured out his story. The weather turned dry, the dust storms came, his cattle died, the bankers called his loans. Major Wilkes had heard the story many times, from Amos and others. No mention of unwise decisions made before or during the downward spiral, but Major Wilkes expected none. After a while the old man's voice began to falter and his eyelids drooped.

"Mr. Fincus, I'm getting awful hot out here in the sun. Sweating like a pig, I am, and my arms is about to fall off, being up like they are. You look sort of tuckered out yourself. Whyn't you let me walk you home, and we'll talk again after you've had some rest?"

"Home? Usually they just call me an old fool and throw me in jail."

"Not this time, Mr. Fincus. You give me that gun, and you can sleep in your own bed."

Major Wilkes got back to the courthouse an hour later, carrying the old man's pistol. Sheriff James slapped him on the back.

"Will, I don't know another man with the guts and judgment to do what you done. I'm making you a senior deputy right now and raising your pay $2 a month. You go down to Ringle tomorrow."

THE WEEKLY Mingus *Times* ran the story in two columns on page one under a bank of headlines.

GUNFIGHT AT COURTHOUSE

SERIOUS INJURY OR DEATH AVERTED
AS YOUNG DEPUTY LAYS WEAPON ASIDE
AND DISARMS DRUNKEN GUNMAN

SHERIFF JAMES PRAISES WILL GOWER'S
"COOL DISPLAY OF COURAGE," PROMOTES
HIM AND ASSIGNS HIM TO RINGLE POST

Major Wilkes mailed a copy of the *Times* to his mother. She slapped on her bonnet and rushed to Minnie, waving the newspaper. "He's a hero! He's a hero!"

Lorena read the headline and story aloud. Listening in his pantry, Amos couldn't help feeling resentful. His name had never appeared in a newspaper headline.

Minnie and Lorena hurried to the Owchicta *Beacon*. The editor agreed to reprint it. When they returned Amos was rocking on the front porch. He spat a mouthful of tobacco juice over the railing, combed his beard, and said, "The boy's a damn fool. He'd better have kilt the old man. Then he'd be a hero for sure."

"Takes a damn fool to know one, doesn't it, Lorena?"

"They're like heroes in that respect, or so I've heard."

Amos ignored them. "I remember Fincus. Settled west of us. Never had the gumption or sense God give a radish. No wonder he lost his land up there in Indian Territory."

"Isn't that just like him?" Minnie said. "Never in his life has he had anything good to say about anybody but himself. He would have shot that poor old man, all right, but in the back."

Amos said, "Now see here," but stopped.

MAJOR WILKES set up bachelor quarters in a roadside cottage owned by the County of Hardcastle in the Village of Ringle.

Spread out along a spur of the Kansas City, Mexico & Oriental Railroad, ten miles from the mainline at Mingus, Ringle was more hamlet than village. It had a permanent population of 26 adults, not counting Major Wilkes, and a child under every foot. Other than the stock-auction shed, feedlots, and corrals that gave it a reason to exist, Ringle offered a general store, which carried everything from horseshoes, plows, and ready-made privies to hardtack, canned tomatoes, female remedies, and fancy boots; a boarding house to put up visiting cattle buyers and herd owners; a cotton gin; two corn cribs, and two grain elevators higher than the Farmers and Merchants Bank in Mingus.

All this plus a one-room school with living quarters over it, nine houses—one of them a big brick house, almost a mansion, distant from everything else at Ringle—16 wells, and 24 privies, of which a number were open-air. The excess of wells and privies over houses had to do with watering the cattle that came to the feed lots and providing facilities for the hands who drove and tended the cattle and camped out in nearby fields. There was no church, saloon, water tower, paved road, or electric light.

One man, Seth Ringle, owned everything and everyone in Ringle except Major Wilkes and the county-built cottage that housed him, his office, and two jail cells. Every resident of Ringle other than the newly appointed deputy was a Ringle, married to a Ringle, worked for a Ringle enterprise or, in the case of the schoolteacher, was the aged aunt of a Ringle daughter-in-law.

Seth Ringle kept a sharp eye on everything that belonged to him, including people, and brooked no backtalk. Short but bulky, Seth looked more solid than he was and made up for his lack of height by the loudness and shrillness of his voice and the ferocity of his temper. Seth's head was pyramid-shaped, broad at the chin and pointed at the top. Jowls and cheeks billowed on either side of his face and quivered like a feeding squirrel's as he talked. The bare crown of his skull thrust upward like a pink mountain peak above a timberline of rusty-looking hair. Like Sheriff James, his belly overhung his belt buckle, which in Ringle's case bore the initials *C.S.A.* The buckle was shiny from incessant rubbing against the underside of its owner's gut, which often hid it from view.

Ringle had three telephones on a party line connecting the not-quite hamlet to Central in Mingus (one long ring). Seth's phone (one long, one short) rang in the kitchen of his big brick house, which stood on a rise distant from feedlots and corrals. The second phone (one long, two shorts) hung behind the counter in the Ringle store that Seth's eldest daughter, Loula, tended and lived in the back of. This phone was available to anyone who needed to make a call, upon payment of a nickel to Loula. (Her ne'er-do-well husband, a hostler at the auction shed, was not allowed to handle cash, because once he got his hands on a nickel it never made its way to Seth.) The third telephone in Ringle (one long, three shorts) was installed on the wall behind Major Wilkes's desk, beyond reach of anyone in the two steel-barred cells.

The kindest thing said about Seth Ringle was that he was the indulgent daddy of pretty Sophie Ringle. Seth's wife had died giving birth to Sophie just about the time his other children were setting up their own establishments in cottages built for them by Seth close by the one in which Sophie was born. As Sophie grew older she found the odors of the feedlots unpleasant.

So Seth built the brick mini-mansion for her. He painted it white and wrapped it with wide porches loaded with wicker rockers and couches, in which he could lounge to survey his domain without smelling it. Sophie spent her summers with her father and his spinster sister at Ringle, but during the school year she lived in Mingus with her aunt, her mother's sister, a widow, at whose home Seth was not welcome.

When Major Wilkes arrived at Ringle, Sophie was preparing for her junior year in high school. Major Wilkes soon heard that Sophie was sure to be elected homecoming queen — the news was everywhere — and thought her a good choice for the honor. He had seen her several times in Mingus, wearing riding breeches — the first Major Wilkes had seen on a female — and mounted on a pinto pony. She was tall, with blue eyes and strawberry blonde hair, and she smiled at everyone, even lowly deputy sheriffs three years her senior.

15.

AMOS HUNGERED FOR an invitation from Major Wilkes to visit Mingus. When the invitation came, it was for Lorena and Minnie; not him. Mary Nell went to stay with a friend. Minnie told Amos to take his meals at the jail. Eph drove his mother and Lorena to Mingus in his new spring-seated buggy behind a high-stepping pair of matched greys. He bragged all the way about the speed and endurance of his team and the smoothness of the ride, nodding his head in agreement with everything he said, without waiting for Minnie or Lorena to express an opinion.

When they passed Seth Ringle's corrals and feed lots, the ladies pressed handkerchiefs to their noses to keep the odors at bay. They were glad to find that Major Wilkes's cottage was beyond the worst stench of the settlement.

It was a white bungalow with green trim and a wide porch across the front. A note on the door said he'd been called away, but, "Come on in. See you in Mingus." Inside, Lorena and Minnie noted that the floor was free of dust. Even the jail cells, seen through the bars, looked clean. Papers cluttered the desk, but in neat piles. In the bedroom, clothes hung neatly on pegs along one wall. The bed was covered with a bright quilt that

Minnie had made. That pleased her, though she saw that he had not squared the tucked-in corners as carefully as he might.

She pointed out this oversight, but added, "He must not have had time."

"I'm sure," Lorena said.

Eph took a different view. "He probably just don't bother."

Minnie and Lorena visited the privy in back and went on with Eph to the Grand Hotel in Mingus, where Major Wilkes had booked a room for them. Eph had made other arrangements for himself.

"The Grand's too rich for my blood," Eph said. "When I'm here on business I always stay at a boarding house, Miss Emma's Home Away from Home for Respectable Ladies and Gentlemen. Get a lot more for my money there."

"I've heard about Miss Emma," Minnie said. "She sounds like an interesting woman. I'd like to meet her."

Lorena also said she'd like to meet Miss Emma. Eph didn't seem to hear. He busied himself with helping the porter with their bags.

The Grand's lobby was elegant—high-ceilinged, paneled in mahogany, floored with Italian tiles, and filled with black leather chairs and brass spittoons so shiny they looked like gold. The heads of exotic beasts, including those of a white tiger, a rhino, and a giraffe hovered on the walls, ready to leap off as soon as their bodies caught up.

"It's the grandest thing I've seen since I was a little girl and went to Vicksburg with my mother and daddy," Minnie said. "That was before the war, of course."

"It don't get much higher on the hog than this, not in these parts," Eph said. "Let's see. This is Thursday. I'll be checking on my oil leases for a couple of days, but I'll be back through here Saturday and pick you up right around 6:00 Sunday morning."

"Couldn't we leave after church?" Lorena asked.

"I gotta get home to Muffie."

"We'll be ready at 6:00," Minnie said. "But I'd surely like to meet Miss Emma."

Eph headed for the door, boot heels clattering on tile.

Major Wilkes had asked for one room with a double bed and a bath down the hall, but the Grand's owner, J. Isaac ("Ike") Watson, insisted on putting Minnie and Lorena in the Presidential Suite at no added cost, in appreciation of their having presented Hardcastle County with such an outstanding young deputy.

The suite had two bedrooms, a sitting room, the grandest bathroom either of them had ever seen, with its marble walls and floor, a tub, a shower, two sinks side by side, a toilet, and a bidet, which neither Minnie nor Lorena admitted to trying, though both were normally open to new experiences. The sitting room's walls were papered in shades of red and gold, and the furniture, even the desk chair, was upholstered in purple velvet. The carpets were so thick Lorena said that taking a step on them reminded her of crossing an Owchicta street after a rainstorm and sinking into the mud, except her feet stayed dry.

MAJOR WILKES LED them on a tour of Mingus. Minnie and Lorena were pleased to see how respectfully he was treated, though they did not hesitate to correct his grammar when necessary, as if he were ten years old. He filled them in on local gossip, which to him was not idle chatter but a guide to the rivalries and alliances that shaped Mingus doings. What he said was often cryptic. After Barney Thrimble, dapper owner of the Thrimble Department Store, planted a lingering kiss on Lorena's hand, Major Wilkes told them, "He's got a hell-raising son and a wife who's a secret drinker. When she gives him the devil you can hear her from one end of Main Street to the other.

Their housekeeper says he likes to wear his wife's pink bloomers to bed."

At the courthouse, Major Wilkes pointed out the damage Abraham Fincus had done to Justice and also the new board that replaced the step the old gentleman's bullet had splintered. He tried to persuade them that disarming Fincus was not a dangerous or remarkable feat, a notion they rejected.

Lorena puffed as they climbed to the porch.

"I understood that the sheriff's office is on the ground floor. Do you have to climb up here and then go down again every time you come or go?"

"The entrance down there is sort of a working entrance. I thought you'd like to use the main one this first time."

Going down a broad stairway from the first floor to the sheriff's office, Minnie brought up Miss Emma again.

"Do you know the lady who runs the boarding house where Eph planned to stay?"

"Oh, that's Mrs. Smith."

"Do you know her?"

"I've seen her at church."

"I'd like to meet her."

"So would I," Lorena said.

"Too bad you won't be here Sunday. Her and her lady boarders go to church every Sunday, all in a group."

"Major Wilkes! 'She and her lady boarders,' please."

"Yes'm."

When they went down the stairs to the sheriff's office on the ground floor, Lorena and Minnie understood why Major Wilkes had wanted them to climb up and then down to get there. On the frosted glass of the office door, his name was freshly painted in the list of deputies: "Will Gower."

"Who in the world is that?" Minnie asked.

"Me. Sheriff James said Major Wilkes was a mouthful."

"Will's not your name, mouthful or not!"

"It's sort of my professional name, Grandma. I don't mind."

"I do. I'll speak to the sheriff."

Sheriff James was all courtliness as he praised "Will," who, he said, was the most accomplished and capable law officer of any age that he had ever served with.

"You have here, Ma'am and Ma'am, a son and grandson who does both of you honor. He will go far in life. You can count on Will."

Minnie could not have improved on what the sheriff said had she described the boy herself, whatever he might be called. She felt no need to protest the "Will."

ON THE WAY BACK to the Grand Hotel they passed McSorley's Pharmacy & Notions Shop. Minnie had not found the ride from Owchicta in Eph's buggy as comfortable as he claimed it was, and she wanted a painkiller for her back. Lorena had lost one of the two red ribbons adorning her bonnet and hoped to match the remaining one.

McSorley's was owned and operated by Mrs. Agnes McSorley, Sophie Ringle's aunt. Twenty years after her young husband's death from consumption, Mrs. McSorley still dressed in widow's weeds. Before he died he taught her all she needed to know about compounding any medication likely to be required by his customers, who were the same ladies that bought her ribbons, needles, and thread. The two lines — potions and notions — went together like Amos and booze, Minnie commented to Lorena.

Mrs. McSorley sat at a roll-top desk in the back of the shop, working on accounts. Sophie sat on a wicker couch with books and papers scattered all around. The new school year had opened just that week, and Sophie was living with her aunt. Both rose, but only Mrs. McSorley came forward.

"Deputy Gower!" She said it emphatically, as though summoning him to the bar for sentencing. "I heard your mother and grandmother were in town. How nice! Would you introduce us? Sophie, come here!"

Beside Minnie, who except when pregnant with the twins had never weighed much over a hundred pounds, Mrs. McSorley looked enormous. Beside Lorena, who was both taller and heavier than Minnie, she looked merely overfed. Major Wilkes stayed out of the conversation the ladies struck up. Sophie stood equally silent except when her opinion was asked about this shade of red ribbon versus that one.

His silence, as Minnie mentioned later to Lorena, made her wonder if Major Wilkes might be more interested in this school girl than he let on. Minnie was soon supplied with a powder that Mrs. McSorley declared would quickly subdue her backache—which it did—and Lorena found a ribbon for her bonnet that exactly matched the old one, even in bright sunshine.

Minnie and Lorena still wanted to meet Miss Emma.

While they napped at the Grand that afternoon, Major Wilkes consulted Sheriff James.

"What should I do?"

The sheriff tilted his chair against the wall and tried to lift his feet onto his desk. "Nothing to worry about. I'll visit Miss Emma and explain your problem. She'll be closed until 6:00 o'clock tomorrow so her girls can rest up for the Saturday night crowd. I'll ask her to invite your folks for coffee in the morning."

"Wouldn't it be better if we could just run into her downtown?"

"Nope. It'd be a scandal, introducing your grandma and mother to a madam right out in public, even if don't nobody admit out loud that that's what she is. And don't worry about

Miss Emma. She's a lady. She knows how to do these things."

Later in the afternoon Minnie and Lorena received a note from Miss Emma on paper embossed *"Mrs. Euphrates Smith."* She invited them to drop by at 10 a.m. the next day. "Please forgive the short notice," Miss Emma wrote, "but I understand that your visit to Mingus will not be long."

"An elegant hand," Minnie and Lorena agreed.

LORENA WONDERED about the bars on the windows. Major Wilkes was ready for the question.

"The bars? I never noticed them until I brought Mrs. Smith your note," he said. "Sheriff James says Mrs. Smith's husband built this house back when this was pretty wild country. Town was just getting settled. Mr. Smith was a circus wrestler and traveled a lot. So he put the bars on. Mayor Powell owns the place now. Mrs. Smith leases it." He did not explain the political circumstances that made it expedient for Mrs. Smith to have the mayor as landlord.

Tessie opened the door. She was dressed not in her usual sheer wrapper but as a maid, in long black skirt, demure black blouse with a white collar, lacy white half-apron, and white cap.

"Yes'm?"

"Mrs. Amos Gower, Mrs. Lorena Gower, and Mr. Deputy Sheriff Major Wilkes Gower to see Mrs. Smith."

Tessie curtsied. "Yes, Ma'am. Mrs. Smith is expecting you."

She conducted them to the front parlor where, as Major Wilkes knew well, unknown gentleman callers were conducted — not during working hours by Tessie, but by one of several "girls" of yesteryear who had grown old in Miss Emma's service — so that Miss Emma or her husband could size up the visitors. It was a formal room furnished with Queen Anne chairs and sofas. The paintings in gilded frames of scantily dressed beauties in seductive poses that usually graced the walls had been replaced with black-framed portraits of stern-faced gentlemen and bonneted ladies—a change of décor achieved in a moment simply by flipping the frames over.

Miss Emma met them with hand outstretched. She was a gray-haired scarecrow of a woman, dressed in black except for a starched white dickey, her customary dress. Her garb bespoke respectability as forcefully as a nun's habit.

"Mrs. Amos Gower, Mrs. Lorena Gower, Deputy Gower, I am delighted to meet you," she said, smiling. "I understand that you ladies are the cultural leaders of Owchicta. Most importantly you are the mother and grandmother of our Deputy Will Gower, whom I have met at church and of whom I hear many good reports."

"We are delighted to meet you, Mrs. Smith."

"Please call me Miss Emma. Everyone does."

The three women were soon discussing the lamentable under-funding of public education, the strides toward nation-wide prohibition being taken by the Women's Christian Temperance Union, and the struggle for women's suffrage. The half-hour that Minnie had allotted for the visit sped by.

As they departed, Miss Emma urged them to call again when they were next in Mingus—"Don't wait for an invitation"—and Minnie extended the same courtesy should Miss Emma find herself in Owchicta.

Tessie saw them out. Handing Major Wilkes his hat, she winked and managed to caress his lower back.

"An interesting woman, Miss Emma," Minnie commented as they walked back into town. "And a nice looking maid, too, I thought."

"Not at all what I expected," Lorena said. "Ladylike, but interesting."

Major Wilkes said nothing.

MINNIE AND LORENA did not mention to Amos that Major Wilkes had taken them to meet Miss Emma. But he heard all about the visit as he lay in bed eavesdropping on their candid discussions in the kitchen. He was shocked to discover that they had gone to a whorehouse and had observed Tessie's caress of Major Wilkes's back. Even more shocking, they had been amused by it. He didn't think nice women—and he regarded his wife and daughter-in-law as nice women to a fault—should acknowledge knowing about such goings-on, let alone talk about them.

He did not, however, point out the error of their ways.

16.

IN 1908, LUCY HINES, daughter of the banker who foreclosed on Amos, married the son of the Englishman who bought Amos's land for next to nothing and the land of many other ranchers for no more.

In the days before Lucy's wedding Mary Nell, 16 and a high school senior, was as bright and chirpy as if she were a little girl again. She went to a party or shower or dinner every day for a week. Minnie was invited to two showers and the wedding as well. If Amos was invited she didn't tell him.

Mary Nell couldn't hide her happiness even when Amos was in his pantry, where she knew he would hear every word she said. She and Minnie spent hours talking about who was there and what was said, with frequent mentions of Jimmy, the skinny soldier who had sent him to his knees in the courthouse square. Amos was glad when the wedding was over.

A couple of months later Amos came home from the jail one morning and found Minnie sitting at the kitchen table in her nightclothes. The range was cold and not even coffee made.

"Mary Nell's gone," Minnie said. She had been crying. Her eyes were reddened and so was the tip of her nose.

"Gone? Gone where?"

"I don't know, Amos. Just gone. Sometime in the night she took the buckboard and your old mare and left."

"The soldier? That Jimmy fella?"

"Most likely. I think she's going to have a baby."

"The slut! Me and the boys'll bring her back, come hell or high water."

Amos rushed into his pantry, collected his gun belt, hid his sword in a bedroll, and headed for the door.

Minnie stood in his way. "Don't hurt her, Amos."

He shoved her aside, not bothering to answer. At the stable he found that the old buckboard wagon was gone, just as Minnie said, and so was his old black mare, the one horse he had been able to keep out of Mr. Hines's hands.

Ben was in his barn, working over the heavy ropes he used in his house-moving business.

Eph was also there, sitting on a bale of hay, just visiting. He and Muffie now lived in Wichita Falls, but were in town for a few days, staying with Muffie's family and showing off their new baby. Eph was doing well, dealing in oilfield supplies and oil leases and once in a while drilling a well himself. On the side he'd gone into politics and got himself elected to the state legislature.

Amos told Ben and Eph what had to be done. Eph offered to round up the rest of the boys. Ben suggested taking along the two sons who were moving houses with him. He thought they should learn what was expected of men when a sister acted up as Mary Nell had. Amos vetoed both proposals.

"We need to keep it small, quiet. Ain't no need to stir up the whole county without we have to. Us three can handle this."

The best thing they could do was find her and get her back before she did something foolish in public, like telling people she'd let herself get with child. No use ruining the girl's life and the family's good name with unnecessary scandal. To preserve that good name Amos would see to it that she got married, if not to her book-reading soldier, then to anyone who would take her off his hands.

He was certain Mary Nell would head for the Owchicta Livestock Auction Co.'s flag stop on the railroad mainline.

They each rode out of town a different way to join up a couple of miles east of town. Mounted on a black mare that Ben had bought at the sale after Mr. Hines foreclosed, Amos followed the buckboard tracks north almost a mile before—as he expected—they turned east. Eph and Ben were waiting for him by the time he got to the meeting place.

"Ain't a chance in hell of stopping her afore she gets to the flag stop," Amos said. "If she catched the midnight local east, which I expect her goddam soldier was on, we'll find the mare and buggy standing beside the tracks and we'll wire ahead and have 'em took off and held for us at Wichita Falls. But if they're taking the westbound, why it ain't due for another hour or so even if it's on time, which it often ain't. We got a good chance to nab 'em right there."

"What'll we do with the son of a bitch?" Ben asked.

"You'll see."

They beat the westbound local to the flag stop. But instead of the fugitives or the old wagon, they found only footprints in the dust and the smoked-down butts of ready-made cigarettes showing where a man had stood around an hour or two, waiting beside the tracks. Jimmy must have got to the siding on the eastbound midnight local and had to wait—Mary Nell wouldn't have been able to slip away before she was sure Minnie was settled for the night. The buckboard tracks came up and stopped in the middle of the butts. The tracks going away were deeper than those coming in. Mary Nell was with her soldier.

"Whore," he groaned.

Ben nodded, but Eph said, "Maybe there ain't nothing happened yet."

"Something's happened, all right. It weren't swallowing a watermelon seed done this to her."

"Maybe they're married."

"That ain't good enough. Not near good enough. Not now."

Amos and his two boys rode hard, not stopping except to relieve themselves. The tracks went one direction and then another—the soldier was trying to throw them off—but generally trended northward, toward Mingus. Now and then the buckboard traveled a main road, where tracking was difficult, but mostly the soldier stuck to trails or went cross-country. He avoided settlements. Amos did the same, except once when his flask needed replenishing. Going after a runaway and certainly pregnant daughter was thirsty business, the thirstiest Amos had ever known. Water could not slake his thirst unless it was dosed with rotgut.

His throat dried out, not just from the dust—which was terrible, with the wind blowing as it was out of the north, out of the old Indian Territory—but also from thoughts of Mary Nell in positions of love. That little girl, pure and sweet as she had always been, what could have got into her? Whatever it was, he vowed to whip it out of her. No surge of pity would soften him or make him turn away. He would not have his daughter a public scandal, known to all as a fallen woman. As for the soldier who corrupted his little Mary Nell—well, as a rancher Amos had cut many a bull calf. When he got through with that soldier, reading books and puffing on ready-mades was all he would be good for.

Late in the day they caught up with them in open country. The soldier spotted them and turned the old mare off the trail to race over the grassy plain, heedless of prairie dog holes. Amos had his flask in his hand. He took a last swallow before tucking it in his belt. Reaching around to the bedroll behind his saddle, he pulled out his sword. He gave a Rebel yell and raced after the wagon, brandishing the sword. He could see the soldier bending forward, snapping reins over the old mare's back, urging her on. Mary Nell clung to the seat with both hands, looking over her shoulder.

He came up beside the buckboard, waving the sword overhead.

"Don't, Pa, please don't," Mary Nell screamed.

Her hair was a wind-blown banner flying around her head. He had always thought she had the prettiest hair in the world, especially loose around her face like it was now, with the setting sun bringing out the red.

Riding full tilt he shifted the sword to the hand with the reins. With the other hand he reached over the wheels and caught the soldier by the scruff of the neck. He yanked him off the seat and dropped him on the ground, flat on his back in grass high enough to tickle a horse's belly. Reins trailing, the old mare pulled the wagon over the prairie at top speed. Mary Nell half-stood in the runaway buckboard, going away from her soldier, looking back, screaming, unable without the reins to stop the mare's headlong rush.

"Get her," Amos shouted. "I'll take care of this'n."

Ben and Eph raced after the wagon. The mare pounded on at top speed with no sign of flagging. Old as she was she was a better horse than her brothers rode. When they caught her, Amos was a mere dot on the prairie far behind.

Mary Nell's soldier looked up at Amos, eyes wide. He looked like Jess Fellows there on the ground under a black mare's hooves, head tilted up, throat exposed, eyes filled with fear. Amos jabbed the point of his sword into Jimmy's neck under the left ear and brought it across to the other ear. Making the cut took all his strength. He was surprised. He had supposed that the Union officer's sword had sliced easily through Jess Fellows' throat. The sudden gush of blood from the neck also surprised him, though it shouldn't have, remembering Jess.

Jimmy thrashed and flipped, just as Jess had—arms and legs jerking this way and that, like there were ropes on them and someone was pulling in all directions. He came to rest on his back, bloodied face up. Amos leaned over and thrust the sword's tip into Jimmy's groin. The black mare reared. One hoof came down on the boy's face.

Far ahead Ben and Eph caught and stopped the buckboard. As Amos rode forward to join them he pondered the uncanny resemblance to Jess Fellows that her Jimmy bore before the hoof came down on him. The same bloody mask. The same astonished look and enormous eyes.

Well away from the buggy Amos called Ben to him so Mary Nell couldn't hear.

"Eph and me'll take care of her. You get rid of what's back there. No trace, understand? After you do what's needed back there, drift on home. Not a word about this here little fracas, hear? We don't want no more scandal than we already got on account of this slut. If'n somebody wants to know whatever happened to Mary Nell and her beau, you tell 'em you don't know what in hell they're talking about. Mary Nell, she's just gone off on a little visit to her brother Eph's to help Muffie with the new baby. And her soldier—ain't nobody seen him since the Hines girl's wedding, not hide nor hair since."

Mary Nell was out of the wagon. She pulled away from Eph and ran screaming over the prairie toward her soldier.

"Catch her. Tie her up."

Eph chased her on horseback.

She dodged and ducked, but he caught her and tied her hands behind her back. He tied her legs, too, and carried her back to the wagon and dumped her over the sideboards like a bag of beans.

"Tie her down, Eph," Amos said.

"She's already tied hand and foot, Pa."

"Tie her down."

"I hate you, Pa. I'll always hate you."

Even after all she had done he could not stand to hear her say she hated him.

"Gag her, Eph."

He thought a minute.

"Listen to me, girl. Your goddam lily-livered soldier hit the ground back there and shat his pants, begging for his life. I told him I'd let him go if he'd stay away from you from now on. He promised and—"

He looked back the way they had come, back to where the soldier lay. Ben was half-way to him.

"Hey! Lookit him go!" he shouted, though there was nothing to see but Ben and waving grass. "He's up and legging it through that there grass like a jackrabbit in a prairie fire. He's a running fool, ain't he, Eph?"

He gave his Rebel yell. Eph whooped too.

"Look it that soldier go!" Eph yelled.

They chortled and slapped their legs with their hats. Mary Nell tried to sit up to look.

"Keep her down, Eph. She don't want to see her fancy man running away from her like he's doing."

There were inquiries, but nothing troublesome. The soldier had taken leave from Fort Sill, not telling anyone where he was going or why. When he didn't return the Army assumed it was just one more case of a young man enlisting and then deserting after finding out he didn't care for army life after all. Mary Nell had not told her troubles or her plans to anyone. No one in Owchicta had known she was still thinking of the book-reading soldier in the weeks after Lucy Hines's wedding. And no one questioned the story that she had gone to Wichita Falls to visit Eph and Muffie and had decided to finish high school there.

As for Amos and Ben, no one connected their brief absence with the soldier's disappearance, word of which did not reach Owchicta until long after the attempted elopement. The sheriff was annoyed that Amos hadn't shown up for work as night jailer for two nights, but supposed he had been on a drunk. Fortunately, there had been no prisoners in the jail on the nights that Amos left it unguarded. The sheriff threatened to fire him but did not. He merely gave him a dressing down, roughly and not with the respect Amos thought was due a Confederate officer and hero decorated by General Lee.

Otherwise Amos took heart from the way things had turned out. By dealing firmly with Mary Nell and her lover, he told himself, he had overcome the hex Dunc's murderer put on him so long ago.

AS MARY NELL'S TIME neared, Minnie announced that she wasn't going to let the girl face her ordeal alone and left for Wichita Falls. Looking ahead to the time when he would have to explain away a new baby, Amos spread it around that it was Minnie who was having the child and had gone to Wichita Falls for special medical attention. No one cared to dispute the claim to his face, though anyone looking at Minnie had to know she was years past her child-bearing time.

Tongues clacked, of course. What the gossips said would have been hurtful to Mary Nell had she heard it, she who had never known anyone other than a friend, Amos aside. But the chatter was so far from the truth that it represented no danger to Amos or his boys.

Mary Nell spent the remaining weeks of expectation in a room under the eaves at Eph and Muffie's big new house in

Wichita Falls, sleeping in the same bed as Minnie but not speaking to her. She said not one word to her mother in all that time. Minnie did the cooking for the family and Mary Nell did the housework. Eph and Muffie had a boy and two little daughters by then, but Muffie regarded Mary Nell as morally suspect and did not allow her near the children. Nor did she speak to her except to issue orders. Eph brought books from the library, and Mary Nell passed her spare time reading. In the evenings, when no one would see her, Eph took her for long walks. He said she talked freely then, mile after mile, but she made him swear not to tell anyone what they talked about. He kept his word.

Amos ruled that he and Minnie would deliver the baby rather than call in a possibly nosy doctor or midwife. It seemed to him that Minnie knew all there was to know about birthing. She had borne nine children and had assisted at the birth of countless others. He'd had some experience along those lines himself, as he pointed out, citing Mary Valentine's Eph as well as hundreds of calves. Minnie protested Amos's decision, but Mary Nell told Eph she was willing to have Minnie help her so long as Amos stayed out of it.

When Mary Nell's time came Amos took the train to Wichita Falls. She was in labor when he arrived. At first she was too proud to acknowledge her pains. She bit her lips, knotted her hands in the bed covers, and turned her face away. But as the pains grew sharper, became constant, she could not help herself. She moaned, and now and again shrieked.

At each scream Amos, listening outside the locked door, tipped up his flask. He could not stand for Mary Nell to suffer. She had sinned, no doubt about that, but he found he could forgive her that. And she was such a little thing. He yearned for her to be whole again, to be again the Mary Nell whose waist he could have spanned with one hand had she permitted it. A day and night passed. Amos could stand it no longer. He put his shoulder against the door and forced it open.

Muffie came in behind him. She whispered to Minnie, "Tell her not to make so much noise. The neighbors will hear."

Mary Nell overheard but misunderstood. She thought it was Minnie worrying about the neighbors.

"I want the neighbors to hear," Mary Nell screamed, speaking to her mother at last. "I want the whole world to know that that old drunk killed Jimmy and you didn't do a thing to stop him."

"Hush, girl," Amos said. "You don't know a damned thing about what happened to that there soldier of yours."

"I do know and I want the world to know."

Amos tipped the flask again.

Mary Nell's ordeal went on and on, a breech birth. Keeping her voice low so as not to frighten Mary Nell, Minnie begged Amos to send for a doctor.

Amos said no. When Minnie tried to go for the doctor herself he stepped in front of the door and would not let her leave the room. He paced the floor, sipping from his flask. Muffie heated water and pleaded through the door for quiet. Eph hauled the water up the stairs. In the end Amos could see nothing to do but push Minnie aside and reach in to pull the baby out as he would have yanked the calf from a suffering cow. As he brought out the head Mary Nell arched, lurched, howled.

Amos heard a snap. It was not a large sound and was almost lost in the tumult.

But he knew a terrible thing had happened, an irreparable thing, and that the sound would echo down the years to haunt him the rest of his life and beyond. Amos was an old man and he cared what his progeny would know of him and even more what they would think of him. He knew that the snap he heard beneath his hands foreshadowed posterity's verdict on a life he had lost track of, his own.

Blood flowed. Minnie sprang forward with the towels and warm water Eph and Muffie had provided. Mary Nell was silent, mercifully unconscious. Amos wrapped the baby in a towel and carried it downstairs. Eph and Muffie were in their kitchen, clinging together.

"A girl," Amos said. He burst into tears. He did not remember ever having cried before, not in his whole life.

Amos and Minnie carried the child home to Owchicta. They buried her as if she had been theirs but Amos would not allow a marker on the grave. Mary Nell did not come home to Minnie ever again. Nor did she write in the years that followed, except now and again to Eph. In those few letters to Eph she sent no message to Minnie or Amos and never mentioned either of them. She placed no blame, asked no forgiveness. Once in a while Eph passed along a scrap of news. Mary Nell had moved to Fort Worth. Mary Nell had gone back to school. Mary Nell was teaching first grade in a country school.

Eph wouldn't say where. She had asked him not to. Amos expected her to soften any day and come back to them. But she did not. Mary Nell was gone.

III. The Trial

17.

EVERY CITIZEN OF Hardcastle County who could make it crowded into Mingus on the last day of 1909, a Friday, to celebrate New Year's Eve and a second full year of Oklahoma statehood. Bonfires blazed, speeches poured forth, and fireworks shook the earth like cannon at Shiloh, filling the evening sky with the fleeting colors of a million shooting stars.

Preparing for what promised to be a night of rowdy celebration, Sheriff James called in all his deputies from outlying offices, Major Wilkes among them, to bolster the local forces of law and order. He also swore in a dozen private citizens as special deputies.

Until nearly 2:00 o'clock on New Year's Day morning, however, Hardcastle County's celebration was without serious incident. It seemed to be ending quietly, leaving only a few boisterous drunks harmonizing in Sheriff James's jail cells. Most of the special deputies turned in their stars and went home. The full-time officers gathered in the sheriff's office to warm up and swap stories about the evening before heading to their beds.

Tessie burst through the door. She clutched a man's black cloak to her. It covered her from head to toe and her face as well. Only her eyes showed. One was blackened and closed. She rushed to Major Wilkes.

"Tess! What happened?"

She was his favorite at Miss Emma's—not especially pretty or exciting, but comfortable to be with. He put his arms around her. She leaned against him, her big shoulders heaving, rocking them both.

"They pistol-whipped me," she said, her voice muffled against his shoulder. "I never been treated like that. Not in my whole life. Never."

She stepped away from Major Wilkes and threw the cloak open. A bruise purpled one cheek and her chin. Cuts on her forehead and chin oozed blood. Blood trickled from her nose, which was twice its usual size. Her working costume, a gauzy red wrapper like the one she had worn the first time Major Wilkes met her, was in pieces. Bruises covered breasts, belly, and thighs.

"Look at me! I ain't going to be able to work for a month. Maybe never. They ruined my looks."

Major Wilkes helped her to a chair. Sheriff James handed her a bottle of brandy.

She tipped it up, took a long swig, and handed it back.

"I needed that." She drew her cloak around her and huddled on the chair, overflowing it, crying like a child.

"Who done it, Tess?" Sheriff James asked.

Between bouts of sobbing, she told her story.

By 1:30 a.m. all visitors at Miss Emma's Home Away from Home for Respectable Ladies and Gentlemen had departed. Miss Emma and her ladies relaxed with champagne after a busy evening. A dozen young men—"just boys, but awful drunk"— burst through the front door. When Miss Emma's husband tried to put them out, a boy beat him on the head with a gun butt and knocked him out. The intruders tore down Miss Emma's red damask drapes and used them to tie him up.

When Miss Emma tried to stop them, they tied her up, too. Some of Miss Emma's resident ladies managed to hide, but the boys grabbed Tessie and several others, beat them with guns as well as fists, and took turns raping them on couches and even the floor, not bothering to take them upstairs. One intruder offered to untie Miss Emma if she would open the vault where she stored the liquor she kept for regular customers—casual visitors had to bring their own. She refused. The young man said she'd better do it or he'd get his daddy to evict her.

"Has to be the Powell kid," Sheriff James said. "His old man owns the place."

"That's him," Tessie said. "Miss Emma told him she'd do no such thing and he ordered me to get the key. I told him I didn't know where Miss Emma kept it, but I knew his daddy real well and he better be careful. That's when he began hitting me with his pistol. Finally he said they was going into town to get booze and would come back later for— more— more—"

She ducked her head and cried into her hands. She couldn't get the word out.

Sheriff James sent a man to get Doc Gorse to treat Tessie's injuries and several deputies to Miss Emma's to clean up there. Others went to check the illicit saloons where the boys might seek booze. He took Major Wilkes and another young deputy, Billy Bowen, with him to cover Main Street. Major Wilkes started out without his gun belt.

"Better buckle up, Will," the sheriff said. "These boys might be a mite troublesome."

Outside the moon was up and the stars were bright. Scattered sounds told of a dying celebration—a few pistol shots, no doubt aimed at some star overhead, the sputtering explosions of firecrackers, raucous hoots of laughter, and a slurred rendition of *O, Bury Me Not On the Lone Prairie.*

On Main Street, a few merchants still stood guard in front of their darkened stores. The sheriff did not pause for conversation except to ask if they'd seen the troublemakers. None had. But as the lawmen neared the Grand Hotel they heard a loud argument and a couple of shots.

Ike Watson and his night clerk, Buck Farragut, stood on the hotel porch. Watson was in his shirtsleeves and cradled a shotgun. The only light came from the lobby; the globes that stood on either side of the entrance had been shattered. Mingus had not yet installed street lights.

"Some high school hooligans—Jimmy Thrimble and Junior Powell and that bunch—come by just now, looking for trouble," Watson said. "They're drunk as skunks and aiming to get drunker. When Buck told 'em to get out, they wasn't going to get nothing here, they started to rough him up, not knowing I was still around. So I brought out Ol' Betsy and run 'em off."

"We heard shots," Sheriff James said.

"They shot out both porch lamps and a couple of windows before they beat it around the corner," Watson said. "Could've killed somebody."

The lawmen moved on. They had not gone far when they again heard gunshots and shouting behind them. They ran back the way they had come, Major Wilkes in the lead and Billy Bowen on his heels. The sheriff lagged, unable to move his bulk at speed. Billy Bowen charged past Major Wilkes in a sudden burst.

As he came to the Grand, Billy was silhouetted against the lobby lights. From across the street someone fired two shots. A window of the hotel shattered and Billy's hat flew off. He dropped to the board sidewalk, struggling to get his gun out of its holster.

Major Wilkes jerked to a halt just outside the ring of light. "Drop your guns!" he yelled.

The sheriff came up, puffing. "Billy, you all right?"

"Reckon so, They got my hat but not me."

Someone brayed, *"Hee-haw. Hee-haw."* Other voices took up a chant: *"Hee-haw, hee-haw, hee-haw."*

A shot shattered another window behind them.

"Take him, Will!"

"Hee-haw! Hee-haw!" Another shot.

Major Wilkes fired at the flash.

"Oh, Christ, I'm hit!" Somebody screamed, breaking into a coyote-like howl of pain.

"Let's get out of here!" other voices yelled.

Major Wilkes heard running footsteps. He saw the flash of another shot from the street. Another window broke.

"Drop that gun," Sheriff James yelled.

Something struck a rock in the street with a metallic thud.

"He's thrown his gun away," Major Wilkes said.

He ran across the street to a figure moaning in the dust. It was too dark to see who it was. Major Wilkes struck a match.

"You trigger-happy son of a bitch, you've killed me." Junior Powell lay on his side, leaning on an elbow. He reached down with his free hand to the inside of his thigh where the match light showed blood darkening his trouser leg and pooling in the dust.

"It's Junior Powell. He's hurt bad," Major Wilkes yelled. "Get Doc Gorse!"

Sheriff James pushed through a fast-gathering crowd. He held a revolver by two fingers. He knelt by the boy.

"This your gun, Junior?"

"Never seen no fucking gun, Sheriff, I swear to God."

"You're lying, son."

"The hell I am, you fat old fart."

Ike Watson came running with a folding cot from the hotel.

Junior Powell screamed and vomited as Major Wilkes and

Billy Bowen lifted him onto the cot. The smell of rotgut soured the air.

"You know who I am?" Junior wiped his mouth with the back of his hand. "You'll hang for this, you Texas son of a bitch. My old man'll see to that." His words were slurred. "Christ, it hurts."

Doc Gorse got to the hotel as Major Wilkes and Billy put Junior Powell down on the porch. The doctor felt for a pulse. He shook his head.

"He's gone."

Major Wilkes ran a finger around his collar. He heard, "*Crwrgh! Eeghwr. Hrckk. Hrckk. Crwrgh!*"

18.

THE WEEKLY MINGUS *Times* rushed out a broadsheet extra on Saturday, New Year's Day, less than twelve hours after Junior Powell's death. Major Wilkes read it standing at his office desk in Ringle. He had mostly outgrown his habit of tapping his front teeth with a fingernail when he concentrated on something. But he tapped now as he read the newspaper's account. It had few details he didn't know and a number of errors. But he was dismayed to learn how others viewed what he had done.

MURDER MOST HEINOUS IN MINGUS!!

'JUNIOR' POWELL SHOT DOWN EARLY THIS MORNING BY LAWMAN FROM TEXAS IN FRONT OF GRAND HOTEL

DETAILS, TO DEGREE KNOWN, OF TRAGIC KILLING OF MAYOR'S SON ON NEW YEAR'S EVE.

DEPUTY WILL GOWER 'FIRED WITHOUT PROVOCATION,' BOY'S FATHER DECLARES. 'HE MUST HANG!'

Never has so unfortunate an affair saddened the hearts of dwellers of this fair city. In the early hours of today, New Year's Day, 1910, the high spirits and patriotic enthusiasms engendered by combined celebrations of the New Year and Statehood were vanquished by the death of one of Mingus' most outstanding and best-respected young gentlemen at the hands of a deputy sheriff from Texas, a well known marksman.

Justin Bartlett ("Junior") Powell, 19, beloved son of Mayor and Mrs. J. B. Powell, Sr. and a football star and outstanding Senior at Mingus High, was cruelly cut down by Deputy Sheriff Major Wilkes ("Will") Gower on Main Street in front of the Grand Hotel in the wee hours of New Year's Day. The dead boy's father is President of the Hardcastle County Farmers and Merchants Bank and Factoring Co. and a leading real estate investor, who owns many important commercial buildings in this city.

Deputy Gower, who will be 21 next week, is stationed at Ringle but was brought to Mingus on New Year's Eve to help City Marshal Dexter ("Deke") Hagenbotham and Sheriff Claudius James deal with overly boisterous celebrants. Deputy Gower is the son of the late City Marshall Duncan Gower of Owchicta, Tex. who was killed in line of duty while heroically thwarting a bank robbery, and the grandson of Amos Gower, well-known Owchicta rancher and hero of the Confederacy who sold his extensive land holdings a while back to join the law enforcement staff of Owchicta County. In Owchicta young Gower is remembered as an expert marksman. At the age of eleven he won a shoot-from-the saddle contest against a large field of grown men and was named Champion Gun Slinger of Owchicta County.

The killing came at the end of a day and evening of jollification throughout Oklahoma, and no place more so than in Mingus. There was bronc riding where the new fairground is being built; a concert and orations, including one lasting an hour by Mayor Powell, in the future city park; a picnic and revival at the First Baptist Church's cemetery; and a fireworks show last night at the high school football field, the site of young Junior Powell's greatest athletic triumphs.

Outside of an occasional pistol shot fired innocently into the sky and the sounds of firecrackers going off in the streets, the celebration was more restrained and peaceful than the sheriff and marshal had feared it would be until after midnight. Marshal Hagenbotham had retired for the night before a report reached the sheriff that an unruly group of hoodlums had invaded the quiet precincts of Mrs. Emma Smith's boarding house, troubling some of her lady guests.

According to Sheriff James's version of events, he sent several men to the boarding house to settle matters there. Meanwhile he and two deputies, Billy Bowen and Will Gower, walked to Main Street to try to head off several celebrants who were said to have left Mrs. Smith's genteel establishment to look for additional excitement elsewhere. The officers were in front of the Grand Hotel when, they claim, a shot was fired at them, knocking off Deputy Bowen's hat. Deputy Gower returned fire, striking young Powell.

By the time Dr. Elmer Gorse reached Junior there was little for him to do but pronounce the terrible words: "He is slain." Mayor Powell soon arrived to weep over his son's body. Deputy Gower tried to express regret and condolences but the stricken father replied, "You're a cold-blooded killer who fired without provocation and must hang by the neck until dead. I shall see to it that it is your fate and hope it will be a slow and lingering death."

Mayor Powell told this reporter that official reports of what transpired on the fatal night were false. Far from being one of the troublemakers sought by the lawmen and the gunman who put a bullet through Deputy Bowen's hat, the Mayor declared, his son had been with high school chums all of New Year's Eve, enjoying a youth party at the Methodist church. Returning to their homes, they were across the street from the Grand Hotel when they heard a shot and saw Deputy Bowen's hat blown off his head. Not knowing where the shot came from, they started running to get out of the way of what they feared would turn into a gunfight. It was then, according to the distraught father and the boys who were with the victim, that Deputy Gower killed Junior with one shot.

Sheriff James immediately took charge of his deputy, saying that he had clearly acted in the line of duty (which Mayor Powell disputes), but formalities would be observed. Within hours of the crime, Deputy Gower appeared this morning before Justice of the Peace Jacob ("Shorty") Duke on a charge of reckless discharge of a firearm. Deputy Gower was freed on $2000 bail, put up by the sheriff, and was given permission to make a brief visit home to his family in Owchicta. A County Court hearing is scheduled for early next week to determine what, if any, further charges will be filed.

Mayor Powell told Justice Duke he will demand that Deputy Gower be tried for murder. "The man is a killer and must be put to death," he declared, "and the sooner the better."

IN LORENA'S KITCHEN, Major Wilkes broke down and cried. The half-truths and outright lies told by Junior Powell's father and friends seemed more plausible to him than the truth. He could feel the rope around his neck.

"I shouldn't have pulled my gun. I should have just gone across the street and got his gun away from him."

"But he was shooting at you, and the sheriff told you to shoot back," Lorena said.

"He wasn't a good shot. I don't think he could have hit me if he'd tried."

"But he did try," Minnie said.

"He was just a kid."

"Two years younger than you. And he was drunk and raising Cain."

"I should have allowed for that." Major Wilkes bent his head to the table, between his outstretched arms.

Amos came into Lorena's kitchen, letting in a blast of frigid air. He stomped his feet on the blue flowers of her linoleum, knocking off snow.

"Cold. Freeze your balls off."

He swayed a bit as he came up to the table. "What's he blubbering about?"

"Drunk again, Amos?" *Sergeant McCandless.*

"Get out of my kitchen," Lorena said.

"Hell, if I kilt a man like he done, I'd square my shoulders and beat my chest. I'd be proud of what I done. I'd be a man."

Major Wilkes lifted his head. "I reckon you would, Grandpa, but I'm not you." He added, "Thank God."

"Thank God," Lorena and Minnie echoed,

Amos lurched home and lay on his bed, fully dressed. He didn't even take off his boots. He was accustomed to being scorned by Minnie and Lorena. But Major Wilkes? Why would the boy do that?

Major Wilkes came to him and said he was sorry. He stuck out his hand. Amos turned on his side, his back to Major Wilkes.

"That's all right," he said, "I reckon I know where we stand."

That too he didn't understand—why he refused Major Wilkes's outthrust hand.

Without Major Wilkes there was hardly anyone left in the world willing to treat him with the respect due a hero of the Confederacy who had fought with Lee and knew the general better than he knew his own father. Without Major Wilkes, he would have no one to whom he could talk freely. And yet he had refused to take his hand.

As he brooded, he realized that once again the hex had done it. He couldn't remember a moment's good luck since the hanging—or even before it, not his whole life, not since his mother died a-borning him. He'd been living under that hex ever since, even if he hadn't known about it until that young man spat it out at the end of a rope.

19.

IN ITS REGULAR WEEKLY edition the Thursday after the tragedy, the Mingus *Times* brought the death of Junior Powell up to date in two stories.

The lead story, under the usual stack of headlines, was about the preliminary hearing. It presented Wilkes little comfort.

JUNIOR POWELL'S SLAYER
FACES MURDER CHARGE

COUNTY ATTORNEY SAYS OFFICER FIRED UNDER ORDERS AND REFUSES TO ACT AGAINST DEPUTY WILL GOWER; BOY'S FAMILY HIRES 'HANG'IM BILL' GROSS TO SEND THEIR SON'S 'VICIOUS KILLER' TO GALLOWS

COUNTY COMMISSIONERS WILL DEFEND
CHAMPION GUN SLINGER GOWER,
ORDER DEPUTY TO STAY ON DUTY UNTIL TRIAL

Deputy Wilkes ("Will") Gower, 21 years old, a Texas lawman, was charged with murder Tuesday in the shooting death of young Justin B. ("Junior") Powell, 19 years old, popular son of Mingus Mayor J.B. ("Shark") Powell, early on New Year's Day. The charge of murder was filed against Deputy Gower by the Powell family after local authorities declined to prosecute during a nearly day-long hearing before County Judge John W.

McFarrley. The defendant pleaded not guilty and was ordered to stand trial at a future session of District Court. No certain date has been set for the trial but it cannot be held earlier than the spring session of District Court, according to local legal authorities.

County Attorney Charles Peyton Frelinghausen refused to prosecute after presenting sworn testimony that armed youths rioting on the city's streets had endangered with gunfire the lives of law officers and innocent bystanders, as well as property. Witnesses testified that Deputy Gower shot at the boy only when he was ordered by a superior officer to do so.

"An officer of the law," Frelinghausen argued, "should not be placed in jeopardy when all credible evidence proves that he was merely responding appropriately to an attack upon himself and other officers of the law attempting to restore law and order to the streets of our city."

Anticipating Mr. Frelinghausen's refusal to prosecute, Mayor Powell had retained his brother-in-law, State Senator William T. ("Hang'im Bill") Gross of Oklahoma City, to bring and prosecute a murder charge on behalf of the family, a recourse permitted under state law and agreed to by Judge McFarrley. Senator Gross, a famous prosecutor in Territorial days, won his nickname for his skill at persuading juries to drop transgressors from the gallows to hang by the neck until dead. Mayor Powell told the Times that Hang'im Bill's lifetime score is 12 hangings for 12 trials. "This vicious Texas killer must die at the end of a rope," said Mayor Powell. "He shall pay with his life for taking my beloved son from me."

Among the witnesses examined were Sheriff Claudius James and Deputy Billy Bowen, who testified under oath as to the occurrences of that tragic night, as seen from the law enforcement perspective. Sheriff James asserted that the victim was in a drunken and riotous state prior to death and that it was he who ordered Deputy Gower to "take him out." Deputy Bowen testified that a bullet fired by young Powell went through his hat, which he produced as evidence. Doctor Elmer ("Doc") Gorse testified that the victim bled to death from a wound in his thigh. Much of the testimony was consistent with the account published in last Saturday's special edition of *The Times* and need not be repeated here.

However, Rev. James Lowry, Pastor of the First Methodist Church of Mingus, attested to the dead youth's sterling Christian character, high moral standards, and bright prospects, as did certain high school friends of the victim, two of whom said that they were with Junior the entire time on New Year's Eve. They swore under oath that Junior was killed when they were going home from a youth party at Rev. Lowry's church (an assertion confirmed by the minister), and had not been near Miss Emma's Home Away from Home for Respectable Ladies and Gentlemen, where a disturbance had been reported earlier. They denied that there had been any drinking, riotous behavior, or gunfire and insisted that Deputy Gower fired on them for no reason.

The defendant was bound over to District Court on an increased bond of $5000.00, ordered not to leave Hardcastle County without permission of the court, and released. At Sheriff James's request, the court agreed to let Deputy Gower return to duty pending further action. "He is a fine young man and a valuable law enforcement officer whose services I need in assuring the peace and security of our citizens," the sheriff told the court. "I have every confidence that Deputy Gower will be absolved of all blame in this sad affair."

Immediately after the hearing, the County Commissioners convened a special session and voted three to one to authorize County Attorney Frelinghausen to defend Deputy Gower at County expense.

THE OTHER FRONT-PAGE story about the case in that week's Mingus *Times* ran across the bottom of the page, under another banner headline.

HUGE CROWD ATTENDS MURDERED HERO'S LAST RITES

Funeral services for Justin Bartlett ("Junior") Powell, Jr., 19, dearly beloved eldest son of Mayor and Mrs. J. B. Powell, Sr., and a star football player at Mingus High, were held at the First Methodist Church Monday afternoon at 2 o'clock, Pastor James

Lowry officiating. The Mingus Military Band, of which the deceased was a highly talented member, marched slowly with muffled drum behind the Mingus Funeral Home's new motor hearse making its first appearance as it carried the slain hero to the flower-filled church from the opulent family residence, where Junior had lain in open-casket state, leading many to comment on how lifelike he appeared. At the church the coffin was again opened for viewing by those who had been unable to pay their respects at the home.

In the service, Rev. Lowry described the dead boy as "our brightest and best" and praised him as an exemplar of Christian virtue. He prayed that those responsible for his death would be called swiftly to final justice. His heart-rending tribute was eloquently echoed in heartfelt words spoken by family, friends, and community leaders, who described the many acts of benevolence that marked the beloved boy's prematurely and brutally ended life and deplored the cruel act that took it. Each and every one joined Pastor Lowry in the hope that his killer might be appropriately and quickly punished by hanging.

At the end of the service the casket remained open so that all of his dear friends and relatives who desired to do so could say a final good-by, while the band played *Nearer My God to Thee, The Old Wooden Cross,* and other appropriate hymns, as members of the football team stood at attention as an honor guard. Leaving the church for the cemetery the funeral cortege was again preceded by the band, this time playing as a last tribute to him whose voice would be no longer be heard among them the fight song of the Mingus Tigers, *Fight, Fight, Fight Brave Mingi,* as a dirge in quarter time.

Junior's tuba horn, draped in black ribbons, was carried in its usual place in the ranks of the band by his friend and fellow football star, who was with him on the night of his sad death, Horace ("Horse") Crosby, 18. son of K. P. ("Parson") Crosby, owner of the Mingus Livery and Stable Co. of this city. The sight of the dead boy's horn brought tears to the eyes of spectators who lined the streets with uncovered heads, though the wind was biting cold.

Behind the hearse came the carriages and motor cars of mourning relatives and friends of the deceased, followed by the entire student body of Mingus High School, members of the Fraternal Order of Elks, representatives of other fraternal groups, and congregants of the Methodist, Baptist, and other churches. The procession to the place of interment was the longest that has ever followed a body to the Mingus cemetery. Funeral participants regathered in the First Methodist Church basement for a lavish repast after Junior was placed lovingly in his grave.

Arrangements by Mingus Funeral Home, flowers by Mingus Floral Bouquets, rental carriages by Mingus Livery and Stable Co., and refreshments by the First Methodist Church of Mingus Ladies Auxiliary.

MAJOR WILKES' TRIAL was scheduled for the spring term of district court, but was postponed to the summer term when Hang'im Bill announced that he would be too busy in the state legislature to prepare.

When June came, Hang'im Bill was on a summer-long trip to Europe. Major Wilkes's trial was postponed to the fall term.

But the docket for that term was too jammed to accommodate a capital case that was likely to tie up the circuit court for several days.

Once again Major Wilkes' trial was put over. It was rescheduled for the winter term, starting in early December, Circuit Judge Elijah J. Bronson of Tulsa would come to Mingus to handle the case. Charley Frelinghausen said he didn't know much about Judge Bronson, except that he had served in the state senate with Hang'im Bill Gross before going on the bench. Frelinghausen wasn't sure whether that was good news or bad.

Each delay was torture for Major Wilkes. He spent as much time as he could in the far reaches of Hardcastle County, looking into complaints he could not resolve.

Witnesses to fence cuttings, misbranding of calves born to range cattle, and outright rustling were usually non-existent or had a stake in the matter at hand. But he welcomed every case, even domestic disputes involving drunken husbands and neighborly quarrels over the ownership of unbranded heifers. Dealing with such matters took a lot of time, kept him away from Mingus, and eased the pain of being trapped in a House of Mirrors, fragmented like a bullet-struck green jar, disintegrated, defined and reshaped by reflected light and the uninformed opinion of others.

Whenever he had to walk down a street in the county seat he felt himself observed by a hundred eyes, most of them, he was sure, hostile. His unease was reinforced in many ways. The Mingus school board voted to build wooden bleachers on both sides of the high school football field and name it the Junior Powell Stadium. A movement to designate Main Street, "Junior Powell Blvd," failed only because merchants balked at the cost of printing new letterheads and other business documents. Little boys shrieked *"Killer Will"* when they saw Major Wilkes on the street and ran around the nearest corner. Ladies drew their skirts away when he passed and whispered to one another behind their hands.

ONE AFTERNOON, Major Wilkes passed the First Methodist Church of Mingus.

The Reverend Lowry called, "Deputy Gower, step this way, please."

The preacher stood in the stairwell outside his basement office. Only his bald head, glistening in the sun, appeared above ground. He did not reach up to shake hands.

"What can I do for you, Reverend?"

"Call me, Padre, son." Rev. Lowry cleared his throat. "Son, I have a difficult request to make of you, and I hope you will take it in the spirit of love and brotherhood with which I offer it."

"Of course."

"I must ask you not to come to church."

"Say that again, please, Padre."

"Now I'm sure that you will understand how it distresses me, but I do believe that all things considered, it will be for the best if you do not join us for our Sunday services."

He held up his hand when Major Wilkes started to speak.

"Don't think for a moment you will be denied God's loving comfort in these unhappy times. No. Indeed, no. You will be welcome to come here to seek counsel and pray for forgiveness with me any evening you like, except of course when there is an event scheduled in the church. And I'm sure you will prefer to use this entrance so you won't be seen."

"I don't understand."

"We shall miss that beautiful voice of yours, which so enriches our holy worship as we lift our voices in praise of Our Lord's merciful bounty and His—"

"Who is it best for that I shouldn't be seen seeking counsel and praying with my own pastor?"

"As I said, I hope you will accept my suggestion in the same spirit of Christian love and brotherhood with which I offer it."

"Reverend Lowry, you are talking nonsense. Why don't you want me in church?"

"Oh, dear! It's not that I don't want you in church."

"What is it then?"

"It's well— It's that—"

"Oh, come on, Padre. Spit it out."

"Well. Well, yes, in a way I suppose that is best." The pastor made a castle of his fingers and studied the sky overhead through them, as though he were praying. "Mr. Powell, the father of the young man you shot to death, has questioned the propriety of having a murderer mingle—"

Major Wilkes did not stay for the rest of the sentence.

MAJOR WILKES TOOK to reading law books lent to him by Frelinghausen and held long conversations with the lawyer about points of law that applied to his case. Impressed by his intelligence, Frelinghausen invited Major Wilkes to read law with him after the trial.

"I'd like that, if I'm alive."

"You'll be alive. Everybody in Hardcastle County knows Junior was no good. A football hero? That kid was kicked off the team last year for drunkenness after the first two games. It was hushed up, of course, but it'll come out at the trial. And look what he did that night—got roaring drunk, shot up the hotel, beat up Miss Emma's husband, tied her up, raped one and maybe two of her girls, and then took pot shots at officers of the law. Will, all we have to do is find twelve good men and true in this county who'll look at the facts with an open mind. They'll see that you did what you had to do."

"How about Junior Powell Stadium? Junior Powell Boulevard? How about Reverend Lowry telling me he doesn't want me in his church?"

"How about the commissioners voting to have the county pay for your defense? And Will, let me tell you, I'm a politician—have to be to get elected county attorney—and they're politicians. And a politician ain't going to vote to spend county money on an issue like this out of sentiment. They voted like they did because they figure the people who put them in office can be persuaded that they are right to do it, as a matter of law and order."

"Only three voted for it."

"And who voted no? Yeah. Ben Olsen, known far and wide as Ol' Skinflint. He ain't never spent a nickel without moaning about it to anybody who'll listen, except maybe on Miss Emma's girls."

Major Wilkes wasn't persuaded.

"The boy's dead. We can't run him down now. And we both know there's no way Miss Emma or her girls can get on the stand and tell what happened out there."

"You might be surprised. As for running him down, we won't have to do it. That fat windbag Hang'im Bill from Oklahoma City will do it for us, not meaning to. Wait and see."

20.

AS HE DID IN late August every year John Pound Giles, owner of the Kansas City, Mexico & Oriental Railroad and many another enterprise, brought a covey of his Eastern cronies to his Rocking JPG ranch, the largest in Hardcastle County, for three weeks of hunting. They traveled on a special train of private cars, which paused in Mingus only long enough to take on coal and water for the steam engine. No locally purchased supplies were needed. The train arrived laden with every comfort required for gracious living, except the iced oysters, tiny bay shrimp, and fresh fish that would be shipped in daily from California.

From Mingus the private cars would take Giles's guests eight miles west on the KM&O mainline, then drop south nine miles on a spur to park in the shade of cottonwood trees, a half-mile from the corrals and bunkhouses that comprised the headquarters of the Rocking JPG. The Wall Street moguls would not be roughing it. Far from the smells and flies of a working cattle ranch, they would sleep in full-sized beds in the private cars, be waited on by Pullman porters, and dine on meals prepared by the Pullman Co.'s finest chefs.

To allay any resentment that Mingus's merchants and gentry

might feel at his neglect of them and their businesses, Giles invited 40 or so of the town's political, professional, and mercantile elite to a barbecue at the ranch on the first Sunday in September.

Sheriff James was among the invited dignitaries, though not in an official capacity. To take care of any trouble that over-indulgence might provoke among the guests, he assigned Major Wilkes to ride the train. But he changed his mind when he learned that Mayor Powell would attend the party, despite having pledged to mourn for his son until Major Wilkes was swinging at the end of a rope.

"He says Junior wouldn't want him to miss the party," the sheriff told Major Wilkes. "I'll have to send Billy Bowen instead. You take over here Sunday for Billy."

Major Wilkes was disappointed. He had never ridden a train. But on Sunday, soon after the last preacher turned his congregation loose, he joined half of Mingus at the train station to watch the local dignitaries board two club cars, a dining car, and a sleeping car. Assisted by white-jacketed porters, the gentlemen guests (wives had not been included in the invitations) mounted the steps with self-conscious dignity.

The sun was hot and the temperature high, but most wore their Sunday best—black woolen suits, starched shirts with stiff collars, and buttoned vests. Their faces were sweaty but solemn, as though they were filing aboard to say farewell to a dying friend. All the shades on the club cars and Pullman were drawn. The sober-sided businessmen were to be welcomed aboard by a receiving line of Miss Emma's girls, temptingly unclad. The switch engine whistled. The left-behind wives and children cheered. Black smoke puffed from the locomotive's stack. The party was on.

When the special train returned at 3:00 o'clock the next morning, Major Wilkes was waiting to see that everyone got home safely. Porters and Deputy Bowen helped the celebrants stumble off the train. Most were hatless and vestless, a few shoeless, and it took a while before all garments and their owners were reunited. To avoid scandal, Miss Emma's young women left the Pullman on the opposite side and were whisked home in two Mingus Livery & Stable Co. carriages.

Various buckboards and carriages, also supplied by Mingus Livery on John Pound Giles's tab, soon departed with the male detritus, except for Mayor Powell and Seth Ringle, who were slow to leave the train. It required two porters to carry Powell off the train and deposit him on the station platform, and three plus Billy Bowen to lay Seth Ringle beside the mayor.

"What'll we do with these two?" Billy asked. "They ain't in shape to go home."

"The Grand," Major Wilkes said. "They must've drank the river dry."

They loaded the mayor and Ringle into a carriage and followed on horseback to the hotel, where they installed them in porch swings. Out of consideration for other sleeping guests, they did not ring the night bell. As Major Wilkes arranged Powell in his swing, the mayor stretched out his arms without opening his eyes.

"Oh, come on, Tess," he muttered, "can't we be friends again? Junior was just funning, like anybody might do now and again. He didn't mean nothing by it."

IN THE WEEK AFTER his Rocking JPG spree, Seth Ringle missed the regular Thursday meeting in Mingus of the Hardcastle County Chamber of Commerce Executive Committee, on which he served. He didn't feel up to it.

By the following Thursday, however, he was on his feet again. Sophie backed his Model T Ford out of the barn and brought it around in front of the mini-mansion. She was the only person other than himself that he allowed to take the wheel, and she only after having undergone extensive training. Seth lavished as much care on his automobile to keep it looking new as he did on his business. He never returned it to the barn without dusting it, inspecting it for scratches, and polishing the brass radiator and headlamps.

Preparing for his trip to Mingus, Seth tipped up the front cushion and put his fuel-measuring stick in the gas tank. He pulled it out and studied the wet end.

"Plenty of gas to make it back, but remind me to fill up tomorrow." He settled the cushion in place and got in. "If it's all right with you, Sweetie, I reckon to just stay the night in town, if the meeting lasts too long. Don't wait up for me."

That's what Seth said every Thursday and what he always did. The Chamber of Commerce membership met at noon at the Palace Café for an instructive lecture on some topic of business interest, along with dinner and refreshments. But the executive committee meeting followed the membership meeting and often lasted to the supper hour, which stretched into the evening. Seth disliked driving at night.

"I'd rather you did stay in town," Sophie said. "I worry about you at night on that bumpy old road with all those old cows you can't see till the last minute. Horses, too. I'll be fine. I'll lock the doors and won't anybody bother me. And Auntie Sarah will be here, of course."

After supper the housekeeper and cook always returned to their own families for the night. Sophie would be alone in the house except for her spinster aunt, who had taken to going to bed with the hens and getting up with the cock.

"You've got the telephone now, too. Anything scares you, and Aunt Sarah ain't awake, call sister Loula. She'll be here in no time." Loula lived in the back of the Ringle Store and could hear the phone day or night.

"And there's always Deputy Gower. He's got a phone, too," Sophie said.

"Don't call him. I don't want that murdering son of a bee no place around here."

THAT SEPTEMBER THURSDAY ended in one of those mild evenings western Oklahoma can get at summer's end, when the light lingers after sundown and gentle breezes blow away mosquitoes and the stench of cattle-feeding lots. Major Wilkes sat on his porch, reading a law book. About the time it got too dark to read, he heard horses coming along the Mingus road and the riders bantering from horse to horse. He had heard such voices in Mingus on New Year's Eve and in Ringle on Thursday nights all summer.

"Moths to the flame," he said. He had talked to himself a lot since the death of Junior Powell.

One of the horsemen said, "I don't mind you coming along, but keep in mind it's my turn to sit beside her on the swing."

"If she'll let you. Last time it was your turn she said you smelled worser than her pa's stock pens."

"Don't you mind about that. I had me a bath just a day or so back."

"Phew. I can smell stable shit all the way over here."

"That ain't me. It's them feedlots up ahead."

"I never said it was you. But I been noticing it ever since we left Mingus."

By their voices Major Wilkes identified the first rider as Horse Crosby, son of the owner of Mingus Livery and Stable Co, and the second as Jimmy Thrimble, son of the courtly mercantile prince, Barney Thrimble. The two were seldom seen except together. Before Junior Powell's death the duo had been an inseparable trio. See one, see three, people had said.

"There's Deputy Gower's place."

"He's on his porch."

"Who cares?" Horse raised his voice. "Picked out your rope collar yet, Willie?"

The boys spurred their horses and raced down the road. The hoof beats slowed and then faded out. The three had turned off the road to ride quietly on a circuitous trail through the brush to the Ringle mansion, skirting the settlement to avoid alerting watchful Ringles.

A little later the phone rang, two shorts.

Major Wilkes said aloud, "Boys got careless. Some Ringle is calling Central to get hold of Papa Bear at Miss Emma's. Goldilocks is in trouble."

He closed his law book and went inside. Lighting a coal-oil lantern that hung over the desk, he brought his official day book up to date and swept his office. The nearly full moon was just rising. He went out on the porch again to rock and smoke. The bang and rattle of an approaching automobile told him that Papa Bear was approaching. The motorcar's headlamps danced like fireflies on the rutted road from Mingus. Its folded-down top stuck out behind the car like a rooster's tail as Seth Ringle sped past. He hunched over the steering wheel, his high-crowned Stetson pulled down over his ears to keep it from blowing off. Dust spewed behind the Model T like smoke from a campfire in a high wind.

"Howdy, Mr. Ringle," Major Wilkes called.

He did not hear the answer, if any.

He had not expected one. He carried his lantern out to the stable behind the cottage and saddled Bess, yet another distant descendant of the black mare that carried his great-grandfather to war and back again. Before long Horse Crosby and Jimmy Thrimble dashed past toward town, shouting to one another, laughing and talking at the same time.

"Thought I'd die when I heard that motorcar! I jumped off

that swing so fast I nearly fell off the porch."

"We'd have heard it sooner if you hadn't been acting the fool and laughing so loud."

"And that shotgun! Sounded like a cannon. Both barrels!"

"Goddam buckshot whistled past my ear. Thought I was a goner for sure."

"What'll Sophie tell her old man, you think?"

"Jesus! Any damned thing but the truth, I hope. Pa don't know I slipped this here horse out of the stable."

Major Wilkes stayed on his porch, smoking and from time to time tapping his teeth. He had about decided to unsaddle Bess when the phone rang—one long, three shorts. Major Wilkes picked up before the caller could crank again.

"Get your ass over here, Deputy, I mean now," Seth Ringle shouted and hung up, before Major Wilkes could say a word or other subscribers on the party line between Ringle and Mingus could lift their receivers to listen in. Moments later, Bess stepped through sagebrush, following the trail taken earlier by Sophie's young friends.

SETH RINGLE'S white brick house was ghostly in the moonlight. He stood on the porch steps, a double-barreled 12-gauge shotgun in one hand and a swinging lantern in the other. Standing on the bottom step, he was not quite tall enough to be eye-to-eye with Major Wilkes.

"What's doing, Mr. Ringle?"

Words and spit sprayed from Ringle's lips like pellets from his shotgun. "Doing? I'll tell you what's doing. My God, will I tell you what's doing!"

"Yessir," Major Wilkes said. He stepped back a pace to avoid a shower of spittle.

He heard Sophie sobbing on the side porch.

"Some nigra tried to rape my little girl, that's what's doing."

"Is she all right?"

"All right! Would you be all right if'n you'd just got out from under a black buck? Course she ain't all right."

"Have you called Dr. Gorse?"

"Doc Gorse? Why would I call Doc Gorse?"

"Well, if Miss Ringle's been—" He stopped. He wasn't sure what word to use.

"Sophie's been nothing, you hear? Don't you go spreading stories about Sophie. My daughter Loula called me in town where I was on Chamber business and said she seen somebody heading up toward my house and thought I oughta know. I jumped in my motorcar and got here just as Sophie was fighting off that coon. I heard her screaming when I stopped. Then I seen him scooting across the yard toward them trees out back. I grabbed this here shotgun I keep in the back seat. I emptied both barrels at him, but I didn't get him."

"You saw the fella, then?"

"Goddammit, I told you I did."

"There aren't many colored folks around these parts, and even with the moon it's pretty dark to make out somebody at that distance. You could tell he was a Negro?"

"I told you I could, Deputy. Open your goddam ears! Besides, Sophie told me, and she seen him close up."

"Reckon I better talk to Miss Ringle." Major Wilkes took a step forward.

Ringle blocked him. "You ain't going to speak to her, not now, not never. She's all upset and I don't want her upset no more'n she is."

"Mr. Ringle, if you want this case investigated, I have to hear her story."

Ringle put down his lantern and shoved the shotgun's double barrel against Major Wilkes's chest. He cocked both triggers.

"Her story? You've *heard* her story, Goddammit. I just give it to you. That's all you need to know and all you're going to know. All I want from you is for you to find that coon and turn him over to me. I'll take care of the rest."

Major Wilkes took hold of the gun and held it to one side until Ringle uncocked the triggers.

"That's not the way it'll be, Mr. Ringle. If I find somebody, I'll take him in. There'll be a hearing. The whole story will come out—not Miss Ringle's name, of course, but everything else—and if just cause is found, the man will be indicted and tried under the laws of the State of Oklahoma."

"Deputy, you drag my Sophie's name through the mud, I'll kill you and the sonabitch, too."

"Mr. Ringle, he's got rights just like you do, including the right to a fair trial."

"The only right he's gonna have is a rope right around his neck. And I'll put it there myself, laughing while I do it."

"And then you'll be indicted and tried."

"Deputy, for a nobody in this county who's headed for a hanging hisself, you're talking right uppity. Ain't nobody going to know about this little fracas but you, me, and the black bastard I'm going to kill as soon as you get him. So get your ass up and running."

"Mr. Ringle, like I said, if you want this case investigated—and I'm not sure you should—it's going to be done right, just like any other case."

"What you mean—*if?* There ain't no need for investigation. I've told you what happened. Are you calling me a liar? Or Sophie?"

"I'm not calling anybody anything. I'm telling you how I'll investigate this case, which is that I'll find out what really happened. It's always possible you won't like everything I find out."

"Deputy, I don't like your attitude and Sheriff James won't either."

"Maybe so. But I'd still like to hear the young lady tell her story herself."

"I told you. You ain't going to hear a goddam thing."

Major Wilkes tapped his fingernail against his teeth. "You see or hear any horses, anything like that?"

"What's that got to do with it?"

"Did you?"

"No."

"Two horses, maybe? Going off fast?"

"Course not."

Major Wilkes tapped his teeth again.

"Well, if I can't talk to Miss Ringle, maybe I can take a look around? Use your lantern, maybe?"

"I want you to get the hell off my property and find the black bastard—find him and turn him over to me. I'll take care of him, don't you worry about that."

"Like I told you, if I find him, which I doubt, I'll take him to jail and to court."

"Forget the whole thing. I'll handle this myself."

Ringle pointed his shotgun at Major Wilkes but did not cock it.

"Get the hell off my property, and I mean now."

Major Wilkes heard Sophie still sobbing on the side porch.

"I'm leaving, Mr. Ringle, but I'll look around first. And I'd advise you to settle down and go to bed."

Ringle yelled threats at him from the porch as Major Wilkes led Bess toward the grove of trees behind the house.

The moonlight showed him what he expected to see in the sandy soil—two sets of footprints going to the house and returning.

The tracks going back to the trees had been made at a run.

The spot where the horses had waited was marked by fresh droppings.

Had Sophie really told her father such an outrageous lie? He didn't want to believe it.

21.

ROCKING ON HIS PORCH in the moonlight, Major Wilkes heard a running horse turn onto the Mingus road from the Ringle Mansion shortcut. He expected to see Seth Ringle arrive on Li'l Sam, the bay gelding Seth used instead of his Model T for moving around Ringle. It was Li'l Sam, all right, that Major Wilkes saw — but it was Sophie Ringle who rushed up the porch steps in her riding breeches.

"Deputy Gower! I've done a terrible thing. I've killed a man."

Major Wilkes pulled her into his office. She was shaking and sobbing. He sat her down in the chair beside his desk and struck a match to light the lamp.

"Please don't," she said.

Major Wilkes glimpsed bruises on both cheeks before he blew out the match. "What happened, Miss Ringle?"

"Daddy hit me."

"And who did you kill?"

She struggled to answer.

Major Wilkes handed her his red kerchief. "It's not real clean," he said.

"Thank you." She wiped her eyes and blew her nose. "I

don't know. It hasn't happened yet, but I know it will. Daddy's going to kill some innocent man because of me."

Her story came out in snatches, interspersed with tearful outbursts. She told how Seth had gone to town and wasn't expected home until morning, how two of her school friends came to visit her on the porch, and how Seth unexpectedly returned and fired his shotgun at the boys as they ran to their horses in the grove.

"Daddy grabbed me and asked me who they were. I tried to tell him it was my friends from school that he saw and that nothing had happened. He was drunk and wouldn't listen. He called me a liar and started slapping me. I had never seen him like that."

Moonlight filtered into the room. She kept her hand over her face, gripping the kerchief in her fist.

"He was going, 'Who? Who? Who?' Every time he said, 'Who?' he slapped me. I kept trying to tell him. I even told him who it was, Horse Crosby and Jimmy Thrimble.

"He wouldn't listen. He shook me and accused me of all sorts of awful things. I thought he was going to kill me. Finally he said he'd seen a man running away and it was a colored man. I told him he was wrong, it was just Horse and Jimmy. He went crazy. He slapped me harder and harder, and kept yelling, 'You're lying I seen him. He was colored. I seen him. He was colored. Admit he was colored.' To make him stop I finally said yes, it was a colored man.

"I didn't think there were any colored in the county. I didn't know he'd seen a bunch of Pullman porters Sunday at the Rocking JPG barbeque. He walked up and down, back and forth, just raving, saying he'd kill the black son of a—you know. I'm sure he knows it really was my school friends visiting me, but he doesn't care. He wants somebody to blame, somebody he can do something to. He'll do it, too. And I'll have the poor man's blood on my hands."

"Where's your father now?"

"He called you and after you left he locked me in my room and took the auto. He said if you weren't going to do what he told you to do, he'd have to do it himself. He rushed off to get my brothers and brothers-in-law and a couple of the hands and go cross-country to the Rocking JPG to lynch that black man."

"How did you get out?"

She stopped crying. "Oh, I used a hairpin and opened the door. I've done it before."

"Good for you."

"I'm so sorry," she said. "I shouldn't have given in and lied. That poor man!"

"Is there anyone who can look after you?"

"My aunt, in town. I'm supposed to move in with her next week for the school year anyway."

"How about your sisters here in Ringle?"

"They're too scared of Daddy to do anything for me, not now."

Major Wilkes sat tapping his teeth. "How long do you think it'll take him to get going?"

"I don't know. At least an hour, and maybe more. It's late, everybody's been in bed for hours, and my brothers-in-law and the others don't move very fast. Besides, their wives won't want them to go. They'll have screaming fits over who's going to stay and protect them from whoever they think is out there. And Daddy will have to gas the motorcar. That takes at least a half hour, and he won't let anybody else do it. He siphons it out of a barrel at the store. He always swallows some when he's sucking on the hose to get the gas flowing. He spits and chokes until he gets his breath back. Then he has to start all over again."

"How many do you think there'll be?"

"Maybe eight or nine, unless he takes some of the hands

who brought in herds today and are camping for the night. But I don't think he'll want anybody he doesn't know."

"Some in the car and some on horseback?"

"Yes."

Thinking aloud, Major Wilkes said, "It'll be about ten or twelve miles to the ranch as the crow flies. It's rough country, hilly, lots of sagebrush and dry washes to cross—slow going through the sand and sagebrush. Even with the moonlight it'll be too dark to run the horses. With one thing and another, like digging the automobile out of the sand a time or two, they won't make it much before dawn. Bess is good and fast—"

"So is Li'l Sam." Sophie was no longer hiding her face or crying.

"—and the ten miles to Mingus is on a good straight road that Bess knows without even looking."

"So does Li'l Sam."

"From Mingus it's only about five or six miles cross-country to the ranch, and the washes run that direction. I can follow them most of the way, with no brush to slow me down. Plenty of time for me to get you to your aunt in Mingus and still head your father off before he does something crazy—and before everybody in the county knows what's going on."

"You'll need help."

"Let me worry about that."

"I can go alone to Mingus. I've done it many times."

He didn't want to risk it. What if Seth returned home, found her missing, and came after her in his automobile?

"No, I'll ride with you, if you don't mind."

"I don't mind."

With Sophie beside him astride Li'l Sam, Major Wilkes was as aware of her as he was of the road. Halfway to Mingus, she looked over at him and smiled, her hair blowing free. He was almost sorry when they reached Mingus.

At the gate of her aunt's house, he helped her dismount into his arms. She pressed against him. "Thank you, Deputy Will Gower."

"Call me Major Wilkes. That's what they call me at home."

HE INTERCEPTED the tracks of Seth's Model T and the hoof prints of four horses in a dry wash where the Ford had stalled in deep sand about a mile from the Rocking JPG. Seth's passengers had dug it out and pushed it to solid ground. At most four Ringle-sized men could crowd into the Ford with Seth. Major Wilkes figured he was up against only nine Ringles—four on horseback, five in the automobile. Once out of the wash, the tracks showed, Seth had plunged toward the ranch straight through sagebrush without regard to the dents and scratches he might inflict on his motorcar.

In the first light of dawn Major Wilkes came upon the Model T and four tethered horses at the base of a low hill. Beyond the hill he could see the tops of cottonwoods growing beside the railroad tracks. Leaving Bess hidden in another dry wash, Major Wilkes climbed the hill at an angle, seeking to position himself where he would be above the private cars housing John Pound Giles and his eastern guests. Near the top he dropped to the ground and crawled forward into a clump of sage, where he could see without being seen until he was ready to show himself.

Lined up with hands in the air alongside a sleeping car he saw ten portly white men, six Pullman porters, and three Pullman chefs. John Pound Giles and his friends were barefoot and wore nightshirts and, in some cases, nightcaps. The others were fully dressed and ready for their day's work—the porters in white jackets and black trousers, the kitchen workers in all-white.

Sheets covered the nine Ringles from the crowns of their

hats to their shins. Hands holding revolvers poked through slits in the sheets.

Seth Ringle, his bulky form and shrill voice unmistakable, stood a few feet in front of the others. "I ain't fooling. Which one of you niggers was it?"

Major Wilkes stood up, drawing his Colts. "Don't turn around. Drop your guns where you stand."

As Ringles spun toward him, a jackrabbit leapt into the open space between the sheeted men and their captives, Major Wilkes shot the jackrabbit in mid-air. It fell to the ground, dead.

"I said, drop your guns. Belts, too."

For emphasis he fired a shot into the ground about a foot from Seth Ringle. Dirt sprayed across Seth's boots.

Guns and belts hit the ground.

"All your guns." He sprayed more sand with another shot. More revolvers dropped from several sheets, including Seth's.

"Now, put up your hands and take three steps backward."

The Ringles did as ordered. In raising their arms, they hiked the sheets up above their knees.

"Lie down on your bellies facing the train. Now stretch your arms out in front of you. You gentlemen in the nightshirts get back on the train and stay out of the way. You porters, pick up the guns and make sure the sheets don't move. You may shoot if necessary."

The porters and cooks rushed to gather weapons. John Pound Giles and his powerful friends crowded up the steps into the Pullman behind them, stumbling in their haste. Their faces reappeared at the windows. Major Wilkes stayed on the hill, but fired a shot now and again to stimulate Ringle imaginations. He was unsure what he should do next. If he took the Ringles into custody or made them take off their sheets so they could be identified, everyone would soon know whose daughter was implicated in the affair.

But what would the sheriff think if he didn't? He decided to deal with that question later.

"Now, on your feet. Keep your sheets on and your hands up. Turn around and walk over the hill to your horses real slow. Then I'd advise you to get out of here fast. Those wranglers up at ranch headquarters heard the same shots you did. They'll be here any minute, loaded for bear."

"How about our guns?" Seth Ringle demanded.

"They'll make dandy souvenirs for these fellows. Get going."

Ringles struggled through sagebrush over the hill with cacti snagging their sheets, with Seth bringing up the rear. Major Wilkes fired one more shot, just behind him. Seth stumbled and fell. Scrambling on hands and knees, he yelled, "I'm going, Goddammit, I'm going."

When he heard the Ford cranked up and moving, Major Wilkes mounted Bess and headed for Mingus.

SHERIFF JAMES SAID he thought Major Wilkes was right not to arrest the Ringles or make them take their sheets off. But he may have sealed his own doom by going after them in the first place.

"Even if the Ringles keep quiet, it's bound to get out from Giles and his pals. Folks'll figure out pretty quick that it took a hell of a marksman to shoot that jackrabbit. Somebody like the winner of that Gun-Slinger Contest over to Owchicta. And breaking up a lynching like you done — that won't please some of the folks who'll maybe be on your jury. Wish you had give me a call so I could let somebody else go after them idiots."

"There wasn't time," Major Wilkes said.

"Well, maybe, and probably no one else could have pulled it off. But it won't do you any good with a jury."

"I can't help that."

MAJOR WILKES SAID NOTHING in his letters to Lorena about his latest scrape, not wanting to worry her and Minnie. But when the Mingus *Times* got the story from John Pound Giles and trumpeted a laudatory account on page one, Major Wilkes sent his mother a copy with a note.

"Don't believe it all," he wrote. "It wasn't all that risky."

AMAZING TALE!

UNSUNG HERO SINGLEHANDEDLY SAVES INNOCENT PULLMAN PORTER FROM LYNCH MOB AT ROCKING JPG

ONE SHOT KILLS JUMPING JACKRABBIT IN MID-AIR, SENDS COWARDLY GANG SCURRYING; MARKSMAN THEN DISAPPEARS

"BRAVEST MAN I EVER SAW—ONE AGAINST NINE," SAYS ROCKING JPG OWNER JOHN POUND GILES; OFFERS HERO $1,000 IN GOLD TO COME FORWARD

On Thursday last, John Pound Giles, principal owner of the Kansas City, Mexico, & Oriental Railroad and many another great American enterprise, was entertaining some of America's richest and most powerful men at his Rocking JPG Ranch southwest of Mingus. After a day of hunting which netted 36 pheasants, 12 turkeys, innumerable doves, six deer, and a heifer calf shot by mistake, the gentlemen enjoyed a true Western feast of wild game and wondrously tender JPG veal, before retiring about midnight to comfortable berths in luxurious private railroad cars provided by their genial host.

Shortly before dawn on Friday morning, while the Eastern visitors were yet asleep, the twelve Negro porters and professional chefs who see to the comfort and slightest whim of Mr. Giles and his eminent guests were beginning a new day and readying a sumptuous breakfast in the dining car. But before the Rocking JPG wranglers who serve as hostlers and guides brought horses from ranch headquarters a half-mile away to take Giles and his guests on another day's hunt, a gang of armed men concealing themselves from head to toe under white bedsheets burst into the private cars, crying, "Everybody out, hands up or we shoot!"

In the dim light of pre-dawn, the cowardly hooligans herded the Eastern guests in their nightshirts and the Pullman porters in their starched and pressed uniforms off the train and forced them at gunpoint to line up by the railroad cars, hands held over their heads. "Give us the dirty coon rapist," demanded the leader of the gang angrily, waving a Colt .45 in one hand and a hangman's rope in the other, "or we shall shoot you one by one."

When Mr. Giles attempted to reason with him, telling him that no one had left the camp the previous night, the would-be hangman called him a Jew moneybags and a liar.

"I am an Episcopalian in good standing," Mr. Giles replied, "and I am telling the truth."

"Somebody tampered with my daughter and I shall have my revenge," the intruder gruffly asserted, adding, "Hand him over. There is no time to lose."

He aimed his revolver at the railroad owner. Suddenly a deep voice boomed out from atop the hill beside which the railroad cars were parked. In the dim light Giles and others could make out only the outline of a Stetson-wearing man holding a six-shooter in each hand.

"Drop your guns and lie down!" the mysterious stranger commanded.

No one complied. The gang leader whirled around and shot at the lone hero, but missed. The hullabaloo flushed a jackrabbit, which jumped between the desperados and the innocent victims lined up beside the railroad car. In an amazing display of marksmanship, the stranger on the hill fired one shot and killed the jackrabbit in mid-jump.

"The next shot will be for one of you!" he warned.

The intruders dropped their weapons and stretched out on the ground, as ordered. The sharpshooter then told the colored servants to collect weapons. They did this with pleasure and alacrity. He next ordered the KuKluxers to depart, which they did with equal alacrity if less pleasure. How they departed is not certain. The servants report hearing an automobile as well as hoofbeats, but Mr. Giles and his guests, who by then were in the safety of a private car, heard only departing hooves.

When the JPG wranglers, alerted by the gunshots, appeared, no trace of the bold stranger could be found. "He is the bravest man I ever saw," Mr. Giles said. "He faced and vanquished nine armed and angry men single-handedly and unflinchingly. If he will come forward to accept our thanks, he shall receive $1,000 in Double Eagles from me. Of course, he will have to prove his identity, perhaps by shooting another jackrabbit in mid-leap."

At press time the reward was still uncollected. Sheriff Claudius James is investigating but has found no positive clue to the identity of the sheeted men or the unknown citizen who averted what promised to be a terrible tragedy. "It is," Sheriff James said, "a mystery that shows us the worst and best of manhood, not just here in Hardcastle County, but in all the affairs of man. Let us all honor him who without seeking credit served God and saved an innocent man's life, not to mention a young woman's reputation, while so bravely averting a terrible miscarriage of justice."

Amen, we say, and so should say all men of good will, adding only the hope that the racial hatred so prevalent in Tulsa and elsewhere in our Great State at this time will not spread here.

LORENA HURRIED TO Minnie with the Mingus *Times* that Major Wilkes sent. Even without his note, they told one another, each knew instantly it could only have been their boy who had been so brave. Amos, back from sitting around the Zouave with his cronies and his flask, said, "Coulda been him, all right. I taught him to shoot like that. Do they mention me in the story?"

"Of course not. They don't mention anybody and if they did, it wouldn't be you," Minnie said.

Amos wasn't listening. "Seems to me I should get some credit. Don't know anybody else could catch a jack in mid-jump and was me taught him. But if it was him, why ain't the young fool claimed that reward?"

He shook his head.

"And that ain't all. Standing up for a colored man like that is about the dumbest thing he could've done, what with his trial coming up. Ain't a jury in this part of the world will acquit him now. He's as good as put the rope around his own neck."

"Amos, you just shush."

"I had hopes for that young fella. But one thing and another, he's showed that he don't have no more sense than he has backbone."

"How would you recognize either sense or backbone? Go to bed."

AFTER STUDYING the story in the *Times*, Sheriff James decided that there might be a way to change the public's unfavorable view of Major Wilkes. Law and order ranked high in Hardcastle County, among Southerners as well as Yankees. Many of those who settled there had lived through lawless times. They wanted now to enjoy peace and quiet with their growing families. Furthermore, they admired courage and liked the notion of one lone man standing up to a gang of desperados and coming out on top—it was, they assured one another, exactly what every man jack of them would have done in similar circumstances. The sheriff concluded the world should know that it was Major Wilkes who had faced down the Ringles in the interest of justice.

"It doesn't seem fair, what gossips would say about Sophie," Major Wilkes said.

"How about that thousand dollars in gold Giles wants to give you? That's a lot of money, Will. Take you years to save that much. Set you up for life."

"I'd like the money. But if I took it, everybody'd know for sure right off who the father of the girl was—would know the whole story. It seems a shame to tar a young girl for life just because her father's a fool and a bully and made her say something silly. You got to give her credit for realizing she'd made a serious mistake and trying to do something about it. That took spunk. She doesn't deserve to be dragged into this."

The sheriff leaned back in his office chair and struggled to get his feet on the desk. "You sweet on her, Will?"

"No. I don't think so. Not that I know of. Maybe."

Sheriff James laughed. He stared at the ceiling for a while, feet on the desk, hands clasped on his belly.

"A lot of folks already have their suspicions. They know about that phone call his daughter Loula made to Ringle at Miss Emma's—it's a party line, after all. You leave this to me. I'll drop a few hints that you're the 'hero or angel' who stood up to nine armed men and saved the county's reputation as a law-abiding place. The rumor'll get around, but one more rumor ain't going to hurt your young lady, and it might get folks thinking you ain't such a villain after all."

MAJOR WILKES TOOK shelter under a Mingus store's canopy from a sudden thunderstorm. A moment later Sophie Ringle's aunt, Mrs. McSorley, hurried in from the storm and joined him. He pretended to be engrossed in studying his boots.

"Deputy Gower," Mrs. McSorley said, "I am so glad to see you."

Major Wilkes took off his hat and bowed. He could not think what to say beyond, "Mrs. McSorley, ma'am."

"I can never thank you enough," Mrs. McSorley said, "for what you did for Sophie that night and for your reticence in the matter since."

"Think nothing of it, Ma'am."

"Sophie was so frightened and so ashamed of what she had done— I don't know what might have happened to her if you had not been so kind." Mrs. McSorley added, "Sophie joins me in everything I've said. She says she believes you must be the kindest and bravest man in the world. You are truly her hero.

She has always been overindulged but has not always known true, disinterested kindness such as you displayed toward her."

"I was only doing my job, ma'am," Major Wilkes said, twisting his hat in his hands. He knew that there had to be a dozen graceful things he could say to express his delight at her words—"Sophie joins me in everything I've said!"—but he was unable at the moment to put his tongue to even one.

"No, what you did later—when you faced down all those dreadful men—when you stopped her father from committing a terrible crime—that is when you were doing your job. When you concealed your part and Sophie's part in it at a financial loss to yourself, you did it for my Sophie out of the goodness of your heart."

"And how is her father?" Major Wilkes blurted, knowing he was indulging in the equivalent of after-church inanity, when everyone stands around making polite remarks that interest no one, least of all the person uttering them. He also recognized that his remark was worse than inane. It was insane.

"I really don't know, Deputy Gower. I have not seen or spoken to Seth Ringle in many years—since before my poor sister died. Nor has Sophie seen him since that terrible night. She intends to make her home with me from now on."

"I am glad to hear that," Major Wilkes said.

"I hoped you might be."

22.

"THAT THERE BOY'S in trouble," Amos said, as the trial date neared. He was just home from a night at the jail. A good selection of bottles had come in with their owners during the night, and he had managed to drink past wisdom. "He's going to hang. I feel it in my bones. He shouldn't never broke up that lynching. Hang'im Bill is going to use it to turn the jury agin him right from the start. Bound to."

"Be quiet. You don't know a thing about it," Minnie said.

"Them folks up in Hardcastle County ain't going to forget that Major Wilkes wouldn't let them hang a colored man who done raped a white girl—"

"Amos, you know that's not true. No such thing happened."

"Her own father said so. It was right there in that newspaper story about the jackrabbit. If I'd been there 'stead of Major Wilkes, you better believe I'd have tied a real hangman's knot and helped 'em string that fella up proper."

"Oh, yes, that's one thing I can be sure of." Minnie poured him another cup of coffee, which he lifted with a shaking hand. "You'd have been screaming for blood without the least idea whether that poor man had done a thing—as we now know he hadn't."

Amos put his sunny-side-up eggs on his grits and spun a fork in them to break up the yolks. He talked right over her.

"No father would say his girl got raped if she didn't. That's good enough for me, and it'll be good enough for that there murder jury. Major Wilkes hadn't got no business getting in the way of honest citizens protecting their women. And they'll make him pay for it."

"Nonsense!" Minnie said.

"You wait and see. Major Wilkes has good as got a rope around his neck this minute. He don't have a Chinaman's chance."

"He's got a good lawyer and witnesses who know a lot more about what happened that night than you do. And he was ordered to shoot, don't forget.'

"Don't matter. Don't matter no more'n a dried pickle. You think that there sheriff will admit he told Major Wilkes to do it? Course he won't."

"Amos, you don't know Sheriff James. He's an honorable man."

Amos brooded over a forkful of eggs. He dropped the fork without getting it to his mouth. He shoved back from the table, stared at the ceiling, and combed his beard with his fingers.

"I got it! By God, I got it! I know how to do it."

"Do what, Amos?" Minnie was washing up the dishes, paying as little attention to him as the loudness of his voice would permit.

"Get that boy off, that's what we'll do—get him off."

"Who's *we?* And what are *we* going to do?" Minnie stood before him, hands dripping suds. *Sergeant McCandless.*

He paced around the kitchen.

"Me and the boys, that's who *we* is. You don't have to do a damn thing, 'cept stay out of it. Once they get 'em a jury, we're going up there to Mingus, and we're going to be packing guns, and we're going to sit in the front row and we're going to stare at that jury, every last one of 'em just like you're staring at me right now. And that's all. We ain't going to make a sound. Not a sound. No disturbance in court. Just sit there with our arms crossed—maybe once in a while we'll drift a hand down toward a gun butt and stare. Just look at them jurors and *stare*. Not say a word. Just stare. Nothing else. But they'll get what we mean. It's the only thing'll keep that boy alive. You can count on it."

"Amos Gower, now you listen to me. You are not going near Mingus. You and the boys are going to stay out of this. I've always known you're stupid when it comes to a lot of things most folks know and do by nature. But this is the first time I've ever thought you were bed-bug crazy."

"Now, see here—"

Sergeant McCandless. "Amos, go to bed and sober up."

"I'm sober now."

"Go to bed."

CIRCUIT JUDGE Elijah J. Bronson of Tulsa arrived in Mingus to preside over the trial, bringing with him his law clerk, his bailiff, and his court reporter.

They stayed at the Grand Hotel, which was jammed with other judicial personages, including the imported prosecuting attorney, State Senator William T. *("Hang'im Bill")* Gross, and his staff—two young lawyers and a secretary. Hang'im Bill was a big man with a loud voice, a florid face, and a well-filled vest festooned with pendant honors strung on a gold watch chain. He occupied the Presidential suite and hosted dinners there on evenings that he did not dine with his sister and brother-in-law, the Powells, or visit Miss Emma's.

Judge Bronson, so thin and gangly that his scrawny throat rose from his starched collars like a newly plucked turkey's neck, bore a resemblance to Abe Lincoln, a resemblance the judge helped along with a closely trimmed beard and an old-fashioned stovepipe hat.

At the Grand he occupied a small room overlooking the alley, the cheapest available. Rebuffing all invitations, he ate his meals at a table alone, placing Teddy Roosevelt eyeglasses on his nose when he read the menu. He spoke to no one but waiters. If someone stopped by his table to visit, he said nothing and brushed them away with a wave of his hand. Each evening after supper, bundled up against the cold, he sat on the veranda for a solitary smoke before going straight to his room. He rose before dawn to stalk the dark streets for exercise. By the time court opened each day, he had been at work for an hour or more in his courthouse office, having spoken to no one but his law clerk and waiters since the previous day.

The circuit lawyers feared Judge Bronson. They said of him that he ran his court like it was a stagecoach. He yanked reins and cracked his whip to keep the dumb-mule lawyers in line and the coach moving. At the end of a day's session Judge Bronson would be fresh as milk squirted from a cow's teat into a child's waiting mouth, and the lawyers would look like they'd just run all the way from Oklahoma City at top speed in a summer dust storm. He brought his own bailiff because he did not trust local officials to keep order in his court.

Judge Bronson could not abide the slightest disturbance and had once made a lawyer remove his squeaking shoes and argue his case with one toe sticking out of an unmended sock. The lawyers said Judge Bronson was a hanging judge with a knack for making his cases come out the way he thought they should. The characterization spread through Mingus and reached Major Wilkes.

Crwrgh! Eeghwr. Hrckk. Hrckk. Crwrgh!

EPH, SWOLLEN WITH eminence as a member of the Texas Legislature, drove Minnie and Lorena to Mingus in his new Ford Model T over a scraped-out road that followed the path of the old cattle drives.

The Model T was new only to Eph, but he said it would take an expert in these matters to realize that it had been down the road a time or two with one or more previous owners. Neither Minnie nor Lorena had ridden in a motorcar. They enjoyed the adventure, though Minnie complained that compared to a buggy behind a good horse, the automobile was noisy, rough-riding, and evil-smelling. The fumes, she said, kept her choking the whole way.

"Just sit back and enjoy it," Eph urged, but she could not. She kept waiting for whatever was making all that clatter under the hood to explode and scatter the three of them over the prairie without benefit of clergy. Besides, she told Major Wilkes, Eph had talked the whole way.

"I hate to say this about my own son," she said, "but Eph has turned into the braggingest man I've ever known—other than your grandpa, that is. He bragged on his oil deals, bragged on his motorcar, bragged on being a state representative, and bragged on being the best chair-racer ever to serve in Austin. Half the time he wasn't even looking at the road!"

Major Wilkes had never heard of chair racing. Minnie explained as well as she could, relying on information she had garnered from Eph. Chair racing, she said, was an athletic contest engaged in by Texas legislators, typically after a long evening of boisterous drinking at saloons in a neighborhood of Austin called Guy Town. Lobbyists put up a purse. Senators and representatives lined up their chairs. At a signal produced by two fingers in a bartender's mouth, the racers seated themselves backward on their chairs. Hooking their heels on the rungs and clinging to the chair backs with their hands, they rocked back and forth to propel their mounts along a designated track to a finish line near the bar, where fresh libations awaited. The winner of the purse paid for drinks and any chairs broken in the heat of battle. Though previously unversed in the sport, Eph had quickly become the legislature's universally acknowledged all-time champion chair-racer, or so Eph bragged.

"I got so tired of his bragging," Minnie said, "I told him, 'You're getting more like your father every day.' Eph was pleased. He thought it was a compliment."

Minnie did not tell Major Wilkes that Eph claimed he had beaten Hang'im Bill Gross in the final heats for the chair-racing championship.

"There ain't no hard feelings, though," Eph had said. "Me and him is good buddies now—most powerful man in the Senate and a hell of a lawyer. Major Wilkes is in real trouble."

This time Eph did not stay at Miss Emma's—had to go home and tend to business, he said—and Minnie and Lorena did not go to the Grand Hotel. Mrs. McSorley had invited them to be her guests and they had accepted with pleasure. Major Wilkes worried that having his mother and grandmother under the same roof with Sophie might expose the girl to censure because of the jackrabbit incident.

"Nonsense," Minnie said. "This will only tell the gossips what they already know, and not a thing more—that her aunt and I are friends. She's still a young thing, of course, and it's natural that she feels bad about not being elected Homecoming Queen and being talked about behind her back. But she's a sweet girl with good sense and a good heart. She'll hold her head up no matter what ugly things worthless people say."

23.

THE TRIAL STARTED on Thursday morning. Major Wilkes spent Wednesday night in the jail—not as a prisoner, but because deputies based outside Mingus always slept there when duty required them to stay overnight at the county seat. Two cells with four cots were kept free and clean at all times just for them, even when it meant overcrowding the other cells. The surroundings were familiar, and he slept well enough, except for a wakeful spell in the middle of the night, when he worried as much about the possibility that Sophie's name might somehow be brought up in the trial as about the danger that he might be found guilty.

Just before escorting him upstairs to the courtroom, Sheriff James relieved him of his gun and star.

"Sorry to do this, Will. No guns today except on lawmen on duty."

Minnie had told him about Amos's scheme for influencing the jury.

Major Wilkes mentioned it to the sheriff.

"My grandmother said you should know."

"Think he'll try it?"

"Grandma told him he better not."

"We'll keep an eye out for him. Big man, you've said. Big as you?"

"About the same height, but heavier. Face gets bright red when he's drunk or excited. He stands out in a crowd—easy to spot. Just look for the fellow you'd least like to tangle with. That'll be him. If he shows up, get me. I can talk him down."

LORENA AND MINNIE dressed in black but, not wanting to appear funereal, they added new hats adorned with wide, ruffled brims and colorful silk flowers, the whole anchored against the wind by dangling scarves tied under their chins. The hats had been made for them in Wichita Falls in what they were told was the latest style. Heads high, confident of their appearance, they made their way through a crowd that spilled from the courthouse steps into the square. Each carried a knitting bag, knowing that their fingers would ache for employment as the courtroom hours dragged by.

"Carrying his last supper, are you?" a young wag shouted. He was tall and thin, towering over Minnie.

Minnie stopped, though Lorena urged her on.

"Young man," Minnie said, "you are speaking of my grandson, who was a better man than you the day he was born."

"Guilty as hell," the young man said. He laughed. The crowd pulled away from him.

"Anyone but a fool would wait to hear the evidence before reaching a verdict. I'm sure your grandmother would be ashamed for you, if she heard you."

"I ain't got no grandmother."

"Nor father, either, I imagine." The crowd hooted with laughter.

Someone called, "You tell 'im, ma'am."

Bill Bowen and other deputies were massed before the

courthouse doors. Bowen escorted Minnie and Lorena up to the second-floor courtroom and seated them in the front row. Beyond the polished oak railing,

Major Wilkes was already at the defense table. He was wearing a new black suit, a light purple shirt with a stiff white collar, and a black string tie. Lorena and Minnie agreed that he was the best dressed man in the courtroom — nicest looking, too. He introduced them to Charley Frelinghausen. A courtly Virginian in his thirties, Frelinghausen assured them that he was confident of acquittal for their son and grandson, of whom, he said, they had every reason to be proud.

After Major Wilkes and Frelinghausen returned to the defense table, Minnie and Lorena agreed that the lawyer was a charming gentleman but should pay more attention to his grammar — his frequent use of "ain't" was not what they expected in a graduate of the University of Virginia. They also thought that he, or perhaps his wife, might pay more attention to his appearance. His light brown hair was tousled and needed trimming, and his well-tailored black suit looked rumpled. Still, everyone had assured them that Major Wilkes was lucky to be defended by him. Not only was Frelinghausen the county attorney and an experienced prosecutor, he was spoken of as the best defense lawyer west of Oklahoma City.

Tall windows lined one wall of the District Courtroom. The December wind whispered and sometimes roared and banged around the sashes, making the building shake. The pine floor was splotched with stains from the tobacco juice spat on it over the years, and it smelled of oil that janitors spread to keep down dust as they swept.

The jury box was on the wall opposite the windows. On bright days it was difficult for jurors to see the lawyers, judge, and witnesses other than as dark shapes in silhouette — a design fault that lawyers and jurors alike complained of. On this day, however, the skies outside were dark, and the courtroom was barely brightened by flickering bulbs strung on wires far overhead; Mingus's municipal power station was new and the courthouse was not yet fully electrified. The judge's bench, a carved oaken beauty, stood on a raised platform atop a stage opposite the entrance, with the windows on the judge's right and the witness stand on his left. Witness and judge could look down on jurors, spectators, and lawyers. American and Oklahoma flags adorned the wall behind the bench.

Circuit Judge Elijah J. Bronson's bailiff strode in. Tall and barrel-chested, black-suited as an undertaker, he had an outsized bald head that sat on his shoulders without benefit of neck—a perfect globe on which a map of the world would not have looked out of place. Nothing was known about him in Mingus except a rumor, never substantiated, that he had once quieted an Osage County courtroom at Pawhuska by tossing three men out a second-floor window. They landed on stone steps below, or so it was said, and rolled step by step down the hill on which the courthouse was situated to the street below. It was not known in Mingus if any of the three survived.

The bailiff banged the floor with his staff.

"All rise!" He might have been announcing Armageddon.

Lincolnesque, robes swirling, Judge Bronson strode on stage, nodded in the direction of the flags, came up the three steps to his platform in two strides, and seated himself in his high-backed throne. He opened a folder, placed his eyeglasses on his nose with two fingers, and appeared to read. The crowd settled back. A man in the rear coughed. The judge's head snapped up. He removed his glasses and stared over the crowd.

The man coughed again.

"Silence!" the bailiff boomed. "Silence in this court."

The man made strangling noises. He sounded as if the bailiff had somehow reached down the length of the room and wrapped his hands around the troublesome throat.

"Eject that man," the judge ordered.

For all his bulk, the bailiff raced down the aisle faster than the startled jackrabbit Major Wilkes had shot at the Rocking JPG. Lifting the man out of his seat, the bailiff carried him into the hall. The judge resumed reading. If anyone breathed it was not audibly.

NATHAN ADKINS, neatly dressed in a flannel shirt, faded bib overalls, and lately brushed clodhopper shoes, was called as the first prospective juror. Senator Gross, a fashion plate in black tailcoat, striped pants, grey vest, and spats, got up and silently studied a paper he held in his hand. Minnie and Lorena thought the senator, for all his splendor, was costumed like the villain in a melodrama.

The witness chair was the twin of the judge's deeply carved throne. Each arm ended in a lion's head, its toothless mouth gaping wide. Adkins inserted his fingers in the lions' mouths.

Judge Bronson rapped his desk with his gavel. "The court is waiting, Senator. Ask your questions so that we may determine if Mr. Adkins will be a fair and impartial juror."

Hang'im Bill continued to study his paper. Judge Bronson lifted his gavel.

"Senator," he said.

"Your Honor," Hang'im Bill said.

Raising his eyes to Adkins, he seemed to wince.

"Now, Mr. Atkin." He might have been calling pigs.

"Yes, sir," Adkins said. His voice quavered.

[From the transcript]:

Sen. Gross: Do you know anyone connected with this case real well?

A.   No, sir, but —

Q.   You've answered the question. We don't need speeches.

A.   Yes, sir.

Q.   I see here in my papers that you call yourself a rancher, Mr. Atkin?

A.   That's what I am, aright.

Q.   How big a spread, Mr. Atkin?

A.   Well, I got me my homestead, and forty head of cattle. Last week I taken four steers to market down to Ringle's.

Q.   Any bull?

A.   Yes, sir, a right good five-year-old. Raised him myself.

Q.   A quarter-section, forty head, and a home-grown bull. And you say you're a rancher?

A.   Yes, sir. I didn't mention grazing rights. Herd's building year by year.

Q.   Wouldn't "nester" better describe what you are?

A.   I don't know what a nester might be. I'm a rancher. I —

Q.   Free of debt, are you, Mr. Atkin?

A.   No, sir, but —

Q.   No buts, Mr. Atkin. Who holds your paper?

A.   Farmers and Merchants, sir.

Q.   Mr. Powell's bank? The father of the murdered boy?

Mr. Frelinghausen: Objection. There is no —

The Court: Sustained. No more of that, Senator, if you please.

Sen. Gross: As you say, Your Honor. Now, Mr. Atkin, who owns the Hardcastle County Farmers and Merchants Bank?

A.   Mr. Powell, sir.

Q.   But you said, did you not, that you do not know Mr. Powell?

A.   No, sir. I didn't call his name. You asked me did I know anybody real well who's got something to do with this case. That's what you asked and I said I didn't, and that's God's own truth. I maybe met Mr. Powell a time or two, sir, but can't say I know him, not real well.

Q.   No more speeches, if you please, Mr. Atkin, and no more splitting hairs. I want a straight answer to a straight question: How did you meet Mr. Powell?

A.   Well, I got a little behind times and —

Q.   A little behind times on what? Wasn't it on payment of interest on a loan Mr. Powell had made to you on this large herd you were bragging on a minute ago?

A.   I wasn't trying not to pay —

Q.   Yes or no, Mr. Atkin. Did you pay him the money you legally owed him on or near time?

A.   No, but —

Q.   You're full of buts, aren't you, Mr. Atkin? You owed money and didn't pay it. So what happened then?

A.   Well, he sent a couple of men out and taken him a yearling calf. Worth twice the payment I owed, that calf was, but when I went to see Mr. Powell, he said we was only even, because of the penalty for late payment. I didn't know nothing about a penalty. They sprung it on me and —

Q.   So you're not exactly impartial about Mr. Powell are you, Mr. Atkin?

The Court: Senator, no need to bully the gentleman, whose name, if you please, is "Adkins." Please use it in addressing him.

Sen. Gross: Yes, Your Honor, thank you. No more questions.

The Court: Mr. Frelinghausen, have you any questions?

Mr. Frelinghausen: Thank you, Your Honor. Mr. Adkins, as a hardworking man, a family man— Am I right in thinking you're a family man?

A.   Yes, sir, I got me four boys and a girl, and another boy on the way — well, maybe not a boy. Maybe a girl.

[Laughter in the court]

The Court: One more such outburst and I shall clear the courtroom.

Q.   Mr. Adkins, as a family man, a property owner in this county, a rancher, knowing that a young man was killed and the life of another young man, the defendant, is at stake in this case, could you consider fairly all the evidence you'll hear and on the basis of that evidence alone come to a fair and impartial judgment in this case, without regard to your lost calf?

A.   Yes, sir. I could do that.

Q.   Mr. Adkins is acceptable to the defense.

The Court: Inasmuch as the prosecution failed to challenge, Mr. Adkins shall be seated.

Sen. Gross: Your Honor! I must protest.

The Court: You may, of course, Senator, but I do not advise it.

HANG'IM BILL challenged all countrymen except owners of large spreads and all townsmen except those who owned their own businesses. Charley Frelinghausen seemed so relaxed in his questioning of prospective jurors from town and country alike that one spectator was later heard wondering if Charley might be getting ready to run for the state legislature and didn't want to offend any possible voter by rejecting him. But the prosecutor exhausted the jury panel with his challenges by noon.

Judge Bronson ordered deputies to create a fresh panel during the recess. The deputies did not have far to go in search of eligible males. They found them among the crowds waiting for seats in the courtroom. Most protested, to no avail, that they didn't have time to serve—they had urgent business elsewhere and had just stopped by for a quick look at the proceedings.

It took the rest of the day to form a jury, made up of four townsmen, three ranchers with big spreads, three homesteaders, and two established but small ranchers, one of them Adkins. Senator Gross left the courtroom with his two young legal associates congratulating him on getting just the jury he wanted.

"Well, you tried," Major Wilkes said to his attorney.

"Ain't that so?" Frelinghausen said. He looked glum. "Everybody said I wanted clodhoppers, didn't they? And yet I didn't challenge anybody but a few stuffed shirts—easy marks. Now we've got us a jury of sensible citizens. Most got mauled by our fancy-pants opponent and wouldn't have made it if the judge hadn't stepped in and seated them, like he did Adkins."

"A lot of Southerners," Major Wilkes said. "They may not think much of me stopping old Ringle from lynching that porter."

"You're a Southerner and so am I—living proof that Southerners ain't necessarily Klansmen. I'm betting these are serious men interested in law and order."

"You can't be sure, once they get in that jury room. You told me that yourself."

"It's a risk. I won't deny it. But I think we've got a good chance. Hang'im Bill is going to blow smoke like a prairie fire, and maybe he'll sway them. But the facts are on our side. You don't succeed as a homesteader or a rancher, no matter how big or small your spread, if you don't face facts."

"But you got six who aren't ranchers or nesters."

"That's right, but look at who they are—three business owners, including a farm machinery dealer who sells to country folks, a store clerk, a carpenter, and a schoolteacher. Good responsible citizens with their feet on the ground—solid folks who know that Gross sees them as a bunch of country bumpkins and small-town rubes who ain't worth a hill of beans. But it's not their natural resentment of the way he treated them that I'm counting on. It's their native good sense. Some in town and some in the country, these folks are taming a frontier and doing a good job of it. They ain't the kind you can bamboozle or push around, and they don't like being looked down on. "

"Senator Gross seems awful happy."

"Let him. He won't be in the end."

Major Wilkes was not persuaded. He remembered the rumor of a hanging judge and Amos's prediction of a hanging jury.

24.

"TAKE IT EASY," Charley Frelinghausen said as he and Major Wilkes waited at the defense table for the Friday court session to open. "You'll hear a lot of things said about you this morning that you ain't going to like. Hang'im Bill is going to take you apart and hang the pieces out to dry. You won't recognize yourself. But the facts are with us, Will. All he's got is hot air. So sit back and enjoy it. You don't often get a chance to watch an old-time stem-winder draw pictures you can see using nothing but hot air and a few twisted facts. Just don't take any of it too seriously."

"I'll try," Major Wilkes said. "But it's me he'll be hanging, not you."

When Senator Gross rose to deliver his opening statement, the courtroom was jammed with spectators from as far away as Oklahoma City, Wichita Falls, and Fort Worth. The senator wore not only his tailcoat and striped trousers, newly pressed, but also a crimson double-breasted vest, the likes of which had never been seen in Owchicta. Judge Bronson pounded down a murmur that rippled through the courtroom at the sight. The senator smiled at the jury, smoothed the vest over the bulge of his stomach, and remarked, "My friends, you'll be interested to know that this is my lucky vest. I have never lost a case while wearing it."

Before Charley Frelinghausen got his mouth open, Judge Bronson said, "Sustained. Senator, remove your vest before proceeding."

"Your Honor—"

The judge brought down the gavel. "You may continue your address to the jury, Sir, after you have adjusted your costume. This court will be in recess for two minutes and I expect you to delay us no longer than that."

"Right here, Your Honor? Two minutes?"

"Wherever you like, Senator. Two minutes." Judge Bronson reached into his robes and brought out a pocket watch in his cupped hand.

A junior lawyer rushed forward to help the senator out of his tailcoat while Hang'im Bill fumbled with a watch chain and vest buttons. Under the vest he wore only long-sleeved gray underwear, suspenders, and a dickey. The young man tried to use the coat to screen him from the jury and the audience. Unable to do both at the same time, he wound up blocking the view of neither.

Judge Bronson put down his watch and picked up his gavel. The senator rushed into a non-stop sentence with one arm still seeking its way into a coat sleeve.

"Gentlemen of the jury, we are here today to fix the guilt for what your fine newspaper has so aptly described as 'murder most heinous,' a crime that took the life of a fine young man, a young man who might—no, no, not might—who would surely have graced the Halls of Congress, perhaps the White House itself, had he not been shot down in his youth on the very doorstep of greatness, at the threshold of a career that might have led to astounding medical discoveries, or perhaps to inventions to rival those of Thomas Alva Edison or Henry Ford, or just as likely to great novels equal to those of Scott or Hawthorne or Kipling—"

Vest gone, coat and dickey adjusted, no period in sight, Hang'im Bill rushed on and on. He waved his arms, pounded one fist into the other, whispered and boomed.

Words flooded from him like water through a broken irrigation gate, unimpeded by a full stop. Looking ceiling-ward, he described angels in glorious array cheering with heavenly fervor as Junior Powell in shoulder pads of pure gold raced past golden goalposts to claim his heavenly reward. Having got Junior well-situated at the side of the Lord, the senator swung around, pointed a finger at Major Wilkes, and contrasted the joys being showered on Junior in Heaven with the horrors the perfidious Texas killer would face on his arrival at the gates of Hell.

He characterized Major Wilkes as Satan in lawman's guise, a dastardly killer-for-hire who at a tender age was named the Gun-Slinger Champion of Owchicta County, Texas, and who—as a certain well-known but unspecified feat of marksmanship had recently proven—had lost none of his gun-handling prowess in the years since. The defendant, Hang'im Bill declared, had an evil heart as twisted as a hangman's knot and was the secret agent of a foreign state, Texas, bent upon destroying the tranquility of Oklahoma's peaceful homebodies.

Only when the great orator tripped at last over a period or was called to the bench for a conference did he pause and wipe perspiration from his face with a sopping-wet kerchief. His young assistant scurried up to replace it with a fresh one.

Major Wilkes's collar had tightened on his neck as Hang'im Bill filled in his lurid portrait of him as a blood-thirsty monster. Charley Frelinghausen leaped to his feet time after time, questioning the relevancy of the senator's flourishes and whether they could be supported by testimony. His objections took the lawyers up the steps to the bench for lengthy conferences, which made what might have been a two-hour speech stretch into four.

Some spectators deserted the proceedings in these intervals, complaining that they couldn't hear a word the opposing attorneys said to the judge, or he to them. The pantomime of attorneys pounding fists on the bench and shoving index fingers into opposing breasts did not provide sufficient entertainment to justify staying in an overheated courtroom grown stuffy with the fumes of floor-oil and sweating bodies.

Long past the usual time for a noon break, Hang'im Bill stopped in front of the jury box and stood silently, staring at the notes in his hand.

After a moment he slowly, softly, as though sharing a confidence that he wanted the jury but no one else to know, "My friends, one bit of advice. The defense will try to confuse you with fact after fact about this case, but keep a clear mind. There is only one fact that must guide you. And that fact—denied by no one—is that this defendant, Major Wilkes Gower, also known as Will Gower, a Texan and champion gun slinger, shot Justin Bartlett Powell, Jr., to death in the early hours of New Year's Day in the year of our Lord 1910. The defense lawyer will do all in his power to besmirch the dear boy's memory. Do not be swayed. Cling to that one all-important fact. Major Wilkes Gower killed Junior Powell."

He paused, took a deep breath, and thundered: "And for that murder he must die! HANG'IM! Hang him by the neck until dead! Gentlemen of the jury—do not shirk your duty. HANG'IM! HANG'IM! *HANG'IM!*"

With the time verging on 2:00 o'clock, Hang'im Bill sat down, vermilion-faced, panting for breath, smiling. His young assistant handed him another fresh kerchief to swab his face. Judge Bronson held his gavel in mid-air, ready to strike down any demonstration. There was none. No one—no juryman, no member of the audience—moved or made a sound. The magic-tongued orator from Oklahoma City had put them in a trance. Before Frelinghausen could stop him Major Wilkes ran a finger around his collar.

"The jury is excused until 3:00 o'clock." The judge's gavel struck the block, lightly.

As the jury rose to file out, a ruckus broke out at the courtroom door. Major Wilkes heard, "The hell I ain't allowed. I'm his grandpa."

Amos burst through the door, dragging Bill Bowen and another deputy. Shaking them off he stood in the aisle swaying from side to side—Stetson shoved to the back of his head, medals on his shirt, elbows thrust out like wings, hands hovering over two Colts dangling from a cartridge-stuffed gun belt. His face was red as a tom turkey's wattles.

"I'm Amos Gower from Owchicta, Texas, and I'm that boy's grandpa. I'm here to see he gets a fair trial."

Minnie stood up, hands on her hips, *Sergeant McCandless* on her face. "Amos Gower, you get out of this courtroom this instant."

The gavel banged. "Silence!"

"Out of my way, woman. I know what I'm doing and I ain't going to let them hang that boy."

Major Wilkes stood up, with Charley Frelinghausen trying to pull him down. "Grandpa, go home. I don't need your help and I don't want you here."

Judge Bronson banged his gavel so hard that spectators feared for its handle. *"Order! Order!* Bailiff, seize that man."

"You don't want me, Major Wilkes?"

"No, Grandpa. I don't."

The bailiff wrapped his arms around Amos. "You don't want me?"

"No, Grandpa. I'm sorry."

"The defendant will be seated and remain silent. Bailiff, bring that man here. And you, Ma'am, please seat yourself. I shall take care of this without your aid."

"Judge—" said Amos.

"The prisoner will be silent."

"I ain't a prisoner. You can't call me a prisoner."

"You are, I can, and I do. I am sentencing you to ten days in jail for contempt of court for disrupting this proceeding. I leave to a lower court any charges of public drunkenness, disturbing the peace, and carrying weapons into this courtroom. You, sir, are a sorry specimen of an Oklahoma gentleman."

"I'm a Texan."

"That may explain your behavior"—some spectators claimed that the corners of the judge's mouth lifted into what might have grown into a smile, had he not cut it short—"but it is no excuse. Take him away."

The bailiff shoved Amos down the aisle, an old man weighed down by unneeded armament.

"Amos wasn't even charged," Major Wilkes said to Charley Frelinghausen. "Can the judge sentence him just like that?'

"Judge Bronson can."

"Silence! Court is dismissed."

Minnie whispered to Lorena. "It was Eph! I know it was Eph brought him."

Major Wilkes took Minnie and Lorena down to the jail to visit Amos. They found him alone in a cell. His cartridge belt and guns were gone. He lay on his back on a cot that was too short for him, hands clasped on his chest, boots on, and his Stetson covering his face. Major Wilkes thought of Dunc lying on pine boards and sawhorses in the front parlor.

"Amos?" Minnie said.

He did not move.

"Amos Gower! You sit up this minute, hear?"

He lay silent.

"Grandpa? It's Major Wilkes. Won't you talk to me?"

"You don't want me, I don't want you." His face was still covered. His voice was thick. "I was only trying to help. That's a hanging jury, boy. They ain't going to pay no attention to anything you say. They'll put a rope around your neck for messing up their lynching, sure as God made little green apples. And I wouldn't blame them if it was anybody but you."

The cell wasn't locked. Major Wilkes went in and sat on the edge of the cot. He tried to take the hat off Amos's face. Amos struck out at him.

"Get away from me."

"Grandpa, give me your flask."

"Try and get it."

Major Wilkes dodged Amos's fists, reached under him, and plucked the flask from his rear pocket. Amos rolled over on his side, turning his back.

"He's awful hot," Major Wilkes reported to Minnie and Lorena. "I think he's got a fever."

When they came out of the cell block to tell Sheriff James, Eph was sprawled in a chair in the outer office. Stetson shoved back and heels hooked on the chair rungs, he was telling the deputy on duty a joke.

"This here parson, he went in the whorehouse—didn't know what it was, see—and he sees this girl with her tits hanging out, and he says—"

"Eph Gower, I want to speak to you," Minnie said. "This instant!"

Eph leaped to his feet, taking off his Stetson. "Ma, I'm glad to see you."

"I am not glad to see you. You had no business bringing Amos to Mingus. You knew I didn't want him here—and now see what's happened. He's sick and in jail, all because of you."

"He's been drunk for a week, Ma. I couldn't stop him."

"But you didn't need to bring him."

Eph bent over her, trying to get under the flowered hat to kiss her on the cheek.

She pushed him away. Sheriff James came in.

"Grandpa's pretty sick," Major Wilkes said.

"I know. I been to tell the judge Mr. Gower ought to be at home. The judge said it was all right with him, but if he shows up here again, he'll get six months."

"He won't be back," Minnie said. "Eph here will take him home and not leave him out of his sight until I get there after this trial is over."

"Ma! I got a business to tend to. Muffie—"

"Eph, I have told you what you are to do."

In the afternoon Frelinghausen outlined the defense case in an opening statement that lasted less than an hour. He kept his tone conversational and promised that the defense would prove that Deputy Gower was doing his duty as a law officer when he fired the bullet that killed Junior Powell. Reminding the jurymen that it was their duty to base their judgment on the facts presented to them, Frelinghausen did not address the character of the dead boy, but deplored his death, calling it a tragedy for all concerned. He outlined the defense case in detail and urged the jury to ignore rhetoric and histrionics and concentrate on provable facts.

Sounding confident, he said they would have no rational choice but to acquit after hearing evidence proving that the defendant fired only when ordered to do so by his superior officer, after an unseen adversary had shot at an occupied hotel in the middle of the night, shattering lights and windows, and endangering the lives of innocent citizens and law officers alike.

Senator Gross found nothing to object to in Frelinghausen's

discourse, but sat relaxed, doodling on a pad and yawning from time to time. The jurors, who had leaned forward in their seats and turned their heads to follow the famed orator as he paced back and forth hurling red meat their way, sat back and looked more patient than attentive while Frelinghausen offered them a menu of dry facts. At times a juror or two yawned with the senator.

Frelinghausen sat down, Senator Gross suggested that it was too late in the day to start calling witnesses, and the judge agreed. Major Wilkes ran a finger around his collar.

25.

SATURDAY MORNING the prosecution presented its witnesses. The first included Deputy Billy Bowen, City Marshal Deke Hagenbotham, Dr. Elmer Gorse, and Sheriff Claudius James.

In questioning them, bombastic Hang'im Bill briefly turned into a bookkeeper adding up the same column of figures over and over again. With witness after witness he doggedly reviewed the bare-bone facts laid out at the hearings that led to the indictment of Major Wilkes for Junior Powell's death.

Witness after witness told and retold what they had seen and done on the morning of New Year's Day. At appropriate times the senator introduced exhibits, such as the dead boy's clothing and the cot on which he died. But he asked nothing about what Junior Powell did that evening and cut off any witness who ventured to do so. It was as though everyone but the victim had been present in front of the Grand Hotel when the fatal bullet was fired. The jury grew restless as the same facts droned repeatedly into the record. So many spectators deserted their seats in the courtroom that no one was left in line, and empty seats went unfilled for the first time since the trial began.

Charley Frelinghausen did little to relieve the tedium in his cross-examination, until it came time to for him to question Sheriff James, the last of the prosecution's witnesses.

"Sheriff James," Frelinghausen asked, "did you receive a report on New Year's Eve about a misbehaving group of youths?"

"I did."

"Were any names mentioned?"

"Yes, sir."

"Tell us about it, please."

"We was sitting around about 1:30 in the morning congratulating ourselves on how quiet things had been, when a lady guest at Miss Emma's Home Away from Home for Respectable Ladies and Gentlemen come busting in, all roughed up and upset. She —"

Hang'im Bill heaved himself out of his chair.

"Objection. Irrelevant and hearsay, Your Honor."

After a 20-minute conference at the bench, Judge Bronson ruled for the defense, and Sheriff James was allowed to continue.

"This lady I mentioned, she said Junior Powell and a bunch of his friends had broke in and done a lot of damage at Miss Emma's a little earlier. I sent several deputies to Miss Emma's and me, Billy Bowen and Will Gower went out looking for the responsible youths.

"In front of the Grand Hotel we run into Ike Watson. Ike reported that Junior Powell, Jimmy Thrimble, and some other young hooligans —"

"Objection!"

"The witness will moderate his language."

"Yes, Your Honor. Ike Watson said this bunch of young men had barged in drunk as skunks, looking for booze. Ike said he run them off with his shotgun but they shot out a lamp and a couple of windows as they left. We went looking for the troublemakers, then heard gunshots behind us in the direction of the hotel. We went back full steam. In front of the hotel somebody fired on us and knocked Deputy Bowen's hat off.

"It was dark. We couldn't see who it was. We told them to drop their guns, but they yelled, '*Hee-Haw, Hee-Haw,*' and one of them shot out a porch window right over our heads."

"Was that when the fatal shot was fired?"

"Yes."

"Who fired that shot?"

"The defendant, Deputy Gower."

A spectator shouted, "Hang the murderer!"

Unable to determine who uttered the offending words, Judge Bronson told the bailiff to eject an entire row. When several spectators tried to protest their eviction, the judge held them in contempt of court and told the bailiff to have them kept outside the courtroom for him to deal with later.

"Why did the defendant fire that shot?" Frelinghausen asked.

"I ordered him to," Sheriff James said. "He obeyed, firing at the flash of a gun. It was an astonishing display of marksmanship at a time of great personal danger."

Senator Gross leaped to his feet, objecting to an expression of opinion.

Judge Bronson overruled him.

"Sheriff James," Frelinghausen asked, "did the victim say anything in your hearing after he was shot?"

"After I picked up the gun, Junior was lying in the street. I asked Junior if it was his. He said, 'I never seen that fucking gun, Sheriff, I swear to God.' I told him he was lying, and he replied, 'The hell I am, you fat old fart.'"

Senator Gross objected again, this time to the use of vile language with ladies present.

"Junior would never have said anything so disgusting."

After a conference at the bench, Judge Bronson ordered the court reporter to strike the objectionable words from both sentences and insert blanks in their place.

"What more did the young man say that you heard?" Frelinghausen then asked the sheriff.

"The next thing was when the defendant and Deputy Bowen were putting him on the cot to carry him to the hotel for medical attention. Junior told the defendant, 'You'll hang for this, you goddamned Texas son of a bitch, my daddy'll see to that.' The last words I heard him speak, just as he died, were, 'Christ, it hurts.'"

One of Junior Powell's many aunts stood and screamed, "Junior never in his life took the name of Our Lord in vain. You are lying, Sheriff James, and I'll never vote for you again."

"Remove that woman," Judge Bronson ordered.

Junior's aunt strode from the room before the bailiff could reach her. Senator Gross demanded that all of Junior's words, as reported by the sheriff, be stricken from the record as irrelevant. Judge Bronson let them stand, with blanks where needed.

A brief wrangle ensued when Frelinghausen asked Sheriff James to describe the gun that he had referred to and tell how and where he found it.

Hang'im Bill objected to mention of the gun, on the ground that the weapon had not been introduced into evidence. Frelinghausen pointed out that it was the senator who had failed to introduce the weapon earlier, as he might have.

Judge Bronson ordered Sheriff James to produce the gun. After a brief recess it was entered as evidence by the defense. At Frelinghausen's request the sheriff described it as a Model 3 Smith & Wesson with an eight-inch barrel and smooth wood grips.

"Sheriff James, when and where did you first see this

Model 3 Smith & Wesson gun?"

"It was lying in the street about eight feet from Junior Powell. I picked it up."

"Were you surprised to see the gun?

"No, sir. I had heard the gun hit the road. I went right to it and picked it up. Smoke was still coming out the barrel."

"How did you know whose gun it was?"

"Junior Powell was the only person left in the street when it was thrown."

With the groundwork laid, Frelinghausen ended his cross-examination of the sheriff.

Before Senator Gross could call further witnesses, Judge Bronson ordered a recess until Monday. He noted that the time was nearly two hours past the normal Saturday closing hour of noon and apologized to the courthouse staff for keeping them from their dinners. Wishing everyone a pleasant weekend, he adjourned the court until Monday morning.

On Saturday night, the *Times* later reported, "Senator Gross and other distinguished attorneys from out of town were entertained at a sumptuous banquet at the palatial new home of Mayor and Mrs. Powell. Other guests included a cross-section of Mingus's business, professional, and social elite. Judge Bronson, though invited, declined with thanks, saying it would be inappropriate for him to participate at this time."

The *Times* failed to note that male guests who were in town without their spouses found further entertainment that evening at Mrs. Smith's Home Away from Home for Respectable Men and Women.

MINNIE AND LORENA attended Sunday services with Mrs. McSorley and Sophie Ringle, hoping to see the weak vessel who had made the un-Christian suggestion that Major Wilkes stay away from church and slip through the alley when he felt the need of pastoral comfort.

Arriving at the church, a white frame structure with a soaring steeple and several stained-glass windows, Minnie and Lorena were disappointed to learn that, while Miss Emma and her lady boarders were there, they were hidden away at the rear of the sanctuary in a ladies' gallery with a private entrance. This arrangement, they learned from Mrs. McSorley, was something new. It had been introduced by Rev. Lowry under the guise of accommodating maiden ladies not wishing to expose themselves to rude eyes.

"The man's a fool, of course," Mrs. McSorley said. "Mrs. Smith and her girls never minded the rude eyes, and we all positively enjoyed seeing them. Very pretty, most of them, and quite devout."

Mrs. McSorley invited Major Wilkes and Sheriff James to Sunday dinner. The sheriff, a widower for whom a home-cooked meal was a treat, accepted at once—Mrs. McSorley was known to set a good table—but Major Wilkes tried to decline. Mrs. McSorley insisted and so did Lorena.

Major Wilkes said little during the meal, and Sophie no more. But the sheriff, gossipy as a Methodist lady, and the three senior females kept a lively conversation going about everything but the trial. The meal began with a gelatin and canned-pineapple salad, continued with roast chicken (carved by the sheriff, as the senior male present), mashed potatoes, baked sweet potatoes, turnips, home-canned green beans and corn, hot rolls, and cherry pie.

Mrs. McSorley had canned the cherries but the pie was made by Sophie, her aunt announced, which led Major Wilkes to declare it the best pie he had ever eaten, a judgment which he was then forced to amend without hurting Sophie's feelings or those of the two previous champion pie-makers present. His floundering led to great hilarity around the table, though afterward he could not recall a word said by himself or anyone else, except for two words uttered by Sophie—or was it three? "You're sweet."

He doubted that he would ever have a happier afternoon.

THE TRIAL RESUMED on Monday morning in an icy courtroom. A winter storm had struck, bringing sleet, snow, and a bone-chilling wind that shook the courtroom windows. To make matters worse, the coal-burning furnace had gone out overnight.

In the jury box, the jurors huddled under blankets, sheepskins, and heavy coats of every sort, fogging the air with every breath. Judge Bronson wore a velvet-collared black cloak under his judicial robe. Senator Gross hid his tailcoat and two vests (neither red) beneath a skunk-fur garment that made him look like a black bear.

He urged the judge to recess. It was, he said, too cold for thought. His Honor refused, saying that he found cold conducive to clear thinking. Minnie and Lorena had had the foresight to bring long underwear with them, as well as warm coats. They stayed comfortable, except for their feet—they had not thought to pack woolen stockings. Major Wilkes was warm enough in an ankle-length sheepskin riding coat, but shivered through the morning as the prosecution built its case against him.

For the first couple of hours a parade of leading citizens and Junior Powell's friends testified to Junior's sterling character and enumerated his athletic and scholarly triumphs, though the latter were scarce as ants on a block of ice.

Frelinghausen did not bother to cross-examine any of them. "Well-intentioned window dressers," he called them.

The last of the character witnesses was Reverend Lowry, sweater-bloated, a green scarf around his throat, and a raccoon-fur hat on his head. In deference to the minister's baldness, the judge agreed to let him keep his hat on while testifying.

His ode to the goodness and piety of the dead boy moved many in the audience to tears amid cries of "Amen!" and "Lord bless him!" Judge Bronson stayed his gavel and did not cut short the emotional recital.

Once handkerchiefs were tucked away in sleeves and reticules, Senator Gross turned Reverend Lowry's attention to what he referred to as "the so-called facts of the case." Lowry testified that he had held a prayer service at the church on New Year's Eve, followed by a party for Methodist youth in the basement at which games were played and hymns were sung.

"Was Junior Powell among the participants at the youth party?" the senator asked.

"Oh, yes. He and his friends were there until it ended. They were on their way home when he was killed by Deputy Gower."

"That will be all, Reverend, and we thank you for your heartfelt tribute to a fine young man, a scintillating paragon of virtue," Senator Gross said.

Lowry stepped from the stand. Hang'im Bill shook his hand and further hailed his testament to the dead boy's fine qualities as "heart-rending." Judge Bronson ordered the minister back to the witness chair for cross-examination, reprimanded the senator for his remarks, and ordered the jurors to disregard them.

Smiling and nodding at parishioners in the jury box, Reverend Lowry settled into the witness chair again as Charley Frelinghausen approached to cross-examine.

[From the transcript:]

Q. Good morning, Reverend.

A. Good morning, Mr. Frelinghausen.

Q. You said, I believe, that you conducted the 7:00 o'clock New Year's Eve prayer service the evening before the tragic death occurred. Is that correct, sir?

A. Yes, sir—and I was pleased to see you there, I might say, Mr. Frelinghausen.

Q. I was pleased to be there, Reverend Lowry. Did you then attend the youth party in the basement?

A. No, no. I was tucked into my own little bed by then.

[Laughter in the courtroom.]

The Court: Silence!

Q. Now Reverend Lowry, you say you conducted the prayer service but were not present at the youth gala?

A. That is correct.

Q. So you did not see the deceased at the party?

A. Well—

Q. Did you, Reverend?

A. No.

Q. Did you see the boy leave the party—no, of course you didn't. You were tucked away in your own little bed. I withdraw the question. However, I am curious. How did you know that Junior was at the party if you were not there?

A. Why, I was told by his friends. They all agreed that he was there and left as I said.

Q. But you have no direct knowledge that he was present?

A. I suppose not.

Q. And no direct knowledge of when he left the party?

A. No.

Q. Do your youth parties generally run after midnight?

A. Of course not. Nine-thirty to 10:00 is about our limit.

Q. Even on New Year's Eve?

A. Even on New Year's Eve.

Q. As the father of a Methodist youth who in a few years will be old enough to attend your church parties, I am glad to be assured of that. But on this particular New Year's Eve, at what exact time did the last person leave the church premises, Reverend Lowry?

A. Well, as I said, I was—

Q. Tucked away in your little bed. Indeed. But from having been at many church-hall affairs, I recall that you keep a record book in which the person in charge of an event is required to enter the time the affair started and when it ended. Is my recollection correct, Reverend?

A. Yes, we keep such a record.

Q. And what does the record have to say as to the time the party ended?

A. I did not think it necessary to refer to it on this occasion.

Q. If you were to run across the square, perhaps in company with a deputy, could you bring that little book back with you in, oh, perhaps ten minutes?

A. Yes, but I don't see—

Q. Your Honor, may I request a brief recess? This is a matter of some importance.

Senator Gross objected, and a lengthy conference at the bench followed, with the minister still in the witness chair. Judge Bronson finally called the recess. Reverend Lowry was escorted across the square by Billy Bowen. On their return, Frelinghausen entered a large green notebook in evidence, over Hang'im Bill's objection.

Q. Reverend Lowry, have you had time to catch your breath and look at your record book? If so, what did you find?

A. The youth party ended at 10:37—that is, the doors were locked at that hour.

Q. So you were in error when you indicated that Junior Powell and his friends were at the youth party until sometime after midnight?

A. It would appear so.

Q. I recall that it is customary to note the names of those attending an event in the hall. Was that done at the New Year's Eve party?

A. Yes, I see a good many names here.

Q. And is the name of Junior Powell entered there?

Sen. Gross: Objection. The document was entered for the purpose of determining a time, not—

The Court: Overruled.

Q. Is the name of Junior Powell there, Reverend? Take your time. Do you find it?

A. No.

Q. How about Jimmy Thrimble?

A. No.

Q. No further questions.

Sen. Gross: Your Honor, I have a further question for the witness.

The Court: You may proceed.

Sen. Gross: Reverend Lowry, did you make that record?

A. No, Senator, I did not.

Q. So you cannot vouch for its accuracy, can you?

A. No, not at all.

Q. No further questions.

Major Wilkes nudged Frelinghausen. "Shouldn't you ask Reverend Lowry who did sign it?"

"Good thinking," Frelinghausen said, "but not this time. The lady who signed it is a social climber and is known to cheat at Whist. She wouldn't want to offend the Powells and would probably swear that Junior was there and she had failed for some reason to write down his name. And she didn't wear a watch so she couldn't be sure if the time she recorded was correct. I'm just glad Hang'im Bill doesn't know he's passing up a friendly witness. There's an advantage to being just a local yokel."

26.

SENATOR GROSS CALLED Jimmy Thrimble to the stand.

Cocooned in a greatcoat that filled the courtroom with the smell of camphor, Thrimble grew tearful as he told how much he missed the dead boy, "my best pal." Senator Gross led him gently through a recitation of his relationship with Junior, from first grade to high school, and then through a list of things he and Junior had or had not done. They had been helpful and courteous to all, had never bullied anyone, never smoked or taken a drink or been disrespectful to their elders, had in fact made a point of helping little old ladies across muddy streets, and had attended church regularly, two and sometimes three times a week.

> Sen. Gross: Now, Jimmy, did you attend a youth party at the Methodist church hall after the Sunday evening service on December 31, 1909?
>
> A. Sure did. Had a swell time.
>
> Q. At what time did you leave that party?
>
> A. It was exactly ten after twelve.
>
> Q. And who did you leave with?

A. Oh, my usual pals. Junior Powell, Horse Crosby, and a bunch of others.

Q. And what did you and your friends do then?

A. Well, there was doughnuts and cookies left from at the party and we sat on the church steps for an hour or so before we headed home.

Q. And to head home you had to pass the Grand Hotel?

A. Yes, sir.

Q. And what happened at the Grand Hotel?

A. As we got near the hotel we heard some yelling and some shooting. We was hurrying to get out of the way when all of a sudden there's another shot and Junior Powell, he kind of howls and then yells, "Run for your lives, boys, I am shot."

[Witness sobs.]

The Court: Compose yourself, Mr. Thrimble. Bailiff, give the witness a glass of water

Sen. Gross: Are you all right now, Jimmy? I know how hard it is for you to recall that terrible event.

A. Yeah, I reckon I'm okay now. It's just that I miss him so, Junior, I mean. He was the best damn friend I ever had. Best friend I'll ever have.

Q. There, there, son. Pull yourself together. I only have another question or two.

A. Yes, sir.

Q. Now, son, did you or anyone else in your group have a gun with you that night?

A. No, sir.

Q. Did you or any of your friends, including Junior Powell, fire a shot that night?

A. How could we? We didn't have no guns.

Q. Were you at or near Miss Emma's Home Away from Home for Respectable Ladies and Gentlemen at any time on New Year's Eve?

A. Oh, no, sir.

Q. What did you and your group have to drink that night?

A. Lemonade, mostly, and Coca-Cola.

Q. Any alcoholic beverages?

A. Oh, no, sir. Never in my whole life. I wasn't allowed.

Q. No further questions.

Hang'im Bill pulled down his vest and seated himself at the prosecution table.

Frelinghausen leaned over to mutter, "Nice show, Senator."

Hang'im Bill smiled. "Why, thank you, sir. It was a pleasure."

To Major Wilkes, Frelinghausen whispered, "Smile, damn it, like you just heard something funny."

Rising to cross-examine, Frelinghausen held a sheaf of papers in his hands. He glanced through, taking his time. Jimmy began to fidget.

Q. Mr. Thrimble, you testified a few minutes ago that it was "exactly ten after twelve" when you left the Methodist youth party, did you not?

A. You heard me.

Q. Indeed I did. Did you determine the time by looking at the 24-karat Elgin railroad watch you got last Christmas along with a 24-karat gold chain?

A. That's right.

Q. The watch that was reported stolen on December 27, 1909?

A. I don't know what you're talking about.

Q. Didn't your father report the loss to City Marshal Dexter Hagenbotham two days after Christmas, four days before New Year's Eve?

A. How would I know? Ask my father.

Q. Your Honor, I ask permission to suspend my cross-examination of this witness and call Mr. Barney Thrimble to the stand.

Sen. Gross: Objection.

The Court: Overruled.

A. Oh, all right. Yeah, it got stolen.

Q. Had it been replaced by New Year's Eve?

A. No. My old man was too sore.

Q. So you had no watch with you on New Year's Eve?

A. I guess not.

Q. How did you know it was exactly ten after twelve when you left the youth party?

A. I looked at the bank clock, of course.

Q. And it said ten past twelve?

A. Like I said.

Q. Did the bank clock have its hands?

A. Sure. That's how you know what time it is.

Q. Did the clock have hands? Remember you are under oath and most everyone in this courtroom knows that the bank clock was out of commission for repairs and its hands were missing for several months around the end of the year.

A. Well, I asked somebody.

Q. Who?

A. I don't know. Somebody.

Q. All right, we'll leave that. But you are sure that was the time when you left the youth party at the church? Remember, you are under oath.

A. Like I said. Ten past twelve.

Q. Did you hear Pastor Lowry's testimony this morning?

A. I been waiting in the witness room all morning. You ought to know that.

Q. You're right. I ought. So you did not hear him say that the youth party broke up long before midnight?

A. How would he know? He wasn't there.

Q. According to the church-hall record book you weren't there either. Were you there?

A. Damn right I was. I don't care what the damned record book says.

Q. Now, Mr. Thrimble, did you have a pistol with you at any time that night?

A. I sure didn't.

Q. Did Junior Powell or any of your friends carry a pistol?

A. Hell, no.

The Court: Watch your language, young man. I have overlooked your profanity up to now, but I shall not overlook it again.

A. Yes, sir.

Q. I believe you said you have never been to Miss Emma's Home Away from Home for Respectable Ladies and Gentlemen. Do you stand by that statement? Again, remember you are under oath.

A. I sure do stand by it. It's the truth.

Q. And do you stand by your statement that neither you nor Junior Powell nor any of your friends carried a gun on New Year's Eve?

A. You heard me.

Q. Do you stand by the statement?

A. Yes.

Frelinghausen returned to the defense table to pick up another set of papers before asking the next question. He smiled at Major Wilkes, who tried to smile back but managed only a grimace.

Mr. Frelinghausen: Are you a football player, Mr. Thrimble?

A. You bet.

Q. Were you a member of the football team at Mingus High during last year's season?

A. Sure was. Right end.

Q. And was Junior Powell also on the squad?

A. You bet. He was left end.

Q. How many games did you play in?

A. About all of them, I reckon.

Q. For a total of two, all season?

A. Huh?

Q. You played in the first two games of the season, didn't you?

A. Sure.

Q. And so did Junior Powell, did he not?

A. That's right.

Q. Did you and Junior play in any later games?

A. You bet.

Q. Which games?

A. I don't remember.

Q. Your Honor, I have here the official rosters for each of the five other games Mingus High played. I would like to suspend cross-examination of this witness and enter the rosters in the record, along with an article that appeared in the *Times*.

Judge Bronson sent both the jury and the witness out of the room while Hang'im Bill argued against having the rosters entered.

After the judge overruled him, Frelinghausen called Coach Cletus Hanson of the Mingus Tigers football team to testify as to their accuracy and that of the *Times* article.

Q. Coach Hanson, is it true, as your rosters indicate, that Jimmy Thrimble and Junior Powell played in only two games last year?

A. I am sorry to say, that is true.

Q. And is the *Times* article accurate in reference to young Powell and Thrimble?

A. It is.

Jimmy Thrimble returned to the courtroom and to the stand. Frelinghausen handed him the rosters one by one. Jimmy pointed out his name and Junior Powell's on the first two rosters.

Frelinghausen handed him the final three.

Mr. Frelinghausen: Look over these, please, Mr. Thrimble. Can you point out your name and Junior's?

A. Well, I guess somebody left them out.

Q. Are you saying you and Junior played in those games even though your names are not on the roster?

A. That's right.

Q. Would you read this newspaper clipping, Mr. Thrimble, and tell me if you find your name.

A. Well—

Q. Is your name mentioned there, Mr. Thrimble, near the end of the *Times'*s story about the third game of the season, with Elmer High School?

A. Yeah, but it ain't right. Newspapers never get nothing right.

Q. Please read what is said there at the end about you.

A. I told you, it ain't right.

The Court: Read the reference, Mr. Thrimble.

A. "Neither Jimmy Thrimble nor Junior Powell dressed for the game. Coach Cletus ('Heavy') Hanson declined to explain their absence." That's a damn lie.

The Court: I have warned you. I do not allow profanity in my court, Mr. Thrimble. I shall hold you in contempt of court next time.

Q. So the *Times* got it wrong. Tell me, Mr. Thrimble, did you play in the game against Elmer?

A. I sure did. Junior, too.

Q Mr. Thrimble, Coach Hanson testified otherwise a few moments ago. Are you calling him a liar?

A. Old Heavy don't know his ass from a hole in the ground. Never did.

Over Senator Gross's objections, Judge Bronson sent the jury out again and ordered young Thrimble booked for contempt. As the bailiff seized the boy's arms, Barney Thrimble, the department-store magnate, rose in the audience and, swathed in raccoon skins that doubled his size, rumbled up the aisle, shouting that no one could do that to his son.

"You, sir, are also in contempt of court," Judge Bronson said. "Bailiff, remove that person to my chambers along with his son."

The bailiff let go of Jimmy Thrimble and seized the father. Barney Thrimble resisted, and it took the bailiff, Billy Bowen, and another deputy to subdue him.

Female Thrimbles in the audience screamed. Jimmy Thrimble dashed down the aisle to the exit, where other deputies stopped him. He sniffled and Barney Thrimble shouted obscenities as the bailiff and deputies hustled them, handcuffed, to the judge's chambers. Judge Bronson put down his gavel and left the bench, taking the court reporter and attorneys with him. Court resumed a half-hour later, but before calling the jury back Judge Bronson ordered the bailiff to produce the Thrimbles.

Judge Bronson turned first to the father. "I understand you wish to say something to the court, Mr. Thrimble."

Thrimble was still red-faced. He kept his head down and seemed to be addressing the crack between the base of the bench and the stage.

"Yes, sir."

"I can't hear you. Speak up."

"Yes, sir. I want to apologize to the court, sir. I was wrong to do what I done, sir, and I will not do it again. I would like to ask you to suspend the sentence you imposed on me in your office."

"And what was that sentence, Mr. Thrimble?"

"Thirty days in the county jail, sir, and a $100 fine."

Judge Bronson suspended the jail time, but not the fine. "And I do not want to see you in this courtroom again. Bailiff, have this man escorted out of the building."

Back on the witness stand, Jimmy Thrimble wiped his eyes and nose with his kerchief. As cross-examination resumed, he admitted that he and Junior Powell had been fired from the football team, had not been near the Methodist church on New Year's Eve, but had spent the evening drinking with other friends in the new "rumpus room" of the Powell home, in the absence of Junior's parents. He also admitted that he and his friends had "maybe caused some trouble" at a local business establishment near the end of their spree. They had been denied liquid refreshment by the proprietress and had gone forth to seek it elsewhere.

Judge Bronson's gavel was unable to quell the buzz that broke out after Jimmy's next admission.

Mr. Frelinghausen: Mr. Thrimble, you have sworn that no one in your group had a pistol on New Year's Eve? Would you like to correct that statement?

A. Yes, sir. Junior had his daddy's old pistol with him.

Q. Was his pistol a Model 3 Smith & Wesson with an eight-inch barrel and smooth wood grips?

A. That sounds right.

(Counsel picks up Exhibit No. 13, hands it to witness.)

Q. Do you recognize this gun?

A. Yes, sir.

Q. Was this the gun Junior was carrying on New Year's Eve?

A. Yes, sir.

Q. Did Junior strike a Mr. Smith over the head with the gun
   that night?

A. Yes, sir.

Q. Did Junior fire his gun during the evening?

A. Yes, sir.

Q. Did he fire it in front of the Grand Hotel?

A. Yes, sir. He knocked Deputy Bowen's hat off.

Q. And did he fire again just before he died?

A. Yes, sir.

Q. Thank you. No more questions.

When Frelinghausen returned to his seat, Major Wilkes whispered a question. "Why didn't Gross object to any of that?"

"For the same reason he's not going to cross-examine. He doesn't want to step in that tar pit. Only thing he wants out of Junior Powell now is silence."

Judge Bronson sent the jury out and called the lawyers to the bench, where he chastised Hang'im Bill for having relied on perjured testimony. Senator Gross assured the court that he had been misled as egregiously as the judge and apologized profusely.

While he was at the bench, he asked for a further conference before calling the prosecution's next witness. Sheriff James was called to join the discussion. There followed the usual long period, when spectators could hear nothing and see little save pounding fists and pointing fingers. Then several deputies hauled in screens, placing them from the judge's entrance to the witness chair. They set up more screens in front and at the sides of the chair. Only the judge would be able to see the witness.

"What's going on?" Major Wilkes asked when Frelinghausen returned to the defense table.

"Gross is calling Seth Ringle."

"The jackrabbit?"

"The jackrabbit. I joined the senator in favor of concealing Seth's identity, because that was the only way to protect Sophie. The judge finally agreed."

"Why was Sheriff James involved?"

"Seth wouldn't testify unless the sheriff agreed not to bring any charges against him for organizing a lynching party. And I had to make the same promise to keep hands off as county attorney."

"I don't like it."

"Neither do I, but Gross has a right to raise the marksmanship question, because the sheriff brought it up in his testimony. Even if Ringle refused to say a word on the stand — which he could, on self-incrimination grounds — the cat would be out of the bag. I had to go along."

Judge Bronson, adjusting his pince-nez, read a statement telling the jury that the next witness's identity would not be revealed, an unusual move justified by the need to protect certain innocent parties from exposure. He assured them, however, that he, the lawyers, and the accused knew who was testifying and had agreed to the arrangements. The jurymen were not to concern themselves with the witness's identity or the effort to conceal it.

There were sounds of movement behind the screens. Only the bailiff was tall enough for his head to be seen as he guided the witness to his chair and administered the oath.

The Court: Senator Gross, you may proceed.

Sen. Gross: Thank you, Your Honor. Now sir, I understand that you have recent personal knowledge of the defendant's prowess as a marksman. Is that right?

A. I seen it up close, you might say.

Q. Excellent. And was this demonstration by any chance at the JPG ranch?

A. That's right.

Q. Now, you need not give us all the particulars about the occasion, but what, in essence, did you observe?

A. I seen him shoot a jackrabbit dead with one shot. Right in mid-air.

The Court: Silence! I will not have this whispering in my court. Bailiff, eject any spectator you see moving his or her lips. Please resume, Senator.

Q. Tell us more, sir. Was the appearance of the animal expected?

A. Sure wasn't. The jack's hiding in some sagebrush, see? He bounces up out of the bush all of a sudden right at the defendant's feet. Makes two big jumps out into the open, right in front of me. That big old jack's so high in the air he looks like he's flying. The defendant draws and shoots. And before that there jack hits the ground he's deader'n a doornail. Never seen shooting like that, not even Buffalo Bill.

Q. And you are sure that the gun slinger—

Mr. Frelinghausen: Objection.

Q. I shall rephrase the question. Are you sure the man who pulled the trigger of a pistol and killed this jackrabbit in mid-flight, so to speak, was the defendant in this case? I know you can't see him, but—

A. I don't need to see him. I know him, all right, a whole lot better than I ever wanted to. He butted into a private discussion where he wasn't wanted and interfered with a citizen trying to exercise his right to make a citizen's arrest of a black son of a bitch who trifled with my daughter.

The Court: That will do. And I warn the witness that I do not tolerate obscenity in my court.

Sen. Gross: No more questions.

Mr. Frelinghausen: I have no questions for this witness, Your Honor. However, I should like to request that the witness's last sentence be stricken from the record as irrelevant to this case.

The Court: So ordered. The jury is instructed to put it out of their minds.

Sen. Gross: The prosecution rests, Your Honor. I have no further witnesses at this time.

The Court: It is now ten minutes after noon. The court will be in recess, to resume at 2:00 o'clock.

Minnie and Lorena joined Major Wilkes and Charley Frelinghausen in the hall.

"Take it easy, Will," Frelinghausen said.

"How could he do it? Her own father! Destroying her reputation like that." Lorena hugged him. "There, there," she said.

Minnie hugged him, too. "He's a cruel man. But it's done. Everyone who knows her will know it's not true."

"But the gossip! It'll kill her, Grandma."

"Sophie's got backbone, dear. And anyway, by now it's old gossip and won't last long."

Charley Frelinghausen said, "I'll see what I can do." He didn't say what that might be.

27.

AFTER THE NOON RECESS Mrs. McSorley appeared in the courtroom and sat between Minnie and Lorena in the first row. Major Wilkes, already at the defense table, went to greet her.

"I am here," she said, "to show the flag after her father's outrageous betrayal of Sophie this morning."

Before the jury came in Frelinghausen moved to dismiss the charges against his client, giving Major Wilkes a glimmer of hope.

The judge refused, giving no reason, and Frelinghausen called the first witness for the defense, J. Isaac ("Ike") Watson, owner and manager of the Grand Hotel. He testified about what he had seen and heard at his hotel on that New Year's Eve in Mingus, but guardedly.

It had been relatively quiet until well after midnight, he said, when "some disorderly youths" came by.

Q. What were these disorderly youths doing?

A. Oh, shouting, demanding booze, that sort of thing. You know kids.

Q. Did you recognize these disorderly youths?

A. Oh, I'd seen some of them around, I suppose.

Q. But you knew some of them by name?

A. Well, not that I recall, no.

Q. Didn't you mention a couple of names to Sheriff James?

A. I might have, in the excitement of the moment, but afterward I realized I couldn't be sure I was right.

Q. And what were the names you might have mentioned?

A. I don't rightly remember.

Q. Was one of them Junior Powell and another Jimmy Thrimble?

A. Like I said, I don't rightly remember.

Q. I see. Did you tell the sheriff these youths, whoever they were, were endangering your guests?

A. Well, disturbing maybe is a better word. High jinks, maybe.

Q. We have had testimony that shots were fired at your hotel, Lights and windows were broken by bullets. Did that happen?

A. Yes.

Q. Did those "high jinks" not endanger your guests?

A. Yes, I suppose they might have, but nobody got hurt.

Q. Mr. Watson, was the shooting done by the disorderly youths you mentioned?

A. Well, you know, I didn't actually see who fired them shots, you know.

Q. Ike—Mr. Watson—you do recall a fatal shooting, a death, in front of your hotel that night, don't you?

A. Sure I do. But I don't know nothing about it.

Q. Your Honor, I have no further questions for this witness.

Senator Gross, smiling, rose to cross-examine the witness. He had a large sheaf of papers in his hand. He studied the papers for a long moment before he said, "Thank you for your fine testimony today, Mr. Watson. I have no questions for you."

"Gutless," Frelinghausen whispered to Major Wilkes. "Mayor Powell and his pals got to him. I always thought Ike was a better man than that."

Major Wilkes felt the noose tighten.

Frelinghausen next called his own window-dressers. They came from both Owchicta and Hardcastle County to attest to Major Wilkes's reputation as a Christian gentleman of good family and good behavior, well trained in the duties of his office, and thoughtful in his dealings with the public.

Among the character witnesses was Abraham Fincus. He praised Major Wilkes's judgment and restraint in not shooting him when, as the old fellow put it, he was "non compis mental" with drink and fired his pistol at the statue of Justice.

"He could've kilt me, and rightly so, but he didn't. He just talked me out of it."

On cross-examination Senator Gross asked, "Mr. Fincus, as you sit there under oath in the witness chair, can you swear you are sober?"

"Yes sir, but I hope it won't be for long."

Even the judge and Major Wilkes laughed. Senator Gross did not. "No more questions."

Sheriff James was called a second time, this time as a witness for the defense, and delivered an encomium of Major Wilkes that brought tears to the eyes of Lorena and Minnie.

Frelinghausen used the sheriff's further testimony to review for the jury the familiar facts about what actually happened on the night Junior Powell was killed. The sheriff emphasized again that it was he who ordered "Will" to return fire after the officers and others were shot at from a dark street.

To the surprise even of Major Wilkes, Frelinghausen next called Mrs. Euphrates Smith.

Miss Emma's appearance set off a buzz—quickly gaveled down—among jurors as well as spectators. Settling herself in the witness chair, she removed black mittens, revealing white gloves, and nodded at Frelinghausen as though she were the headmistress of a private school, secure in her respectability, and he a student preparing to recite.

After establishing that Mrs. Smith was a long-time businesswoman in Mingus—"I was here when Mingus was six tents and a corral"—Frelinghausen asked if she had known Junior Powell.

A. Very slightly. Mayor Powell, who is my landlord, introduced his son to me on the boy's 16th birthday, and I saw him occasionally at church.

Q. Did you see him in the early hours of January 1 of this year?

A. I did.

Q. Tell us about that.

A. At about 1:30 a.m. or thereabouts, I heard a great commotion at the front door. I was in my kitchen enjoying a bedtime snack and rushed to the front. Eight or ten drunken young men led by Junior Powell and Jimmy Thrimble, whom I had also met on his 16th birthday, had used my landlord's key to enter the premises. My husband tried to stop them, and they attacked him. When I got to the door, Junior Powell was standing over him, beating him on the head with the butt of a gun, rendering him unconscious. A number of my resident ladies tried to help my husband. Junior and his friends seized the ladies, mauled them, ripped their clothes, and—ah—mistreated them. It was terrible. Terrible!

The Court: Compose yourself, Ma'am. Take your time. Bailiff, bring the witness a glass of water.

A. Thank you, Your Honor, I am all right. Junior Powell demanded more liquor for himself and his friends and declared that his father would close down my business if I did not comply with his wishes. I refused and warned him that I would tell his father what they were doing. Junior and his friends finally left. The next morning I heard about his tragic death.

Q. Did you tell Mayor Powell about the events of that evening?

A. I did, though reluctantly, immediately after reading in the *Times* what the mayor said on learning about the death of his son. I realized that he did not know the truth. Painful though it was, it seemed imperative as a matter of business that he should know exactly what had occurred on and to property he owns.

Q. What did Mr. Powell say about the information you gave him?

A. He said he could not and would not believe a word of it.

Q. Thank you, Mrs. Smith. I have no further questions. Your witness, Senator.

Sen. Gross.   Now, Miss Emma —

The Court: Please address the witness by her proper title, Senator.

Sen. Gross.   Mrs. Smith, you say you spoke to Mayor Powell on this matter. Have you proof of that?

A. My word is my proof, Senator, and it has never been successfully challenged.

Q. As to the key you claim these so-called unruly youths used to enter. How do you know whose key it was?

A. The only key to my premises that I did not control was one I had given my landlord, Mayor Powell. I demanded how they got it. Junior Powell boasted that he had "snitched" his father's key. That was his word — snitched. Moreover, they had carelessly left the key in the lock. I retrieved it and have retained it.

Q. Now, Mrs. Smith, what kind of business do you conduct at No. 4 Jolly Roger Road?

A. Why, Senator, as you know very well, since you have been my honored guest many times over the years, most recently Saturday evening, it is a quiet, comfortable refuge for respectable ladies and gentlemen, just as the name says. You have often said there is nothing in Mingus you find more enjoyable than an evening spent at my home when you visit your brother-in-law, the mayor, who is not only my landlord but also a valued customer, as he has been for many years.

Q. No further questions, Your Honor.

The Court: Bailiff, eject the entire back row. I will not countenance laughter in my court. Mr. Frelinghausen, your next witness, please.

"MISS SOPHIA RINGLE," the bailiff roared, setting off a greater courtroom bustle than even Miss Emma's appearance had created.

"Damn! Why did you do this to her?" Major Wilkes asked Frelinghausen.

"She asked to testify and her aunt agreed."

"I don't like it."

"Don't worry. She'll do fine."

Sophie entered, not from the witness room, but the judge's chambers.

Dressed for the cold, she wore a black coat and black gloves. Her hat was also black, with a broad brim and black veil. As the clerk of the court administered the oath Sophie threw back the veil. Gripping the chair's arms, she buried the tips of her gloved fingers in the lion mouths carved there. She did not look at Major Wilkes.

Frelinghausen walked up close to the witness stand, positioning himself so that when she looked at him she would also be looking at the jury.

"Miss Ringle, may I ask how old you are?"

"I will be 18 in February, sir."

"Were you subpoenaed to appear?"

"No, sir. I asked to testify."

"And why did you wish to testify?'

"For two reasons, sir. First, I did something foolish two months ago that could have led to a man's death if Deputy Gower had not intervened and I wanted to tell about it so that people would know what a wise and gentle person he is. Second, I learned that a member of my family said something about me in court this morning that is false and will blacken my reputation forever if I don't correct it now."

Hang'im Bill leaped to his feet.

"I object, Your Honor. There can be no conceivable connection between this young woman's alleged problem in September and the murder—I beg your pardon—the *death* of Junior Powell nearly a year ago. Furthermore, she has revealed the identity of a witness who testified only on the court's assurance of anonymity."

Judge Bronson called the attorneys to the bench. Sophie pulled down her veil. She sat clutching the lions' heads while the lawyers shoved fingers at one another and pounded fists on the bench. Major Wilkes felt that she was looking at him through the veil and he smiled—a real smile, not one that felt like he was bending leather.

In a few minutes Senator Gross, shaking his head, returned to his seat. Sophie lifted her veil.

Judge Bronson said, "You may proceed, Mr. Frelinghausen."

"Now, Miss Ringle, what was the 'foolish thing' you did two months ago? Just tell the jury in your own way and take all the time you need.

She spoke haltingly at first and softly. Judge Bronson asked her to speak louder.

"I'm sorry. Is this better?"

"Indeed it is. Please continue."

She told her story much as Major Wilkes had first heard it, leaving nothing out—how Seth had come home and found her with two friends, Jimmy Thrimble and Horse Crosby.

"We were sitting in swings on the side porch, acting silly, laughing, and making lots of noise, when we heard my father's motorcar stop in front of the house. The boys had left their horses in the grove of trees behind the house. They jumped over the railing and were running for their horses when my father came around the corner of the house. It was moonlight and he could see them. He fired his shotgun, both barrels, but missed.

"They rode off real fast. He rushed up on the porch and grabbed me. He shook me and asked who he was. I told him it was Jimmy and Horse, but he wouldn't listen. He said he had seen him and it just one man and a colored man at that. He started slapping me, yelling 'Who was he? *Who? Who?'* He called me names, awful names, and accused me of doing all sorts of things—things I had never even heard of before. And he was slapping me in the face and all over. He was drunk, awful drunk. I had never seen him like that. I had always loved him."

She broke down, sobbing. Judge Bronson offered to call a recess, but she shook her head, blew her nose, and told him she was all right and wanted to go on.

"Finally I couldn't stand it anymore. I told him, yes, it was a colored man. I thought it was safe to say that, because I didn't know of any colored in the county.

"He called Deputy Gower, who came right away. But my father ordered him off the property when he said he needed to hear my story from me. Deputy Gower said he wouldn't turn anyone he arrested over to my father but would take him to jail for trial. That made Daddy madder than ever. He ordered Deputy Gower off the property and locked me in my room. He said there were some Pullman porters at the Rocking JPG and he was going to kill them all.

"I realized I had done a terrible thing—that he was going to kill an innocent man, maybe more than one, because of the stupid things I had done and said. I should never have invited a couple of silly boys to visit me without his permission. I'm ashamed to admit that I didn't ask permission because I knew he wouldn't approve. I waited until he drove away, then I saddled Big Sam, our best horse, and rode to Deputy Sheriff Gower's office by a back way as fast as I could. Deputy Gower was very kind and gentle and didn't scold me, though I had done a terrible thing. He took me to my Aunt Agnes McSorley in Mingus and then went off alone to stop my father before anyone got hurt."

> Mr. Frelinghausen: You say you went by a back way from your home to the sheriff's office at Ringle. Why was that?
>
> A. Because I didn't want my aunts and uncles who live down near the feed lots and store to hear me and tell my father.
>
> Q. You also said that your father locked you in your room. How did you get out?
>
> A. My Aunt Sarah Ringle let me out.

Q. Didn't you tell Deputy Gower that you picked the lock with a hairpin?

A. Yes sir. Aunt Sarah was really scared of my father. She was afraid what he might do if he knew she had helped me and asked me not to say anything about it. But today after she heard what my father said in court about me being 'trifled with,' Aunt Sarah called me to say it was all right to tell the whole story, that she's got some money saved up and would be all right even if he kicks her out.

Q. Was there something else your Aunt Sarah Ringle did for you that night that you have not told us?

A. Yes, there is. Aunt Sarah likes to go to bed real early, but whenever I invited boys to visit when my father was gone, she would stay up. She always fixed lemonade and cookies, and that's what she did that night, too. She was there the whole time.

Q. Did she tell your father that?

A. She tried to, but my father wouldn't listen to her. He told her to shut up and go to bed.

Q. Is there anything further you would like to tell us?

A. I understand my father claimed in this courtroom today that I was "trifled with." That is not true. It was an innocent evening, as Aunt Sarah can tell you, and nothing happened to me except what my father did. I don't know what else would have happened to me that night if Deputy Gower had not helped a foolish girl who had caused so much trouble get to a safe place before he went off alone to save the life of an innocent man. And he did it without hurting anything but a jackrabbit. A lot of terrible things have been said about him here. I want people to know that they are not true. He is a good man, the best man I have ever known.

Q. Have you seen your father since that night, Miss Ringle?

A. No, sir. He has disowned me and I now make my home
with my Aunt Agnes, Mrs. McSorley, here in Mingus.

Q. I have no further questions.

Sen. Gross: No questions, Your Honor.

Sophie pulled down her veil and left the stand, not by way
of the judge's chambers, but down the main aisle. She held her
head high and did not hurry. Mrs. McSorley, Minnie, and
Lorena joined her in the aisle and left with her.

"At least he didn't cross-examine her," Major Wilkes said.

"He's too smart for that," Frelinghausen said.

MANY IN THE COURTROOM, including members of the jury,
expected Major Wilkes to take the stand next. But their hopes
for a lively cross-examination by Hang'im Bill were
disappointed. Frelinghausen rested the defense's case as soon as
Sophie Ringle left the courtroom, followed by her aunt.

The prosecution also rested.

Judge Bronson announced that final arguments would be
heard the next morning, Tuesday, and adjourned court.

"Why didn't you let me testify?" Major Wilkes asked
Charley Frelinghausen. "I look like a coward?"

"I didn't call you because I didn't need to. Believe me, Will,
this is a smart jury. Thanks to that puffed-up windbag's own
witnesses they know what Junior Powell was really like.
Tearing down a dead man's reputation is a terrible thing. Juries
don't like it. We couldn't open an attack on Junior, but after our
simpleton preacher and the Thrimbles dealt out a pack of lies
we were able to bring out the truth about Junior by refuting
their lies with honest witnesses—Sheriff James, Mrs. Smith,
your Sophie, and even old Fincus. You're as good as free."

"You always say not to count on a jury until the foreman
speaks."

"That's true as a rule, Major Wilkes, but this time count on it."

It was the first time Frelinghausen had called him anything but Will. But Major Wilkes was not encouraged. Amos's words rang in his head.

"Hanging jury."

28.

TUESDAY DAWNED SUNNY, cold, and windless. Would-be spectators stood for hours on the steps and in the square out front, stomping their feet in yesterday's snow, waiting for the courthouse to open. Once inside, they found that the furnace had been repaired. Heat poured from it as though it were roasting turkeys. Without wind to blast refreshing drafts of cold air around the windows, the courtroom was stifling when Judge Bronson invited Senator Gross to sum up the prosecution's case.

The senator rose. He took a gold watch out of a black vest's pocket, snapped its top open, and held it out before him as far as its chain would allow. It was 8:38 a.m., although the senator did not announce that fact. He snapped the watch shut and restored it to his pocket.

Pulling down his vest he approached the jury box. He stopped in front of the foreman and stared unblinkingly into the man's eyes. Saying not a word, he moved to the next juror, the next, the next. Some blinked, some looked away, but all seemed to shrink before that unrelenting gaze. He thrust a fist into the air and unfolded an index finger until it pointed straight up. Slowly, slowly he brought the finger down and aimed it at each juror in turn, saying nothing and holding his breath until his face changed from florid to bright red. Still pointing, he expelled his breath in a shout:

"Gentlemen of the jury!"

Even Judge Bronson recoiled. Major Wilkes forgot where the finger was pointing and felt that every eye in the courtroom had turned on him. Senator Gross continued in a voice so low that he could barely be heard but gradually increasing its volume and timbre.

"You have a momentous decision before you, my friends, a decision that will mark each man-jack of you as a free man or a slave to the powers that be, wrapped in chains, mired in great puddles of incongruity, of puzzlement, of multitudinous lies and libels against a dead boy, the beloved son of a bereaved mother, innocently celebrating the coming of a New Year and the coming of the third year of statehood for our great state of Oklahoma, struck down in the spring of his existence by a merciless killer, and that decision you must make is whether the trigger-happy Texan gun-for-hire sitting there in the guise of a lawman—" the pointing finger moved to Major Wilkes "—that champion gun slinger who took from us all that dearly beloved young man, one of our own—*murdered* him in cold blood on a dark night—in a word, whether this desperado now looking blandly at you—indeed, looking so smugly at you—should or should not be made to pay the penalty for the young and valuable life he took from Junior Powell—took when you stop to think of it not just from Junior but from his heart-broken family, from Hardcastle County, from Oklahoma, from this great country of the United States of America—from, when all is said and done, from us all and from the world that was a better place before this beast from Texas savagely slew our Junior Powell."

All this Hang'im Bill poured forth in one window-rattling roar with no stops and scarcely a breath.

Clasping his hands to form a megaphone around his lips, he continued by again lowering his voice to a whisper that the jurors strained to hear. Some even cupped their hands behind their ears, the better to catch every linguistic pearl shot forth by the prosecutorial lips. "The choice is yours, gentlemen of the jury, the choice is yours: Will you vindicate Junior Powell and hang his despicable killer, or will you let him go free, mayhap to kill you or mayhap your son or who knows whom on another day?"

Hang'im Bill continued to alternate between bellows and whispers, with gestures so sweeping that at times he appeared to be pumping air into his lungs with his arms or fencing with an unseen adversary, lunging and parrying.

In three hours of exertion in the overheated courtroom, he worked up such a sweat that jurors were forced to shield themselves from the spray as he paced back and forth before them, waving his arms and swinging about from time to time to point his sword-like finger at the defendant as he condemned the "hasty, reckless, uncalled-for action by a gun-slinging Texan, a vicious gunman masquerading as an officer of the law."

He did not dwell on the circumstances or details of Junior's death, saying only that the truth of who shot whom was too well-known to need repeating. Time after time he deplored what he called the defense strategy of attempting to "defame the memory and blacken the reputation of a model son and exemplary human being, cruelly cut off in the prime of his youth by a barbarian from Texas."

Frelinghausen objected sparingly, winning some points, losing others. Twice Judge Bronson gaveled the senator down before Frelinghausen could get on his feet. The first time was when Hang'im Bill declared that Major Wilkes had a record of interfering with the rights of ordinary citizens to defend themselves. He added, "Remember, it was the defendant who shot and killed a jackrabbit at the Rocking JPG as he sought to prevent a citizen's arrest of a Negro rapist." After a long wrangle at the bench, Judge Bronson ruled that the statement should be stricken from the record and the minds of the jury.

Even the jackrabbit had to go. Senator Gross bowed to the judge, smiled at the jury, and returned to extolling the virtues of Junior Powell.

The judge again reined him after he asked the jury "to keep in mind that beyond question or any reasonable doubt Junior Powell, the very paragon of a young Oklahoma gentleman, was the innocent victim of a vicious Texas marksman, a professional killer who smiled as he pulled the trigger to smite down one of the finest young men who ever drew breath in Hardcastle County." He swung around and pointed. "Look! Look at him — look at the Gun-Slinging Champion of Owchicta County, Texas, smiling even now!"

Major Wilkes was not smiling. Senator Gross was forced by the judge to acknowledge his error.

Major Wilkes had begun to find the repetitious attacks on him tiresome and hoped the jury would feel the same. But he felt the noose tighten around his neck when the great orator abruptly quit orating and attacked the defense case head-on.

He asserted that ownership of the Smith & Wesson the sheriff found in the street had not been established. Junior Powell had denied that it was his, and no persuasive evidence or testimony connected him with it, except that of a frightened young witness who was testifying under duress. Smith & Wesson revolvers of that vintage were no rarity in Mingus. Sheriff James had not seen the gun thrown. He had only heard it hit the road.

"The one established fact known about the ownership of the gun in the road," Senator Gross said, "Is that when Junior

Powell declared as he lay dying that he had never seen it, he added, 'I swear to God.' Those are powerful words, coming as they did from a religious boy facing death. Junior would not have used them lightly. Remember those words, gentlemen of the jury. '*I . . . swear . . . to . . . God!*'"

He then asserted that the defense had failed to prove that Junior had not attended the youth party at the Methodist church.

"Much was made of a church record book and what was supposed to be entered in it. But we never learned important—nay, essential—facts about that record, not even who was in charge of taking the roll and noting the time the party ended. Nor did we learn whether in fact the responsible party could swear under oath that he or she took a complete roll and accurately recorded the time the party ended and who attended. All we know for certain about the church party is that a frightened young witness whose memory was befuddled by the defense attorney's cruel bullying was forced to change his sworn testimony."

Frelinghausen objected, but Judge Bronson overruled him.

"Even more telling," Hang'im Bill continued, "is how little we were told about what happened that evening at Miss Emma's Home Away from Home for Respectable Ladies and Gentlemen. What little we know from direct testimony about those alleged events came from the confused recollections of young Thrimble and from the proprietress of that so-called 'Home,' to which others might apply another name, who was clearly more interested in concealing the true nature of the place than in speak king the truth."

"*Objection!*"

"Overruled. You may proceed, Senator."

"As I say, we heard from only two witnesses, one confused and another whose interest lay in telling as little as possible about what happened that fateful night, while claiming that a great deal did happen. We did not learn who brought the report to the sheriff. We did not even learn her identity. Why was she not called to testify? And what about the other young women at the so-called 'Home,' what did they see and hear? How were they, as we were told, 'mistreated' by these young boys? Not one of those witnesses was called to testify under oath what happened to her, if anything, that fateful evening.

"Be not swayed, gentlemen of the jury, by unproved and unsupported allegations of misconduct. Put the incident entirely from your minds—it has no place in the judgment you must make. Did or did not a cold-blooded killer, hiding behind a lawman's badge, murder Junior Powell? That is the question, the only question, before you."

Senator Gross appeared ready to conclude his address to the jury. But he shied away and, arms flailing, roamed again through rhetorical byways. After a final recitation of Junior Powell's virtues and the great things the boy might have achieved had he lived, he added horns to his portrait of Major Wilkes by charging that the cowardly lawman sought to hide behind the skirts of a naive young woman with no connection to the case.

Concluding at last, Hang'im Bill pulled a hangman's noose from his pocket. With tears or sweat—it wasn't clear which—running down and dripping off his cheeks and nose, he leaned into the jury box waving the noose.

"HANG'IM!" he roared. "Drop him through the trapdoor to hang by the neck till he is dead, dead, *dead*—and let the vultures peck his eyes out! HANG'IM, I say. HANG'IM! *HANG'IM!*"

The dead boy's family wept with him and rose as one, clapping as Senator Gross bowed and Judge Bronson hammered.

THE MORNING SESSION ended late. In the afternoon, Charley Frelinghausen spoke for 50 minutes, spending most of the time doggedly reviewing the factual evidence the jury had heard. Relying heavily on the testimony of Jimmy Thrimble—"a participant in a drunken rampage, a friend of the dead boy and, as you saw, a reluctant witness"—he reconstructed what he called "a reckless evening of youthful excess that ended in tragedy." He said nothing about Junior Powell's unsavory past and expressed sympathy for "the bereaved parents and family of a young man whose untimely death sadly dashed their hopes and expectations."

He asked the jury to consider the situation the defendant found himself in when he fired the fatal shot.

"A band of boys of good families, their judgment impaired by drink they should never have been able to obtain, roamed the public streets, firing pistols indiscriminately—firing into the windows of an occupied hotel, firing even at an officer of the law, and succeeding in knocking off his hat. Only an inch or two lower, and that bullet would have gone into his head. No one could condone such irresponsible behavior, no matter by whom. When yet another shot was fired from the dark street in the direction of the officers—a shot that broke still another hotel window—Sheriff James ordered Deputy Gower, 'Take him, Will.'

"What would you have done, gentlemen of the jury? Would you have refused to obey the lawful order of your superior officer to stop an armed lawbreaker—not knowing whether he might be man, boy, saint or sinner—who was at that very moment shooting at you, endangering your life and the lives of others? You would do the only proper thing, just as Deputy Will Gower did. You would do your duty—you would 'take him' to the best of your ability. I ask you to consider carefully all the evidence in this sad case and acquit Deputy Major Wilkes

Gower of the unjustified charge of murder."

Judge Bronson's instructions to the jury took an hour and a half. Few spectators left the courtroom; most seemed to expect a quick verdict, one way or the other.

Sheriff James took Major Wilkes down to his office to wait. Frelinghausen, Minnie, and Lorena joined them.

Major Wilkes told the lawyer that he thought his restrained summation had been brilliant, and the others agreed. But Major Wilkes doubted the outcome. He could not bring himself to believe that Hardcastle minds could withstand the assault on reason launched by the Demosthenes of the Senate as he scaled oratorical heights not previously ascended in Hardcastle County.

He paced the floor, avoiding the sympathetic murmurings of his mother and Minnie, and steeled himself for the moment when the jury would file in, eyes averted from him, and the foreman would announce: "We find the defendant, Major Wilkes Gower, guilty of murder as charged." *Crwrgh! Eeghwr. Hrckk. Hrckk. Crwrgh!*

After two hours, with the jury still out, Minnie and Lorena also began to dread the outcome. The case was so clear! Men with any sense should have reached a verdict of acquittal without even closing the door of the jury room! They feared that Major Wilkes's heroic action in preventing the lynching of the Pullman porter was now threatening their dear boy's own life, just as Amos predicted.

It was another hour before the bailiff sent word that the jury was coming in.

The sun was long down and the courtroom was dim, lighted only by the shadow-casting bare bulbs strung overhead. Major Wilkes took his place at the defense table.

Minnie and Lorena, wearing the beflowered and beribboned bonnets they had worn throughout the trial, were in their usual front-row seats. Senator Gross strolled in, wearing his red vest and surrounded by Junior Powell's family. The senator looked over at Major Wilkes, shook his head, patted his vest, and smiled.

Major Wilkes looked away. He ran a finger under his collar, amusing the spectators crowding in.

The jury entered, a single file of twelve solemn-faced men in Sunday-go-to-meeting clothes, except for a couple of bib-overalls over flannel shirts.

The foreman was the farm-equipment dealer. He handed a folded paper to the bailiff, who handed it to Judge Bronson. Light from the nearest bare bulb bounced off the judge's Teddy Roosevelt nose-pinchers in the midst of Lincolnesque whiskers as the judge studied the verdict.

Charley Frelinghausen nudged Major Wilkes.

"For God's sake keep your hands away from your neck. And smile! We're going to win this and I want you to look like you know it."

Major Wilkes hooked his thumbs in his belt and tried to smile but could not. He dared not open his lips too wide for fear he would vomit.

When he heard "Not guilty," he put his head on the table and cried.

He felt sure the foreman had handed the judge the wrong folded paper, though Charlie Frelinghausen and Sheriff James were beating him on the back and shoulders. Not even the shrieks of the Powell family and friends and the sight of Hang'im Bill in his lucky red vest sitting with his mouth open, unable to speak, made the gift of life seem real.

When Major Wilkes finally managed to thank Frelinghausen, the lawyer shook his head.

"The only thing I needed to do, Major Wilkes, was get you a jury of good sensible folks who wouldn't be bowled over by the folderol old Hang'im served up. I knew we deserved to win on the facts, and he cinched it."

Lorena, Minnie, and Mrs. McSorley swarmed through the watching crowd to hug, laugh, and weep with Major Wilkes. In their wake came Sophie. She seized his shoulders, stood on tiptoe, and kissed him on the mouth. Major Wilkes suddenly found it easy to smile. He was alive, Sophie was in his arms, and he was free.

IV. The Hero

29.

A BLIZZARD RAGED, and Owchicta's new municipal power plant failed. Amos came awake to find himself staring into the yellowish light of a coal-oil lamp held over his head. He couldn't make out who held the lamp.

"Mary Nell?"

"She's not coming, Amos."

"She knows?"

"She knows."

"I want to see Mary Nell."

"She doesn't want to see you, Amos. She doesn't want to see either of us, thanks to you." Minnie was talking city, sounding like her mother.

"I don't know, I don't rightly know what I ever done—"

"You've never known, Amos. Not ever. Not right from the start. You have just never known."

It was true.

It was not what he wanted to hear.

He threw back his head and groaned as loudly as he could, hoping for sympathy.

Receiving none, he went back to sleep.

Over the months that Amos lay dying there had been so many false alarms that no one bothered to gather at his bedside unless it was convenient to do so, which it had not been for Major Wilkes. This time the telegram from Eph said,

    DOC SAYS NO HOPE COME NOW YOU
    WANT SEE HIM.

Major Wilkes cranked the Model T he had bought after Eph moved up to the State Senate and a Packard. Ten miles from Owchicta he ran into the blizzard. The wind was so powerful it stripped away the snap-on canvas door on the driver's side. By the time Major Wilkes stomped his feet on Minnie's screened kitchen porch, his sheepskin riding coat—fleece on the inside and split to the tailbone in back—was plastered with blown snow. So was the scarf wrapped around his face. It crackled as he took it off.

The kitchen was hot and crowded—noisy, too, and cloudy with cigar smoke and fumes from candles and a couple of coal-oil lamps that cast flickering light and shadows around the room. The children and grandchildren of Amos's sons and their flibbertigibbet wives swarmed through the house. So many children of early-marrying, long-bearing couples darted in and out of the kitchen that no one could be sure to whom or to which generation any one of them belonged. Most were boys and even the great-grandsons among them favored Amos in both appearance and behavior, as Amos liked to note, Minnie not so much.

Food brought by neighbors and Methodist ladies covered tables, countertops, and the big kitchen range—soups, stews, beef roasts, pork chops, whole turkeys browned to perfection, hams glistening with glaze, casseroles of more varieties than anyone had yet lifted a lid to identify, fresh-baked bread, cookies, angel-food and upside-down cakes, along with apple, sour cherry, and sweet potato pies. Food to feed an army, as Lenore said, and just as well. Gowers devoured provisions like locusts in a garden, while talking up a locust-like uproar. Every Gower shouted to be heard because every other Gower shouted to be heard.

Before Major Wilkes could get his coat off Lorena hauled him over to the big kitchen range, where pots and skillets bubbled, steamed, and smoked. She rubbed his cheeks and hands and ordered him to hover over the stove with his coat spread open to catch the heat. Melting snow slid off the coat and droplets danced over the hot surface to disappear in bursts of steam.

His uncles, big men with big bellies, sprawled on benches around Minnie's over-sized oaken table. They talked and laughed with their mouths full and reached long arms down the table to spear another steak or pork chop or well-browned turkey leg or thick slice of that fresh-baked bread, on which they spread great dollops of new-churned butter. They looked up and waved greetings at Major Wilkes with half-chewed turkey legs and steak-laden forks. Every motion sent shadows spreading in all directions. Only Eph spoke.

"You look like somebody stuck an icicle up your ass," he said.

Minnie came from Amos's room carrying a hot-water bottle. She went straight to Major Wilkes, hugging him despite his dripping coat.

"How's Grandpa?" Though she was in his arms, he had to speak up to be heard.

"Hanging on. He can't last, but he's a stubborn old goat."

Major Wilkes hung his riding coat on a wooden peg by the door. Lorena shoehorned him into a space at the end of a bench next to Eph.

"A sad day," Eph said, sopping up the last bit of gravy on his plate with a hunk of bread. He wiped his lips with a monogrammed handkerchief he pulled from the breast pocket of his coat. Unlike his elder brothers, who wore their usual clodhoppers and bib overalls, he was—as they had already commented—"dressed to the nines" in a funeral-going suit.

"Sad day, for sure," Major Wilkes said.

"What'd you say? I can't hear you over all this noise. Everybody talking and laughing. Nobody showing respect. Don't they know why we're here?"

Eph stood up and clapped his hands for silence. His becoming a senator had cemented his position as the family's acknowledged spokesman. Eph always knew just what to say no matter the occasion. Could have been a preacher, the family said, if and so he'd been called that way.

Eph yelled and clapped until the kitchen stilled.

"Well," he said in his deepest speechifying tones, "a giant of a man is about to leave us. Let us pay him due respect. He was an officer and a gentleman, a hero of the Confederacy, decorated by General Lee. One day we'll find the name of Amos Gower in the pantheon of Texas heroes, you mark my words."

"Nonsense," Minnie said, loud enough to reach every ear in the stilled kitchen. She stood at the stove, refilling Amos's hot-water bottle from a steaming teakettle.

Eph ignored her. "A lot of great men had feet of clay. But if Amos Gower had a fault, I don't know what it was."

"I do," Minnie said. "And it wasn't just clay feet. It was head and heart, too."

Eph talked over her, but even he couldn't keep a crowd of Gowers quiet for long.

The room was noisy as ever when the undertaker and four of his men arrived, brushing snow off their Stetsons.

"It won't be long now, Mr. Ross," Minnie said. "Will you

have a bite of supper while you're waiting? There's plenty."

"We done ate, thank you kindly, ma'am, but a cup of coffee might go well."

Among the undertaker's men was Jeff Hines, son of the Owchicta banker who foreclosed on Amos's ranch and then went broke himself after a run on his bank. Now Jeff Hines had to fend for himself instead of living off his daddy. He crowded in at the end of the bench opposite Major Wilkes.

"Still like it up there in Indian Territory? Rough crowd up there, everybody says."

"It's been a state for a good long while now and I like it fine. Nice people. They're treating me good."

Lorena was filling his coffee cup. *"Well,* Major Wilkes! Treating you well."

Major Wilkes smiled. "Treating me well."

"Heard they let you off for killing that fella. How's it feel to be a free man?"

"That's ancient history now."

"Wonderful what a good lawyer can do." Hines spooned sugar into the cup of coffee Lorena handed him.

"Helps if you done it in the line of duty, after being shot at." Major Wilkes corrected himself before Lorena could. "Did it."

"Somebody said you and Old Man Ringle's daughter was getting together."

"I heard that too."

Major Wilkes might have added, but didn't, that he and Sophie had been married for some time and were expecting in the spring. He never had liked Jeff Hines, who had a mouth like a pump, always pouring out words, most of them meaningless. Hines was almost as big a talker as Eph.

Hines wasn't done.

"And how about the thousand dollars in gold that railroad man—Giles, his name is—promised you. He paid up yet?"

"Giles doesn't owe me a thing."

It was none of Hines's business that Giles had given him fifty Double Eagles after Sophie appeared at the trial and confirmed what everybody was already sure of, that Major Wilkes was the mysterious stranger who had dispersed Ringle's lynching mob with one shot at a passing jackrabbit. Seth Ringle had testified to it before Sophie spoke up, of course, but Giles said he wouldn't accept Ringle's unsupported word if he swore water ran downhill.

The windfall had allowed Major Wilkes and Sophie to marry even before he went to reading law with Charley Frelinghausen.

MINNIE PUT THE hot-water bottle under Amos's feet and smoothed his sheets. He reared up on an elbow.

What he saw was the skinny little blue-eyed girl with freckles and brown hair glinting red swinging on the gate of a burned-out Mississippi plantation and smiling at him as the column marched past what he didn't know then was the Wilkes place. His vision cleared. She was old, old, old, almost as old as he. Where had that little girl gone?

"What you doing, woman? Who you got out there?"

"The family and Mr. Ross."

"Why you got him here? I ain't died yet and don't know that I aim to."

"You will, Amos, soon enough." She still sounded city, which Amos found unsettling, he couldn't remember why. "Is flags at half-mast?"

"Of course not. Why would they be?"

"I'm a officer and hero of the Confederacy, that's why. I got my medals, woman, my sword—my hat, too. Oh, them was the days! I remember at—at Shiloh, was it? Maybe Manassas? Anyways, there I was and—"

"That's right, there you were, no medals in sight. I can see you now — a scared boy hiding in that old shed and begging for food after deserting your post under fire."

"*Deserted!* I never. And scared? Why, what I done — "

"Amos, I know all about what you 'done.' The first minute I saw you I suspected you were a deserter, and knew it for sure when your company came by again after the battle. Your captain told us about being surprised by a troop of Federal cavalry. Sergeant McCandless was killed, he said, and so were lots of others, including the young soldier who was on lookout with you before the battle. They went to where the two of you were on sentry duty and found him with his head almost cut off. You were missing. They followed your trail through the brush for a way and then lost it. There was no sign you'd been taken prisoner. The captain told Father if you came around he should turn you over to the nearest Confederate troops to be shot for cowardice and desertion in the face of the enemy."

"I weren't no deserter. No coward, neither! Why, General Lee hisself said I — "

"General Lee said nothing!"

"What about all them battles I was in? Ain't you heard me tell about them?" He took his hand out from under the covers and shook his fist.

She tucked his hand back under the blanket.

"Amos, I know as well as you do that the only battle you were ever in was the one you ran away from. You were a coward, never a hero."

"What about them medals General Lee pinned on me?"

"You bought those medals in Fort Worth! You think I didn't know? You never in your life saw General Lee. You're a hero of brag, Amos — nothing more. They don't give medals for brag."

"I'm a hero of the Confederacy, woman. Ask anybody. Ask Eph. He'll tell you."

"He already has."

"See? What's a woman know about being a hero?"

"Amos, if it comes down to which of us is some sort of hero, I think I'm more likely than you to get the medal."

"What you ever done worth a medal?"

"I knew what you were and what you would always be, but I married you anyway and I've stuck with you. That was heroic, medal or no medal."

She put her hand on his forehead. It was hot. She felt his feet. They were still cold, though the hot-water bottle under his feet was warm.

There was warm water in a basin, and she sponged his face with a damp cloth.

"I never asked you to marry me."

"That's true, but—"

"You was pregnant and claimed I done it. But I never. No, I never."

"The tunnel, Amos, the tunnel!"

"I never!"

"Listen to me, Amos! I didn't marry you because I was pregnant. I did it because I couldn't bear to send you back to the Army to be shot for deserting. Much as I hated you I didn't want your blood on my hands. And the only way I could save you was to marry you."

"I tell you, I weren't no deserter. I got my medals. General Lee, he said—"

"Oh, bother General Lee!"

"It ain't right, a woman talking to her husband that way."

"Don't you tell me what's right, Amos Gower! I'm proud of that little girl who had the courage to do what she thought she had to do, even when she knew what it would cost her. Many's the time I've wanted to leave you, Amos, but the thought of that brave child always stopped me. I couldn't betray her by quitting.

"Now I'm tired, Amos. You cost me my daughter and I want you out the door the minute you're gone. Mary—not Mary Nell, but Mary Valentine—always said you were the easiest led, least trustworthy—"

"And fastest?" he suggested, not sure why.

"And fastest. That's what Mary Valentine used to say. 'The fastest man in Texas,' she said. And that's part of what I'm talking about. You never thought about anybody but yourself. You had no friends and believed the world was full of enemies. If you hadn't been at war with everybody all the time, even me, if you—"

He quit listening and settled back against the pillow. It was just woman-prattle, the kind he'd tried all his life to straighten out. But Minnie was the strong one, too strong for him, and stubborn. So were the two Marys—his Mary Nell and Mary Valentine.

Lorena, too. All it proved, so far as he could see, all he had ever been able to see, was that he had been unlucky in his women. He had understood that it was a man's world and acted accordingly. His women had not agreed. They had refused to obey what he supposed were God-given rules. His women had minds of their own and would not listen to him, as they should have. They and the hex put upon him by Dunc's killer had driven him to the edge of the grave.

"I want to see my boys, just them."

They filed in, gray-headed and gray-bearded, most of them, and squeezed in between the foot of the bed and shelves laden with neatly labeled Mason jars filled with jams, jellies, fruits and vegetables. Not a tear except maybe in Eph's eye, and that could have been a reflection from the coal-oil lamp on the chiffonier.

"It won't be long now," Minnie said.

They all nodded, agreeing with her. Eph, too. Even his boys were against him. His own sons! He didn't know what to think.

He tried to protest. Couldn't catch his breath.

Couldn't speak. Couldn't remember what he was wanting to say or why.

"Major Wilkes," he whispered.

He heard Minnie open the door. "He'd like to see you, Major Wilkes."

She added, speaking to Mr. Ross and his men, "You gentlemen might as well finish up your coffee."

Amos didn't like the sound of that.

Major Wilkes went in, not wanting to. He was unwilling to say to a dying man what he felt was the only honest thing to say, which was, "I love you. I'll miss you," with its implicit acknowledgement that death was certain. He doubted that Amos would ever admit the possibility that he, among all men, was mortal.

Amos lay in the bed on his back, the covers pulled up to his chin. His eyes were open but unfocused. His lips moved but made no sound.

"Amos, here's Major Wilkes."

"Who?"

"Major Wilkes."

"Canvas bag on the black mare. I seen him."

"Lorena and Dunc's Major Wilkes."

"Oh."

Major Wilkes stroked the bump in the blankets that showed where the old man's hands were clasped on his chest.

"Grandpa, it's me, Major Wilkes."

"Mary Nell," Amos muttered, barely aloud. "I want my Mary Nell."

Major Wilkes stepped back and stood beside his uncles, taller than any of them. The room was crowded and very warm. The lamp smoked. Soot crept up one side of its glass chimney.

"Mary Nell's not coming, Amos," Minnie said. "I told you."

"She knows?"

"She knows, Amos."

"She'll come, won't she?"

"I told you. She won't come."

He paid her no mind. Little Mary Nell was right there at the foot of his bed standing at Eph's side, pretty as a picture in her Sunday dress, the white one with a flaring skirt, his favorite. He was surprised she still had that dress, more surprised that it still fit her. Here she was a grown woman with a woman's form and yet able to get into that little white dress she had worn when she was not much more than a baby.

His arms flew from under the covers and stretched toward her. "Mary Nell!"

Major Wilkes looked at the door. It was closed. No one had come in.

"Got a smile for your pa?" Amos sounded like himself, not an old man on the knife's edge of death.

She wasn't crying, which it seemed to Amos she might have been, but she was not frowning either. That was something.

"Got a smile for your pa?" he asked again, weakly this time.

She turned her back to him. Looking at him over her shoulder she lifted her skirt and dropped her bloomers. Red welts crisscrossed her little behind, one livid streak after another. There were bruises, too, ugly bruises, black and purple. He could not bear the sight. Nor could he bear the *Sergeant McCandless* expression on her face. And there, standing right beside her, was the sergeant himself, big as life and still in uniform, looking at him like something smelled bad.

"Sergeant McCandless!"

"He's not here, Amos. The war's over. You're safe."

Jess Fellows leaned against the sergeant. Amos caught a glimpse of a moonlit chin, a brief glint of steel. Jess's head fell backward off his neck, like a hinged coffeepot lid. Blood welled.

Jess lifted his head into place again. Only a red line showed where the Yankee sword had sliced across his throat. Next to Jess, Mary Valentine's young lover *F* crouched with a gun-shaped candleholder in his hand and dealt a flurry of cards one at a time from the starched cuff of a ruffled shirt stained with river mud.

And there, too, slumping against *F* like a rag doll needing support, was the curly-haired young bank robber, Dunc's killer, seemingly unable to hold his head up. Deep rope burns circled his neck. His chin wobbled against his chest as he turned his head to stare aslant at Amos. He spoke: *"Crwrgh! Eeghwr. Hrckk. Hrckk. Crwrgh!"*

The curse straight from the dead man's lips burned into Amos's ears, reinforcing what he had long known. Nothing had been his fault, not from his mother's dying to this moment with an undertaker waiting.

The hex accounted for everything. It explained why Minnie never got over what happened in the tunnel. Why she kept an arm over her face when he was on her. Why an old woman who looked like a young girl held a lamp over him and told him she'd called in the undertaker and him not dead yet. And not going to be, neither, not if I got a say about it. Why the wind came up and sent him sailing out of the Owchicta town square with everyone laughing as he pulled the tarp off the Zouave on the day that up to that moment had been the happiest of his life. Why he lost the ranch to drought and Banker Hines. Why Mary Nell turned against him and stayed that way, right to this minute, with him maybe on his deathbed. Why her book-reading, good for nothing young soldier—Jimmy, his name was—had been able to put him, Amos, on the ground with fire in his groin while Sheriff Barnes watched and courthouse idlers hooted.

And there he was, that scrawny soldier, that seducer of the

sweetest, purest little girl in the world. He stood between Mary Nell and Sergeant McCandless. He was hugging Mary Nell, hugging her right there in front of Amos. Amos couldn't stand it. He closed his eyes. When he opened them, Mary Nell was lifting her lips to her lover and Jimmy was in the tall grass, scrambling to avoid the black mare's hooves and the sword that Minnie's hero father had carried in the war. The boy looked up with startled eyes so big they shouldn't have fit in his head but somehow did. Blood spurted, as it had when the Yankee officer's blade slashed Jess's throat. The blood-spooked mare's hoof crushed Jimmy's face, and Mary Nell thrashed in a bloody bed while Eph's wife, Muffie, scratched at the door. Mary Nell screamed and screamed, heartbreaking shrieks.

"Tell her to be quiet," Muffie whimpered. "The neighbors'll hear."

"Get the doctor!" Minnie said.

What could the doctor do that he couldn't? He did the thing he had to do, the only thing anybody could do. He seized the tiny body and jerked it from between Mary Nell's arched legs as he would a breached calf. Snap! He did not see the baby's face, only tufts of dark hair, blood-wet and curly. But he heard the snap echo down the years to this moment and on and on for generations not yet born to hear.

At the foot of his bed Mary Nell held the baby in her arms. Her eyes, green as a cat's, shone with tears.

"Her name is Nellie, for my grandmother. You never let me hold her."

The child had Mary Nell's face and cat's eyes. She could have been Mary Nell in Minnie's arms.

"You killed her."

"I never. No, I never."

No one in the room knew what accusation he was denying or who had made it.

His mouth fell open. The few teeth he had left were rotted stumps, stained walnut brown by ten thousand chaws of tobacco. His eyes glared at the ceiling as though at another world.

Minnie motioned her boys and Major Wilkes out of the room. Major Wilkes was the only one to look back or speak.

"Goodbye, Grandpa. I'll miss you."

Minnie closed Amos's eyes and mouth. She smoothed his beard and hair with her fingers. Crossing his arms on his chest, she leaned over and kissed his forehead.

"I can't forgive you, Amos," she said, "but I can pity you." She pulled the blanket over his face and went to the door. "All right, Mr. Ross. Take him away."

The family fell silent and pressed back to the walls to open a path through the kitchen for the stretcher, a man on each handle. Mr. Ross brought up the rear, carrying clothes to dress Amos.

Major Wilkes opened the door. Cold air rushed in, welcome after all the heat and smoke. The thud of boots on the frozen boards of the screened porch rang like a dirge on a taut-tuned drum. The undertaker's men grunted under the weight of Amos's body as they tilted the stretcher down snow-packed steps in the dark. They might have been carrying the Amos of long ago, not a frail old man shrunken by illness, with no meat on his bones.

THE OWCHICTA *Beacon*, Thursday, January 16, 1913:

FLAGS AT HALF-MAST!

SENATOR EPH GOWER ANNOUNCES DEATH OF OWCHICTA'S BELOVED CONFEDERATE HERO

GENERAL LEE HONORED MAJOR AMOS GOWER AS

'THE BRAVEST MAN IN AN ARMY OF BRAVE MEN!'